"Thank you for catching me."

"You gave me quite a scare." Would she notice the tremble in his voice that he couldn't hide?

"Me, too."

To keep from touching her, Wyatt pressed his hands to the new boards. If only he had the freedom to pull her close and comfort her. But he didn't, and never would, because he would never be free from the sting of his past.

Cora sucked in air. "I owe you for saving my life."

He tried to snort, but it sounded more like a groan. "Let's hope you wouldn't have died."

She faced him, but he kept his gaze riveted to the spot where she almost fell. "Wyatt, if you need or want anything, feel free to ask. If I can, I'll give it to you."

Slowly his gaze sought hers and he fell into the darkness of her eyes and the sweetness of her invitation. He had needs and wants. Acceptance despite his past, someone who trusted him, believed in him, loved him. His throat tightened. His heart ached with longing. If only she could give him what he needed.

Linda Ford

Big Sky Cowboy
&
Big Sky Daddy

LOVE INSPIRED
INSPIRATIONAL ROMANCE

LOVE INSPIRED®
INSPIRATIONAL ROMANCE

ISBN-13: 978-1-335-45670-0

Recycling programs
for this product may
not exist in your area.

Big Sky Cowboy and Big Sky Daddy

Copyright © 2021 by Harlequin Books S.A.

Big Sky Cowboy
First published in 2014. This edition published in 2021.
Copyright © 2014 by Linda Ford

Big Sky Daddy
First published in 2014. This edition published in 2021.
Copyright © 2014 by Linda Ford

This edition published by arrangement with Harlequin Books S.A.

For questions and comments about the quality of this book, please contact us
at CustomerService@Harlequin.com.

Love Inspired
22 Adelaide St. West, 40th Floor
Toronto, Ontario M5H 4E3, Canada
www.Harlequin.com

Printed in U.S.A.

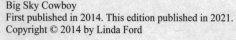

CONTENTS

Linda Ford lives on a ranch in Alberta, Canada, near enough to the Rocky Mountains that she can enjoy them on a daily basis. She and her husband raised fourteen children—four homemade, ten adopted. She currently shares her home and life with her husband, a grown son, a live-in paraplegic client, and a continual (and welcome) stream of kids, kids-in-law, grandkids, and assorted friends and relatives.

Books by Linda Ford

Love Inspired Historical

Big Sky Country

Montana Cowboy Daddy
Montana Cowboy Family
Montana Cowboy's Baby
Montana Bride by Christmas
Montana Groom of Convenience
Montana Lawman Rescuer

Montana Cowboys

The Cowboy's Ready-Made Family
The Cowboy's Baby Bond
The Cowboy's City Girl

Visit the Author Profile page
at Harlequin.com for more titles.

BIG SKY COWBOY

For I know the thoughts that I think toward you,
saith the Lord, thoughts of peace, and not of evil,
to give you an expected end.
—*Jeremiah* 29:11

To adoptive parents who, like the Bells,
welcome into their family children not born to them.
May love and joy shine forever on your family.

Chapter One

A farm near Bar Crossing, Montana
Summer, 1889

*S*quee.

What was that awful noise?

Wyatt Williams eased back on his reins and glanced over his shoulder to his brother, Lonnie. The sixteen-year-old shrank back as if he wished to disappear into the saddle.

Squee. Squee.

The sound came again, rending the air and filling it with tension.

Wyatt stared at the farm ahead. From where he sat he had a good view of the place. A pretty little house with a bay window and a little veranda faced the road. A tumble of flowers in every hue of the rainbow surrounded the house. A garden as precise as a ruler ran from the river to the trees at the back of the lot. There were several tidy buildings, some pens and the naked skeleton of a barn.

Wyatt considered his brother and the mare he led.

Fanny was heavy with foal. The weeks of moving had taxed her strength. He couldn't push her farther.

His gaze went past Lonnie and the horse. He couldn't see the other mares that he hoped to start a new ranch with, but he knew they were tied securely down by the water. He only wanted permission from the farmer to camp by the river until Fanny foaled, and she and the newborn grew strong enough to resume their journey. Plus their supplies were running low and he hoped to restock here. He could ride to the nearby town for what he needed, but it seemed unnecessary. Wyatt studied the sign nailed to the gatepost.

For Sale—Eggs, Milk, Cheese, Garden Stuff.

His mouth watered. Fresh food had never sounded so good.

"Wait here," he told Lonnie, and rode forward.

From around one of the outbuildings came a squealing pig with a floppy-eared, big-footed dog barking at its tail.

A young woman skidded around the corner, blond braids flying. "You get back here, you little trouble-maker." She dived for it, catching the animal for about ten seconds before it slipped away, squealing righteous indignation and leaving the gal in the dirt.

Wyatt drew to a halt and grinned.

The woman picked herself up and shook a finger at the dog. "Grub, enough. I'll never catch the crazy pig with you barking and chasing after it."

Wyatt took *Grub* to be the dog's name, for it stopped and yapped and then turned back to pig chasing, which seemed to be the sport of the day. The young woman took off after them. The pig veered from side to side. She pounced on it again, but it wasn't about to be captured. It wriggled free and headed in Wyatt's direction.

His horse snorted.

"Rooster, you never mind. He's just a wee oinker." Wyatt reached for his lariat, swung a lazy loop and dropped it over the pig's head.

The little pig yanked on the rope, trying to get free. The squeals that erupted about deafened Wyatt and, he guessed, anyone within a hundred yards.

The gal blinked at Wyatt. "I just about had him." Her brown eyes challenged him. Seemed she didn't care to have someone interfere in her work.

Her attitude tickled Wyatt clear to the pit of his stomach. He grinned. "You're welcome."

She planted her hands on her hips. The flash in her eyes told him how hard it was for her to maintain her annoyed look.

He tipped his head toward the pig, who continued to fight the rope and put up an awful fuss. "Ma'am, if you don't mind me suggesting it, why not let me lead the pig to his pen." Though he guessed "lead" was only a wish.

She nodded decisively. "No doubt that would be wise. Come along, then." She moved toward an enclosure while Wyatt dragged and tugged and generally fought his way after her, Rooster snorting his protest at the indignity.

She held the pen gate open. Wyatt dismounted and pushed the pig through the space she gave him, then slipped off the rope. Five other little pigs rushed forward, joining in the melee. An old, fat sow huffed over to them.

The young woman sighed and wiped her hand across her brow, leaving a streak of dirt to match the three on her dress.

The dog sat on his haunches watching the pig.

Wyatt gave the dog further study. "Does he always wear a grin?"

"A grinning dog and a crying pig. Who'd believe it?" The girl hooted with laughter.

Wyatt couldn't remember when he'd last heard such a freeing sound. His grin widened, went deep into his heart.

She calmed her chuckles, though her quivering lips warned him it might resume at any moment.

From behind him came a strange sound. He jerked around to see the source. Lonnie had moved close enough to see and hear, and he laughed, too. A sound almost foreign to Wyatt's ears.

Lonnie noticed Wyatt watching and immediately sobered.

Oh, how Wyatt wished his brother would stop being so tense around him. Lonnie was even more jumpy around strangers, and yet…

Wyatt looked at the woman before him. Had her laughter drawn Lonnie forward? He shifted his gaze toward the pigs. Was it the animals that attracted Lonnie?

Whatever it was, Wyatt was grateful.

"I don't believe I've seen you around before." The pretty young woman drew his attention back to her.

"Nope. Name's Wyatt Williams. This is my brother, Lonnie."

"Pleased to meet you both. I'm Cora Bell. What can I do for you?"

"My mare needs to rest." He indicated Fanny. "The rest of my animals are down at the river. We want permission to stay there until she's ready to travel again. We could use some supplies, as well. I saw your sign on the gate and thought…"

"I can certainly sell you anything we have. You'll

need to talk to Pa about your animals, though. Come along."

He dismounted, handed Rooster's reins to Lonnie and strode after her.

She led him to a small outbuilding and stepped inside. He followed into the dim interior.

"Pa, I brought you company."

A man emerged from behind a stack of wood pieces, old barrel hoops and broken wagon wheels. He wiped his greasy hands on a stained rag.

Cora introduced the pair.

Mr. Bell held out a soiled hand. "Pleased to meet you. What brings you to our part of the country?"

Wyatt repeated his request. "I'll only stay until my mare and her foal are ready to travel, then I'll be on my way."

"Got someplace to be, do you?"

Mr. Bell likely only meant to make conversation, but the question made Wyatt face the fact that he didn't know where they were going. How far would they have to in order to get away from their past? How far before Lonnie could forget their abusive father? How far before people would forget Wyatt had gone to jail for beating up the old man?

Not that he'd done it. Lonnie, sensitive and quiet, had snapped one day and turned on their father. Knowing his brother would never survive in jail, Wyatt had confessed to the crime. Now, a year later, he was out. Of course, no one would let that be in the past. Pa had died while Wyatt was in prison. Perhaps the beating had done irreparable damage. Or maybe Pa's hard life had caught up with him. Ma, God rest her soul, had lived long enough to see Wyatt free again. Then she'd wearily given up as if life was just too much effort.

Wyatt had sold their farm in Kansas and was headed as far away from there as possible. He planned to buy a bit of land someday and start over. He'd be a rancher. Raise horses. Find peace. He'd brought along a half-dozen mares to start a herd with. He and Lonnie—wanting to forget their past and hoping for a happy future. Somewhere. Sometime. He rubbed at the tightness in his neck. Maybe in Canada they could start over without him constantly looking over his shoulder.

He shuddered, then sucked in a lungful of air and forced his thoughts under control. He would not think of those who might recognize him from the trial. Or even those who might have their own reasons for tracking him down. For instance, a certain jailbird who hated Wyatt and vowed to make him pay for Wyatt's interference when the man tried to bully his way into power in jail. Not that he figured Jimmy Stone had enough get-up-and-go to ride after them. But the man had gotten out of prison a few weeks after Wyatt, and Wyatt hadn't been able to forget the man's threats.

"Headed north," he said, answering Mr. Bell's question.

"You've about run out of north." The old man scratched his whiskered chin. "Unless you're headed for Canada."

"Might be." Even if he had particulars about his destination, he wouldn't be sharing them.

Mr. Bell studied him a moment. "You sound like a man running from something."

"Could be I'm running to something."

Mr. Bell didn't blink. "So long as your running poses no threat to me or my family."

Wyatt didn't answer. He couldn't give that kind of assurance. "My mare's about to foal."

Mr. Bell limped toward the door. "Let's have a look."

They made their slow way toward Lonnie and the mare. Lonnie tossed the mare's rope toward Wyatt and backed away at their approach. No one but Wyatt seemed to notice Lonnie's odd behavior. The others were too busy eyeing Fanny. He introduced his brother to Mr. Bell, who greeted him, then returned his attention to the horse.

Mr. Bell ran his hand along Fanny's sides and walked around the horse then tsked. "She needs to rest. Where did you say you come from?"

"Didn't say."

Mr. Bell straightened and fixed Wyatt with a look that caused him to hastily add, "Been on the road awhile."

"That's no excuse for exhausting a mare this heavy in foal." The look Mr. Bell gave him would have made many a man stammer some kind of apology, but Wyatt had faced harsher looks and far bigger men without revealing a hint of weakness.

"Been looking for a decent place to stop for a few days now."

"Huh."

Apparently that wasn't a good enough excuse. And Wyatt wasn't about to tell anyone that every time he mentioned stopping Lonnie had begged him not to. Until now, he hadn't been able to ignore his brother's request.

Cora grinned at Wyatt. "Best you know Pa can't abide any carelessness with God's creatures or His creation."

"I gathered."

"Cora, run and get some of Ma's tonic. Be sure to tell her it's for a mare in foal."

"Yes, Pa." She trotted away.

Wyatt watched her go, then realized Mr. Bell was studying him, and shifted his gaze back to the mare. "Do I have your permission for me and my brother to camp down by the river with my stock?"

Mr. Bell rocked his eyes from Wyatt to Lonnie to the mare and out to the river a couple of times as if measuring…considering.

If he knew the facts he would no doubt be asking them to move on.

Mr. Bell nodded. "Can't hardly ask you to take this mare any farther. You're welcome to pen them here and throw your bedrolls in the shed."

Wyatt didn't have to look at Lonnie to know his face would be pinched. "Thanks, but we'll be comfortable camping down by the water."

"Fine. Before you take the mare there, I'll give her some tonic to strengthen her. Do you have oats?"

Wyatt shook his head. "I'm out. Would you have some I could purchase?"

"I'll see to it." Mr. Bell faced Wyatt. The man looked almost old enough to be Cora's grandfather. He had a strong face, lined from years of both good times and worry. His hair was thick and gray. "I'll be keeping an eye on you." The look he gave Wyatt said a whole lot more than his words.

Wyatt understood the man's warning. Wyatt's vague answers had given him reason to be suspicious. If Mr. Bell knew the truth—a history of family violence and time in prison—he'd chase Wyatt and Lonnie away in spite of Fanny's condition.

Wyatt kept his gaze on Fanny.

Would he ever escape the shame and regret of his past?

* * *

With a smile on her lips, Cora made her way to the garden shed. How quickly and easily Wyatt had dropped a loop over that silly piglet's head. But, oh, the fuss the pig had made. Better entertainment than a circus.

Wyatt had laughed easily, but she'd seen so many secrets behind his dark eyes. She'd also noticed how his brother had pulled away from them all. It wasn't simply shyness. No, there was something unusual about his reaction.

Her amusement fled. She suspected he hid something. Secrets, in her opinion, made people forget things they'd promised to those they pretended to care about. She might be considered innocent, but despite being only twenty years old, she knew that much for certain. Like her supposed beau, Evan Price. Pretending to really care about her while all the time planning to leave for the goldfields. Goodbye came far too easy for him. She drew in a deep breath and forced her thoughts to things she needed to do yet today.

Between the wandering pig and the visiting cowboy she was way behind in her chores, and she picked up her pace. She had butter to churn and cheese to start. The sale of these products, plus whatever people offered in return for the healing powders that Ma made from medicinal plants, brought in the cash to pay for what they couldn't raise themselves.

A quick glance at the garden informed her that Lilly had not pulled weeds as she'd agree to. Heaven alone knew where she'd wandered off to. Likely she was searching for the mama cat and her newborn kittens.

Ma and Rose were in the garden shed, and she turned her steps in that direction.

Rose stepped from the garden shed, saw her and waved. "We're making progress." Rose wanted Ma to write down all medicinal remedies. That meant Rose was writing as Ma recited them.

"Good," Cora said. She stepped into the shed. "Ma, can I have some tonic for a horse?"

"Horse tonic?" Rose asked.

Cora jabbed her finger over her shoulder. "Company."

"Really?"

"Yup." It wasn't as if they never had company. Lots of people dropped by to purchase eggs or butter or cheese or garden produce or something for an ailment.

She explained to Ma and Rose about the mare.

Ma shook dust from her ample apron. She ran her hands over her gray hair and patted her skirts smooth. "Let's have a look."

The trio walked to where Pa and Wyatt stood talking next to the mare. Lonnie and the other two horses were gone. As she expected, Pa had allowed them to rest down by the river. "Ma, this is Wyatt Williams. Wyatt, my mother, Mrs. Gertie Bell. And this is my sister Rose."

As the others studied Wyatt, Cora also took a good look at him. Dark hair showed around his black cowboy hat. His brown eyes were fringed with long lashes. And despite the shadows in his eyes, he looked as though he smiled often.

Eighteen-year-old Rose's red hair drew Wyatt's gaze like a moth to flames, but he shifted his gaze past her and said hello to her mother.

Ma nodded to Wyatt, then turned her attention to the

horse. "Poor thing looks exhausted. This tonic ought to make her feel better."

Lilly drifted by, saw the crowd and shifted direction. "What's everyone doing here?"

Rose and Lilly were twins, although as different as the flowers they'd been named for.

Lilly cradled one of last year's kittens.

Cora moved to Lilly's side as she introduced Wyatt yet again. "That's our family."

"Pleased to meet you all," he said. "I don't plan to be a nuisance. We'll be down by the river until Fanny here and her new baby are ready to move."

Another wanderer. Here today, maybe tomorrow or even the next day, then gone as fast as he could pull his boots on…or, in this case, as soon as he deemed his horse fit to move on.

Cora'd had her fill of wandering men. First her birth father had abandoned her and the twins when she was five and the twins just three. The day was burned into her memory.

Papa in a wagon, riding away with a promise to return. "Wait for me. I'll be back," he'd said. But he'd never returned and she'd never known why.

And then Evan. Cora wondered how she could have let herself care for him in the first place. Once bitten, twice shy. She'd not be so willing to trust a man again.

"You're fortunate you ended up here," Rose said. "Our ma is known for her healing powders and ointments."

"I'm grateful, though it was the sign on your gate that caught my attention. Then I saw your sister chasing after a pig and had to ride closer."

Cora groaned. Now Lilly would get all concerned.

"What pig?" Lilly looked about ready to cry. How

many times had Cora told her sister that, at eighteen, tears shouldn't be so close to the surface?

"One of the little pigs," Cora said.

"But which one?"

"I couldn't say. They all look the same to me." Fat, pink or otherwise, and noisy. She darted a glance at Wyatt. He flashed a grin as if recalling the chase they'd had.

She almost laughed and choked the sound back so she wouldn't be called upon to explain herself. She drew curious looks from both sisters. She patted her chest as if she had a tickle.

But Lilly had not lost sight of her concern over the pigs. "Was the pig all pink or did it have spots?"

Cora honestly could not say. She'd been entirely focused on getting the creature back into the pen before it had decided to root in the garden the way one had done last week. She'd managed to salvage some of the bean plants, but half a dozen were beyond help. After all her hard work planting and weeding.

"There was a black spot on its rump," Wyatt said.

Cora stared at him. How had he noticed when she hadn't?

"That was Mini," Lilly said. "I hope you didn't hurt him. He's the littlest one, you know."

"He looked fine to me," Cora said.

"I'll check on him." Lilly dashed off with Rose after her.

Pa gave the horse the tonic, then he and Ma wandered away, leaving Cora alone with Wyatt.

She wasn't sure what to say. Was she supposed to escort him down to the river? She blurted out the first thing that came to mind. "My sister worries so much about those pigs." She realized she might not appear to be sympathetic and she truly was. "Don't get me wrong. I adore my sister. Both of them. They mean the world to me."

He studied her a moment, his eyes filled with those dark secrets she'd noticed before. "I guess your family is your life."

She'd never thought of it that way, but it was true. "Yes, they are." She wanted to ask about his family, but before she could, he spoke again.

"Your pa said I could buy some oats for my horses. Could you tell me where I can find them?"

She went to the shed and pointed to the bins in the corner. "I'd better get back to my work." She returned to the workroom off the kitchen to churn butter. Even with all the windows open, the room was far too warm. She needed to get a springhouse built so there'd be a cool place to store the butter and cheese during the summer. But she never had enough time, and Pa, bless his heart, tried to help, but he was getting far too old and sore for heavy work.

As she pumped the handle of the churn, her thoughts returned to the cowboy.

When she'd first seen him, she'd hoped he'd come in answer to the notice she'd nailed up in the store several days ago, offering a job to someone who would help her build a new barn. It seemed Mr. Frank, the store owner, was right. No one was going to risk displeasure from the Caldwells by helping the Bells.

The Caldwells objected to the Bells farming in the midst of their ranch land. It was only a mistake, they insisted, that the Bells had been able to file on that particular piece of land. They'd made it clear the Bells should pack up and leave. Pa was equally convinced that the little bit of land they owned next to the river shouldn't matter to the Caldwells. The cowboys and cows could access the river for miles on either side. So he refused every effort the Caldwells made to convince him to relocate.

But Wyatt had only stopped to take care of his horses, not to help with the barn.

A thought grew. Maybe he'd be interested in helping with the construction work in exchange for oats for the animals and supplies for himself and Lonnie. He certainly looked strong enough to handle the work.

The man hid secrets, but did it matter? He meant to move on. All she cared about was getting the barn finished this summer.

But first she'd make sure he posed no threat to her family.

How was she to find out?

Chapter Two

Wyatt led Fanny to the river. Lonnie scrambled to his feet and backed away at their approach. Wyatt hoped to see the fear and tension disappear when Lonnie saw who it was, but neither did.

He sighed. "Lonnie, why do you act like I'm going to hurt you? You know I won't."

Lonnie nodded and mumbled. "I guess."

Guess? Was that the best the boy could do? Wyatt let it go. He could only hope that time would heal Lonnie's wounds. "Mr. Bell said we could stay here. Help me make camp." He tossed the end of a rope toward Lonnie. "Stretch it between those trees." They'd make a rope corral to hold the mares.

Lonnie jumped to do as Wyatt said. Jumped too fast, Wyatt figured. As if he thought that if he dillydallied, Wyatt would boot him. How long would it be before Lonnie stopped expecting to be treated the way their pa had treated him?

Wyatt had set his mind to being patient and soft-spoken with the boy, even when his fearful attitude made him want to shake him.

"That ought to hold them for now. I bought oats from the Bells. How about you give the mares a ration?"

Lonnie eagerly did so. The only time he truly relaxed was around animals. Not that Wyatt could blame him. He, too, had plenty of reason not to trust people. Jail had been a harsh teacher in that regard.

"Now let's get a camp set up for us."

"How long are we going to stay?" Lonnie rocked back and forth on the balls of his feet.

It was his usual worry stance. Wyatt remembered him doing it from the time he started to walk. Wyatt secretly smiled as he recalled those good memories before their family had been affect by their pa's moods. Pa hadn't always been violent. Wyatt could say exactly when it happened. Seemed it was sometime after Lonnie was born.

"We'll have to stay until Fanny foals and the baby is strong enough to travel."

Lonnie held one corner of the tarpaulin they were securing between trees for shelter. "But didn't she have some kind of tonic? Won't that make her able to go farther?"

"No, it won't." As Mr. Bell said, they had pushed the poor animal too much already.

Lonnie let his corner of the canvas droop.

"We can't run forever." Wyatt kept his voice calm and soothing. "Can you hold your corner tight?"

Lonnie jerked the canvas taut. "Why not?"

"We'd run out of money, for one thing." Besides, he ached to settle down. Had from his first day in jail. One thing he'd promised himself while behind bars—once he got out he'd find a place where he could belong and find peace. He still clung to that dream, though he didn't know the when or where of it.

"We could go into the bush, and hunt and fish."

"I suppose we could. We'd be hermits. You think you'd like that?"

"Maybe."

He tied Lonnie's corner of the tarpaulin and stepped back. "There. Looks like a nice home for us." He reached out to drape an arm across Lonnie's shoulders.

Lonnie shrank away.

Wyatt closed his eyes. It hurt like crazy to be treated this way by Lonnie. "We'll move on after Fanny's foal is born and it's strong enough to travel."

"How long will that be?" Lonnie asked.

"I expect a month or so."

"A month!" Lonnie stalked away to the bank of the river, mumbling under his breath. "What if they find out?"

"We'll make sure they don't."

He wanted so much for Lonnie to feel safe with him. To feel safe around other people.

During his days in prison, Wyatt's only consolation had been reading his Bible and praying. Prayer was unhindered by bars. He'd promised himself to trust God every day and in every way. If he meant to keep his vow, he had to believe they'd been led to this place. Seemed the Bells were the kind of people to extend hospitality for the sake of his animals.

Could it be they would also accept a jailbird? But he wasn't ready to cast aside his doubts and caution. Not until he'd had a chance to see what sort of folk they were. Even then, parts of his past must remain a secret. But he wanted Lonnie to feel at ease with them. Lonnie's constant nervousness would surely make people suspicious that something wasn't right.

"The Bells seem like nice people." The thought of Cora laughing brought a smile to Wyatt's face. "You didn't meet the twins."

Lonnie turned, an eager expression on his face. "Boys? Are they my age?"

"Girls. And they're about as big as Cora."

"Oh, well." Lonnie moseyed over to Wyatt's side and sank down beside him. "How old you figure Cora is?"

"I don't know."

"You could ask me." At the sound of a lilting voice, Wyatt jerked about to see Cora standing nearby. "You said you were out of supplies so I brought you some things." She held up a sack.

Lonnie jerked to his feet and hurried over to the horses.

Wyatt did his best to hide his disappointment at Lonnie's retreat and turned back to Cora with a smile that didn't chase the throb from behind his eyes.

At the way her gaze followed Lonnie, he knew she wondered at the boy's sudden withdrawal.

"He's shy," he said by way of explanation.

"Lilly is much the same way."

"So how old are you?" He hoped it was the kind of question that would divert her from following any suspicions she had about Lonnie's behavior.

"Twenty," she answered, her gaze still on the boy. "And you?"

"Twenty-one." He felt a lot older. Old enough to be weary, though that was as much the result of a year in prison as from being on the road for weeks. "Lonnie's sixteen."

She took a good look around. "You've got a pretty good setup here."

"It suits us."

She nodded. Her gaze came to him and she gave him serious consideration.

What did she see? He banked every thought but survival. She must never guess his secret. "Care to sit a spell?"

She sat on a log to his right.

"I'd offer you cookies and coffee, but I have no cookies and haven't built a fire yet, so I don't have any coffee."

She smiled, sending golden light through her eyes. "Maybe I can help."

She opened the sack she carried and pulled out new potatoes and carrots so fresh he could smell them. She held up a jar of milk, then set it by him. She unwrapped a generous piece of cheese and set down a half-dozen eggs.

Despite his practice of hiding his feelings, he felt his eyes widen with pleasure at such delights. He swallowed a rush of saliva. He hadn't seen food such as this in so long it was but a hungry memory.

Then she removed another packet from the sack and unfolded the paper. "Cookies. Ma said you looked hungry." She grinned with such innocent happiness that his heart twisted into a knot.

Her smile would not be so warm and welcoming if she knew the truth about him.

She would never know.

His gaze clung to the cookies. They'd had nothing but hard biscuits and jerky for three days. "Lonnie, she brought milk and cookies," he called. "Come have some."

"What kind?"

Wyatt almost laughed. As if it made any difference. Lonnie was every bit as hungry as Wyatt. "Cow's milk."

Lonnie snorted. "I mean the cookies."

"Oh." He knew what Lonnie meant but he went out of his way to force his brother to talk to him.

"Oatmeal and raisin," Cora said. "Ma made them, and she's a very good cook."

"Your favorite, if I remember correctly," Wyatt added.

Lonnie still hesitated.

Wyatt pulled three tin cups from the supplies and held them out to Cora. She unscrewed the lid from the jar and poured milk into each cup. He handed her one cup and took a long drink from another.

"This is so good. I haven't had fresh milk since—" He smiled as Lonnie moved closer and sat down as far away from Cora as possible and took the cup of milk Wyatt offered.

Cora passed around the cookies. "Have two." They needed no urging.

For a moment they enjoyed the snack without need for words.

Cora, who only ate one cookie, finished before Wyatt and Lonnie. "Where do you plan on going?"

He'd answered the question when her pa had asked and she knew it. And her quiet tone didn't make him believe she only made conversation. She wanted to know more about him. And he couldn't blame her. Two strangers camped so close to their home posed a risk. But not the sort she probably imagined.

"We'll know when we get there."

"I suppose. When did you leave your home? Where did you say it was?"

"Didn't say. We've been on the road a couple weeks." Give or take. He didn't intend to offer any more information. Out of the corner of his eyes he saw Lonnie's leg bouncing and shot him a look of assurance.

"You have any other family?"

Wyatt choked back the mouthful of cookie, suddenly as dry as dust. He took a sip of milk to wet his mouth.

Lonnie grew as still as the log on which he sat. Wyatt wondered if he even breathed.

"No other family," Wyatt said softly.

"No ma and pa?" She sounded shocked.

"Ma died a couple months back." Wyatt figured she'd hung around just long enough for Wyatt's return. Long enough to make Wyatt promise to take care of Lonnie. Even without Ma's admonition, he'd have made sure Lonnie was okay. He'd been Lonnie's guardian and protector since Ma had put the tiny baby, only one day old, in Wyatt's arms. She'd hugged them both. Wyatt had put his finger in Lonnie's palm and the baby's tiny fingers had curled around it.

It probably wasn't manly to say it, but it had been love at first touch.

He loved his troubled little brother even more now.

"I'm so sorry." Cora's voice thickened as if she held back tears. "I can't imagine not having a ma."

The river rumbled by, on its way to the ocean, where it would become part of something so much bigger it would disappear. Was that how death was? Or maybe it was only how it felt to those left behind, because he knew Ma had gone to something better where her pain and fear disappeared and she became whole and happy again.

"What about your pa?" Cora asked.

Her words vibrated through the air. Wyatt kept a firm look on Lonnie, silently begging him not to overreact.

Lonnie met his eyes, correctly read Wyatt's message, and didn't speak or move.

Relieved, Wyatt smiled and nodded reassurance. He didn't break eye contact with Lonnie as he answered Cora.

"Our pa's been dead several months now." He'd survived the beating but from what Ma and Lonnie said, it seemed something inside him had been broken. He never regained his strength but slowly faded away to a shadow before he died, which was a mercy for Lonnie. It had freed the boy from the fear of more abuse. But from what Wyatt had put together about the year he'd been missing, he figured the boy was made to feel ashamed because he had a brother in prison, and he remained afraid even after Pa was dead and gone.

Cora touched the back of his hand, bringing his attention to her. "I'm so sorry. You're both far too young to be orphans." She pulled her hand back to her lap.

His skin where she'd touched him burned as if he'd had too much sun in that one spot. He'd not been touched in a compassionate way in so long he didn't know how to respond.

"At least we have each other." He managed to squeeze out the words. He gripped Lonnie's shoulder, felt the tension and held on until the boy began to relax. "We will always have each other."

Cora stared at her empty cup. She tipped it as if she could dredge up another drop of milk and that would somehow give her the words to express her sorrow at their state. No wonder Lonnie acted as though the world was ready to beat him up. Likely that was how it felt.

It was enough to make her want to offer Wyatt and

Lonnie a home with the Bells, where they'd find the welcome and warmth she and her sisters had found.

Mrs. Bell had found five-year-old Cora and the twins two days after their real father had ridden away.

Cora remembered how she'd been ready to defend them. "My papa's coming back," she'd told Ma Bell. She'd looked down the trail as if he might suddenly appear. "He'll be here any second now." They were the same words she'd spoken to the twins throughout the lonely, fear-filled days and night. But the twins had gone readily into Ma Bell's open arms and been comforted.

Cora had needed a little more persuasion.

"Your sisters are tired and dirty and hungry," Ma had said. "Why not come with us? I'll help you take care of them."

It was the only argument she would have listened to. Their mother had died a few weeks previously, but not before she'd made Cora promise to take care of the twins.

Their father had never returned, though Cora had watched for him for several years. She'd given up looking for him, but she would never forget the promise she'd made to her mother, which meant she must be very careful about every decision she made. On the other hand, Ma and Pa Bell made the promise easy to keep.

The Bells had loved the girls from the first. She wished everyone could have people like them—loving and true. They'd never once given her any reason to doubt them or their word.

"I'm sorry you don't have parents," she said as she handed Wyatt the empty cup.

Wyatt nodded as he took it from her. "How much do I owe you for the oats and the food? They're very much appreciated. Thank you, in case I forgot to say that earlier."

Normally she would name the price and take the money, but his question gave her a way to see more of him, assess how honest he was. "You can settle up with Pa later."

"I'll do that."

She rolled up the sack she'd brought the supplies in and rose. "If there's anything else you need, don't hesitate to ask."

Wyatt rose, too, and smiled at her. "Much obliged."

She studied him. He had a nice smile, but it didn't erase the dark shadows that lingered in his eyes. It was those shadows, and his reluctance to say where he and Lonnie had come from and where they were going, that made her wary of him. "Bye for now."

He nodded. "Goodbye."

She glanced past him to Lonnie. "Bye, Lonnie."

The boy's head jerked up, his lips parted, his eyes wide. "Bye." The word squeaked from him.

Was he afraid of her? But why?

His eyes went to Wyatt, who stood with his back to his brother.

Was Lonnie afraid of his brother? That gave her cause for concern. One thing was certain. There was something not quite right with this pair, and until she knew it wasn't anything that threatened anyone in her family—including herself—she would not be encouraging any contact. She silently prayed as she returned to the farm. *God, make the truth known, clear and plain. Protect my family. May we serve You in sincerity and truth.*

Rose and Lilly watched for her return. "Did you find out anything?" they asked in unison.

"Their parents are dead." Her voice trembled. "I can't help feeling sorry for anyone whose parents are dead."

The girls nodded.

Cora said, "Makes us all the more grateful for being adopted by the Bells."

"We need to tell them again," Rose said.

The girls agreed they would be more faithful at telling their parents how much they appreciated their love.

Cora knew the twins wondered about their birth parents, but she was the only one with any recollection of them. Not that it mattered. They were now the Bell sisters.

"Did you find out where they're going?" Rose asked.

"How did the mares look?" Lilly added.

Cora chuckled. "I could tell which one asked each question without seeing either of you. Lilly's first concern is the animals. Rose's is to have all the questions answered."

The girls faced her as a pair. "Well?"

She grinned and teased them. "Well, what?"

"The mares?" Lilly prodded.

"They looked all right to me, but I honestly didn't look very closely at them. Wyatt and his brother built a rope corral that looked fine."

Lilly sighed long. "The mare he had here was foot weary and about ready to foal. I'm wondering how the others are."

Cora gave a little shrug. "I'm sorry, but I can't say."

"Did they say where they were going? Or where they were from?" Rose demanded.

"No more than they told Pa."

"Hmm." Rose's brows furrowed. "Why do you suppose they don't say?"

Lilly shrugged. "Could be any number of reasons. No need to imagine some deep, dark secret."

Rose huffed. "I'm not imagining anything. I just don't like unanswered questions. Or unfinished business. Seems to me if a person has nothing to hide they can answer civil questions."

Lilly gave her twin a fierce look. "Or maybe they just want to be left to themselves."

"Girls," Cora soothed before the pair got really involved in their differing opinions. "I've decided we should give the two of them a wide berth until we're certain they pose no risk."

"Risk to who?" Rose demanded.

"Their poor animals." Lilly shook her head.

"A risk to us," Cora corrected. "To you two. To Ma and Pa. They seem harmless enough, but I don't intend to believe first impressions. Now let's get the chores done and help Ma with supper."

She brought in the two milk cows and milked them while Lilly fed the pigs and chickens. Rose gathered the eggs and went to help Ma.

That evening they kept busy with shelling the peas they'd picked earlier. It gave them plenty of time to talk and even more time to think.

Even without the conversation circling back to the two newcomers and their horses, Cora's thoughts went unbidden to Wyatt sitting down by the river in his crude little camp. Hungry, orphaned and caring for a younger brother who seemed troubled, to say the least.

Or was she being like Rose and, in her search for answers, making up things that had no basis in fact?

One thing was certain. She would not let down her guard until she had some assurance that it was safe to do so.

* * *

Wyatt didn't come to pay Pa that evening. Perhaps he'd taken the feed and victuals and moved on. In the morning, Cora slipped close enough to see that they were still there. Lonnie was brushing Fanny until her coat shone. Where was Wyatt? She looked around. Then she spotted him, headed up the hill toward the house.

She bolted to her feet and scampered back before he got there. Slightly breathless, she hurried to meet him.

"Good morning. I came to pay your pa," he said, snatching his hat from his head. His face was slightly reddened, as if he'd scrubbed it hard in cold water. He was freshly shaven. She hadn't noticed his well-shaped chin yesterday. His damp hair looked black.

"He's in his work shed. I'll take you to him." She led the way to the weather-stained building where Pa spent many happy hours.

"Pa," she called. "Mr. Williams has come to pay for the oats and the food I took him last night."

Pa's head poked around a cupboard. "Can't you take care of it?"

"Not this time, Pa."

He considered her a moment, seemed to understand she had her reasons and emerged. "So what did you take him?"

She told him. "I'll leave you to it." She backed away and ducked around the corner of the building to listen. Perhaps she'd see his true character in how he treated Pa. To many, her pa appeared a crippled old man. But he had his wits about him and saw far more than most realized.

Pa named a sum and coins rattled as Wyatt paid the amount.

But Wyatt didn't move away.

"What do you think of this?" Pa asked and Cora knew he wanted Wyatt to look at his latest invention.

"Interesting. What is it?" Wyatt sounded sincere.

"I'm trying to figure out how to hoe four rows at once."

Cora smiled. Pa was always experimenting and inventing. Some things turned out well, others not so well, but like Pa said, you had to try and fail before you could succeed.

"I'm not sure I've got the angle of the hoes just right. Could you hold it so I can check?"

Wyatt's boots clumped on the wooden floor as he moved to help Pa. "It's a mite heavy," Wyatt said.

"Do you think it's too heavy for the girls? Bear in mind they're good strong girls."

Wyatt grunted a time or two. "Seems as if it would be a big load, especially if they're supposed to pull it through the soil."

"You could be right. Maybe if I shape the hoes to a point?"

"Might work."

A thump, rattle and several grunts came from the shed.

Cora edged around the corner so she could see what they were doing.

They'd turned the hoe over on its back and Wyatt squatted next to Pa. "Maybe like this?" He indicated with his finger.

"That might do it."

"You maybe should get some metal ones. They'd cut through the soil better."

Pa gave Wyatt an approving smile. "Yup. Figured to do that once I get the working model figured out."

He rubbed his crippled leg. "Sure can't move about the way I used to."

Cora saw Pa's considering look. She didn't want him to get it in his head that he'd return to work on the barn. He was getting too old and had already had one fall. No, she'd do it by herself before she'd let that happen. She sprang forward.

"Pa—oh, hi, Wyatt. Did you two sort out the payment?"

"Sure did."

Pa turned back to his hoe. "I'm going to try that."

Wyatt patted Pa's back. "Don't hesitate to ask if you need help with it. Or anything."

"Maybe you'd like a tour of the place." Now, why had she offered that? She didn't have time for a social visit. Not with beans to pick and potatoes to hill and hay to cut and stack. She could be three people, and the twins could be doubled, and the work would never end. Which, she supposed, about described the lot of most farmers. But having offered, she had little choice but to show the stranger around and learn more about him.

One way or another.

Chapter Three

Wyatt would enjoy seeing more of this tidy little farm. He didn't mind the company, either. The young woman's chatter was a pleasant change from Lonnie's dour complaints about having to stay in one place. No amount of explaining about the necessity of stopping for Fanny's sake satisfied him. Wyatt had been grateful to leave the boy cleaning up the campsite after breakfast.

He and Cora fell in, side by side. The lop-eared dog trotted alongside them. He tripped over himself and skidded into the ground.

Wyatt chuckled. "What kind of dog do you call that?"

"He doesn't mind what we call him, so long as we don't call him late for supper."

Wyatt laughed. She sure did have a way of easing his mind.

As they walked beside the garden, Cora explained that they grew enough to supply their own needs and sell to others. But she stopped when they reached an overgrown patch of wild plants.

"We don't ever touch that," Cora said. "It's Ma's healing plants. She is the only one who can tell which ones are good and which are weeds. To me, they all look like weeds. She lets them grow wild and untamed. I've suggested she should tidy them to rows so we can clean up the patch." Cora sighed. "By her reaction, you'd think I'd told her I planned to plow it under. So it stays that way."

Wyatt studied the unruly growth, and compared it to the rest of the neat garden. He understood the need for order, allowing the plants to be better tended, but something about the untamed patch pulled at his thoughts. Wild and free. He shifted back to study of the tidy garden. Order and control. He'd had enough of the latter while in prison, but the former didn't satisfy him, either. Was it possible to have something in the middle?

Cora cleared her throat to get his attention. He must have been staring at the plants long enough to make her wonder why they interested him so much.

"Maybe it could do with just a little taming," he said, as if that had been his only thought.

"That's what I said to Ma."

They proceeded down a pathway between the two gardens. Grub, seeing the direction they headed, loped ahead of them.

"Ma and Pa have planted berry bushes of all sorts—raspberries, gooseberries, currants, chokecherries—and fruit trees. We get lots of berries, but not much fruit. Seems we always get frost too soon and the winters are too severe. Pa's been grafting fruit trees to wild trees to see if that will work."

The idea intrigued Wyatt. Was this a way of combining wild and free with tame? Would it work for a tree? How about a man? "Has it?"

"There is a lot of winterkill, but a couple of trees have

given us sour little apples. Pa is determined to produce a decent apple. Says he'll call it a Montana."

They passed the bushes and reached a fence. Three cows grazed in a little pasture.

"I'm currently milking two of them."

A flock of sheep nibbled in another fenced area of grass, and a field of green oats lay beyond.

"The sheep are Lilly's project."

A trail led toward the river and they followed it. When they reached the water's edge, she stood in the shadow of the trees. They were downstream and out of sight from where Lonnie waited at the camp Wyatt had set up. He stood at her side with the sound of the water rumbling through his thoughts.

"This is one of my favorite spots." She sighed. "I can see so far. Look." She pointed. "The prairies roll away like giant waves."

He followed her direction. Indeed, the prairies were like a golden ocean. They went on and on. No walls. No bars. A man could fill his lungs to capacity here.

She shifted, brushing his arm as she pointed to his right, sending a jolt through his nerves. Even an accidental touch startled him. He wondered if she noticed, and if so, what did she think? Would she put it down to unexpectedness? Of course she would. She had no way of knowing that any contact in jail had signaled violence, and before that, Pa's touch had taught him to jerk away.

No wonder Lonnie was so anxious about even gentle touches. But Wyatt would teach him…teach them both to welcome such.

Cora spoke softly. "In that direction you see the hills with their hollows full of trees." She turned still farther.

"And the mountains in the west. 'Tis truly a beautiful land, and like Pa says, we are to be good stewards of it."

"I never thought of being a steward of the land."

"I take it you're planning to have a ranch and raise horses."

It was an obvious conclusion. "Kind of hope to."

"Are you opposed to farmers?

He shrugged. "Not opposed to much of anything."

She shifted and pinned him with a look. "Don't you believe in seeking good and avoiding evil?"

Her look reached into his chest to squeeze his heart. He stiffened as pain and regret oozed out. "I hate evil." She'd never know how much of it he'd seen.

She nodded silent approval and his heart beat smoothly again.

He heard the sound of horses' hooves and turned to see two riders approach. Beside him, Cora stiffened, alert and cautious.

Wyatt gave his full attention to the pair. Nothing out of the ordinary as far as he could tell. Medium build, lean as cowboys usually were. Dusty, work-soiled cowboy hats pulled low to shade their eyes. They rode slowly, as if studying the surroundings, or perhaps looking for a wayward horse. But he'd seen no sign of a wandering animal.

They rode closer, seemed to be aiming at the river. One spoke to the other. He couldn't hear their words, but mocking laughter carried across the distance. They were fifty yards away when they reined up and stared at Cora and Wyatt. He realized they were in the shadows and the pair hadn't noticed them until then.

The bigger of the men pushed his hat back, allowing Wyatt to see a swarthy man with a deep scowl. There was something about him that sent sharp prickles up Wyatt's spine. He'd seen the same expression many times in prison, usually on the face of a bully. Someone who used intimidation to make people obey him.

He guessed Cora felt the same because she tensed even more. Her fists curled so tight her knuckles were white.

The man turned his horse and the pair rode away. Not until they were out of sight did Cora's shoulders sag.

"You know those two?" he asked.

She sucked in air with such force he figured she hadn't breathed for several minutes. She coughed as her lungs filled.

Wyatt patted her back gently, as if calming a frightened animal. "Are you okay?"

She nodded. "I'm fine. The big cowboy is Ebner. He works for the Caldwell Ranch." Her lip curled. "I believe he is responsible for almost all of the harm we've suffered."

He nodded. Just as he thought. He'd dealt with men of that sort before and ended up with an enemy or two. Not that it bothered him. He refused to back down from any bully.

"What kind of things?" he asked her.

"He's cut our fences, chased the milk cows until he might have killed them. He's turned Caldwell cows into our garden and let the pigs loose." She waved her hands as she described the events. Her voice rang with the injustice of it.

He caught her hands and stilled them. Realizing the liberty he'd taken, he dropped his arms to his sides. But not before a longing as wide as the prairie swept into his heart, making him aware of how empty and barren his life was. He wanted so much more than the right to hold her and comfort her. He longed for a home and love. He hoped to gain the first for Lonnie's sake as well as his own. Winning Lonnie's trust would have to satisfy his desire for love. He'd never ask or expect a woman to share the shame of being associated with a jailbird.

"Why do these men bother you? Doesn't their boss know?"

"Mr. Caldwell likely orders them to do it. From the time we settled here, he's been trying to drive us off."

"Why would he care about your farm?"

She shrugged, her eyes full of anger. "I've asked that question many times. He told Pa it breaks up the perimeter of his ranch and blocks access to the river." She snorted. "As if a few acres of farm are any hindrance to his animals watering at the river. But sodbusters are not welcome."

"Isn't there a marshal in the area? Surely he can protect your rights."

"The Caldwells manage to stay within the law. They claim they can't help it if the cows don't understand fences. Only once has the sheriff been convinced the wires were purposely cut, and of course no one confessed to it, so there wasn't anything the sheriff could do."

"Well, you'd think the man would realize how unimportant a few acres are." Even as he said it, he guessed it wasn't about the acres but about the man's pride. A rich man, likely used to getting what he wanted, and for whatever reason, he wanted the Bell farm. Or to be rid of the settlers in his midst.

"It's mostly that he's a Caldwell and wants to own everything on this side of the river," Cora commented.

She turned her gaze from the trail of dust kicked up

by the cowboys' retreating horses and looked at him. Her dark eyes flashed with anger. "Maybe they saw you and thought we'd hired a guard."

His plans did not include being a bodyguard to anyone. Except wasn't that what he'd been for Lonnie? And continued to be?

But neither would he stand by and watch a bunch of cowboys bully the Bells. Not just because they had been kind to him, though that was reason enough, but because he would never stand by while people were pushed around for no reason. People could be pushed too far. He'd seen that with Lonnie and vowed to never again stand by and not take action. It had been the reason he'd stood up to Jimmy Stone. While he was here waiting for Fanny to foal, he'd keep his eyes open to any sort of trouble.

Cora turned and stepped away from the river. "I need to get at my chores."

He followed her. They reached the edge of the garden and she stopped.

"Is there anything you need?" she asked.

"No, thanks. I enjoyed the tour of your farm."

She met his eyes and smiled, and he was struck by the friendliness of her look. Her brown eyes were bottomless, as if she had nothing to hide.

Of course she didn't. She'd been open with him.

He jerked his gaze past her lest she see the vast ocean of secrets he hid, and must always hide, if he and Lonnie hoped to have any chance of starting over.

"I need to get back to Lonnie," he mumbled, and trotted away. His mind whirled with so many things—the beauty of the well-developed little farm and the endless land and the look on the face of that Caldwell cowboy, but mostly Cora's pride in who she was and her fear at the approach of those riders.

It wasn't right that this idyllic home should be marred by bullying cowboys. Cora had been kind to him from the start and he wanted to do something to show his gratitude.

He passed the partially constructed barn. Did they have neighbors or friends who were going to help finish it?

Seeing the building gave him an idea. A way he could repay the Bell's kindness and watch the Caldwell cowboys. He'd offer to work on the barn.

He'd talk to Mr. Bell about it as soon as he'd checked on Lonnie.

"Cora, our prayers have been answered," Pa said to her later that morning.

She straightened from hilling the potato plants and tried to think which prayer he meant.

The one for good weather? Well, seemed they had that to be grateful for.

Enough rain and sunshine to promise a bountiful crop? Again, it seemed that prayer had been generously answered. *Thank You, God.*

Or did he mean the one about protecting them from the mischief of the Caldwell cowboys?

Or perhaps the one he and Ma made no attempt to hide—to provide good, Christian husbands for the three girls and to give them many grandchildren while they were young enough to enjoy them. She grinned as she thought of that prayer. Then her amusement fled. They'd actually thanked God when Evan had ridden off.

"He wasn't the man for you," Pa had said.

Ma had hugged Cora. "You'll see it's true, once you get over being hurt."

Cora knew they were right. It was her pride that was hurt more than her heart.

"Which prayer is that, Pa?"

"The one asking for someone to help finish the barn."

She jerked to full attention and glanced around. "Someone came in answer to my advertisement? Guess Mr. Frank was wrong." She wondered who was prepared to ignore the Caldwells' displeasure, but saw no one and returned her attention to Pa.

"In answer to our prayers, not your notice."

"What do you mean?"

"He didn't see the notice."

Cora shook her head as if doing so would make her understand what Pa was talking about. "Who?"

"Wyatt, of course."

"Wyatt?" She'd been thinking about it all morning—weighing the pros and cons, mentally listing what she knew about him against what she didn't know—and she still wasn't ready to take a chance on him, lest he be hiding something that would bring danger into their lives. "But, Pa, what do we know about him?"

"What do we need to know except he's big and strong and willing to help?"

"Indeed." Except maybe where he was from and where he was going and what was in between the past and the future. Wyatt Williams made her want to know all his secrets.

"When's he planning to start?"

"I said you'd tell him what to do."

She was glad Pa didn't want to climb up the ladder and show Wyatt what to do, but she glanced at the potatoes yet to hill, then over to the barn. She couldn't be in two places at the same time. Rose and Lilly were helping Ma can peas and make rhubarb preserves. She sighed and took the hoe to the shed.

Grub stirred himself from the cool garden soil and ambled after her. Despite her frustration, she smiled as she looked at his grin. Something she'd not really noticed until Wyatt pointed it out.

Maybe working with the newcomer wouldn't be so bad.

She patted Grub's head. "Are you coming with me to find him?"

Grub wriggled so hard his hind legs got ahead of him and he almost tumbled into a tangle.

Cora laughed and patted his head again, then turned toward the river and the place where Wyatt and Lonnie camped.

"You looking for me?"

She cranked her head around, feeling about as awkward as Grub.

Wyatt leaned against the corner of the bare barn walls, so relaxed and at ease it made her want to suggest they forget work and go for a walk. But he wasn't here to waste time and neither was she.

"Pa said you offered to help build the barn."

"Yes, in exchange for feed for my horses and some supplies for Lonnie and me, and he agreed."

"I'm glad to have some help." She stopped a few feet from the building and studied it. "We got this far—" The external walls were up, holes in place for windows and doors. "But Pa fell and hurt his leg." She shook her head. "He's getting too old to be running up and down the ladder." She had to admit, though, his movements were more of a crawl than a run.

She closed her eyes against the fear that claimed her every time she thought of Pa falling.

"Is he hurt bad?" Wyatt's quiet voice made it possible to talk again.

"He says it's nothing, but I see the pain in his face when he moves too fast or turns too suddenly. It could have been so much worse." Her voice broke and she paused to take in two calming breaths. "I saw him fall and thought—" Her throat clogged with tears and she couldn't go on.

Wyatt unwound from his casual position and closed the distance between them. "God protected him."

She nodded, grateful for his kind words. "And gifted us with more time with him." She shook the depressing thoughts from her mind. "Do you have experience with construction?"

"I've helped put up a few buildings. Guess I know enough to put the right board in the right place and nail it solid." His face wreathed in a grin. "If not, I hope you'll correct me."

She chuckled. "All I know is what I've learned from Pa. But I was only twelve when he built these other buildings, and mostly I handed him nails." Her amusement grew as she thought of those days. "He let me hammer in a few nails and praised my efforts, but I believe he pulled out the bent nails and hammered them in straight when I wasn't looking."

"Sounds like he's a good father."

"The best." A movement caught her eye and she saw Lonnie hiding in the shadows. "Are you going to help, too?" she asked him.

Lonnie ducked his head, as if he didn't plan to an-swer, then lifted it and faced her squarely. "I mean to do my share."

"That's all anyone can expect, isn't it?"

Even though he remained in the shadows, she saw a flicker of acknowledgment in his eyes. The boy seemed hungry for approval. Too bad Pa wasn't going to be su-pervising. He was the expert on giving encouragement and approval but she'd be second best if she could.

"The tools are in the shed."

"I already got them," Wyatt said, pointing toward the saws and hammers next to the stack of lumber.

"Then let's get at it." She headed for the lumber pile. "Stu Maples, who owns the lumber yard, said we'd never be able to build the barn on our own—a bunch of women and a man getting up in years." She chuckled. "But he didn't mind selling us the lumber."

Wyatt grabbed a board, laid it across the sawhorses, measured and cut it. "Lonnie, help me put it in place."

Lonnie raced forward and grabbed an end.

Cora followed them. As soon as the board was in place, she started nailing.

Wyatt left her and Lonnie to do that while he cut another piece. They soon worked in a smooth rhythm.

"How long have you been here?" Wyatt asked.

"Eight years. Before that we lived in town. But Pa wanted us to be able to grow and produce more so we'd be self-sufficient."

"Seems you got a little bit of everything."

"Chickens, sheep, pigs, milk cows, the garden. I guess we have most everything. We make cheese, spin the wool and can the produce." She knew her voice rang with pride.

Wyatt chuckled. "And you're very proud of all your family has achieved."

She straightened and grinned at him. "Guess I make it pretty obvious."

Wyatt handed her the next board. "I'd say you have good reason to feel that way."

"It's my family I'm most proud of. We're strong and... survivors, I guess you'd say."

"Huh?" He paused from sawing a board to look at her. "Survivors? Oh, I suppose you mean the Caldwells."

"That and other things." Their gazes connected across the distance as he seemed to contemplate asking her for further explanation.

She didn't mind providing the answer, whether or not he asked the question. "Not all fathers are like my pa."

Lonnie dropped a board and jerked back, a look of such abject fear on his face that she automatically reached for him. She meant to comfort him, but he threw up his arms as if he expected her to—

Hit him?

She looked to Wyatt for explanation.

He focused on Lonnie. "It's okay, Lon. No harm done. Just pick up your end again."

Lonnie shuddered. His wide dark eyes slowly returned to normal and he bent to retrieve the board.

Cora continued to stare at him, then shifted her study to Wyatt. There was something seriously wrong with Lonnie, and if Wyatt planned to stay on the place, she needed an explanation.

Wyatt met her look and shook his head.

She nodded. Now was not the time or the place, but she would be sure to find an opportunity very soon. If whatever caused Lonnie's fear threatened the safety and security of her family in any way, she would insist they move on.

But would he tell her the truth?

Her experience with men didn't give her much confidence that he would.

Chapter Four

Cora returned to the task of building the barn for another half hour, then straightened. "I'm thirsty. Let's get a drink."

Wyatt dropped everything and followed her toward the pump. Even Lonnie didn't hesitate.

She pumped and Wyatt filled the dipper.

"Thanks. I'm about parched." He drank three full dippers, then took off his hat and poured some over his head. He shook the water from his face and planted his hat back on his wet head. "That's better. Thanks."

Her eyes followed the trails streaking from his wavy, dark brown hair down his sun-bronzed face and dripping off his chiseled chin. Chiseled chin! She snorted. What kind of observation was that? Right up there with her mental description of his chocolate-colored eyes with flashes of evening shadows in them and a certain sadness that she'd noticed before and put down to something in his past that he hid.

She drank from the dipper and considered pouring the rest of the water over her head. It might cool her face, but it would do nothing to cool her thoughts.

She splashed cold water on her face and handed the dipper to Lonnie, who drank his fill. Then, with a grin teasing his lips, he lifted his hat and poured water over his head.

Wyatt stared at him.

Cora laughed, which brought two pairs of eyes toward her. She couldn't tell which of the two was more surprised, but Wyatt recovered first and tipped his head back and laughed. Then, his eyes sparkling, he squeezed Lonnie's shoulder.

Cora could see the boy start to shrug away and then stop himself, and the pleasure in Wyatt's eyes went so deep that it made her eyes sting.

She could hardly wait to hear Wyatt's explanation for his brother's odd behavior.

Rose trotted toward the garden, likely to get potatoes for supper.

Lilly sang as she went to feed the pigs.

"I need to do chores," Cora said.

Wyatt nodded. "We'll work a bit longer." He and Lonnie returned to the barn while Cora made her way to the pasture to get the cows. First, she did her usual check on the pasture fence. It had a habit of mysteriously breaking down and letting the cows wander away. Not that there was any mystery about the cause of the frequent breaks. The cowboys from the Caldwell ranch broke the wires and generally made life as miserable as possible for the Bells.

She found no breaks in the fence. The cowboys must be too busy to harass them at the moment. The sun headed toward the mountaintops, signaling the end of the afternoon as she finished inspecting the fence and took Bossy and Maude home, lowing for feed and milking.

She gave them each a few oats, grabbed the milk buckets and milked the cows. As she rose to turn the cows into the pen, she almost ran into Wyatt as he rounded the corner at the same time.

He clamped his hands on her shoulders to steady her. "Whoa there, girl."

His warm and firm hands held her like an anchor. His fingers pressed into her shoulders, easing an ache she'd developed while hoeing in the garden and then hammering nails. A scent of warm soil, hard work and strength filled her nostrils and tugged at something deep inside. She fought to right herself—not physically but mentally. When had she ever reacted so strongly to a simple touch? Or the nearness of a man? She certainly hadn't had these unexpected feelings around Evan.

Evan! Remembering him made her pull back.

Wyatt's hands dropped to his sides.

She sucked in air to keep from swaying. "Sorry," she murmured. "Wasn't paying attention. Truth is, I don't usually see anyone around when I'm milking." It was one of the times she could count on solitude.

"Let me guess. No one else wants to share the task."

She couldn't decide if he teased or not and wouldn't look directly at him to gauge. She was finding it much too difficult to think clearly already. "Did you want something?" Of course he did. What other reason would he come to the shed?

"I think you and I need to talk."

"Yes, we do."

"Would you like to go for a walk after supper?"

Her thoughts hammered against the inside of her head. It sounded like a courting request, but of course it was only a way for them to talk.

No reason for her to be on edge.

"That will be fine." She took the buckets of milk and headed for the house. She could walk with a man without her heart racing ahead with possibilities.

Wyatt knew Cora would demand to know about Lonnie's reaction. He thought of what he'd say while he and Lonnie tended the horses and built a small fire to fry up the potatoes and the last of the eggs. He hated to always be asking, but he needed more eggs and meat if the Bells could spare some. Lonnie needed to eat better. The boy was as scrawny as a poplar sapling.

"Did you like working on the barn?" Lonnie asked.

Wyatt wasn't sure what the boy wanted with his unexpected question. "I like building things. Always have."

"Huh. What have you built?"

"Have you forgotten I built that rocker Ma had?"

"Pa broke it after you went to jail."

Wyatt glanced both ways out of habit.

Lonnie jerked around and studied the surroundings. "Sooner or later they're gonna find out."

"Maybe so, but I don't intend to tell them." He turned the conversation back to building.

Lonnie looked interested for about thirty seconds, then his expression soured. "Suppose that's why Pa broke it? 'Cause you built it?"

"Likely. But I still had the fun of making it and seeing her rock in it."

Lonnie stared at the fire.

Wyatt waited, hoping he would say something more. When he didn't, Wyatt returned to Lonnie's original question. "The Bells have been hospitable to us. Mr. Bell is finding it hard to get around, and the womenfolk shouldn't be trying to build a barn on their own. So maybe God brought us here to help them."

"God don't care where we go or what we do." Those few words carried a whole world of misery that Wyatt would erase if it was possible, but he knew it wasn't. He could only pray Lonnie would find his way to trust. Not only trust God but trust people.

"I guess I have to believe otherwise or life looks mighty uninviting."

Lonnie's only reply was to sag over his knees.

"Supper's ready. Hold out your plate."

Lonnie did so and ate in a distracted way.

Wyatt waited, hoping his brother would open up and say what he was thinking.

Lonnie finally spoke. "Did you see the pigs?"

"Uh-huh."

"They sure are cute, aren't they?" Lonnie's eyes lit with joy in a way Wyatt hadn't seen in a long time.

"How about we have pigs on our new farm?"

Lonnie nodded, a genuine smile on his face. "I'd like that."

"Me, too." If it made his brother smile like that he'd raise a hundred pigs. "I asked Cora to go for a walk with me this evening."

Lonnie bolted to his feet. "You're going to court her? What's gonna happen to me? Nobody will want a young brother tagging along. You ever think of that?"

"You don't need to worry. In the first place, I don't think anyone is going to want a jailbird. But even if that wasn't the case, you and I are brothers. We stick together no matter what." As an afterthought, he added, "This isn't courting. Just need to straighten up a few things with her."

"Like what?"

Wyatt wasn't about to tell him the whole reason—that Cora had grown curious about Lonnie's odd behavior. Instead, he said, "What all she needs done so we can earn our keep."

"Oh." Lonnie sat down again and nodded, but the fearful look did not leave.

Wyatt squeezed the boy's shoulder. "If it ever comes to choosing between you and someone else, I promise I'll choose you."

Lonnie nodded, but kept his eyes on the dying flames of the fire. "Want me to wash the dishes?"

"We'll do them together." He filled the basin with hot water from the fire and Lonnie grabbed a towel. The few dishes were soon done.

"What are you going to do while I see Cora?" Wyatt asked. He must talk to her but didn't care for leaving Lonnie alone.

"Guess I'll watch Fanny. Maybe she'll have her foal tonight." Worry lined his forehead. "What if she foals while you're gone? Something might go wrong."

"I expect she'll be fine, so don't worry."

"But what if—"

"You go up and find Mr. Bell. He'll know what to do."

Lonnie rocked his head back and forth.

Wyatt grabbed his chin to stop the movement. "Would you let your choices hurt Fanny and her baby?" He waited as Lonnie considered the question.

"Guess I wouldn't."

He released Lonnie's chin. "I knew you wouldn't, but kind of figured you needed to know it, too."

Lonnie snorted but a smile tugged at his lips and Wyatt knew he'd gained a small victory. He almost wished Fanny would foal while he was out walking with Cora so Lonnie would go to Mr. Bell for help. Wouldn't that be a giant step forward for his brother?

"I'll see you later."

Wyatt climbed the hill and leaned against the corner post of the garden fence to wait for Cora. The scent of flowers wafted through the air on a gentle breeze. Birds sang and scolded from the trees and fence lines. Grub wandered over and flopped down at Wyatt's feet. He scratched behind the dog's ears and earned a moist lick of Grub's tongue.

The dog equivalent of thanks.

Wyatt filled his lungs to capacity with the warm, sweet air. If only life could be like this always.

The screen door squawked open and Cora stepped out. She glanced around until she found him. The air between them shimmered with tension. She would demand answers. He must say only enough to satisfy her questions. At all costs, he must protect their secret.

She smiled, and the tightness in his chest eased.

He continued to lounge back as she crossed the yard toward him. All day, as they'd worked on the barn, she had worn a floppy straw hat. Now her head was bare. The sun shone on her hair, making it shine like gold. Each stride she took said she knew who she was. Moreover, she liked who she was and was confident of her place in the world.

He wished he could share that feeling.

As she approached, her smile never faltered. Her eyes said she had purpose.

He knew all too well what that purpose was. And he meant to delay the moment as long as he could. He pushed away from the fence post that had been his support for the past fifteen minutes and smiled at her. He was glad of her company despite the reason for it.

"Let's walk," she said.

His smile deepened. Maybe she wasn't any more anxious for the moment of truth than he.

He fell in at her side and they made their way to the river and turned to the left to walk along the bank.

"The wildflowers are so bountiful this time of year. I love the summer flowers." She pointed out a patch of brown-eyed Susans and bluebonnets. "There's some balsamroot. Ma uses the root to make a tonic and cough medicine."

Content to let her talk and simply enjoy the evening, he turned toward some flowers. "Does your ma use these for anything?"

She squatted by the patch of flowers, touching the blossoms gently. As she lifted her face to him, a smile filled her eyes. "Yes, she does." Cora straightened. "Every year, when the brown-eyed Susans—or, as she prefers to call them, black-eyed Susans—are at their best, she fills a jug with the blossoms and puts it in the middle of the table." She looked into the distance, the soft smile still on her lips. "And she repeats a poem about the black-eyed Susan who was a woman. Her sweet William was sailing away and she feared he would forget her. He said she would be present wherever he went. Her eyes would be seen in the diamonds they found, her breath would be sweeter than any spices and her skin prettier than any ivory. Every beautiful object he saw would remind him of his pretty Susan." She drew in a slow breath. "It's a lovely poem." She shrugged. "Now you'll think me a romantic, and I'm not."

"What would be wrong if you were?" She'd certainly

sent his mind on a lovely romantic journey. Oh, that he could promise some sweet Susan such fidelity. His heart hurt at the knowledge that the best he could offer any Susan was to protect her from sharing the shame of his past. For, although he'd done nothing wrong, he'd learned people only saw the fact that he'd spent time in jail.

She laughed, a merry little sound. "I'm Cora, the practical sister." She turned her steps back to the riverbank. "I take care of business."

"Because you have to or because you want to?"

She stopped dead and turned to face him squarely. "Why, both, of course."

"You mean your sisters or your ma or pa couldn't look after business if you didn't?" He didn't know why it mattered one way or the other to him, but for some reason it did. Perhaps because he felt as if she was creating a prison for herself—one with no walls or bars or guards except of her own making. And jails, real or otherwise, were not pleasant places.

She shrugged. "I suppose they could, but they don't have to. Come this way. Shh." She pressed her finger to her lips as she tiptoed toward a swampy area. "I like watching the baby ducklings." She plopped down as if prepared to stay awhile.

He sank to the ground beside her. He'd been dreading this walk and the talk that was to accompany it. But sitting by the slough and watching birds was fine with him.

The mother duck had flapped the ducklings into hiding in the reeds at their approach, but as they sat quietly, the little family soon emerged and resumed looking for food.

He realized Cora had shifted her attention from the birds to him and studied him intently. Slowly he brought his gaze to hers. The moment had come, and he drew in a deep, steadying breath.

"I want to know why Lonnie is so afraid," she said, her voice soft, as if she thought he might react the way Lonnie had.

He'd considered how to answer, had even rehearsed what he'd say, but now it didn't feel right, so he stared at the water before them and tried to shepherd his thoughts into order.

"The reason he acted like that was because you said not all fathers are like your pa. He knows too well the truth of those words." Wyatt slowly returned his eyes to her, wanting to see her reaction, assess her response.

Her brown eyes softened and he drew in courage at the thought that she was sympathetic.

"My father beat us regularly." He recalled so many times being kicked or hit with something—whatever his pa could lay his hands on. One time, the old man had come after him with an ax. It had been one of the few times Wyatt had defended himself.

She touched the back of his hand. "That's awful. I'm so sorry. Poor Lonnie. No wonder he shrinks back when someone gets too close."

Wyatt nodded. The pressure of her fingers on his skin unwound a tightness behind his heart. "The worst part was not knowing what Lonnie endured the last year of Pa's life."

The movement of her fingers stilled. Slowly she withdrew her hand.

He tried to think what he'd said to make her pull away and look at him as if he'd admitted to some terrible behavior.

"Where were you that you didn't know?"

He resisted an urge to thump his forehead. He'd opened the door a crack and she meant to walk right through.

"I had to be away."

"You left him?" Her shock echoed through his head. Every day he'd prayed that Lonnie would be safe. In fact, it was in prison that he'd learned to pray and been forced to trust God, simply because there was nothing else he could do.

"I had no choice," he murmured.

She shook her head and turned to stare ahead. "I would never abandon my sisters."

"Sometimes you don't have any alternative." Misery edged each word, but she didn't seem to notice. Or perhaps she didn't care.

"I can't imagine any reason strong enough except death." The look she gave him seemed to point out that he was very much alive, so he couldn't claim that excuse.

His eyebrows went up. She had laid down a challenge—*give me a good reason or face my censure.*

He could not give her a good reason. That secret remained locked up for Lonnie's protection as well as his own.

She jumped to her feet. "I'd better get back before Pa comes looking for me."

He rose more slowly, aching with disappointment, though why it should be so he would have to reason out at a later date. He only knew he wished their time together could have ended differently. He touched the spot on the back of his hand where her fingers had rubbed.

Then he flung his hands apart. Bad enough to be condemned for supposedly abandoning his brother. Think how much worse it would be if she learned he'd been in jail.

No woman would ever touch him in a gentle, accepting way once the truth was discovered. It hadn't taken many days of freedom to learn this truth. People crossed the street to avoid him. Fathers and mothers dragged their daughters away as if a mere glance at him would ruin them for life. And discovery was always a possibility no matter how far he and Lonnie went. Nor had he forgotten the threat of one Jimmy Stone. Jimmy knew where they lived. He'd made a point of reminding Wyatt of the fact when Wyatt had got out of prison. Wyatt didn't doubt the man's intention to get revenge. He wasn't even that surprised when he heard a man fitting Jimmy's description had been asking about him. If Jimmy meant to find him, he would, unless they could outrun him. They had to move on as soon as possible to escape their past.

Wyatt had even considered changing their names but drew a line there. He was Wyatt Williams and he'd live and die with that name.

Cora steamed away. How could Wyatt have left Lonnie, knowing full well the abuse he would suffer? Had he done it to escape his father's wrath? He claimed he'd had no choice. She snorted. A person always had a choice. Some chose to fulfill their responsibilities. Some chose to abandon them.

All her life she'd lived with not knowing why their papa, as she always referred to the man who had been their father, had walked away from them. She couldn't even remember their last name. Not that it mattered at all.

What mattered to Cora was that a man had shirked his role as a father. For whatever reason. No doubt he would also say he didn't have a choice, but she couldn't believe there was any good reason to abandon three little girls in the middle of the prairie. They would surely have perished if Ma hadn't been out looking for her medicinal plants and found them.

The twins had quickly responded to her hugs and kisses and the food she'd shared with them from her satchel. Cora had been more guarded. Her papa's promise to return had sustained her the two days and a night of fear.

Ma had asked a few questions—enough to know Cora's papa wasn't coming back.

Agitated by the memories, Cora spun to confront Wyatt, who had followed her. "There is no good reason for abandoning family. Ever."

"You certainly have very strong opinions about it. But how can you possibly understand? You enjoy your parents' love and have two sisters to share it with. You simply couldn't begin to understand."

"Oh, I understand far better than you think." She stomped three more paces. She would not blurt out the words on the tip of her tongue, but she knew exactly how it felt to be left behind, and no excuse in this world or the next would be enough. She might just tell him that. She turned again. A hornet flew in her face and she brushed it away. It didn't leave but stung her on the cheek.

"Ouch."

Others buzzed around her, a swarm of angry hornets bent on attack. She swatted at them, shook her skirts to discourage them and stepped backward. Her heel caught on a clod of dirt and she fell down hard, smacking her head on the ground.

The hornets buzzed about her, stinging her hands and face.

Wyatt scooped her up and raced for the river. "What are you doing?" She hung on as he jostled her.

They reached the edge of the water and he set her down. "You were standing on their underground nest." He pushed aside her hair to examine her stings, pulled up her hands to look at the exposed skin. "You were fortunate. Only six stings. Sit here." He scooped up some river mud and returned to her side. "This is the best way to stop the pain. Close your eyes."

She did so. There was no denying the stings hurt. He held her chin as he plastered mud on the three on her face.

Her face grew warm. Surely he would put it down to the aftereffects of the stings, not to the sharp awareness of how gently he spread the mud, how firm his cool fingers were on her chin. Yet she felt no fear. He would not hurt her. How could she possibly know that? Hadn't she learned not to trust so easily? But none of her lessons applied to Wyatt. Or was she blindly ignoring what her head told her?

He released her chin and picked up her hand.

She quietly drew in a calming breath and watched him apply mud to the backs of her hands. "You must have had a good mother." The words came out of their own accord.

She waited, wondering how he'd respond.

He shook the rest of the mud from his hands and wiped them on the grass, then he raised his gaze to hers.

"I did. But how do you know?" His eyes were almost black as she looked at him, silhouetted against the bright sky behind his head.

"Because you have a gentle touch." Again, she spoke

the truth from her heart without any thought to how he would react.

His gaze held hers, unblinking and as dark as a starless midnight.

She held her breath, waiting for him to speak or shrug or somehow indicate he'd heard and maybe even show what he thought about her words.

He laughed.

She stared. Of all the reactions he might have had, this was the most unexpected. "Why is that funny?"

He stood to his full height and grinned down at her. "Here I was thinking you would find me rough. After all, you have a mother and sisters who would normally tend your needs. I kept expecting you to tell me I was a big oaf." He laughed again. "A gentle touch, you say. I will never forget that."

He squatted in front of her. "How is your head? You took quite a fall."

Her head buzzed from the swirling confusion of her thoughts. Not from hitting the ground.

"I'm fine." She pushed to her feet. "What about you? Didn't you get stung?"

He shifted his gaze to a spot over her shoulder. "Nothing to be concerned about."

"Really? And yet you drag me over here and plaster mud on each bite?" She tried to sound teasing, but her voice caught with an overwhelming sense of tenderness. "Let me see." She grabbed his chin just as he'd done with her and felt him stiffen. He wasn't a lot different from his brother. Afraid of touches. Expecting them to be cruel. If he stayed here long he'd learn otherwise. Ma and Pa were the gentlest pair ever.

She saw no sign of stings on his face but detected

three on his neck below his ear. "You have been stung. I'll get some mud." But when she tried to stand, he shook his head.

"There's some here." He pointed toward a clump that had fallen from his hands.

She loaded her finger with some and applied it to his bites. Beneath her fingertip his muscles knotted. She ignored his tension. Being this close gave her plenty of chance to study him more closely. Tiny white lines, from squinting in the sunshine, fanned out from the corners of his eyes. His black whiskers roughened suntanned skin.

When the stings were well bathed in mud, she wiped her fingers in the grass.

She turned her eyes toward him. His gaze jerked away as if uncomfortable with all the touching of the past few minutes, even though it had been impersonal for both them. Hadn't it?

Swallowing hard, she put eight more inches between them.

"Are you feeling up to walking home?" he asked.

His tender look caused her throat to tighten. Then some little imp made her press the back of her arm to her forehead dramatically and wobble slightly.

His arm came around her shoulders and steadied her.

"Do you think you could carry me all the way?" She managed to make her voice quaver.

"I think I'll go get my horse."

She laughed. "I'll walk. I'm fine."

He nodded, a wide grin on his face. "I figured you were."

They gave the area of the hornet's nest a wide berth.

"I'll be sure to tell the others its location." She surely didn't want anyone else to be attacked. Though, on second thought, if Ebner or some other troublemaking Caldwell cowboy got a sting or two, it sounded like justice to her.

As they neared home, she slowed her steps. "Wyatt, why would you leave Lonnie with your pa, knowing what he was like? I need to understand. I want to understand."

He stopped, faced her squarely. "I'm afraid I can't tell you anything more. I had to, and that's all I can say."

She sighed. It wasn't enough and yet she couldn't believe his reasons had been selfish. Or was she letting his taking care of her for a few minutes erase her sense of caution?

Chapter Five

Wyatt kept his gaze straight forward as they returned to the farm. His fingers tingled from touching her tender skin. His neck muscles twitched at the memory of her ministrations.

When he'd seen the hornets attack her and then heard her head smack the ground, his heart had raced. He'd had to force himself to release her when he got her to the river. Something almost primitive had urged him to hold her and protect her.

He swallowed a snort. If Mr. Bell learned the truth about Wyatt, he would reveal his wrath. How would the man do that? In Wyatt's experience the only way was with fists and boots.

Rose was in the garden when Wyatt and Cora tramped by. She looked up, saw the mud on her sister's face and her mouth fell open.

Wyatt would have slipped away to avoid being questioned, but since Cora had banged her head hard he couldn't leave until he'd informed her ma.

Rose trotted over to join them. "Looks like you fell into some mud."

"I stepped on a hornet's nest," she said. "The mud takes out the pain."

Rose turned to Wyatt. "You got stung, too?"

He nodded. "It's nothing."

"Ma will want to check on you both." Rose hustled them toward the house. "Ma," she called.

Wyatt glanced over his shoulder. "Lonnie will wonder where I am." But before he could escape, the Bells crowded around them, all asking questions at the same time. Cora explained about the hornet attack and where the nest was.

"Wyatt rescued me."

Mr. Bell eyed Wyatt closely.

Wyatt couldn't tell if the man was grateful for the rescue or wondering if Wyatt had been too forward. He didn't intend to hang around waiting to find out, and edged past Lilly.

"Did Ma look at your bites?" she asked.

"I've got to get back to Lonnie," he mumbled.

"I'll let him know you've been detained." Before he could utter a single word in protest, Lilly trotted away.

He groaned. Lonnie would not welcome a visitor.

Mrs. Bell caught his attention. "You did the right thing in applying mud, but I have an ointment that will help even more. You wait here while I get it." She hurried over to the shed near the garden.

Wyatt shifted from foot to foot and looked longingly toward escape.

Cora patted his arm. "Relax. Ma's remedies are the best."

He nodded. How could he hope for her or anyone to overlook the fact he'd been in jail? If the Bells ever learned the truth, Wyatt would be run off the place. And yet...yet...what was the harm in enjoying the ministrations of a loving family until they learned the truth? Perhaps they never would. The depth of his longing frightened him, and his mouth puckered with the anguish of such futile hope.

Mrs. Bell returned. "You two come in the house and let me take care of those stings."

Cora smiled at his helpless shrug. "It won't hurt a bit, I promise."

He nodded. It might not hurt now, but it would eventually. There was no point in hoping for any other outcome. But he allowed himself to be shepherded inside, where Rose washed Cora's stings. Mrs. Bell cleaned away the mud on his neck and applied the ointment while he stared at the floor. Every touch of the older woman's cool fingers reminded him of Cora's gentle touch and tightened the tender strands of hope about his heart.

Lilly burst into the house. "I brought Lonnie back with me."

Wyatt jerked to his feet and stared at his little brother hovering at the open door.

Lonnie's eyes were wide, his fists curled into white-knuckled balls.

"Come right in and join us," Mr. Bell called from the end of the table where he watched the proceedings.

Lonnie slid in and plopped on a chair next to Wyatt. "Heard you got stung. You okay?"

So worry over Wyatt's well-being had spurred him into joining them. It certainly made a few hornet stings worthwhile. "I'm fine. Nothing that requires all this fuss."

Mrs. Bell tsked. "The girls will tell you fussing is what I do best."

"That's right," her daughters chorused, and Mr. Bell added a deep chuckle.

Mrs. Bell moved away toward the stove. "Let's have some tea and cookies."

"There's more." Wyatt remembered what had brought him here in the first place. And it wasn't to share tea and cookies with Cora's family, as appealing as that sounded. "Cora fell on her back trying to get away from the hornets. She banged her head pretty hard."

Mrs. Bell shifted direction toward Cora and the twins rushed to her side.

"Let me have a look." Mrs. Bell took Cora's chin in her hands.

Wyatt squeezed his hand into a ball. He'd done the same thing, and despite his genuine concern about her injuries, longing had risen within him. A need to hold and comfort her. A desire to let her see into his heart, to confess his secrets and receive her understanding. Fortunately, he'd been too busy to give in to such foolish thoughts.

"Where did you hit?" Cora's ma asked her.

"Back of my head."

Mrs. Bell's fingers explored through Cora's hair, loosening wisps from the braid to feather around her head.

Wyatt ducked his head to keep from staring at the shiny strands.

"I feel quite a knot," Mrs. Bell said. "How does your head feel?"

Cora laughed. "Like someone messed my hair."

The twins laughed and Mrs. Bell made a dismissive sound.

"You be sure and let me know if you feel sick or have a headache."

"Yes, Ma." She grinned at Wyatt then turned back to her mother. "Didn't you say something about tea and cookies?"

Mrs. Bell hustled away with Rose at her side, and soon the goodies were placed on the table.

"I saw the rest of your horses," Lilly said.

Cora groaned. "Lilly, he's been on the road. They won't look like horses kept in a pasture and fed oats every day."

Wyatt leaned back. "Did you think I neglected my horses?" Did Cora think the same? After he'd stopped his journey to care for Fanny? After he'd personally taken care of Cora's bites?

But when he saw Lonnie perched on the edge of his chair, his fists on his knees, Wyatt sat back. He knew it would only take one loud word for his brother to jump to his feet and race out the door.

Cora's hands grew still.

He guessed his question had caught her off guard.

"I guess I didn't know what to expect." Her voice was low as if she meant the words as a warning.

He took them as such. She wasn't prepared to trust him until all her questions were answered. And he couldn't answer most of them. That left a vast, uncrossable chasm between them.

"I saw them for myself and they look well cared for," Lilly said.

Mr. Bell murmured approval. "How is Fanny?"

"No foal yet," Lilly and Lonnie answered at the same time.

Mrs. Bell poured the tea and passed the cookies.

It was nice. Like a family ought to be. But Wyatt had to work to keep from jiggling his legs. Families talked about everything. Asked all sorts of questions. At least, that was what he'd seen with his friends' families when he was a youngster. He had to get out of there before the questions started. He ate his cookie in three bites and drank his tea in four swallows with little regard for the way it burned on the way down. Then he pushed to his feet.

"We need to get back to the animals." It seemed an excuse that the Bells would approve of. "Thank you for the tea and cookies and ointment. Come on, Lonnie."

The boy was already on his feet, headed for the door.

"Wait." Mrs. Bell pushed her chair back.

Lonnie reached the door and made his escape.

Wyatt's breath stalled halfway up his throat. Was she about to demand to know more about them? After all, they'd sat around her table. Didn't that require a certain amount of honesty and openness? He considered bolting after Lonnie.

"I'll send some ointment with you. Put it on if your stings hurt and for sure in the morning." She handed him a small jar.

"Thank you again." He strode toward the door, grabbing his hat on the way out. Not until he reached back to shut the door did he realize Cora had followed him.

"I'm sorry for sounding as though I thought badly of you," she said.

He twisted his hat round and round. "No need to apologize."

"I believe there is. You rescued me from the hornets and knew enough to plaster on mud, and I repaid you by being doubtful of you. I'm sorry." She planted herself in front of him so he couldn't escape.

He met her look for look, banking his surprise and

the thrill of her fledgling trust. But despite his best intentions, her look probed deeper than he wanted. He feared she would see into the depths of his heart. See his secret. Perhaps even see the shame and sorrow he carried as a daily burden. With a great deal of effort, he shifted his gaze away.

He meant to say again that there was no need for apologies, but the words that came out of mouth were "Glad I could be there to get you out of trouble." Where had that come from? Certainly not from any spot in his brain that he was familiar with.

She laughed, bringing his gaze back to her. The bite below her eye had swelled a bit, making her smile somewhat crooked, and he laughed in spite of himself. She stepped aside. "See you tomorrow?"

"Yup. Got a barn to build." His words were filled with amusement, anticipation and a dozen other things he should be better at resisting. Things like enjoyment of a young lady's company.

"Good night, then," she murmured.

"Good night." He had to force his feet to move, but once started they hurried after Lonnie as though he couldn't wait to get away.

Which, to his dismay, couldn't have been further from the truth.

Ma and Pa waited at the table for Cora to return. Rose and Lilly had already gone to the bedroom the three girls shared.

"Good night, Ma and Pa," Cora said, crossing the room to give them both a hug. "Have I told you lately how grateful I am that you found us and adopted us?"

Ma kissed her cheek and Pa squeezed her to his side.

"We love you like our own," Ma said.

"I know it." Perhaps God in His mercy had saved them from a father like Wyatt's.

She kissed both their cheeks, then went to her bedroom.

"Is he as nice as he seems?" From where she sat on the side of her bed came Rose's voice, filled with longing. Cora knew Rose hoped for a beautiful future. Of course, if any of the three could hope for such, it would be Rose. She was as beautiful as her name. Her red hair attracted lots of attention, some good, some not so good. But most of all, Rose had a loving heart.

Cora studied her sisters.

Rose, intent on fixing things. Lilly, clinging to the present, sure it alone provided happiness. They couldn't have been more different in their outlooks.

"Wyatt seems like a decent man. He told me his father beat them. That's why Lonnie is so nervous."

Both of her sisters gasped.

Rose spoke first. "It always amazes me how cruelly people can treat their own flesh and blood."

Lilly shifted to her twin's side and hugged her.

They all understood Rose meant more than a man like Mr. Williams. Their birth father had been so cruel as to leave the girls, never to return.

After a moment, the girls sighed and crawled into their separate beds.

"Cora, Lilly, do you dream of getting married and having your own family?" The silence lengthened as Rose's question hung in the air, quivering with hope, yet so full of risk and danger.

Lilly sighed heavily. "People always want to know who our real parents are. I can't remember them. Ma and Pa are the only parents I want." She paused, a moment full of heaviness. "Or need."

Rose persisted. "Are you afraid to fall in love?"

"Maybe." The word from Lilly beat against Cora's thoughts.

"I thought I loved Evan," she said. "But he left. Just like our birth father."

Cora's reminder silenced them. She had to say something to lift the pall. "Wyatt says Grub looks as if he's grinning all the time."

Her two sisters chuckled at the idea. For a few minutes they laughed about their silly, useless—but well-loved—dog. Then silence settled about them, filled with contentment. Here they knew they were loved, and Ma and Pa would never hurt them.

Cora shifted, trying to get settled. Her thoughts drifted to Wyatt. Despite his confession that his father beat them, she saw something more hidden in his gaze.

As she lay there waiting for sleep, her thoughts flooded with the memory of Wyatt's touch. She touched her cheek where the hornet had stung her and where Wyatt had so tenderly applied mud.

A smile curved her lips. She tried to inform her wayward thoughts that it meant nothing. She'd only been surprised by the warmth of his hands and amazed that he could be so gentle, given his confession about a cruel father.

But she failed so badly to make her brain settle down that she curled her hands into fists and insisted she knew better than to let such things affect her. It was only because it was late at night and they had talked about their papa that she ached for such touches. Only she wanted them to be meaningful, given from a heart of love and

faithfulness, not casual, given out of necessity of dealing with stings.

Tomorrow, in the light of day, her common sense
would exert its hold on her and her thoughts would return to normal.

Despite her mental warnings, a smile clung to her
lips as she fell asleep.

The next morning, after breakfast and chores, she
made her way to the barn. Wyatt and Lonnie had already arrived, and the sound of sawing and hammering had begun.

As she crossed the yard, she reminded herself that
she was the practical Miss Cora Bell.

She grabbed a hammer and went to join them.

Wyatt climbed down from the ladder and stood studying her with such intensity she almost shied away from
his look. "What?" she demanded when it seemed he
would never stop staring.

"Are you winking at me?"

Lonnie, standing at Wyatt's back, smothered a giggle.

"I am not. Why would you say such a thing?" Then
she remembered her eye had swollen almost shut from
the hornet bite. She made a sound of exasperation. "You
know it's a bite. And one would think you'd be polite
enough not to mention it."

"Oh, sorry." His unrepentant grin said quite the opposite. "Guess I've forgotten how to be polite." He drawled
the words. "With just me and Lonnie and some horses
we got kind of sloppy, I guess." He turned and winked
at Lonnie. "Isn't that right, boy?"

Lonnie laughed again. "I have to say, Miss Cora, you
do look a little—" He seemed to search for a word.

"Funny?" she asked. "Strange? Odd?" She planted her fists on her hips and silently waited to see if they would push the matter further.

Wyatt crossed his arms over his chest and did his best to make her think he wasn't still amused. "He means no insult. Do you, Lonnie?"

Lonnie crossed his arms over his chest and rocked back in a perfect imitation of Wyatt. Only Lonnie looked worried, as if he thought one of them would object to his teasing. "No insult meant, ma'am."

"Now it's ma'am? From odd to ma'am? What did I do to deserve that?"

Wyatt understood she was teasing and laughed. "It's awfully hard to take you serious when you keep winking."

"Oh, you." She bent down, yanked out a handful of grass and tossed it at him. "Now, are we going to get to work or not?"

Wyatt studied her again. Then shook his head. "I don't think *we* are. We are working up above our heads, using a ladder. With your eye swollen like that, I'm afraid your balance might be off. Not to mention you fell on your head."

"I am fine." She ground the words out. Since when did he tell her what she could do?

"Not for climbing up a ladder."

"Says who?"

"Me."

Lonnie tapped Wyatt's shoulder. "Don't argue."

Cora immediately repented. "It's okay, Lonnie. I'm not angry."

"Neither am I," Wyatt assured him.

"But," Cora continued, "I haven't changed my mind. I need to help."

Wyatt sighed. "Why? Don't you think I'm capable?"

She stared at him. "Do you have to turn everything into some kind of personal attack?"

His mouth grew into a tight line and his eyes narrowed. He looked at her without blinking.

So he meant to be stubborn about this, did he?

"Do you have to always be in control of everything?" He spat each word out as if it tasted bad.

"I do not." They glowered at each other.

Lonnie shifted from foot to foot and watched them nervously.

Cora knew she was overreacting. In fact, she was being as stubborn as he. How ludicrous. "We're acting like little banty roosters." She burst out laughing.

He stared and then a grin slowly grew until his whole face relaxed. He tipped his head back and roared with laughter.

She sobered as she watched him. Goodness, but the man had a nice laugh. His merriment rippled through her insides.

He stopped chuckling but continued to grin at her in such a way that she felt blessed.

She must have hit her head harder than she thought to be so silly.

He nodded toward the garden. "Weren't you in the midst of hilling potatoes?"

"That's not very subtle." Yet she couldn't help but be amused by his attempt to divert her from the barn.

He took off his hat and rubbed his hair, mussing it into a riot of waves, making her want to smooth it back into place. "I'll tell you what. Lonnie and I will help in the garden today."

Cora considered the idea. "I haven't had such a good offer in a long time." She let a beat of silence follow her words, then added, "Maybe forever. Usually I have to beg people to help hoe."

He nodded. Did she detect a look of regret? But what better way to see what the man was made of? Would he find excuses not to work or would he put his back to the task and dig in?

"Like I said, we'll work in the garden this morning."

Lonnie groaned. "Do I have to help?"

Wyatt considered his younger brother for a full twenty seconds then shrugged. "Do you have another way of paying for your food?"

"I could snare a rabbit and roast it."

"Fine. You do that."

The boy scampered off.

Cora stared after him. "I thought you'd insist on him helping." It disappointed her that he hadn't.

"Unwilling help isn't much help most times, wouldn't you say?"

She nodded. But still she wondered if Wyatt shouldn't ask a little more of his brother.

"Besides, I want him to learn he can disagree with me without me getting angry."

Her disappointment gave way to respect. Wyatt had made a noble choice, not a lazy one. He really cared about his brother.

Which made it all the more confusing to know he'd left Lonnie to face their pa's beatings alone. Why would he do that? What could have constituted an "unavoidable" reason?

There were too many unanswered questions about Wyatt Williams to let herself be influenced by gentle touches and noble choices.

Chapter Six

Cora led the way to the garden, retrieved a pair of hoes from the shed and handed him one. "There's weeding to be done." She pointed toward a row of carrots, moved to the next row and set up a steady rhythm of chopping down weeds.

Wyatt hadn't used a hoe since he was a boy at home, and within half an hour remembered how much he hated it. Hoeing was hard work. Where was Mr. Bell with his four-in-one invention?

Cora didn't pause for anything but worked steadily up and down the rows.

He wiped his brow. The sun was way too hot. His mouth grew dry but he would not stop to get a drink. His admiration grew for the tough young woman working at his side. Seemed she didn't let challenges slow her down. He let his thoughts go in a direction he knew he should not allow. What would she do if she learned the truth about him? Would she turn her back on him, or would she fearlessly face the dishonor of his past? Not that he'd ever make her choose.

He bent his back to the task and started down another

row. In a short while, Cora appeared before him with a bucket of water and a dipper.

"Thought you might be getting thirsty by now."

He leaned against the hoe. "I'm about parched."

"You're welcome to stop and get a drink or pour water over your head anytime. I don't expect you to work non-stop. After all, I'm not a slave driver."

"Good to know."

"Did you think I was?"

He shrugged. "I didn't know what to think." He'd learned to work without complaining or expecting a break long before his prison days. He drank his fill of cold water and returned to hoeing.

Cora set the bucket at the end of the garden and picked up her hoe again.

A few minutes later, Rose and Lilly joined them.

"With all this help we'll have the garden clean in no time," Cora said, sounding as relieved at the thought as he was.

Again he wondered if Mr. Bell had finished adjusting the four-in-one hoe.

Then, as if Wyatt's thoughts had called him, Mr. Bell crossed the yard dragging the massive hoe behind him. He reached the edge of the garden and turned the blades over into the soil. Each of the four matched the spaces between the rows.

"Let's see if it works. Who wants to try it first?"

To Wyatt's surprise, none of the girls volunteered. "I'll give it a try. Anything that makes this work easier would be a great invention." Did the three girls smile behind their hands?

He grabbed the sturdy handle and tugged the hoe. He grunted and leaned into it with all his might. His muscles strained and then the inertia gave way to motion. Slow, torturous forward movement. The hoe stalled. His neck spasmed in protest. He looked behind to see what caused the problem. Nothing but a lump of dirt. He pulled and pulled and pulled.

The hoe refused to move, and he bent over his knees gasping for breath. As soon as he could breathe halfway normally he faced Mr. Bell. "Sir, it would take a small horse to pull that thing."

Mr. Bell nodded as he studied the useless tool. "You might have something there." He turned the hoe over so he could drag it and trotted back to the workshop.

Cora groaned loudly, making no attempt to hide her frustration.

Cora looked at Wyatt, her eyes narrowed and accusing. "Next we'll have a herd of small horses dragging clunky hoes in the garden, ripping up everything in sight. I can see it already."

Rose and Lilly came to her side.

"You have to understand something about Pa." Cora explained to Wyatt. "He's always coming up with these really good ideas, but usually they end up causing more work for us. But we love him, so we generally laugh and carry on."

Rose continued the story. "Like the time Pa bought turkeys."

Lilly said, "He figured he could get them to eat the weeds from around his fruit trees."

Rose took over from her sister. "Pa soon discovered he couldn't teach turkeys anything. They raided our garden so often it became a full-time job to keep them out."

"So Pa thought he'd get a dog to herd them," Cora added.

Beside her, her sisters chuckled and she nodded. "Wait until you hear what he brought home to herd the turkeys." Unable to stop laughing, she pointed to Grub sitting at the end of the garden, his head cocked as he listened to them.

"Grub? He got Grub as a herding dog?" A chuckle began in the pit of his stomach. "Did he keep them out of the garden?"

Three heads shook in unison. Cora waited, her eyes filled with expectancy.

She didn't have to wait long. Wyatt tried to picture the flop-eared dog trying to control turkeys. He wondered if Grub would end up tripping on his ears or falling over his feet or barking after the turkeys had all disappeared into a safe hiding place. No wonder the girls laughed. Chuckling, he returned to his work.

His smile lifted his lips throughout the morning and seemed to lighten the work, as well.

Lilly started to sing and the others joined her, the twins singing soprano and Cora a throaty alto.

"She'll be coming round the mountain when she comes…."

They paused and looked at Wyatt.

He continued to hoe as if he wasn't aware of three pairs of eyes on him.

"Sing with us," Cora said.

He continued to attack the weeds.

"Wyatt?"

"You wouldn't want me to."

"Why not?"

He stopped hoeing and looked at her. "I don't sing. I growl." Fellow inmates had jeered at him, so he knew it to be true. Not that he hadn't been aware of the fact long before then.

Cora glanced at the others, who both listened intently. "Surely it can't be that bad."

"Or it could be worse."

"Oh, come on. Join us. Singing is fun."

"Yeah," the twins echoed, and taking his silence for agreement they began again.

"She'll be coming round the mountain when she comes...."

Aware of three sets of eyes on him, he growled, "Yee-haw."

Cora nodded soberly. "We accept your yee-haw." And she started the song again.

He good-humoredly contributed his part.

The sun rose overhead. Shouldn't Lonnie be back by now? Wyatt looked toward the spot where he'd appear if he came from the campsite. No sign of him. He glanced around but didn't see Lonnie in any direction. He bent back to the hoeing but every few seconds looked about for him.

"Are you worried about Lonnie?" Cora asked.

"He's a big boy." Still, Lonnie had spent so much time hiding from people, Wyatt wasn't sure he could handle himself in the open.

"You're plainly worried. Why don't you check on him?"

"I think I will." He returned the hoe to the shed and jogged toward the camp. "Lonnie."

No answer. No boy stretched out sleeping in the shade.

Wyatt shaded his eyes and searched the prairie for signs of his brother. Nothing. He scanned the trees along the river, straining for movement in the shadows. A crow stirred the treetops, but nothing else.

Should he be concerned? Should he start looking?

"He's not back?" Cora called from up the embankment.

"No." Wyatt told himself Lonnie was old enough to look after himself, but he wasn't convinced.

"Do you want help looking for him?"

He wanted to say no. Because he wanted to believe Lonnie was okay. But if the boy had stumbled into trouble...

"I'd feel better if I knew he wasn't lying injured somewhere."

She trotted down the incline to his side. "Do you want us to search together or split up?"

"You know the country better than I do, so maybe we should stay together." Besides, he rather preferred to have her company.

They made their way downriver, calling Lonnie's name often and stopping every few feet to look around them.

He was the one who spotted a bit of twine and snagged it up. "He's been this way." He would have used the twine for snaring a rabbit.

"Then we'll keep heading in this direction." She marched past him.

Wyatt stared at the bit of twine he held and was hit by a memory, strong and vibrant.

"Wyatt?" Cora came back. "What is it?"

He couldn't stop staring at the bit of rope and remembering. "It was the summer I was sixteen and Lonnie eleven. I'd gotten a job working in the hardware store, hoping to use the money I earned to buy myself a horse. Pa raised fine riding stock but refused to give me my own horse. Said it didn't hurt a boy none to walk. 'Shank's mare will take you any place you need to go,' he used to tell me. So every day I walked the five miles to town to work at the Kansas Hardware and Supplies." He'd liked the job just fine. "Mr. McIver was a fair man to work for and seemed to like what I did. Every day I thought about what sort of horse I'd get. Maybe a mare so I could start my own herd. Or a fast gelding so I could win money racing at the local fairs." He stopped as bitterness surged up his throat.

Cora brushed his upper arm. "What happened?" she asked in a quiet, caring way, as if she guessed it was an unhappy story.

Her gentle touch and sweet concern neutralized the bitterness and he sighed. "My father happened." A moment passed and then he continued.

"To this day I don't know what he was mad about, but he was in a rage when he rode up to the store and bellowed my name. Mr. McIver went outside to suggest he calm down, which only made Pa worse. He jumped from the horse, pushed Mr. McIver aside and stormed into the store." He held up the bit of twine. "I'd been cutting some store string when my pa came in. Still held it in my hands when we got home. He grabbed me by the scruff of the neck, cuffed my ears until they rang and dragged me from the store."

He couldn't go on as he thought of his humiliation.

"Wyatt." Her hand smoothed up and down his arm. Soothed his shame and sorrow at the memory of that day.

"Several upright citizens stood on the sidewalk watching. One man had his daughter at his side. A pretty young thing I thought was my friend. Her father hurried her away and informed her she was to have nothing more to do with me. Ever."

"Oh, Wyatt. As if it was your fault."

"Well, you know how it is. The sins of the fathers will be visited on their children." His rejection by decent folk had started long before he'd gone to jail. His jail time had only provided more reason to look at him with disfavor.

"Or maybe man judges by outward appearance but God looks on the heart."

He took a moment to digest her comment. "It would be nice if man also judged by the heart."

"How do you know that some don't?"

"I suppose I haven't seen much evidence of it."

She looked thoughtful a moment, then asked, "Did you buy yourself a horse that summer?"

"Never went back. My pa made sure of it." He had ridden his horse home while Wyatt had walked. He'd been tempted to dawdle but Pa would have known if he did, and Wyatt hadn't intended to provide him with any reason to strap him. Though Pa hadn't much cared whether or not he'd had a reason. His own bad mood was motive enough.

Wyatt didn't wait for Cora to say anything about his lost job. Or his lost dream of buying a horse. He'd eventually purchased his own just before he'd gone to jail. Pa had gladly taken over the horse. But now Wyatt and Lonnie owned all that was left of Pa's once fine breeding stock.

"I need to find Lonnie," he said. Perhaps he, too, had been overwhelmed by bitter memories. Wyatt couldn't guess what Lonnie would do if he took a mind to run.

Cora fell in step with him as they continued to follow

the river. They reached the rocky ford that led to town and Wyatt halted. "He wouldn't go into town."

"Okay. Then where would he go?"

Wyatt turned full circle to study his surroundings. Trees along the river. Hills undulating to the west. Open prairie to the east. For some reason, the open spaces called to him, speaking freedom. "What's over there?" He pointed east.

"It looks flat, doesn't it?"

She waited for him to nod. "But there are hollows where a horse can disappear."

If Lonnie had discovered he could hide from view, wouldn't he think that a good thing? "Let's go see."

They crossed the river on rocks and tramped over the grassy land. If he wasn't concerned about Lonnie he might have enjoyed the sun on his shoulders, the scent of wild grass wafting up to him and the swing of Cora's sure stride at his side.

"Look around you," she said, and he did. "See how the ground rises up around us."

"I see what you mean." They had gone down enough of an incline to be in a wide hollow. "Lonnie could be hurt in a place like this and we'd never find him."

"God sees him. He will lead us to him."

She spoke with such confidence he stared at her. "You believe that completely, don't you?"

"God sees everything. His eyes wander to and fro across the land."

Wyatt didn't doubt that for a moment. "I mean, how can you be so sure He'll show us where Lonnie is?"

"Because I asked Him to. Doesn't the Word promise if we ask, we will receive?" She stopped in front of him. "Don't you believe in God and His love?"

"I do, but I sometimes have trouble trusting Him when things aren't going the way I think they should." Her faith put him to shame.

"Oh, you mean you think you know better than God what is best."

Said that way, it sounded presumptuous. "No. I don't think so."

"If God asks you to trust, do you decide you can't? Or won't?"

"Lady, you sure are blunt."

"I believe in speaking the truth. Kindly, of course."

"Of course." They had climbed to a spot that gave them a wide-open view. And he saw nothing but miles of grass. "For all we know, he is twenty miles away."

"'You have not because you ask not.' So ask God to show us where Lonnie is."

He wanted to point out that she'd asked and believed, but she'd no doubt have forty-five arguments as to why he had to do the asking.

"That is, if you believe God can show you."

Believing God *could* had never been a problem. Wondering if He *would* was an entirely different matter. But with Cora watching him, silently challenging him, he knew it was time to put his faith to the test. "Do you expect me to pray aloud?"

"Do you object to doing so?"

Surprisingly enough, he didn't. Somehow her faith reinforced his and he felt an invisible link between them. He bowed his head and closed his eyes. "God in heaven, You see everything. You know everything. Could You please show us where Lonnie is? And please keep him safe. He's all I've got left. Amen."

"Amen," she said. "Now let's find him."

She headed off.

"How do you know that's the right direction?"

"Does it feel wrong to you?"

He shrugged. "Can't say one way or the other."

"Then it will do."

"I can't argue with that." He caught up to her and they walked on. They approached a small rise.

"Let's go there," he said. "We'll be able to see farther."

They climbed to the top and looked about. In the distance, he spied a small animal and pointed it out to Cora. The animal moved. "It's not an animal. It's Lonnie." He shouted his brother's name but Lonnie couldn't hear.

Cora picked up her skirts and raced toward the boy but Wyatt outdistanced her and reached him first by seconds. They both crouched by Lonnie's side.

Lonnie sat with a frightened rabbit in his hands. He looked up at Wyatt. Dried tears streaked his cheeks. "I couldn't kill it."

Wyatt eased the rabbit from Lonnie's grip and set it free. It sat huddled and afraid for a moment, then hopped away in a crazy zigzag.

Wyatt watched Lonnie. He didn't know how to deal with this situation. The boy had gone out to snare a rabbit for their meal. How did he expect to do that without killing the animal?

"I never killed an animal before." Lonnie shivered. "I couldn't do it."

Wyatt nodded.

Cora sat cross-legged in front of Lonnie, her elbow brushing Wyatt's arm. Wyatt took comfort in her presence.

"Lonnie, I don't know what to say," Wyatt said.

Lonnie rubbed his leg, brushed away a bit of fur. "I'd sooner go hungry."

"That's fine." Though he doubted Lonnie would enjoy being hungry.

"I don't understand how someone could hurt an animal."

Wyatt waited, hearing the agony in Lonnie's voice and knowing the boy had sat there, maybe for hours, trying to sort out his feelings.

"If I can't hurt an animal, how could I hurt a person? Especially someone I knew and was supposed to love? How could anyone do that?" He groaned as if feeling real physical pain.

Wyatt knew the pain was in his memory. As was the reality of being treated cruelly by a father who was supposed to love him.

Cora took Lonnie's hands.

Lonnie ducked his head, likely not wanting her to see his dried tears or the depths of his pain.

"Lonnie, you ask a very good question. How can people hurt each other? How can love hurt?"

He raised his head and nodded.

"It isn't supposed to. But sometimes things get broken and don't mend. Like this man in town who broke his leg and it never healed properly. He has to use a crutch, and Ma says he endures a lot of pain."

"Does it make him mean?"

"Not that I know of. But what if his heart had been hurt and it didn't get tended to, so it never healed? Maybe that person wouldn't be able to love."

"And he'd be mean?"

Cora nodded. "I guess so."

Lonnie shook his head. "Can someone fix him?"

"I think God could, but I also think there are people who were hurt when they were so young they don't know they're broken. It's all they've ever known."

Wyatt sat back on his heels. Was he broken inside? Was Lonnie? About all they'd ever known was hate and anger. Was that to be normal for them?

Not if he could help it. God had led them to Lonnie. Perhaps He'd also led them to the Bells so he and Lonnie could learn how to be different from their father. If that was so, he needed to spend as much time as possible with Cora and her family, learning everything they could and maybe getting fixed inside.

Cora got to her feet. "Let's go home." She held out a hand to both Lonnie and Wyatt.

Wyatt took her hand and held it even after he was on his feet. She didn't pull away or he would have put some distance between them. Perhaps she sensed that he felt the need of healing and she didn't mind doing what she could to help. A smile started deep inside and claimed his entire being before it settled on his lips.

Cora knew God had provided the words she'd offered Lonnie. But as she spoke them, she realized they were for herself, as well. Her papa had left them. There had to be something broken inside him that he did such a vile thing. Thinking of it that way made it less hurtful.

She clung to Wyatt's hand as they tramped across the prairie, needing the strength his presence provided. He was so patient and gentle with Lonnie. Whatever secrets he hid that had forced him to leave Lonnie with an abusive father, she grew more and more convinced he was a good man.

They crossed the river and returned to the farm. When

she saw Pa waiting at the end of the lane, Cora slipped her hand from Wyatt's and eased away from his side.

Pa sheltered his eyes with his hand and waited until they drew closer to speak. "I was beginning to get worried."

"Everyone is fine," Cora said. "Lonnie lost track of the time."

"Ma saved some dinner for you. You'd best hurry in and eat it so she can clean up."

"Yes, Pa." It was on the tip of her tongue to suggest Wyatt and Lonnie might like to eat, too, but at Pa's look she hurried away. Just before she stepped inside, she glanced back. Pa and Wyatt were talking, while Lonnie made his way toward their camp.

She'd check this afternoon and make sure they had plenty of food. After all, they were working in exchange for supplies.

The kitchen was empty when she stepped inside. Ma would be napping and the twins were out doing something. Maybe they'd finish hoeing the garden and hilling the potatoes so she could go back to working on the barn.

She quickly ate the cheese sandwiches Ma had left for her, then cleaned the kitchen.

Ma came out as she finished. "You were gone a long time."

Cora explained how she'd gone with Wyatt to find Lonnie and discovered him upset about hurting the rabbit. "Can people broken inside be fixed?" she asked.

Ma sat across from her and took her hands. "It's a shame that people get their hearts and souls hurt. Usually it's at the hands of another person. That is so wrong." She shook her head. Her thumbs rubbed the back of Cora's hands in a comforting way.

Again, Cora's heart welled with gratitude that she and the twins had been adopted by such loving parents.

"I'm sure God can heal such a person," Ma continued. "But often He uses other people to do it." She thought a moment. "I expect God brought Wyatt and Lonnie here so we could be part of their healing. Especially Lonnie. That poor boy." She'd told her parents how violent Wyatt's father had been.

Cora smiled. If God wanted her to be part of healing for Lonnie and Wyatt, she'd gladly do what she could.

That afternoon she persuaded Wyatt she was fit as a fiddle and able to return to helping build the barn.

"We're doing the joists next." His voice revealed a hefty dose of doubt.

"I can help with that." She eyed the timbers that would support the floor of the loft. No way would she shirk from helping with them. She pulled on her leather gloves. "I'm ready."

He quirked his eyebrows and signaled for Lonnie to bring a rope. Wyatt fashioned a pulley, then they carried a beam to the ladder and Wyatt climbed to the top of the walls. "Lonnie, you guide it." Wyatt pulled the wood steadily upward.

"What am I going to do?" Cora demanded.

"Help Lonnie steady the beam."

Was he trying to appease her? But she stood with Lonnie and did as directed. One by one the beams were lifted up and nailed in place. And the afternoon slipped away.

Wyatt climbed down and wiped his brow. He downed three dippers full of water and poured two more over his head.

Cora watched the water wash over his skin and tried

not to be distracted. How was she to be part of their healing if all they did was grunt and lift all day long? She turned to the ladder. "I want to see how it looks." She climbed to the floor of the loft—or what would be the loft when the barn was completed. All it was now was open beams.

She nodded her approval and began to back down but only got partway before Wyatt's hands clamped around her waist and he lifted her to the ground. Her heart caught in her throat at the unexpected touch. She calmed her jittery nerves and turned to face him, determined to show him the kindness she experienced every day. "Thank you," she murmured, and at the way he looked at her she could manage no more.

At that moment, Ma crossed the yard toward them and Cora stepped back two feet, not wanting Ma to think she'd been acting inappropriately with their guest.

"Would you please join us for supper?" Ma asked.

Lonnie stiffened as if he feared to sit around the table with them, even though he'd been persuaded to join them for tea and cookies. Come to think of it, that day he'd perched on the edge of his chair the whole time, expecting danger and ready to flee.

She shifted her gaze to Wyatt. He gave Lonnie a reassuring smile, then turned to Ma. "It's most generous of you and we accept."

Cora wondered how it was that Wyatt wasn't as fearful as Lonnie. Did it have something to do with his having to leave for a year? Or had it been a year? She tried to recall exactly what he'd said and realized she might have assumed the time period.

Where had he been and what constituted an unavoidable reason?

Chapter Seven

Wyatt fought for mental equilibrium. When he'd noticed that the ladder was listing to one side with Cora partway down the rungs, he'd hurried to lift her down, never once thinking how she would feel to be swept off her feet in such an unceremonious way. When she'd turned to confront him, exuberant color had stained her cheeks.

His own face had stung with embarrassment and his throat had closed off, making it impossible to explain why he'd done such a brash thing.

He had about regained his voice when Mrs. Bell had extended her invitation.

He should likely have refused her offer, but he was tired and didn't feel like making a decent meal. Besides, if they were to learn about family from the Bells, he needed to spend time with them.

He fell in beside Cora as they crossed to the house.

But the first step inside the door caused him to hesitate, Lonnie at his back. The entire family gathered in the kitchen, Mr. Bell sitting at the end of the table, Lilly and Rose carrying steaming dishes forward.

He didn't belong here. If his past should be discovered, it would bring shame and disgrace to these innocent people. And he would lose something he grew to cherish more each day—the acceptance of a normal, loving family.

He tried to back up but Lonnie pressed forward, making it impossible.

"You can sit here." Mrs. Bell indicated a chair.

Still he hesitated, then he breathed a lungful of savory scents. A homemade meal sure beat beans and biscuits, even with fresh farm produce added. He stepped forward and sat on the chair.

They all took their seats. Mrs. Bell sat at the opposite end of the table from her husband, Rose and Lilly facing him, Cora to his right and Lonnie to his left.

"We'll ask the blessing." Mr. Bell held his hands toward a daughter on each side. The twins joined hands and reached for their mother's.

Cora held her hand toward Wyatt. He swallowed a huge lump. Was this what families did? Hold hands around the table? The idea lived and breathed welcome and acceptance.

Again, he fought against allowing such feelings. But he meant to learn how a decent family behaved.

Mrs. Bell had taken Lonnie's hand.

Wyatt felt his brother stiffen, and then he grabbed Wyatt's hand and squeezed hard. Knowing how much Lonnie needed family lessons, Wyatt tried desperately to shed his caution. But he seemed stuck between wanting to guard the shame of his past and wanting to move forward and take part in family life with the Bells.

"Cora," Mr. Bell said. "Let's pray."

She placed her hand close to his plate, her fingers open and inviting.

Wyatt stared at it, felt the expectant waiting from everyone at the table. He quickly considered his options: push away from the table and run from the room, giving up a hot meal that had his taste buds working hard, or hold hands with a young woman who had made him laugh, bossed him about and offered him something he couldn't remember ever having—acceptance.

He took her hand and bowed his head. Her warm fingers curled around his. A thousand emotions erupted inside him with such force he thought they'd explode from his skin—longing as deep as the deepest mine, hope as wide as the ocean and an emotion he could only name as anger. Anger at the way he'd been raised. At a violent father who had pushed Lonnie to the breaking point.

The year Wyatt spent in prison had irrevocably changed him, making him less trusting, and it would always change how others viewed him.

He even admitted a shred of anger toward his ma, who had seemed unable to stand up to her husband, and who had simply been a shadowy figure in the background. Though, he soothed his ruffled feelings, it hadn't always been so. He remembered far better times, but they'd been swallowed up by the bad things that followed.

Mr. Bell said, "Amen."

Wyatt didn't know who jerked away faster—him or Cora. The girls passed the food around and chattered up a storm, making it unnecessary for Wyatt to make conversation. The conversation also made it possible for him to cork the bottle of his agitated emotions.

"Ma and I are almost finished cleaning the garden shed," Rose said.

Beside him, Cora spread butter on a thick slice of homemade bread. "Good to hear."

Wyatt also buttered on his bread and bit down. His taste buds thanked him profusely. "Sweet-cream butter. It's very good."

"Cora's specialty," Lilly said. "People come from miles around to buy her butter. And her cheese."

"I can see why." Right then and there, he decided he could live on freshly baked bread and sweet-cream butter the rest of his life. But the meal offered more than that— mashed potatoes and rich gravy, new carrots bathed in butter, cooked green beans fresh from the garden and roast pork.

A few minutes later, he cleaned his plate and leaned back. "Thank you. That was an excellent meal. I'm trying to remember when I've had better." He tapped his chin. Sure did beat the unpalatable rations they'd lived on for the past week. As a child, every meal had been off flavored by the fear of what their father would do. "Nope. Can't recall a time. How about you, Lonnie?" The boy had eaten a goodly amount and then some.

"Sure better'n what you make." The words had slipped out unguarded, and he ducked his head as if expecting Wyatt to take objection.

Wyatt laughed. "Sure was." How he wished Lonnie would stop acting as though Wyatt was about to whip him.

The others chuckled.

"We still have dessert," Cora said, and from the cupboard Lilly brought a chocolate cake so rich it was almost black. Mrs. Bell cut generous slices and served each with spoon-thick cream.

Wyatt's stomach thought he'd died and taken it to heaven.

From the barely audible sighs at his left, he knew Lonnie felt the same. Their ma had seldom bothered with what she called "fancy baking." As her strength dwindled, and her interest in life faded, so had her efforts at preparing meals.

Once they were all finished, the girls took away the dishes and poured tea for everyone while Mr. Bell opened a well-worn black leather Bible.

"We always have a time of Bible reading after supper," he explained to Wyatt. "I hope you don't mind joining us."

He felt Mr. Bell's silent waiting and knew the man was asking Wyatt where he stood on faith matters. He didn't mind telling. "Mr. Bell, I am a firm believer in God's grace. I'd be honored to be part of your Bible reading time."

Mr. Bell considered him unblinkingly for a moment, then nodded.

Wyatt couldn't tell if his answer had satisfied the man or not.

"We are reading the last chapter of Matthew," Mr. Bell said. "'Lo, I am with you always, even unto the end of the world.'" As the older man continued reading, the words refreshed Wyatt's soul as much as the food had refreshed his body.

"We'll pray now." The Bells again reached out and held hands. This gesture no doubt knit the family members together. He wasn't likely to be woven into this family, but he and Lonnie could do something similar.

He reached for Cora's hand, again feeling a warm rush of emotions threatening to blow away his control.

Rather than try to understand what it meant, he focused on Mr. Bell's prayer as he asked God to bless all sorts of friends and neighbors. When he said, "Bless the Caldwells," Cora's fingers squeezed Wyatt's hard. She'd said the Caldwells didn't welcome the farm in the middle of their ranch.

Seemed she wasn't quite as concerned with their well-being as her pa.

Upon Mr. Bell's "amen," the family pushed from the table.

Wyatt and Lonnie did the same. "Thank you again for a wonderful meal and your hospitality." Wyatt backed toward the door with Lonnie at his side.

"No need to rush off," Mr. Bell said. "Stay and visit awhile."

Wyatt glanced about the room. The evening sun flashed through the window and splashed light on the back of Cora's head as she leaned over the table to gather up teacups.

She turned and smiled at him. "Of course, we expect you to help with the dishes." She tossed each of them a towel.

And as easy as that, he decided to stay.

Red-headed Rose had her hands in a basin of soapy water and handed him a plate to dry. Lilly took a dish of scraps out to Grub. Mrs. Bell lifted a basket from a nearby shelf and began to darn a sock while Mr. Bell sat at the table, scratching away on a piece of paper. Wyatt glanced at what the man did. Seemed he worked on a design for that four-in-one hoe. Wyatt knew there was a serious flaw in the design. It weighed too much to be practical. Would Mr. Bell find a solution?

Cora took the dishes from Wyatt and Lonnie as they

dried them and put them into the cupboard. Their hands brushed each time and Wyatt's skin grew warmer with each touch.

"We're done." Rose carried the wash water outside and dumped it on the flowers.

"I'll take the slop to the pigs," Lilly said.

"Can I help?" Lonnie asked, and received an invitation to join Lilly.

Wyatt stood near the kitchen cupboard wondering if he should wait for Lonnie or excuse himself.

Cora took the towel from Wyatt's hand and went outside to hang it to dry.

He followed her out of the house. He moseyed over to the corner of the garden and leaned against the post.

Cora joined him there. "Lonnie seems to have forgotten about the rabbit."

"I hope so." Wyatt tried to think how to express his appreciation for her family's kindness, but everything he thought of sounded like an invitation for her to ask more about his family. He'd said about all he meant to say on that subject. His teeth creaked as his jaw clenched. There were so many secrets to protect. He would never forget the sight of Lonnie standing over their bleeding father, trembling, tears running down his face.

He shuddered.

Cora no doubt took it to be because of Lonnie and the rabbit. "He is so tenderhearted. I believe that means he can become a strong, confident man who is no longer afraid people will treat him as his father did."

Wyatt forced himself to relax. "He's young. He can change." With good examples like the Bells to teach him. Unless someone learned the truth of their past. He silently vowed that if anyone discovered he'd been in jail, he would never reveal it was Lonnie who had beaten their father.

Cora touched his arm. "God led us to find Lonnie this afternoon. I truly believe He directs our every step. Remember that verse in Jeremiah where God says His thoughts to us are for peace and not evil, to give us an expected end?"

An expected end? Wasn't that a warning not to think he could change anything?

He hadn't asked the question aloud, but she addressed it anyway. "Pa says the expected end means the kind of end we can expect from God. So it means good things, blessings, His tender care."

Wyatt couldn't take his eyes from her glowing face as she spoke. His heart caught her faith and swelled with joy at what God had promised. "You believe so deeply."

She nodded. "The more I choose to believe in God's love and goodness, the more blessed I feel." She smiled up at the sky. "Sometimes I could dance for joy."

He'd like to see that. He'd like to dance with her. What better time than now, he thought as he reached for her.

But Lonnie jogged toward them just then and Wyatt stepped back. He realized how foolish it would be to let his guard down. "We'll be going now," he said to Cora. "Good night."

He and Lonnie made their way back to the campsite. "We need to give the horses some oats." If he fed them well while they rested they would be in good shape for more travel when the time came. His insides twisted at the thought of leaving. He shook his head hard. Had he so quickly forgotten who he was?

Wyatt paid special attention to Fanny. "She'll have that foal any time now."

"Lilly let me help feed the pigs," Lonnie called from where he fed the horses. "They're so sweet. At least, the baby ones are. Do you know Lilly names each of them and they come when she calls?"

"Uh-huh." He had a hard time keeping his attention on talk of pigs when his thoughts hovered between hope and despair.

"Lilly says they're a lot smarter than people think." Lonnie continued to chatter about the pigs as they tended the horses and while they prepared for bed. At least he seemed to have forgotten the incident on the prairie.

Later, as they lay side by side in their bedrolls, Lonnie sighed. "Do you think I'm broken inside like Cora talked about?"

So the incident hadn't been forgotten after all. Wyatt considered his answer carefully. "I think our pa was broken. We might be broken a little because of that, but didn't she say sometimes people don't realize they aren't normal? So they don't know they need fixing."

"I guess."

Wyatt continued, silently praying Lonnie would understand he could one day become whole. "The Bells seem nice, don't they?"

"Uh-huh."

"The sort of family we wished we had. Maybe if we watch carefully we can learn to be like them."

"Did you like how they prayed together?"

"It was good."

"Cora's nice, don't you think?"

"They all are." Though he'd taken little note of Rose and Lilly. Natural enough, he reasoned, seeing as he spent most of his time working beside Cora.

"But Cora seems extraspecial. She's so smart and kind and—I don't know. Just real nice."

"Indeed." He could add more description—beautiful, full of faith, generous, determined, loyal—

That stopped him. Her loyalty belonged to her family. She'd do everything she could to protect them.

He flipped to his side and tried to find a comfortable position. Tried desperately to ignore the mocking words in his head.

He posed a risk to their security and acceptance. She'd defend her family against him if she learned he was a jailbird. He'd grown used to the idea that people would shun him because of his past. Had figured he could survive without their approval. But he hadn't figured on meeting someone like Cora who made him want to start over with an unblemished slate.

He flipped to his other side and groaned. No matter how hard he tried to make it happen, he knew his heart would bear a permanent wound when she found out the truth and—

He couldn't even think how she'd react.

How he'd continue to breathe and eat and walk.

Cora and the twins retired to their bedroom. She saw Lilly and Rose exchange knowing looks.

"What?"

Lilly perched on the edge of her bed. "He makes you laugh."

"Don't I usually laugh?"

Lilly nodded. "But you sounded real happy talking to him in the garden."

Cora tapped Lilly's arm. "I'm always happy."

"But not that kind of happy. Aren't I right, Rose?"

The pair nodded.

"Honestly, I have no idea what you mean."

"We know you don't, which is really sad."

Cora wouldn't admit there was a hint of truth to their observations and didn't reply.

Rose sighed. "It was kind of fun telling our stories, wasn't it?" She glanced from Cora to Lilly and back again. "I like having company."

Cora tipped her head. "I never thought of it before." They attended church every Sunday in Bar Crossing and each Saturday went to town to sell their goods and buy supplies, but their friends very rarely visited the farm. No doubt they didn't want to get involved in the feud the Caldwells wouldn't abandon.

She and Anna, the preacher's daughter, always found plenty to talk about when they got together. Though, on closer examination, Anna did most of the talking.

It *was* nice to have visitors on the farm, but she didn't want to admit how much she enjoyed Wyatt's company. Not even to herself. "Life is simply fun if you let it be."

The twins agreed.

The three of them crawled into their beds and opened their Bibles to read a passage—something Ma had taught them. At first, she'd read to them, but as they grew older they were each presented with Bibles of their own. In the flyleaf of each Ma had written a blessing. Although Cora knew the words by heart, she turned to that page first. "To the daughter of my heart: You are strong and bold in life. May you also be strong and bold in your faith. May our love hold you close all the days of your life." Their parents had given each of them a special verse, and Ma had penned Cora's below the blessing. "Proverbs 3:5-6: Trust in the Lord with all thine heart; and lean not unto thine own understanding. In all thy ways acknowledge him, and he shall direct thy paths."

She breathed in the words, let them settle deep into her heart with a comforting touch. Throughout the day, she'd discovered surprising longings and desires welling up. Always when she was around Wyatt. When he touched her. When he revealed tenderness and strength at the same time.

She needed to keep her thoughts focused on God's will and God's ways and not be drawn aside by her silly reactions to a man she barely knew.

She read a few verses and closed the Bible. Rose turned out the lamp and the twins' deep breathing soon informed her they had fallen asleep. Cora lay awake thinking of Wyatt and Lonnie. What could she—all of them—do to help the pair?

The next morning, she waited until breakfast was over, the dishes done and the twins had left the house to do chores.

"Ma, Pa, can I talk to you?"

Her parents returned to their chairs. She sat between them.

"Ma, remember how you said that God had brought Wyatt and Lonnie here so we could help them?"

Ma explained to Pa what Cora meant.

Cora continued, "Maybe we could help them more by having them join us for dinner and supper." She turned to Pa. "They need to see how a good father behaves."

Pa smiled at her praise.

Then her parents looked at each other. They never spoke a word and yet she knew each somehow understood what the other was thinking.

Cora always marveled at how they could communicate this way.

Pa spoke first. "We know so little about them."

Ma nodded. "Only enough to know they've been badly hurt." She turned to Cora, who was about to point out that Wyatt had said their father beat them. "Yes, he's told you about his father. But my concern is that badly hurt people can sometimes be dangerous."

Cora stared. "You think Wyatt or Lonnie might hurt us?" She couldn't believe it, though her only evidence as to his goodness was the way her heart jumped when he touched her and the tenderness he showed toward Lonnie. And Lonnie? Why, he couldn't even hurt a rabbit.

Pa touched her hands. "If I thought Wyatt presented a danger to us I wouldn't let him stay. But I fear you might grow too fond of him."

She ducked her head to avoid his probing stare. She'd warned herself of the same thing, but nevertheless had grown more fond of him than she cared to admit. Not that she meant it to get out of control.

Pa continued. "I just don't want to see you get hurt again."

She nodded. "I think I've learned to be careful about trusting a man."

Ma shook her head. "I don't think that's what Pa meant. It's okay to trust, but only when you know the truth, the whole truth."

"No dark secrets. No mysterious past. No unanswered questions." She listed the things she considered necessary.

Pa patted her hands. "Exactly. You're a sensible girl. I know you'll follow your head and act wisely."

"I believe you're correct in suggesting we ought to invite them to share our meals," Ma added.

Cora thanked them both for their wisdom and left to do her chores. She was sensible. She would offer help to Wyatt and his brother, but she'd also guard her heart.

When she went outside, Wyatt and Lonnie were already working on the barn, nailing the loft floor into place. She should be helping them but had the cows to tend first.

Wyatt looked up and waved. His hat shadowed his eyes but his smile flashed. Her heart picked up its pace in response. Too many unanswered questions, she reminded herself, but smiled as she continued on her way. She hurried through her chores so she could join Wyatt working on the barn.

Wyatt and Lonnie, she corrected herself.

But it wasn't Lonnie's smile she wanted to see more of.

She sought Pa's words of advice and pushed them to the forefront of her thoughts.

Somehow, with loads of determination, she'd work with Wyatt, she'd help them both and she'd keep her thoughts and heart firmly under control.

How hard could it be?

Chapter Eight

Later, Cora hurried up the ladder so fast that Wyatt called down a warning.

"Careful. There's very little floor for you to stand on." He reached out a hand and held hers firmly as she climbed to his side. He didn't immediately release her hand, and she didn't think to pull away as she looked into his dark eyes and smiling face.

Lonnie pounded a nail. The sound made her remember her purpose in being there. To help, she reminded her stalled brain.

"You started early," she said.

"Yup. I wanted to get some solid footing up here before you came." He continued to smile at her, making it difficult to tear her gaze away. "I don't suppose I can persuade you to leave the work to us?"

"Why would you want to?" Her tongue felt stiff, making her words slow.

"What if you get dizzy? What if your foot slips?"

His concern delighted her. When did anyone ever worry about her like that? Pa was protective but thought her self-sufficient. The twins looked to her for direction much of the time. Ma was affectionate but had taught her to be independent. And her papa—well, he hadn't concerned himself about her safety even when she was five.

She realized that Wyatt waited, as if thinking she might take herself down to the ground. She laughed. "I won't fall."

"Promise?" A smile lingered on his lips, but his gaze was dark and demanding.

"I promise."

His eyes said he would guard her and make sure she didn't stumble. And then he blinked and the thought was gone.

She wondered if she'd only imagined it. How foolish she was getting, and only a while after assuring her parents she would be wise. But somehow she struggled to keep her wits about her when he looked at her with his dark eyes full of feeling.

She jerked her attention to the task before them. "Let's get this done. Tomorrow is Saturday and we go to town." She picked up a hammer and a handful of spikes and began to nail a plank into place. "We take a supply of cheese, butter and eggs, and trade them at the store for things we need." She pounded on the nail. "Ma will likely take some garden produce, too. She sells out of the back of the wagon. We do all right, you know?" She rattled on without giving him a chance to answer. "Sometimes the ladies bring their complaints and ask for one of her medicines." *Pound, pound, pound.* The noise made further conversation impossible.

Wyatt set another board in place and knelt beside her to hammer in nails.

She sat back and watched how easily they went in for him.

Noticing she had stopped work, he turned to her, two spikes protruding from his mouth. He took them out so he could talk. "Something wrong?"

"Only that it takes me three times as long to drive a nail home."

He grinned and flexed his arm. "So you're willing to admit I'm better than you?"

She sighed dramatically. "At pounding in nails, I have to concede you're better."

His eyes narrowed. "That's all?"

She pretended to consider the question seriously, then shook her head. "Can't think of anything else. Of course, I'm willing to admit it might be because I know so little about you."

His expression tightened. His eyes grew cold. "There's nothing to know."

"Really? I can think of a lot of things." Would he tell her if she asked some of the many questions she had? Seeing the tension in his tight jaw, she guessed he wouldn't. She examined the nail in her hand as if it might supply answers. She could drop the subject entirely or she could probe just a little. Perhaps make him realize it wasn't dangerous to answer questions.

"Where did you grow up?" she asked.

He shrugged. "Mostly in Kansas."

"Was your father a farmer?"

"Of sorts. But mostly he raised horses."

"So that's why you want to ranch and raise horses?"

He nodded his head. "All that's left of his breeding stock is the few head I have. It's good stock, and I hope to improve it." He pounded in spike after spike, making further questions impossible.

"Help me set this plank," he called to Lonnie.

The boy was perched on the last board, his feet dangling as something beyond the barn held his attention. He smiled slightly and appeared relaxed.

Cora followed the direction of his look. He must be watching the pigs.

Lonnie jumped up, a guilty look on his face. "I'll help." He scurried to adjust the board and hammered nails with much more vigor than accuracy.

"Slow down," Wyatt said, without a hint of rancor in his voice.

Lonnie stopped and sucked in air. "I'm sorry."

"Nothing to be sorry about. Take your time. We're not in any sort of race."

Lonnie nodded and his movements grew deliberate.

Cora ducked her head to hide her reaction. The poor boy was so leery of everyone, including Wyatt. That seemed a little strange, but then she didn't know what it would feel like to duck every time Pa lifted his hand, so maybe the reaction was normal.

An hour later, Wyatt sent Lonnie to get a bucket of water.

Cora rolled her shoulders.

Wyatt watched her. "Are you sore?"

Her instinct was to deny it. Normally she would. She'd pretend she didn't hurt and would work without complaining, but something in his voice and in his look made her answer honestly. "My arms aren't used to this kind of work."

"Then why not let us do it?"

She shook her head without considering it. "I wouldn't feel right about that."

"Why?"

She couldn't tell him it was because she liked working

with him, liked watching the way he moved, the way he instructed Lonnie, the sureness of his every action. Her cheeks grew warm at her wayward thoughts. "I kind of like helping," she finally murmured.

He got a silly grin on his face and she knew her answer had pleased him.

Maybe he even shared the same pleasure in working with her.

The idea brought an answering smile to her lips.

Wyatt drank the water Lonnie brought and returned to the job of making a floor. He couldn't stop smiling. Cora liked working with him. And he liked working with her. He would not think any deeper than that.

They worked until dinnertime. He hurried down the ladder to hold it firm as she made her way to the ground. His heart stalled every time she stepped on a rung. If she caught her foot in her skirts or leaned too far to one side...

He and Lonnie were about to head to their camp when she stopped them.

"Ma's expecting you to join us."

Wyatt looked at Lonnie. Did he detect in his brother's eyes the same mixture of eagerness and reluctance he felt? Then he calmed his thoughts. This was the opportunity he sought to teach them both more about healthy family life.

"Thank you." The three of them fell in step as they crossed the yard.

The meal was more hurried than supper the previous night. Mr. Bell did not read from the Bible, but they held hands around the table as they prayed. And, most important, Lonnie did not seem to mind. Neither, Wyatt confessed to himself, did he as he held Cora's.

They enjoyed a generous feed of huge slices of golden bread and thick pieces of cheese. Raw carrots and freshly picked peas crunched in contrast.

Lonnie sighed his pleasure as he finished. "Good food. Thanks, Mrs. Bell."

Mrs. Bell patted Lonnie's hand. "Glad you enjoyed it."

Lonnie snorted. "You should see what Wyatt feeds us."

Wyatt groaned. Was the boy going to point out his deficiencies as a cook at every chance he got? "I never had a chance to practice cooking."

At the reminder of one reason why Wyatt had had no such chance, Lonnie ducked his head.

Wyatt tried to think of a way to make it clear he didn't mean just the past year. "Ma didn't like anyone messing about in her kitchen." He squeezed Lonnie's shoulder, hoping to signal he didn't mean to remind him of jail.

The meal ended and the younger ones returned to their chores.

"Ma and Pa will have a nap," Cora said. "You're welcome to do so, too, if you want."

Lonnie choked back a snort.

Wyatt ignored his brother's reaction. "I haven't had an afternoon nap since I was three."

"Just offering," she said. "No shame in taking a break from your labors. Pa says it makes him more vigorous for the rest of the day."

"Uh-huh," Wyatt said.

"Sure you don't need a nap?" Lonnie jeered.

"I'm absolutely certain. Now, be sure *you* don't fall

asleep and tumble off the roof," Wyatt said as they returned to the job.

Lonnie and Cora both laughed.

Wyatt grinned as he bent to hammer in nails. He'd made his little brother laugh. Lonnie had allowed physical contact.

His pleasure lasted throughout the early part of the afternoon. But as the sun beat down mercilessly on them, and sweat dribbled from his face, he tried to think of a way to suggest they forget about the project for a few hours. He'd come right out and give his opinion of working in the hottest part of the day, except he didn't want to look like a slacker. Now, if she'd suggest it…

"Push the plank into place," he told Lonnie as Cora sat back, wiping her face on a handkerchief.

Lonnie moved as though his limbs had turned to lead.

Wyatt understood how he felt, but the boy didn't complain. No doubt because he feared retaliation from Wyatt.

"That's good." Wyatt sat down beside Cora and Lonnie flopped to the finished portion of the floor. On the ground, in the shade of the house, Mrs. Bell, Lilly and Rose sat shelling peas. He'd do most anything to get out of the blazing heat, but not unless Cora suggested it.

She didn't. They continued throughout the hot afternoon, though their movements grew slower and more sluggish as the hours passed. Lonnie kept them supplied with water. A bucket disappeared quickly between three people drinking copious amounts and he and Lonnie pouring it over their heads.

Cora splashed it on her face.

"Sure is hot." Lonnie fanned himself with his hat.

"Finally," Cora said with feeling. "I thought no one would ever complain, and I wasn't about to be the first."

"Well, I'm hot." Lonnie sounded defensive.

"So am I," Cora said. "Aren't you?" she asked Wyatt.

"I am baked, fried and toasted."

"But are you hot?" Her voice was bland but her eyes twinkled.

He laughed. "I didn't want anyone to think I couldn't handle it."

"Well, I've had enough. Let's get off this fry pan."

Lonnie was down the ladder before she finished her sentence.

She scrambled to her feet but jerked to a halt and tumbled forward.

Wyatt grabbed her, his heart thudding in his ears. He held tight as he struggled to his feet on legs that had turned to butter. He pulled her back to the floor beside him. "The heat is making you dizzy."

Her eyes had widened to the size of dinner plates and she held on to him with both hands.

She sat safely on the loft floor, but he couldn't release her any more than he could tear himself from her gaze. It demanded a dozen things from him—his protection, which he'd freely given, but also the truth about his past, his time in prison, his hopes and fears and failures—things he could not allow her to know. He tried to close the emotional door that had been flung wide-open when he'd thought she was about to fall to the ground. A door that concealed the secrets he must guard the rest of his life. But the door jammed and he could not close it.

She swallowed so hard he figured it must hurt. "I wasn't dizzy."

"You almost fell."

She withdrew her hands slowly. Their eyes held each other's. "My skirt is caught."

"Your skirt?" He echoed her words without understanding her meaning.

She blinked and shifted her gaze to her feet. "Yes. Between the boards."

He forced his brain to start functioning. Indeed, the hem of her skirt was caught, jammed between two boards he and Lonnie had pushed into place.

At the realization of how one bit of carelessness could have been the cause of a disaster, he sucked in air in a futile attempt to calm his pounding head.

"Wyatt?"

The concern in her voice made him concentrate. "I'll get it. Don't move." He pried the board away enough to pull the fabric free. But he made no move to climb down from the loft. If Cora's limbs were as shaky as his, they wouldn't be safe on the ladder.

"Thank you for catching me." She stared at the hem of her skirt.

"You gave me quite a scare." Would she notice the tremble in his voice that he couldn't hide?

"Me, too."

To keep from touching her, Wyatt pressed his hands to the new boards. If only he had the freedom to pull her close and comfort her. But he didn't, and never would, because he would never be free from the sting of his past.

She sucked in air. "I owe you for saving my life."

He tried to snort, but it sounded more like a groan. "Let's hope you wouldn't have died."

She faced him, but he kept his gaze riveted to the spot where she almost fell. "Wyatt, if you need or want anything, feel free to ask. If I can, I'll give it to you."

Slowly his gaze sought hers and he fell into the darkness of her eyes and the sweetness of her invitation. He had needs and wants. Acceptance despite his past, some-one who trusted him, believed in him, loved him. His throat tightened. His heart ached with longing. If only she could give him what he needed.

He forced himself to take slow, steadying breaths. Grabbed at reality and pulled it back where it belonged—in his head and in his heart. "Thanks. I'll be sure to let you know if there is." It was time to leave behind this sweet moment and he pushed to his feet. "Do you feel ready to crawl down the ladder?" He held out a hand to pull her to her feet.

She grabbed his hand and let him help her. She stood facing him without moving.

"Are you feeling dizzy? Weak?"

She shook her head. "I'm fine." She headed for the ladder.

He stepped around her. "Let me go first so I can help you." She didn't protest as he descended, one rung at a time, and waited on each to help her down.

They reached the ground and he stepped aside.

Lonnie straightened from petting Grub. "What took you so long?"

"My skirt was caught in the boards." Cora smiled at Wyatt, her fingers pressed to her throat as if she tried to contain the memory of her fright.

Only it wasn't fear he saw in her eyes. What was it? Gratitude? Or something more? Something that grew from having shared a moment full of raw emotion? How could he tell? He was ill equipped to read the silent mes-sage contained in her eyes. He'd grown up with a mother who grew more distant with the passing years, a father who had one emotion in varying degrees, and he'd spent a year with men who calmly said one thing and meant another without revealing any emotion.

Mrs. Bell called out to them, "I've got fresh lemonade. Come and have some."

They traipsed across the yard to plunk down in the shade of the house, where it was several degrees cooler than on the top of a half-finished barn. Lilly poured them all lemonade and Wyatt drank eagerly. So did Lonnie and Cora.

A smile tugged at the edges of his heart and teased his lips.

Cora noticed. "What are you grinning about?"

"Us." He turned to explain to the others. "We about melted up there, but none of us wanted to be the first to admit the heat was getting to us."

Lilly and Rose gave all three of them considered study.

"Who was first?"

"Me." Lonnie sighed. "Those two are too stubborn to admit it."

The twins laughed and Mrs. Bell tsked.

Cora looked around. "Where's Pa?"

"He went to check on his fruit trees. Wouldn't be surprised if he found a shady spot and fell asleep." Mrs. Bell's voice rang with affection.

The peas were done and the Bells seemed content to rest in the shade. So Wyatt followed their lead, quietly observing them. They were so relaxed around one another. Even Lonnie sat with Grub at his side, as relaxed as he ever got. Which meant he slid his gaze from one to the other as they talked, alert for any sign of tension.

Wyatt leaned back to watch. How long would it take for Lonnie to realize this family didn't operate that way?

Grub trotted off, found a stick and dropped it at Lonnie's feet.

"He wants to play," Cora said.

"With me?"

Wyatt understood that Lonnie wondered if he had permission to play with the Bells' dog.

"Seems he's chosen you," Cora said. "Go ahead. Throw the stick for him."

Lonnie did and laughed as Grub tripped over himself in his rush to chase it.

Wyatt's muscles relaxed. Guess he, like Lonnie, needed to learn that people could be trusted to be kind.

How long would it take him to learn it?

Mrs. Bell took the peas inside. The others continued to lounge in the shade.

Lilly got to her feet and stretched. "I'm going to take the pea shells to the pigs."

Lonnie stilled. "Can I go?"

"Certainly. Come along. Grab that basket."

Rose joined them and the three carried the baskets of peapods to the pigs.

Only Cora and Wyatt remained.

"We go to town tomorrow," she said.

"Yes." She'd already mentioned it.

"If I go, I can't help with the barn."

"That's fine." He'd be happy enough if she kept her feet firmly planted on the ground.

"Guess I don't have to go." She sounded disappointed.

"Why wouldn't you?"

"I couldn't leave you working alone."

"Lonnie will be here."

She brightened. "Or you could come with us. Yes.

Why don't you? You'd get to see our little town. Besides, you and Lonnie deserve a break."

Town was the last place he cared to be. Too many curious people. But if he refused, he had no doubt she would opt to stay home, too.

He simply wasn't ready to see her on the loft floor again.

"A trip to town might be a nice change," he finally said.

He could only hope no one in town asked questions of him or cared enough to look for answers.

Chapter Nine

Cora sat with her sisters on quilts in the back of the wagon, crowded in amidst the vegetables and other things they'd brought to sell and trade.

Wyatt and Lonnie perched at the end of the wagon. They'd get dusty in the cloud that rolled up from the wheels.

Ma and Pa rode on the wagon seat, as always.

They rumbled across the rocky ford of the river. The Bell farm was three miles from town—an easy walk. The girls had walked it to attend school and they often walked to church, but on Saturdays they took the wagon to carry in their produce.

The wagon rattled past several ladies who lifted their hands in greeting. Cora smiled at the way they eyed the wagon, trying to see what vegetables Ma had to sell.

They passed a livery barn where several men conducted business. Next to that was a blacksmith shop. Cora pointed out each business, though likely Wyatt could read the signs for himself.

They came to a pretty white church with a steeple.

"That's where we go to church," Cora said.

Then Pa turned the wagon down another street. False-fronted wooden buildings were crowded by impressive brick structures. Cora wondered if Wyatt noticed how the town seemed determined to escape its early frontier beginnings and move into regal permanency.

She watched him, saw he studied each business they passed, so she didn't point out the lawyer, newspaper office, freight station and three mercantile stores. Pa stopped in front of Frank's Hardware and Necessities, where they did their business, and got down. He trotted to Ma and assisted her to the ground.

Wyatt and Lonnie jumped down. Lonnie stared at the store, his eyes searching. What did he want? Cora wondered as Wyatt helped each of the girls down. The twins hurried to their ma's side but Cora waited for Wyatt.

"I could use some help getting supplies at the feed store," Pa said.

Wyatt needed no more urging. He jumped up beside Pa and Lonnie climbed back into the wagon, his gaze lingering on the display in the store.

Cora turned to see what held so much interest for the boy. Just the ordinary tools Mr. Frank sold—an array of shovels, some leather goods—nothing to hold a young man's attention that she could see.

She followed Ma and the twins into the store and breathed in a myriad of scents. Linseed oil on the dark floorboards. Canvas rolled up in the back. Tangy dill from a barrel of pickles. A jumble of tools and cast iron ware occupied one corner and another held ladies' wear. The store was crowded from the roof to the floor and from wall to wall.

Cora stuffed back unreasonable disappointment. Yes,

she'd hoped to show Wyatt around the store and then the town, but of course he'd sooner spend the time with Pa.

Her visual assessment stalled at Anna Rawley, Cora's best friend since grade three. Anna saw her and waved her over. Rose and Lilly followed on Cora's heels as they crossed the floor, edging past the coffee grinder and a display of pitchforks.

Two other young ladies left off the examination of a new shipment of buttons and joined them, Nancy White and Mary Ann McHaig. Nancy lived with her family across from the school and Mary Ann had recently started up a milliner's shop and wore a specimen of her work—a fancy affair in green satin, frothy feathers and big bows.

Rose pointed to it. "Very nice. How is your business doing?"

"Flourishing," Mary Ann assured them. Her smile faded. "Though I would sooner have my uncle back." Her uncle had been her guardian, and upon his death several months ago she had inherited money enough to start her own business.

Cora squeezed her arm. "If you get lonely you can always come and visit us." Silently she thanked God that she had her sisters, and Ma and Pa Bell.

The town girls were full of news about who had been seen with whom and the newest merchandise in every store, all of which interested Cora and her sisters. She and her sisters likewise told their news, including the arrival of Wyatt and Lonnie and their need to rest their horses until Fanny foaled.

She knew the moment Wyatt stepped into the store. She felt his eyes without even turning in his direction. A smile curved her lips as she shifted to look at him.

Wyatt stood alone in the doorway. Ma had gone across the street to speak to a friend she'd spied. Pa had no doubt gone to fetch her.

She'd never taken into account how tall Wyatt was until she saw him framed by the screen door. He stood with his fingers tucked in the front pockets of his trousers and his hat tipped back, which allowed her to admire his dark brown hair. He'd gotten it cut. That surely explained why she studied him so thoroughly.

His bottomless eyes met hers. A smile barely touched his lips but filled his gaze.

He tipped his hat forward and strode toward her.

She jerked around, breathing slowly, hoping to calm the wild fluttering of her heart.

When he reached them, Rose and Lilly shifted so he could join their circle. He favored each girl with a smile and greeted each of the young women in a charming fashion.

Cora's lips tightened as Anna and the other two town girls preened like a trio of peacocks.

"Girls," she managed in a neutral voice, "I'd like you to meet Mr. Wyatt Williams." She left it at that, then introduced each of the girls.

"This is the man visiting at your farm?" Nancy sounded as if she'd run all the way from Fort Benton.

Anna nudged Cora. "The cowboy with the herd of horses?"

Cora was beginning to wish she hadn't mentioned anything about him. In truth, she'd said very little, but Rose and Lilly had run over with information.

Mary Ann leaned forward and offered her hand. "I own the new milliner's shop. I guess you won't be needing a new bonnet for yourself. But perhaps for your wife…"

He grinned. "I don't have one."

Mary Ann beamed. "Or your mother."

Wyatt's grin lingered, though Cora thought it lacked the usual amusement. "I think my ma would have little use for a fancy bonnet even if she was still alive."

His response made her want to cheer. Why would any woman spend good money on such foolish things? But she'd seen enough women wearing elaborate hats to know not everyone shared her opinion.

She couldn't fault his manners, though he remained aloof despite the girls' attention.

"Mary Ann was about to tell us some interesting new about the Caldwells." Cora hoped to distract the girls from practically falling over themselves trying to impress Wyatt.

Mary Ann nodded, sending the feathers on her bonnet into a furious dance. A little curl of black hair fluttered across her cheek. Her dark eyes rounded. "I hear Duke Caldwell is returning."

"His name is Douglas." Duke was his nickname, which Rose refused to use. "I thought he was gone for good."

Lilly nudged her in the ribs. "You only wish it were true."

Anna tsked. "You don't really want that!"

"I sure wouldn't," Mary Ann said, fluttering her eyelashes at Wyatt.

Nancy nodded agreement.

Cora had noticed Mary Ann's particular interest in men before, but now it had grown downright annoying.

"We can only hope he'll be kept busy and maybe keep the Caldwell cowboys busy enough they won't bother us."

"He was always unkind to us, as I recall." Rose adjusted her gloves as she spoke, worrying them until Cora caught her hands and stilled them. Rose sighed. "Just like his father. I don't expect we'll see any changes. Certainly not for the better."

Lilly nodded, her face tight with worry. "It might get worse."

"Here's Pa," Cora said, grateful for the diversion. She whispered to the girls as they crossed the oiled floor to join their parents. "Don't repeat your concerns about Duke to Ma and Pa. They'll worry needlessly."

They conducted their business, Mr. Frank taking the cheese, butter and eggs and noting the amount in his little notebook.

Ma ordered syrup, cocoa and a few other items they were low on.

Cora watched Lonnie, who was now studying the display in the window. She turned to Wyatt, saw he, too, watched his brother. "What has him so interested?"

Wyatt shook his head. He poked his head outside and called to his brother. "Lonnie, let's get some candy."

The boy jerked as if he'd been lassoed at a full gallop. He drew in a shuddering breath and hurried in to the candy display. Between them, Wyatt and Lonnie filled a bag rather generously, Cora figured.

"I'm done here," Ma said, and led them outside. Pa helped her to the wagon. She turned to study the girls as Wyatt helped them into the back. "Is something going on I should know about?"

Ma could always see through any secrets the girls

tried to keep. Cora knew there was no point in trying to hide the news.

"Mary Ann says Duke Caldwell is coming home."

Pa grunted. "The younger Caldwell returns. Maybe Philadelphia has had enough of him."

Ma faced forward, her shoulders stiff. She did not like the feud between the families. "Neighbors should get along. You never know when you'll need help from each other."

"Sadly, the Caldwells do not share your philosophy," Cora said.

Wyatt sat on the back of the wagon, looking as self-satisfied as one of Lilly's cats at milking time.

Cora pretended to adjust her skirts so she could study him. Had he enjoyed the attention the girls had paid him?

Ma and Pa chatted as they journeyed home. Pa seemed satisfied with his purchase—new wooden planks that filled the air with a piney scent.

Ma nodded and made agreeing noises at the appropriate times as Pa talked, but Cora wondered if she really listened to him. Was she worrying how Duke's return would affect them?

Cora turned to her sisters. "Did Mary Ann say when Duke is expected to arrive?"

Rose snorted. "Too soon for my liking."

"You've never forgiven him for teasing you about your red hair, have you?"

"That was only one of many things he did."

Lilly interrupted before Rose could itemize Duke's faults. "According to Mary Ann, Mrs. Caldwell said he was making a leisurely trip, stopping to visit a few places. They are anxious for his return, but Mary Ann didn't know a specific date." She turned to Rose, her expression so guileless few would guess she meant to tease her twin sister. "Rose, did you hear when he would arrive?"

Lilly and Cora darted amused glances at each other. Rose and Duke had their own personal feud going on, and the sisters didn't mind reminding Rose of it.

"I don't care." Rose managed to look glum.

"Nice town," Wyatt murmured as they drove away. He settled back, pulled out the bag of candy and passed it around.

They crossed the river and turned homeward. She sat up and looked toward the farm. Out of habit, she ran a practiced eye about the place, mentally checking each pasture, the orchard, the sheep—

Whoa. She jerked her gaze back. The sheep pasture stood void of the little wooly animals. She rose to her knees. "Where are the sheep?"

At her question, Pa and Ma strained forward.

Lilly jumped up and pressed to their backs. "The pasture is empty."

Rose leaned around Ma.

Wyatt crowded close to Cora's back, not touching, but she breathed the lemony scent of his freshly groomed hair.

"There." He pointed past her, his arm brushing her shoulder, sending startled awareness up her spine and down to her fingertips.

The small flock huddled at the water's edge a hundred yards farther down, half-hidden by the rocks and a scraggly bunch of bushes at the river's edge.

Lilly staggered toward the back of the wagon.

Cora and Wyatt both reached for her at the same time and steadied her.

"Sit down and wait until Pa stops," Cora ordered.

Lilly jerked to one side and then the other to escape their grasp but finally sank to her knees. "It's those Caldwell cowboys again. If any of the animals are hurt—" Her voice broke.

Cora turned to Wyatt, knowing full well her concern filled her face. "Why must the Caldwells constantly harass us?"

Wyatt touched her arm. "We'll get them all back safely."

She nodded, grateful for his reassurance and comforting touch. She could not remember a time when she didn't feel she had to be the one to stand strong to protect her family.

She shook away the foolish thought. She would never let harm come to them so long as she could prevent it.

Wyatt hung on to Lilly. He figured if she could, she would launch herself out the back with no heed for life and limb. Were these girls intent on killing themselves over the farm and their animals? Over family? Someone ought to inform them they were of more value to family and home alive than dead.

Before Mr. Bell pulled the wagon to a halt, Wyatt jumped to the ground. He reached up and helped Lilly down. She grabbed up her skirts and ran toward the bleating sheep.

Wyatt turned back in time to help Cora alight. "Does this happen often?"

"If not this, then something else." Her words were tight, as if it hurt to move her jaw.

Rose jumped to their side. "Come on, you two. Lilly

needs help." She raced to her sister. "Now, now, Lilly. Don't fret. We'll get them all back safely."

"The poor things." Lilly's hands fluttered helplessly.

"I'll take Ma to the house," Mr. Bell called, the wagon rumbling away.

Wyatt watched them depart. The man was likely grateful for an excuse to escape the near hysteria of his one daughter.

He turned to Lonnie, who had the look of a trapped animal. "It's okay," Wyatt said softly. "You can help or go to the house with Mr. Bell."

Lonnie looked about. "I'll help him unload." He scurried away and Wyatt turned his attention back to the girls.

"We'll get them all back," Cora said as she hurried to Lilly's side.

Lilly sobbed hard.

Wyatt pressed the heel of one hand to his forehead. If all three of them started weeping he'd… He wasn't sure what he would do, but being locked up with a bunch of angry men sounded safer at the moment.

He dismissed the thought as quickly as it came. Surely crying lasted for only a moment. Being locked up was endless.

He kept to Cora's side as he took in the scene. Some of the sheep were in the river. He figured all that kept them from being swept downstream were the rocks that corralled them. Other sheep stood in the bushes.

Heedless of her dress and shoes, Lilly rushed into the stream. "They'll drown." Only the weight of the water around her legs slowed her frantic hurry.

"Sheep can swim," Cora said. She turned to Wyatt.

"She'll drown herself before she'll let something happen to one of those creatures."

Wyatt didn't stop to think about his actions but plunged in after Lilly, calling to Cora over his shoulder, "You stay there and pull them from the water when I shove them in your direction." The cold made him gasp. The water sucked at his legs.

He grabbed the nearest ewe and shoved her toward Cora, who helped the animal climb the rocky bank to safety.

Meanwhile, Lilly had her hands full trying to persuade another animal to back away from the rocks so she could push it to Cora. The animal bolted, was caught in the current and would have been carried downstream if Wyatt hadn't reached out and snagged it.

In a few minutes, all the sheep stood on grassy ground. Wyatt helped Lilly out of the river and then began to scramble over the slippery rocks.

Cora held a hand out to him. Without hesitation he let her help him out of the water, but he dropped her hand as soon as he stood on two feet. He needed to keep his distance from her. Each time he saw her it grew harder. He thought of the moment he'd stepped into the store and seen her dark blond hair hanging in a braid down her back. She'd met his gaze, her eyes dark and watchful across the cluttered shop. She'd stood surrounded by five young women, but none of them were half as beautiful as she, and their expressions revealed nowhere near as much character. Cora was a force of nature—strong, independent, protective. Her family came first with her. The thought swept through his mental wanderings, leaving him with one solid surety. Nothing would ever entice her away from her sisters and the Bells. Nothing would be allowed to endanger them in any way.

The bracing thought enabled him to ignore how warm and firm her hand had been in his.

"It's cold." He shivered.

"Thanks for helping get the sheep out." She favored him with a sunlit smile that slipped right past his defenses and plopped into his heart like a stubborn squatter.

She cast a troubled look at the wet sheep bleating in a huddle nearby. "Lilly would have been devastated if one of them drowned."

Poor Cora, always trying to protect her sisters from anything bad. What would she do if she failed or thought she had? "Where did Lilly go?" Cora searched for her sister, though she must be as cold as he.

They saw her at the same time, tromping through the bushes. "The sheep are caught in the branches."

Ignoring his wet clothes and waterlogged boots, Wyatt went over and helped free the animals.

Cora worked at his side. "Lilly, they're unharmed. All we have to do is get them back to their pen."

Rose shepherded each animal back to the pasture as it was freed.

Finally, the last ewe was back, the lambs bleating after them. The smell of wet lanolin filled the air. The warm breeze dried the edges of Wyatt's shirt, but his trousers hung heavy about his waist and his feet stood in boots full of water.

The four of them stood together in the gap of the fence. The posts were tipped over.

"I know those posts were in solidly." Cora ground the words out. "But those Caldwell cowboys know how to make it look as if they had nothing to do with it."

Wyatt looked for signs in the ground, but the sheep had trampled away any clue. His fists curled; his insides tightened. This was beyond causing trouble. It was vindictive. Mean-spirited. Harsh. The sheep might have drowned if the Bells had been gone longer. He couldn't abide someone bigger, tougher and more powerful treating those weaker and more vulnerable this way. It reminded him too sharply of his father.

"Why don't you—" He meant to ask why they didn't go to the sheriff or approach the boss at the Caldwell ranch, but his question was cut off by a howl from Lilly.

"Lambie Four is missing."

"Lambie Four?" Wyatt turned to Cora for an explanation.

"She numbers them when they're born. Doesn't give them real names until they're weaned." She shrugged. "Don't know why."

Wyatt didn't miss the way her shoulders slumped forward. Or how her arms hung at her sides.

"Poor Lilly." Her voice dripped with sympathy. "The animals are so precious to her."

He touched Cora's hand. "Maybe the lamb is still out there. Come on. Let's look." He returned to the bushes. But no little white lamb was caught in the branches.

He pressed his lips tight. The Caldwells were cruel people. He turned and came face-to-face with Cora.

"Don't you think we would have seen a lamb if it was there?" she asked him.

"Of course you would have. I didn't mean otherwise. But I'm not about to give up and provide those two more reason to cry." He tipped his head toward the twins. Rose held Lilly in her arms, her sister's head pressed to her neck. Their muffled sobs hit him harder than an iron fist. Women shouldn't be made to cry. They should be protected, though—he darted his gaze to Cora—if she heard him say so she would likely inform him she didn't need protection.

Cora stared at the river. "It might have drowned."

Remembering how the sheep caught in the current had passed him, he grabbed Cora's hand. "Or it might have been carried downstream. Let's see."

Her fingers, warm and strong, gripped his. "Oh, please, God. Let it be alive."

His muscles tightened as he silently echoed the prayer. He could understand why Cora felt so strongly about protecting her sisters. He wanted to do the same for her. Strange thought from a man who'd known little but darkness and violence in his life.

They trotted along the bank of the river. Bushes reached the water's edge in places and Wyatt clambered down to examine them, both relieved that he didn't find a dead animal and disappointed he hadn't found Lambie Four alive and well.

Half a mile later, Cora caught his arm. "We might as well go back." She rocked her head back and forth. "I don't know how I'm going to deal with Lilly." She plunked down on a nearby rock. "I try to protect the girls, but how am I to shield them from the Caldwells? From the hurtful teasing like Duke hands out?" Her hands hung between her knees and she stared at the gurgling water.

Wyatt sat at her side. "You live on a farm. Isn't birth and death part of the experience?"

Cora spared him a pained look. "But not senseless like this."

He nodded, understanding the difference, and sat as

dejected as she. He looked past her, avoiding the anger in her face. He knew the look wasn't directed at him, but the set of her mouth made him nervous. In his experience, anger led to uncontrolled actions.

She sucked in air. "I'm going back to console Lilly and fix the fence." Her expression softened and he relaxed. Her anger seemed short-lived and controlled.

The breeze snorted down the river. Despite the heat of the sun, he shivered in his damp clothes.

The breeze bent the willows growing along the water. Something flashed. He squinted. Was it his imagination or had he seen a bit of white? "There's something in those bushes." He hurried toward them.

"What is it?" Cora kept pace at his side. She watched the bushes, trying to catch a glimpse of whatever he'd seen.

"I don't know, but I thought I saw a bit of white."

She sucked in air as if he'd promised her a sure thing.

"I can't be certain." He no longer saw it.

They reached the willows. "You wait here." He slid into the water.

"I'm coming, too."

"I'm already wet." He waved her back, hoping she would heed his suggestion. The last thing he needed now was to worry about her. He already felt as if his heart was near to shattering with all the emotional upheaval of the afternoon.

She clung to a tree, almost falling into the water, but remained on shore while he pushed into the bushes.

That was when he saw it. A little lamb caught in the branches, bobbing in the flow of the water. Wyatt drew his mouth back and hid his reaction when he could detect no movement from the animal.

"Did you find anything?" Cora called.

"I think so. Just a minute." He wanted to pretend he hadn't, but he couldn't lie to her. Besides, she'd demand to see for herself. He parted the bushes and untangled the limp creature. His insides boiled that someone had deliberately caused this needless death, not to mention the pain and sorrow for Lilly and the frustration for Cora that she couldn't protect her sisters from such agony.

He edged back toward Cora.

She saw the lamb and her face lit up. "You found it. How wonderful."

Unable to tell her the truth, he cradled the creature close as he made his way to the bank. Cora held out a hand to help him from the river.

He turned so she couldn't see the lamb and knelt. But he couldn't release it, couldn't let her see the truth.

She pulled at his arms. "Let me see."

He shook his head.

Sitting back on her heels, she stared at him. "You mean…?"

He nodded and slowly, reluctantly lifted his head to see her reaction. If only he could spare her this. Spare all of them. He sat back, staring at Cora. Instead of sadness, her eyes flashed hardness, punching a hole in his sympathy. She bolted to her feet and stalked toward the river. He half rose, but she spun around, her fists bunched at her sides, and he settled back, withdrawing at the fierceness of her look.

"I would like to march over to the Caldwells and toss this poor dead lamb on their table. I wonder how they'd like that."

"I can't think they would." He watched her carefully, not sure how she'd handle her anger.

Cora dropped her gaze to the lamb in Wyatt's arms. "Poor little thing." She sucked in air as if preparing for battle. "Poor Lilly. Well, there's nothing for it but to go home and tell her the news."

He shifted his weight back on his heels to push himself up. The lamb shifted as he moved. And then it shifted again. He sank back to the ground and stared. "Cora!"

"Come on. Let's get this done with."

"Cora, come here."

"What's wrong with you? You object to carrying a dead lamb? Maybe you don't like sheep."

He ignored her accusing tone. "I like sheep just fine. But I don't think I'll be carrying a dead lamb."

She pushed him aside. "For goodness' sake. Give it to me. I'll carry it."

The lamb bleated weakly.

Cora fell back, landing on her rump, her eyes so round that Wyatt nearly laughed.

"It's alive?"

"That's what I was trying to tell you." He grinned at her.

"God be praised." She sprang to her feet and threw her arms about him. "God be praised." Her words were muffled against the hollow of his shoulder.

He didn't move. Didn't raise his arms to hold her. Couldn't. She only hugged him because of her joy over one live lamb. She didn't realize what she did. Any more than she knew how warm and inviting her arms were. Or how her hair tickled his nose and made him want to bury his face in it.

His heart beat at an alarming rate. As if he'd swum a mile in the cold river. Or climbed the tallest mountain. Or run all the way to town carrying a heavy pack.

He blinked hard. He was an ex-con. He ought to remember that.

She stepped back and tipped her head to consider him. "You're ice-cold."

A weak grin touched his mouth without reaching his eyes or coming anywhere near his heart. "I've been in the river twice now."

The lamb bleated again and tried to stand up.

"Maybe he was only cold." She patted Wyatt's cheek, sending tension to his eyes and hope to his heart. "You are a hero, Wyatt. Wait until the girls learn what you've done."

He shook his head. "I didn't do anything." He didn't expect Rose and Lilly would throw themselves into his arms, but if Cora did it again…

He swallowed hard. He couldn't let himself get too drawn to this family. His past could hurt them. Especially if Jimmy Stone showed up. Wyatt knew the man wouldn't hesitate to hurt the Bells if he thought it would hurt Wyatt. He needed to remember that.

Needing to escape Cora's gratitude, he turned to the lamb. "Lambie Four, I presume."

Cora chuckled. "I'm sure he's pleased to meet you."

"He's awfully weak." He scooped the lamb into his arms. "We'd better get him back to his mama."

"Which one?" The words gurgled from her throat. "The ewe or Lilly?"

Wyatt laughed as every remnant of tension slipped from him. "I expect they will both fuss over him."

Cora patted his shoulder. "I expect they will. Best you be prepared for gratitude and joy."

He gave an exaggerated shudder. "Please tell me they don't cry when they're happy." He tried to concentrate on the unfamiliar smell of wet sheep, paid attention to the ground before him so he wouldn't trip and drop the lamb. He thought of how waterlogged his feet were. He would have to hang his boots by the fire tonight to dry them out.

"Wyatt, what's wrong?"

He shook his head. "Nothing." Except all this crying and hugging was so unfamiliar he wasn't sure how to react. Should he enjoy it as much as he did? At least the hugging part? "Did you know wet sheep smell like damp clothes?"

She laughed. "'Cause it's the same thing. Wool on the critter becomes wool in a garment."

He knew that, of course. He released the air in his lungs quietly, lest it draw attention to the fact he'd acted so strangely.

Cora patted his cheek. "Wyatt, you're a hero."

"So you said, but don't believe it. I'm just an ordinary man."

She snorted. "No man thinks he's ordinary."

Her statement made him plumb forget his past and his need for caution. "Really? How do you know this?"

She quirked an eyebrow at him. "From my vast experience with men, of course." She held his gaze, her eyes wide.

Except he didn't believe her. She was far too innocent and fresh to have had a lot of experience with men. On top of that, he knew firsthand how carefully Mr. Bell watched his daughters. Wyatt tipped his head back and roared with laughter. "Your vast experience! Now I've heard it all." He hooted again.

She shrugged and grinned as if pleased with herself. "You sound as though you doubt me."

He shook his head while his chuckles continued to erupt. "Oh, not at all," he choked out.

They drew close to the farm. Mr. Bell and the twins were repairing the fence. Rose glanced up and saw them. She called to Lilly, who stared at the white bundle in Wyatt's arms, her eyes wide.

"He's okay," Cora called, and Lilly raced toward them.

Wyatt couldn't miss the joy in her face. He shifted his attention to Cora, who beamed at her approaching sister, then flicked him a smile that touched him like a gentle caress and turned his heart to a quivering mass that longed for such approval every day of his life.

Lilly reached them with Rose at her heels.

He realized that laughing with Cora, receiving her hugs and approval, had soothed some part of him inside that had hurt all his life. Something he'd not been aware of until he felt the lightness when it was gone.

For a heartbeat he wondered if she had the ability to heal other wounds. Wounds left by his angry father, by a year of sharing his life with criminals who cared nothing for his feelings other than to mock if they thought they'd found a tender spot, and by the hurt heaped on him by cruel comments and rejection from people he had considered friends and neighbors.

He'd gladly let Cora be the one to heal him. Only he didn't want to bring disgrace or danger into her life.

Chapter Ten

Cora wondered if she'd ever felt so alive. Knowing the lamb was safe and then hugging Wyatt in her excitement... Something had shifted between them at that moment. The joy of making him laugh, seeing the tension in his eyes disappear, was rivaled only by that of returning Lambie Four safely to Lilly.

Wyatt released the lamb to Lilly, who took it to the ewe. She dried the little one with her skirts and no one protested. Together she and the ewe hovered over the lamb, petting and comforting it.

Rose stayed close as well, reassuring herself that Lilly was going to be okay now.

Cora stole a glance at Wyatt. He stood with his hands on his hips, his stance wide, grinning at Lilly. He whispered to Cora, "Two mamas, just like you said. That little one is getting his fair share of care, I'd say."

She laughed. "I expect it will last for days, weeks." She tossed her hands in the air as if exasperated. "Months more than likely."

Pa joined them. "The fence is repaired." He looked

Wyatt up and down. "Looks as if you should find some dry clothes."

Wyatt glanced down. "Guess I should, at that."

But before he could make one step toward his camp, Lilly and Rose spoke to each other, nodded and trotted to him.

Rose hesitated, but Lilly didn't lose a moment. She hugged him hard. "I'm so grateful to you for finding him. I can't believe the rest of us were ready to give up so easily. It shames me."

Rose patted Wyatt's arm. "We are so grateful. If there's anything we can do for you, name it."

Cora smiled gently. Her sisters' joy had been restored and that was all that mattered. Then she noticed how easily Wyatt patted Lilly on the back and grinned at Rose. Why had he stood stiff and awkward when she'd hugged him? It had only been a gesture of joy and gratitude, but still. Would it have hurt him to respond just a little? She turned away from the trio and stared at the repaired fence.

Her anger and confusion focused on the damage the Caldwells had done. Perhaps they'd intended for the whole flock to drown. She kicked at a clump of sod and sent it sailing over the fence.

Wyatt touched her shoulder. "Don't let them get to you. Everything is back to normal. Now I'm going to get out of these wet things." He patted her shoulder in a fatherly way and trotted toward the barn.

Cora's insides boiled. She'd had a father who left her. She had Pa, who took real good care of her. She didn't need a fatherly pat from Wyatt. And he was wrong. Things weren't back to normal. Thanks to his presence on the farm, things might never be normal for her again.

He made her long for things she couldn't allow herself. Her place was here on the farm, watching over her sisters. Besides, hadn't she learned her lesson about trusting any man but Pa? Twice she'd been hurt by men with no regard for her feelings. First her papa and then Evan. There would not be a third time.

Not that Wyatt had in any way suggested he might have feelings for her. It was only her own silly reaction to an emotionally fraught moment that had even made her think such things.

She was far too practical to let her thoughts get out of control.

Between them, Cora and Rose persuaded Lilly to leave the lamb long enough to change into dry clothes.

Lonnie wandered over. "Where did everyone go?"

Cora explained about finding the lost lamb. "Wyatt has gone to change."

Lonnie's face wrinkled in worry. "Is he okay?"

"He just got wet. He's fine." She didn't add that he had been rather cold, and she chafed her arms where his skin had chilled hers. Her heart longed to take care of Wyatt—wrap him in a cozy woolen blanket, rub his hands and arms until they glowed with warmth, give him hot, sweet tea.

She closed her eyes, sucked in air and forced a reminder into her brain. She had no right to be imagining such intimacies.

Wyatt returned a few minutes later in dry clothes, though she knew his boots would still be wet inside.

She half expected Lonnie to rush to his side, but the boy hung back. He'd picked up one of the kittens and held it close. His eyes went to Wyatt, then darted away.

How strange. It was one of the many unanswered

questions about the pair that warned her she must be cautious.

Yet despite what her brain said, she struggled to keep from watching Wyatt's every move. In helping rescue the sheep, he'd revealed so many different facets of his character—tenderness, caring and determination. Combined with all she'd already observed and the way she'd seen him with fresh eyes at the store, it created a very appealing package. He was a man of honor and character.

A man with a past he refused to talk about.

She'd hugged him. Out of gratitude for the rescued lamb. But she'd felt much more than gratitude. There was a fluttering in her heart as she tried to identify her emotions. Admiration and concern. When she'd realized how cold he was, her nerves had tensed. What if he got sick?

Looking back, she realized how foolish it was to be so concerned. He was a tough cowboy, used to riding long hours in any weather. A little soaking wouldn't hurt him.

Please, God, keep him safe.

It was a prayer that she might have said for anyone. Except she'd never before prayed it for anyone outside her family.

Ma called them to come to the house.

Cora gladly turned away from the pair and pulled determination into her thoughts. She had her head on straight and meant for her heart to follow.

Lonnie trailed along behind Wyatt, carrying the kitten.

"Ma doesn't allow cats in the house," Cora warned.

Lonnie pulled to a halt. "I'll stay out here with it." He sank to the grass and trailed a bit of string for the kitten to chase.

"You all need a good strong cup of my red rot tea." Ma guided them toward the table.

"Red rot tea?" Wyatt asked, swallowing hard.

Cora hid a smile as he glanced toward the door, his eyes wide, his shoulders tensing.

"Best thing to ward off a chill from your dunking." Ma waited for everyone to sit, then poured tea into cups and passed them around.

Wyatt sat with his hands under his knees staring at his cup. He turned to Cora. "Red rot?" he whispered.

Lilly could not stop talking about her sheep and all they'd suffered, so the others did not hear his question.

Cora leaned closer. "Would you sooner be sick?"

He contemplated the tea. "Maybe."

"Would it help to know that the plant Ma uses to make the tea eats ants?"

He jerked back. "You're joshing." He gave her such a doubting look she pressed her hand to her mouth to keep back a laugh.

"No, I'm not. It's a carnivorous plant with excellent medicinal qualities."

By now, the rest of the family had grown still and was listening to the conversation. Lilly and Rose sucked in their lips to stop from laughing.

Wyatt sat back in his chair and stared at the tea as if it might bite him.

Cora cleared her throat so she could speak. "Not to worry, though. Ma puts a few other things in with it to tame it."

Lilly and Rose no longer tried to hide their amusement and giggled.

Ma smiled gently. "Wyatt, it's perfectly harmless. Don't let these girls tease you so. Why, people come from miles around for a supply of red rot tea each fall. It keeps them healthy and fights off chest infections."

Pa sipped his drink. "Ma's right. Look at me. An old man now and never sick with a chill. All thanks to Ma's medicinals."

Cora turned to her pa. "You aren't old." It bothered her to think of him in those terms.

He patted her hand. "I'm sure not as young as I used to be."

A shiver snaked up her spine. "Don't you even talk about getting old." She didn't want to think of losing either of their parents. Not for a long, long time.

"Age is not something I can control," Pa said. "But no need for any of you to fret. I'm healthy as a horse."

Cora studied him a moment. She couldn't recall him being sick a day since he and Ma found them. Reassured by the knowledge, she turned back to Wyatt. "Don't tell me a big strong cowboy like you is afraid of a little cup of harmless tea."

He squinted at her. "How harmless can something called red rot be? You're sure my insides won't disintegrate?"

Cora shrugged. "Who knows? I suppose it depends on how tough you are." She drank from her cup and gave him a daring glance. "Maybe you aren't as tough as us Bells. Especially as, apart from Pa, we're all females."

As if to prove their toughness, Rose and Lilly lifted their cups and drank. Even Ma gave him a challenging look over the rim of her cup.

Wyatt's gaze went from Rose to Lilly to Ma then to Cora. Finally, he considered his cup. He edged one hand from under his knee and grasped the handle gingerly, as if even touching it carried risk. He shuddered and slowly lifted the tea to his lips.

She laughed, and at the exact moment he swallowed she said, "Might be your last moment on earth."

He sputtered but it was too late. His eyes widened. "It doesn't taste bad."

The Bell family chuckled.

But Cora couldn't resist one last tease. "Let us know if your stomach starts to hurt or you begin to bleed from your pores."

Wyatt squinted at her, informing her he didn't believe a word of her warning.

"Cora," Ma scolded. "Stop tormenting the poor man."

Wyatt gave her a superior look. "Your ma is defending me." He set his cup down and shifted, making his chair squeak. He glanced around the table. "I hope you don't mind me asking, but why don't you report this mischief to the sheriff? Wouldn't that put an end to the Caldwells bothering you?"

Five cups clattered to the table. Five pairs of eyes stared at him. Cora had told him the sheriff could do nothing.

"Or go to this Mr. Caldwell and ask him to stop his cowboys from doing this?"

Lilly shook her head. "It might make things worse. The Caldwells might get more aggressive."

Rose planted her fists on either side of her cup and pursed her lips as she looked around the table, spearing each of them with her gaze. "The Caldwells aren't the only people with a right to own land."

Cora looked at her sister. Rose always wanted things fixed: have the Caldwells put in their place, get Ma's remedies neatly noted in a little book, learn the facts about who their birth family had been and if any of them lived. Perhaps even search for them. In Cora's opinion, Rose simply asked for more hurt, more reminder of how little they mattered to their birth father if she pursued the subject.

Cora would protect her younger sisters from feeling the devastation of such rejection.

Pa pushed back from the table. "While Ma makes supper, we'd best get some work done." He trod toward the door.

Cora listened to his footsteps. Did they seem heavier, slower than the last time she gave it thought? She shook her head. She only considered it because of his reminder that he grew old.

Lilly grabbed Ma's hand before she could push to her feet. "The sheep had a good soaking. Those that didn't have been under a lot of stress. Ma, do you think some of this tea would help them? Maybe keep them from getting sick?"

Ma sank back and studied Lilly. "Sometimes we do all we can and still don't get the result we want."

Yes! Exactly what Cora wished Rose would accept. She shot her redheaded sister a look and gave a little nod. *Listen to our wise ma.*

Rose only widened her eyes to inform Cora she didn't plan to change her mind. Rose could be so stubborn. So single-minded. To her own harm.

"But I must do all I can," Lilly beseeched Ma.

"Of course you must, but how are you going to get a dozen ewes and their lambs to drink tea?"

Lilly shrugged, misery in her eyes and posture.

Ma patted Lilly's hand. "I have a tincture that has the same medicinal qualities. I'll get it for you."

Ma hurried to the garden shed where she kept most of her herbs and healing plants.

Rose grinned. "There you go, Lilly. Your sheep will be just fine. Do you want help doctoring them?"

Lilly smiled at her twin. "I won't be able to do it on my own." She darted a glance toward Cora and then Wyatt.

"We'll help, too," Cora said.

The twins trotted out to get the tincture from Ma.

Cora faced Wyatt. "Do you object to helping with the sheep?"

His eyebrows rose. "Should I?"

"I don't know. Seems cowboys often hate sheep."

"Cowboys have the reputation of hating farms and farmers. Do I act like I do?"

She shook her head, mesmerized by the teasing gleam in his eyes. She forced her tongue to work. "You aren't like most cowboys I know."

His grin flashed. "And with your vast experience with men, you've known hundreds, I suppose?"

She gave an airy wave. "So many I couldn't begin to count them."

"And not one of them has cared for sheep?"

"Not a one." Her smile flattened as she thought of the Caldwell cowboys. "In my vast experience—" she tried to sound nonchalant "—they would like to see all sheep drown in the river."

His grin fled. "That was downright stupid and callous and—" He lifted his hands in a gesture of defeat. "I can't even begin to say all the things I feel about that dreadful deed."

Cora admired his passion and ushered them outside. "You are not like any cowboy I ever met."

He thrust his shoulders back and held his chin high. "I take that as a true compliment."

As they walked out together, a wonderful warming feeling spread like sweet honey throughout Cora's insides.

Wyatt looked about. "Where did Lonnie go?"

Cora saw him first. "He's over by the pigpen."

Wyatt called to him. "We're going to help Lilly with the sheep. Do you want to come?

"Mr. Bell is going to show me how to make a rope."

"Okay."

Cora smiled. Pa would do more to heal Lonnie's fear of men than anyone she knew.

They had reached the fence of the sheep pasture and she stepped away from Wyatt's side. She enjoyed his company far too much for her own comfort. She would do well to listen to the same advice she wished Rose would heed. A person could be the cause of their own hurt if they didn't take care.

Hadn't she promised Pa and Ma and herself that she would not be hurt by Wyatt? She had no intention of being too free with her trust.

Grub sat outside the fence and jumped to his feet, wagging all over when he saw they were venturing into the pasture.

"No, you stay here, boy," Cora said.

"Wouldn't he be a help?"

Cora snorted. "You heard how good he is at herding turkeys. He's even worse at herding sheep."

"I have to ask why you keep such a useless dog."

She gave him a wide-eyed look of shock. "Why, that should be obvious. It's because he's so cute."

Wyatt roared with laughter. "He's the ug—"

"Don't say it," she warned him.

He stifled a chuckle as he closed the gate behind them.

In the pasture, Lilly and Rose held a sheep as Lilly inserted a dropper in its mouth and held its jaws until it swallowed. Only then did she glance up. "If you two can catch them and bring them to me one at a time, it would sure go a lot faster."

Rose marked the treated sheep with a little colored chalk and turned it loose.

"You know how to catch sheep?" Wyatt murmured.

"Sure. Reach out and grab it and drag it to Lilly."

He leaned back on his heels and grinned at her. "It sounds as easy as catching a little pig."

She rolled her eyes and pretended to ignore his reference. Inside, she chuckled at the memory of their first meeting. "How hard can it be?"

"If you say so. Grab that one. She's close."

They lunged for the ewe, but she bleated and trotted away, leaving Cora with had a handful of wool.

She sat on her rump and stared at the animal.

"You're going at it all wrong," Lilly said. "Just call them to you and hold each one under their chin. It's not hard."

Wyatt groaned. "Seems I've heard that before."

Under her breath, Cora murmured, "I don't much care for sheep."

Wyatt choked. "And you accused me of not liking them. As if it was the worst possible crime a man could commit."

She ignored him. This teasing brought her perilously close to the invisible line that she would not, must not, cross.

He nudged her with his foot.

Still she ignored him.

He pushed her over.

She gasped and stared up at him. "Why'd you do that?"

He planted his hands on his hips. "Why did you pretend you liked sheep?"

She scrambled to her feet and gave a dismissive toss of her head. "I never said anything of the sort."

"You might as well have."

She shrugged. "I can't help it if you make huge assumptions."

He took a step toward her.

Not caring for the look in his eyes, she edged away and considered the sheep. "We'd better get to work."

He growled, "I should have brought my rope. I could lasso them."

"Go around them," Lilly called. "All you have to do is herd them my way. I'll call them."

As they moseyed around the animals, Lilly called, "Watch out for the ram. He's harmless but he likes to butt."

Wyatt jerked, looking around for the animal. "Cora, watch out."

The urgency in his voice sent tremors up her spine, but before she could turn, something hit the backs of her legs and propelled her forward.

"Cora." Wyatt could barely push her name past his teeth as the ram hit her from behind. He raced forward, intending to beat the animal off with his bare hands if he must. But the ram trotted off, his head high, as if pleased with his actions.

Cora lay facedown in the grass.

Wyatt squatted at her side. He reached out, wanting to roll her over and make certain she was okay but afraid she might be too injured. "Cora." He touched her shoulder gently. "Cora, say something."

Her ribs expanded in a great gasp. She lifted her head, spit out grass and rolled to her back to stare up at him.

"I don't like sheep," she muttered.

He chuckled, more from relief than any other reason. "Good to see you alive and kicking."

She sat up and groaned. "I'm not kicking, but if Lilly wasn't so blame fond of these horrible, smelly creatures, I'd sure be tempted to kick a ram."

Suspecting she didn't mean a word of her threat, he watched her closely. "I tried to warn you, but it was too late."

"Seems to be the story of my life."

There was a whole lot of information hidden in those few words, but now was not the time or place to ask about it. "Are you hurt anywhere?"

"Only my pride. Imagine my chagrin to be knocked over by a silly ram, especially in front of a cowboy." She closed her eyes and managed to look pained. "Why is it you always see me at my worst?"

"I can't imagine what you mean." He couldn't recall a time when he'd seen anything but her best.

"I'm sure you can. First, you find me falling on my face chasing a little pig. Then I trip on my skirt and almost fall from the barn. Now I'm falling on my face over sheep."

"Best moments of my life." He held out a hand to help her up.

She looked ready to slap it away, then accepted defeat and grabbed on.

He pulled her to her feet and kept hold of her hand even after she was upright. He looked into her eyes and smiled. "Yup, best moments of my life."

"Oh, you." She pushed him hard.

He staggered back but kept his feet. "What was that for?"

She shrugged. "You figure it out."

He grinned. He liked teasing her. Liked seeing her chasing little animals and helping her sisters. Guess he liked most everything about her.

He spun away and reached for one of the ewes.

It mattered not if he liked anything or everything about Cora. Indeed, if he cared the least little bit about her, he would leave this minute, before he brought shame and censure to her and her family.

He looked toward the river and the campsite he and Lonnie shared. Fanny hadn't foaled yet and couldn't travel. Even after she did, they'd have to wait until the foal was strong enough before they moved on.

With a sigh of resignation, he bowed his head. How was he to give his horses a chance to rest, allow Lonnie to learn about normal family and yet protect the Bell family from being affected by his reputation?

How was he going to keep his secrets locked away? Even more important, how would he keep his heart safe?

Chapter Eleven

Cora accompanied her sisters to their shared bedroom to prepare for church.

Pa had informed Wyatt that the Bells attended church every Sunday. He hadn't come right out and said the words, but his meaning was clear—Wyatt and Lonnie were expected to attend, as well. Poor Wyatt had looked as if he wanted to sprout wings and fly away. Lonnie had shrunk back into the shadows, so Cora hadn't seen his expression, but his actions had said it all. They'd both acted as though church attendance threatened their safety.

Cora could think of no reason why anyone would think such a thing unless they were afraid of someone or something. But what could they possibility be afraid of? It wasn't as if they were evil men with their likenesses on a wanted poster. She'd seen enough of them to be certain of that.

Their father was dead. They couldn't be expecting him to turn up at any moment.

So who or what did they fear?

If only he would answer the question should she pose

it to him. There were so many things she didn't know about him. Reason enough to cling to her guardedness, she told herself.

She turned her attention to selecting a dress.

Every other day of the week she wore cotton dresses, some stained and mended. Normally, she didn't give much thought to what she put on, so long as it was practical and allowed her freedom to work. She had two dresses saved for Sundays. She'd always thought the dark red one looked rather nice on her. But it was heavy satin with a high collar that would suffocate her in the summer heat. The other one, a cotton in blue-and-white stripes, would be cooler. She had worn it every Sunday for the past month without giving it a thought, but now she stared at it. The simple style seemed a little childish.

She realized Rose was watching her and brushed her hand over the skirt as if removing specks of dust.

"Something wrong with your dress?" Rose asked.

Cora shook her head. "It's fine."

Lilly and Rose moved closer and studied the gown.

"You could wear that lacy white shawl Anna gave you last Christmas. That would make it look nice," Rose said.

"And why not pin that lovely brooch Ma gave you to the neck?" Lilly added.

"Why in heaven's name would I do that?" Yet she already pictured how those two additions would make the outfit more grown-up.

"To look nice," Lilly said.

Rose nodded. "After all, you know Mary Ann and Nancy and half the young women in Bar Crossing will be flocking to Wyatt likes bees around Ma's flowers."

"And why would I care about that?" Cora couldn't decide if she should be cross or amused.

"I like Wyatt," Rose said. "I wish he would stay here."

Cora gave Rose a look of disbelief. "You are begging for pain and sorrow if you grow too fond of him. That man has deep, dark secrets. Who knows how they might threaten our family?" She hadn't meant to blurt out her own concerns. She pressed her point with another shake of her head, then turned to Lilly. "You two need to learn you can't count on any man hanging around."

The two backed away and stood shoulder to shoulder, denial and stubbornness drawing their mouths into tight lines and narrowing their eyes.

Lilly sniffed. "You always think every man will leave you just because our real pa did."

Rose nodded. "And Evan."

"Thanks for the reminder." Cora slipped the blue-and-white dress over her head. "But it isn't me who needs reminding. It's you two."

Rose and Lilly silently consulted each other. Lilly shook her head but Rose turned away. "Cora," she said. "Why won't you tell us anything about our parents?"

"What's to tell? I was five years old. About all I can remember is staring after a wagon and waiting for it to come back. I know our father was on that wagon, but that's about all I remember." All she cared to remember. "He didn't care for us then. We don't need him now." The girls looked teary eyed so she added, "Then Lilly started to fuss, and all I thought of was how to take care of you two." She smiled at them.

"It's still all you care about," Rose pointed out. "But we're grown up now. Besides, you must remember something."

Lilly tapped Rose's arm. "Let it be. You know she's

not going to tell you anything, and maybe she's right. Maybe we're better off not knowing."

"There you go." Cora arranged her hair in a floppy roll around her head. How did Anna make it look so easy? "Rose, listen to your sister."

The girls turned back to preparing for church, but Cora felt their restlessness. Rose wanting to know who their parents were and why their father had left three little girls behind. Lilly wanting to avoid information for fear it would hurt.

Cora took the suggested brooch and pinned it at her throat. The silver of the oblong embossed brooch looked quite fine. She glanced at the shawl wrapped in tissue on the shelf of the wardrobe and dismissed the idea of wearing it.

Rose noticed her hesitation and picked up the shawl. She draped it over Cora's shoulders. It was as light as morning dew and lacy as the first frost of winter.

"You look great," Lilly said. "Wait a minute." She retrieved her best straw bonnet from the top shelf. "This will be perfect."

"I couldn't," Cora protested. "It's your favorite."

"Nonsense. What are sisters for if they can't share?" Ignoring Cora's objection, she tied it on Cora's head then turned her to the looking glass.

Cora stared at her image.

"You look very nice," Rose said. "I'm sure Wyatt will think so, too."

"I'm not wearing this so Wyatt will notice." She reached for the strings of the bonnet, intending to remove the hat, but her sisters pushed her to the door before she could accomplish it.

"This isn't about Wyatt," she murmured as they left the room.

"Uh-huh." The girls might make agreeing sounds, but they obviously didn't mean it.

She wanted to argue but they reached the kitchen and she wouldn't say anything in front of Ma.

Ma waited, wearing her usual dark blue dress and matching bonnet. Cora tried to recall if she'd ever seen Ma wear anything else for church.

"Pa is ready," Ma said, pulling on black gloves. "It's time to go."

Pa waited at the side of the wagon to help Ma up.

Wyatt stood at the back, Lonnie behind him.

Cora stared at him. He cleaned up nice. He wore black trousers, a black-and-white striped shirt with a black string tie at the collar and a brown leather vest.

"Oh, my!" Lilly whispered.

"Good thing you fancied up a bit," Rose murmured near Cora's ear.

Cora ignored them both and waited as Wyatt assisted her sisters into the back of the wagon, where Pa had spread an old quilt for them to sit on. Then Wyatt reached for her hand. Even with gloves on, she felt the warmth of his touch. He'd slicked his hair back with something lemon scented that had the power to turn her brain to mush.

She climbed into the wagon box and sat beside Rose, spreading her skirts to keep them smooth.

Wyatt waited for Lonnie to climb up, then jumped in and pulled the tailgate closed to keep out dust. He settled between Lonnie and Lilly, facing Cora, his black-clad legs stretched out. He'd polished his boots until they gleamed.

How was she to ignore him as they rattled toward

town? Three miles of torture. She shifted her attention to the scenery and kept her attention on the view.

Rose patted her arm. "Cora, tell us about the time you rescued Evan from the mad cow."

Cora sent her sister a look rank with protest. It wasn't the kind of story she cared to share with Wyatt.

"Oh, yes, do," Lilly echoed.

Wyatt looked interested. "Who is Evan?"

Cora signaled her sisters to be quiet but they ignored her.

"Evan Price was her beau." The twins rattled off the information like well-oiled gears working together. "He left to go looking for gold."

"He wasn't the man for our sister."

Cora closed her eyes and hoped the twins wouldn't say any more about her and Evan. She felt foolish enough that she'd trusted the man. She surely didn't intend to repeat her mistake. Her resolve allowed her to face Wyatt and his teasing grin.

Rose continued with the story. "I think it began when Evan thought he would hurry Cora along so they could go to the church social." She turned to Cora. "Isn't that right?"

Cora barely nodded. They knew the story as well as she.

"One of the cows had just freshened—"

"Bossy," Cora said. She turned to Wyatt. "Bossy can be very cranky."

"How cranky?" His eyes sparkled.

He was enjoying this far too much. "Let's just say she doesn't care for strangers around her newborns."

Rose said, "We tried to warn Evan, but he said he knew how to handle animals."

"Of course, we didn't see what happened to start with," Lilly added. "But when we heard Cora yell, we rushed out. There was Evan, perched on top of the fence, waving his feet wildly." She turned to Cora. "What did he do?"

Cora rolled her eyes. "I've told you before."

"I know but we weren't there."

A chuckle rolled up Cora's throat. It pleasured her a little to picture Evan up on the fence, begging her to rescue him. "He walked up to where I was milking Maude. Bossy's calf was nursing. He didn't even look at her. I doubt he saw her. He saw me and got all huffy because I wasn't ready to go. I didn't listen to his fussing because I saw Bossy jerk her head up at the sound of a stranger. The calf had skittered away. I knew he was in danger and tried to warn him. 'Evan,' I said. 'You best be getting behind that fence.' Of course, he thought I meant he should wait out of my way and started to argue. Bossy caught him in the rear end with a head butt. Did he ever get over the fence in a hurry then! I had to push Bossy away from him and persuade her he wouldn't hurt her baby."

Rose and Lilly laughed. "It was quite a thing to see."

Cora snorted. "In hindsight, if I'd known he meant to go looking for gold I might have left him there to fight his own battle."

Wyatt grinned, though she detected a glint of something else in his eyes. Perhaps he felt he had been warned. She regarded him steadily to let him know she didn't take kindly to people hurting her. Or worse, one of her family.

They arrived at the church and Pa stopped the wagon. She allowed Wyatt to help her down because it would be foolish not to. As Ma said, pride goeth before a fall and she didn't care to provide proof.

As they walked toward the church, they saw Mary Ann and a cluster of young women huddled together, watching and chattering.

Cora sighed. Mary Ann had no doubt told all her friends about the cowboy staying at the Bells'. Mothers of eligible young ladies also studied the visitor.

Lilly chuckled. "Seems we're attracting a lot of attention today."

Rose snorted. "I don't think it's us." She gave Wyatt a pointed look.

"Me?" he said. He'd left his hat in the wagon and ran his hand over his hair. "Is my hair sticking up? Do I look funny?" He glanced down at his outfit. "Don't my clothes fit properly? The man that sold them to me said they did, but perhaps he only meant to make a sale."

The three girls stared at him.

"Are you serious?" Cora asked. Surely he understood they looked because his hair looked fine, his clothes fit fine and he looked good enough to eat.

"What?" How did he manage to look so confused?

Cora couldn't believe he was serious. "Wyatt, you're joshing, aren't you? They are looking because they like what they see."

He stared at her, then a slow grin curled his lips and lit his eyes. "They're admiring how fine I look?"

"Yes." She'd as much told him she thought he looked rather nice. Heat stung her cheeks and she knew she surely glowed like a ripe apple.

"The mothers are plotting how to get you to marry their daughters, and the young ladies are wondering if you'll accept an invitation to dinner."

Amusement fled and his jaw muscles tightened. "The answer is no."

She wasn't pleased at his instant refusal. It wasn't as if she'd grown fond of him.

Seeing as it was Sunday and they were about to enter the church, she had to be honest with herself. Maybe she'd grown just a little fond of him.

They trailed into church and sat in their regular pew. Somehow Cora ended up between Rose and Wyatt. How had her sisters managed that?

Mary Ann followed them down the aisle and paused to speak. "So nice to see you again, Mr. Williams."

"Nice to see you, too." He introduced Lonnie.

Mary Ann barely gave poor Lonnie a look as she practically swooned at Wyatt's feet. The half-dozen girls with her sighed. When had her friends ever been so blatantly foolish?

Mary Ann fluttered her eyelashes. "Will you be visiting long, Wyatt?"

"Not long."

"Maybe we can plan a social while you're here."

Cora barely constrained a groan.

"I wouldn't think I'll be here that long."

Thankfully the bevy of girls moved on and settled into pews. Several of them turned and smiled in Wyatt's direction.

But he had opened the hymnal and was turning the pages.

Cora breathed slowly. In and out. In and out. Church was not the place to let petty emotions rage through her. She glanced around the congregation, seeing familiar faces in familiar places. She frowned at Mr. and Mrs. Caldwell sitting front and center. At least they had the dignity not to look back at the Bells. And later, out of habit, the Caldwells and the Bells would exit without crossing paths. It had been that way for eight years, and she didn't expect it would change in her lifetime.

Anna's father took his place behind the pulpit and the service began. Pastor Rawley announced the first hymn. Rose shared her hymnal with Lilly, which left Cora to share with Wyatt.

He held the book toward her. As she grasped the corner, their fingers brushed, and awareness of his warmth and solidness and handsomeness sent a jolt up her arm, branding the inside of her heart.

He smiled at her then. She swallowed hard, hoping he hadn't noticed her reaction.

Then the wheezy organ pumped out the hymn and they turned forward to join the singing.

At first he didn't sing, and she recalled his earlier confession that he growled rather than sang. She jabbed him in the ribs.

When he glanced at her, she nodded toward the hymn book, silently suggesting he should sing.

He shook his head and rolled his eyes.

She managed to keep singing despite the bubble of laughter in her throat and ignored the little glances Mary Ann tossed their way.

Wyatt let the familiar words of the hymns fill his heart. Sitting in church with Cora holding the hymnal between them and listening to her sing at his side felt right and good and refreshing.

Those silly girls giggling and glancing at him had annoyed Cora. Just as they annoyed him.

The sermon was based on the passage, "No man, having put his hand to the plow, and looking back, is fit for the kingdom of God." Before the last amen, Wyatt's resolve had returned. He had vowed to move far enough away that his past couldn't follow him. He'd promised himself he would not let anyone he cared about be hurt by being associated with a jailbird. He dared not forget it.

The service over, he joined the general exodus, glad he could escape before Mary Ann reached him.

The Bells paused to speak to their neighbors but carefully kept to one side of the yard.

Cora leaned toward him to explain. "See that man and woman over there? The ones dressed in such fine clothes?"

He nodded.

"That's Mr. and Mrs. Caldwell."

His eyes widened. "You attend the same church?" Wyatt looked at Mrs. Caldwell more closely. A regal woman with steel-gray hair, she wore a fancy bonnet, perhaps one of Mary Ann's designs, and a velvet cape that was surely too warm for the present weather. Her expression could only be described as pinched, though Wyatt had no way of guessing if she always looked that way or only when she must be in the presence of the Bells.

Mr. Caldwell wasn't a big man but nevertheless carried an air of authority and power.

"It's the only church here. It's either go to the same one or don't go to any, so we've all decided to ignore each other on Sunday for the sake of worship."

He studied the idea. Somehow it didn't seem right. "Doesn't the scripture say if you have something against your brother you are to make it right before you come to church?"

"It doesn't say exactly that, but how are we to make peace when they want our land badly enough to try to drive us off?"

They had walked ahead of the others and stood by the wagon.

Mary Ann and her entourage headed in their direction.

Wyatt groaned. "Any hope we can leave before your friend starts asking me more questions?"

Cora waved to her sisters and they trotted over. "We'll all get into the wagon. That way Mary Ann will realize we don't plan to stay and visit."

Wyatt gratefully helped the girls into the back, waited for Lonnie to jump aboard, then climbed in, pulling the tailgate closed. He wondered what Lonnie thought of attending church, but the discussion would have to wait until they were alone.

Mary Ann slowed, waved prettily and pouted a little.

Wyatt silently begged Mr. Bell to hurry along. But the man made his way slowly toward them, his wife at his side, as they spoke to several neighbors.

Finally they climbed onto the wagon seat and headed out of town. Wyatt let out a huge sigh.

As they passed the livery barn, a swarthy man ducked into the shadows.

Every nerve in Wyatt's body jerked. He pulled his hat low and squinted at the man. Was it Jimmy Stone? He shook off the thought. No, this man was heavier. Though if Jimmy wanted to find him, he could. It wouldn't take a skilled tracker to follow the trail a herd of horses left behind. And Jimmy had vowed revenge.

Wyatt sank back against the side of the wagon. He

was only letting his fear of discovery—it never quite left his mind—make him unnecessarily nervous.

Later that evening, when he and Lonnie were alone, he turned to the boy. "What did you think of church?"

Lonnie shrugged. "It was okay." He grinned. "The girls sure did like you."

Wyatt groaned. "I hope they stay away. Young ladies are always full of demanding questions."

Lonnie sat back on his heels. "I never thought of that. What if they find out?"

"We'll just have to be careful of what we say." He tried not to think of the man he'd seen as they left town. It couldn't be Jimmy Stone. Could it?

Chapter Twelve

The next morning, Cora, Wyatt and Lonnie resumed work on the barn. Having had a serious talk with herself the night before, Cora concentrated on pounding in spikes and refused to let her mind wander to thinking of Wyatt as handsome, kind, gentle, helpful—

Whoa. She wasn't going to think like that anymore. No. If she couldn't keep her mind occupied with measuring where to place the spike and hitting it with each blow then she'd think of less positive things.

Such as how Wyatt had pulled his hat down when they'd passed the livery barn yesterday. As if he didn't want anyone to see him. How could he be concerned about that when he'd gone to town Saturday and church on Sunday? Most everyone in the community would have seen him by then.

Suspicion scratched at her thoughts.

Everyone except for those just passing through. Maybe the man she'd glimpsed near the livery barn knew Wyatt. If so, why didn't Wyatt greet him?

Many questions but no answers.

And as she'd told Ma and Pa, she'd guard herself and the family from a man with unanswered questions.

By midafternoon the floor was completed, and the three of them admired their work.

"Next, we'll tackle the roof," Wyatt said.

She felt his gaze on her and turned to meet his look. "What?"

"Are you sure I can't persuade you to let Lonnie and me do it on our own?"

"Huh?" Lonnie had been watching Lilly feed the pigs.

"We could manage on our own, don't you think?" he asked Lonnie.

"I guess." Lonnie's attention had already drifted away as he watched Lilly.

Cora refrained from pointing out how often Lonnie's attention had wandered. Usually to observe the pigs.

Lilly noted Lonnie's interest and called up to him, "I found the other batch of kittens. Do you want to see them?"

Lonnie scampered down the ladder before Wyatt could say a word.

Cora laughed at the confounded expression on Wyatt's face. "He likes the animals every bit as much as Lilly does. She gets a lot of satisfaction out of tending them. Not just the pigs and the sheep, but also the cats and their yearly batches of kittens. She hates to give the little ones away, but kittens from the Bells are known to be good mousers and are in high demand."

"I promised him we'd have pigs when we find a place to settle down."

"Have you decided where that might be?"

He shook his head, his eyes revealing nothing but secrets.

If she needed any reminder of the distance that separated them, he provided it at every question.

She shifted her attention to Lonnie and Lilly as they went to the cow shed to find the kittens. It reminded her of their first kittens on the farm. "We moved out here when I was twelve. Even though I liked the thought of living on our own farm, I didn't like change and I was sad. One day, Ma brought home a kitten for each of us. I remember how mine comforted me." That gave her an idea. Something that might help Lonnie get over his bouts of worry and fear. "Lonnie loves the pigs."

"He sure does."

"I would like to offer him two little ones in return for his work." Perhaps the pigs and the pleasure of working to earn them would comfort him as much as the kitten had comforted her.

Wyatt shook his head. "Our work here is to pay for the feed for the horses and our meals."

"I could ask him to do some other chores."

"Such as?"

"Feed the pigs."

Wyatt laughed. "He already does that. No, in order to be fair, it would have to be a job that needed doing."

She pressed her finger to her chin and considered the matter. "There's always something to be done." She refrained from pointing out that Lonnie often got distracted while helping with the barn, so he wasn't really doing his share anyway. "Like picking potato bugs off the plants. Or cutting the grass around the trees in the orchard."

He nodded. "So long as he does enough work to warrant earning the pigs."

"I'll see that he does. Do you want to tell him?"

"It's your deal. You tell him."

"Let's tell him together."

He helped her down the ladder and they crossed to the shed where Lilly and Lonnie sat cross-legged, each holding two kittens while the mama cat hovered nearby.

Lonnie looked up and guilt blanched his face. "I'm only going to spend a minute or two with them."

Cora again wondered at the tightness in him when he spoke to Wyatt.

Wyatt spoke gently. "I'm not here to scold you. Cora has a business proposition for you."

Lonnie turned an eager look toward Cora.

She stole a glance at Wyatt, and if she didn't miss her guess, he was hurt that Lonnie seemed to trust her more than him. If only she understood the reason. Could it be that Lonnie thought Wyatt would act like their father if angered? But she'd seen no evidence of raging anger, even when he corrected or instructed Lonnie. But there had to be some reason for Lonnie's odd behavior around Wyatt.

For now, she had a deal to strike with Lonnie. "Every year we sell most of the pigs."

Lilly sighed. "I hate that we do, but we can't afford to feed them all winter long. Besides, there are new ones in the spring."

Cora continued when Lilly gave her a chance. "I see you like pigs, and Wyatt says you want to raise them when you get your own ranch." No reason why it should hurt to think of them moving away, but she couldn't deny a stabbing pain in her heart.

"Has he changed his mind?" Lonnie's voice carried a bitter edge.

"No. Not at all. In fact, he and I have discussed letting you do extra chores around the place in exchange for two of these little pigs."

Lonnie transferred the kittens to Lilly's lap and bounced to his feet in one swift movement. "Really? You mean it?" He looked from Wyatt to Cora and they both nodded.

"If you think it's a good idea." Cora wanted to hear him continue to express his pleasure as openly as he did at the moment.

"Wowee! Do I ever! Thank you." He grabbed Cora's hand in a hard grip and pumped her arm up and down.

"You're welcome. Be sure to thank Wyatt, as well."

Lonnie faltered for barely a second, but his joy would not be thwarted. He slapped Wyatt on the back. "Thank you, big brother. Come on, Lilly. Help me choose which ones I want." The pair trotted over to the pigpen.

Cora grinned after them. "That went rather well, I think."

Wyatt's face wore a look of wonder and amazement as he stared after his brother. He nodded without speaking.

Sensing how Lonnie's customary fear around him hurt Wyatt's heart, Cora pressed her hand to his upper arm. "He's cautious of trusting people. Who can blame him when he's been hurt over and over by the very person who should have protected him? Give him time. He'll learn to trust—" She thought to say trust *you,* but perhaps that was too direct. "He'll learn to trust others in time."

Wyatt nodded again.

They didn't return to work on the barn before supper, but Lonnie trotted over to ask what chores he could do and Cora put him to work picking potato bugs off the plants. To his credit, he didn't complain about the disagreeable task.

Rose and Lilly sidled up to Cora. "Sure glad he likes the job," one of them said. "'Cause we don't," the other added, and they both shuddered.

The next two days Lonnie scampered up the ladder, eager to get done the work on the barn so he could do chores to earn his pigs.

Cora wondered if Wyatt had spoken to him about paying more attention to the building of the barn or if the boy was motivated of his own accord.

During the hot afternoon sun, and because she had other things to attend to, she insisted they take a break.

Lonnie scurried to do whatever jobs she assigned him.

She had to smile at his eagerness.

Pa, aware of her bargain with Lonnie and supportive of it, came to her side as she watched him scouring the potato plants for more bugs. Besides that, he had swung a sickle and mowed a patch of grass in the orchard. Once it was dry he'd stack it in the cow shed.

"He's a hard worker when motivated," Pa said.

"Certainly is." Her gaze went toward the path that led to Wyatt and Lonnie's campsite. Wyatt had gone there an hour ago to check on Fanny.

"I wonder if Fanny is okay," Cora said.

"Seems she should have delivered by now. Perhaps you should run down there and see if she needs help. Come and get me if she does."

"Okay, Pa." She trotted to the camp.

She hadn't been there since the first day and was surprised how neat and tidy the place was. She'd seen cowboy camps on occasion, and they were usually anything but clean.

The horses cropped the grass contentedly. Wyatt had moved the rope corral to give them ample grazing. A couple of the horses whinnied at her approach, then ignored her.

She didn't see Wyatt anywhere and edged along the herd. There he was. He signaled her over, holding a finger to his lips to indicate she should approach quietly.

Tiptoeing and moving slowly so as to not disturb the mare lying nearby, she moved to his side.

"Look," he said.

"Oh." A newborn foal lay on the ground.

"It was just born," he whispered.

The mare struggled to her feet and turned to lick her baby, cleaning it and encouraging it to stand.

The newborn put one front foot and then the other in place, lurched to its feet and fell as it failed to get its hind legs in place.

Cora held her breath, willing the little one to get up.

It struggled twice more, then took a break.

The mare waited beside it. Then the mare licked the baby again until it staggered to its feet and lurched forward on incredibly long, wobbly legs, nuzzling as it looked for milk.

Cora dashed away tears with her free hand. When had she taken Wyatt's hand? Or had he taken hers? All she knew was they held on tightly and neither made any move to break free.

"That was beautiful," she murmured.

"My first foal." His words resounded with awe.

"May it be the first of many, and may they be as perfect as this one."

He looked deep into her eyes, letting her see clear

through his thoughts, except all he allowed her to see were his hopes and dreams of a successful ranch.

Far away from here, if he followed his plan.

She slipped her hand away. "What will you call her?"

He studied the little one, apparently unaware they no longer held hands.

For a heartbeat she regretted breaking the contact. But only for the length of time it took for her thoughts to register in her brain. He made it clear he meant to leave. He refused to share his secrets and she knew there were plenty. Truth be told, she knew little about this man.

Except his generosity, his gentleness with his brother and with animals and his honor in wanting to help to pay for feed that others might have accepted without offering anything in return.

"I think I'll call her Bell Flower. Because she was born on the Bell farm and you three girls are like flowers in a summer bouquet."

She added one more asset to the list. He was poetic.

He tipped his head to look into her face. "Do you like it?"

Feeling responsible for the uncertainty in his voice, she met his eyes. "I like it very much."

His gaze went on and on, laying claim to her thoughts, forbidding them to recall her reasons for caution. It went past her fears and her doubts to a tender spot inside that she kept covered, hidden from view. A spot that yearned to be touched in an affectionate way. To be protected through every danger. To be loved until life was no more.

She knew she had good reasons for keeping that place tucked away, but at the moment there seemed no reason at all and she could only smile with an open heart.

He touched her cheek. His gaze dipped to her mouth and then lifted to her eyes.

"Wyatt, Cora, are you here?" Lonnie, Lilly and Rose called them.

"They will all want to see the newborn."

"Yes, they will."

But neither of them moved.

The others called again. The mare whinnied, protective of her baby.

Cora sighed. "We'd better go warn them to be quiet before they start a stampede."

"Yes, we should."

Still they continued to look at each other, then he nodded and took one step away.

She blinked. What had just happened? How had she been mesmerized like that?

"Are you coming?" Wyatt waited for her, and she hurried to join him.

They reached the others, warned them to be quiet and led them back to watch Fanny and Bell Flower.

"Oh, the baby is so sweet," Lilly whispered.

Everyone agreed, but after a few minutes, Wyatt indicated they should leave the pair alone. They made their way back to the campsite and sat on logs pulled into a circle.

Rose and Lilly talked at once, joined often by Lonnie, oohing and aahing about the baby.

"I think my pigs are just as cute," Lonnie finally said, reducing the whole lot of them to laughter.

Cora jerked to her feet. "Come on, girls. Pa will wonder where we've disappeared to."

The twins rose more slowly. "He'll understand. After all, we've not seen a newborn foal before."

"You've seen calves and pigs, kittens and puppies born," Cora pointed out.

"It's not the same," Rose insisted.

"No, it's not," she agreed. "Besides, can one ever get tired of seeing the beginning of new life?" She smiled around the circle but her gaze rested on Wyatt. "A reminder that we can start fresh. Every day is a new beginning." She hadn't meant to suggest he should start over, build a new life, leave behind whatever secrets dogged him. The words had come out without such forethought.

But perhaps he would consider it.

And if he did? Would she be willing to open her heart to him? Trust him?

She wasn't sure. Wasn't it easier and safer to guard her thoughts and heart and mind?

It wasn't until after he and Lonnie lay in their bedrolls that night that Wyatt got a chance to think through the events of the day.

The birth of Fanny's foal had changed his relationship with Cora. Or at least it would if he let it. They had shared a special moment. He'd allowed himself to open his heart to her in a way he'd never done before. And then she'd offered him the hope of starting over.

But she didn't know what she offered or to whom. He was a man convicted of a crime and could not accept the hope of a new beginning.

"Are you awake?" Lonnie asked.

"Yes. Are you?"

Lonnie laughed. "No, I'm talking in my sleep."

Wyatt grinned. He loved it when Lonnie relaxed enough to joke and laugh with him. "What's on your mind?"

"So many things don't make sense. Like how nice the Bells are. But what would they think if they found out the truth?"

Wyatt had no answer. "I hope they never do. You know what people are like when they learn about me. I wouldn't want the Bells to have to deal with that." All the name-calling, the refusal to do business with anyone who associated with a jailbird and the accusations every time someone lost something.

Lonnie grunted. "Me, either." He perched up on one elbow. "It's nice for a while, though, isn't it?"

"It surely is." But Wyatt knew deep inside that he couldn't keep his past hidden forever. There was always the threat of someone journeying through who would recognize his name or face and recall the story of his going to jail. All he could hope for was to stay until Fanny and Bell Flower were ready to travel.

Please, God, keep the truth concealed until we can leave and then after so the Bells are never touched by my past.

He would leave as soon as possible, but he meant to enjoy every minute of the few weeks it would take for Bell Flower to get strong enough to travel.

Surely there was no harm in that.

He closed his mind to the warning bells jangling in his head.

Chapter Thirteen

The rafters were in place by early afternoon the next day. It was time to start building the roof. Wyatt eyed the height and slope and swallowed hard. How was he to persuade Cora to stay on the ground and let him and Lonnie do the work? He'd mentioned it three times yesterday and she'd scoffed. But he simply couldn't think of her in such a dangerous place.

"No one is going up there until I make some footholds." He climbed the ladder and nailed boards into place.

From his vantage point he saw a wagon crossing the river. Five minutes later, he called, "You got company coming."

Visitors weren't unusual. Three times in the past week someone had come for one of Mrs. Bell's medicines, or eggs or milk or any of the various things the Bells sold.

Until now, the arrival of callers had set his nerves to twitching. Each time he feared it was someone to inform the Bells they harbored a jailbird who was not welcome in the community. But today he breathed a prayer of thanks. This wagonload of people might be enough to keep Cora on the ground for the rest of the afternoon.

He recognized Anna, Nancy and three other young ladies from church whose names he didn't recall. Apparently this was to be a social call. All the better.

The wagon drew to a halt before the house. "Hello, Cora," called Anna.

Cora sighed loudly enough that Wyatt heard her from his perch atop the roof. "Hello, girls."

Wyatt wondered if the visitors heard the resignation in Cora's voice. If so, it didn't deter them. They hopped down, patted their skirts and adjusted their bonnets. One young lady removed her hat to reveal a mass of golden curls. She looked around, spied Wyatt on the roof and waved.

Five pretty faces turned in his direction and smiled.

He ducked away and hammered nails, successfully drowning out anything they said.

"Rose, Lilly, we have guests," Cora called, and the girls left the garden where they'd been picking beans.

Wyatt saw a lot more eagerness in their faces for the interruption than Cora had expressed.

Lonnie had watched the proceedings from the ground but now climbed the ladder. "Suppose they're going to have a tea party or something?"

"Do you want to join them?" Had Lonnie noticed that one of the girls was a younger sister?

"Nah."

Rather a halfhearted response, but Wyatt let it go. He meant to make the most of this time with Cora otherwise occupied and he placed boards and nailed them in place as quickly as he could with Lonnie struggling to keep up.

The young ladies and the Bell sisters spread quilts in

the shade of the trees next to the house. He could have wished for them to go around the corner out of sight so they couldn't all watch him, but such was not to be the case.

Cora brought out a tray of glasses filled with lemonade and Rose passed around cookies.

Eight heads tipped together and laughter reached Wyatt. He told himself it was normal girlish behavior, but he couldn't help wondering if they found him amusing.

Cora rose and crossed toward the barn.

Wyatt watched her every step. His lungs tightened as she approached the barn. Had they sent her on an errand? He guessed they had, and guessed, as well, that it involved him in a way he might not like.

Cora reached the bottom of the ladder. "Wyatt?"

He slowly turned to look down at her. "Do you need something?"

"Yes. You."

The girls giggled.

Pink raced up her neck and pooled in Cora's cheeks. "My visitors accuse me of having bad manners by not inviting you to join us. So would you both please join us?"

He should refuse. There was the roof to finish. Besides, he had no desire to share the afternoon with a bevy of giggling females, but Cora appeared to need help in dealing with her friends. "Thank you. We accept your invitation."

She nodded and stepped back as Lonnie descended the ladder.

Wyatt climbed down more slowly. At the bottom he whispered to her, "I'm hardly clean enough to join your friends." Perspiration soaked his back. He swiped his arm across his face to dry it.

"They'll no doubt be impressed by your muscles and sweat." She rolled her eyes.

He grinned at her. "Is that what young ladies like?"

"If so, you're all set for success."

Their gazes locked. Did he read admiration? Reluctant, if so. But he also detected uncertainty. Why? Then it hit him. She thought he might enjoy the admiration of those young ladies.

"Success if I want admiration, but not if I much prefer conversation and sharing of similar tastes." He wished he could express himself better, explain to her that her honesty and hard work were a lot more appealing to him than giggling admiration.

She smiled, the tension gone from her eyes. "Let's see if you can't enjoy a bit of each."

He accompanied her to the tea party where Lonnie hovered, waiting to be invited to sit down.

"Ladies," Cora said. "You remember Wyatt and Lonnie from church." Ignoring their wide-eyed admiration, she introduced her friends. Besides the two he recognized there was a Miss Sally Jones, as well as a Miss Inez Burroughs and her younger sister, Ellen, who smiled sweetly at Lonnie.

Cora indicated they should sit.

Wyatt sat next to her and took the offered glass of lemonade and two cookies.

"Where are you from, Mr. Wyatt?" one lady asked.

"Kansas," he said. They might want more information but he didn't mean to provide it.

"Are you planning to settle here?" Nancy asked.

"Going north." The same answer he'd given Mr. Bell. The questions continued to fly. Where north? Why?

Did he have a wife and children waiting for him? Had he been in the army?

"Army? No. Why would you think that?"

Sally, who had asked the question, shrugged. "I thought the way you carry yourself, your short answers—" She shook her head. "It made me think of my uncle who was a soldier."

Lonnie's hand halted half to his mouth with a cookie. His shoulders tensed.

Wyatt didn't want anyone to look at the boy and wonder at his reaction, but he struggled to control his own movements. Did something about the way he talked and moved provide clues that he'd been in jail? He'd hardly think it would be similar to being in the army.

Cora, who'd watched in silence as he fielded the many questions, spoke to the young women. "Is there anything new in town?"

The preacher's daughter, Anna, bounced with eagerness. "Indeed, there is much news. Someone stole a bunch of stuff from Mr. Frank's store."

Miss Nancy interrupted. "The cash box was stolen from the feed store."

"Two houses were broken into, and silver and jewelry taken," Miss Sally added.

Cora looked shocked. "Really? There have never been robberies in Bar Crossing before that I know of."

"That's what everyone is saying."

"No one in town would do something so awful," Anna said. "My father says it must be a stranger doing it."

Wyatt kept his eyes lowered. Bad enough to be among those under suspicion because he was a stranger, but he'd be found guilty without evidence or a trial if anyone discovered his past.

Fortunately, no one pointed out the fact that he and Lonnie were strangers, and the conversation moved to other things. Wyatt wanted to excuse himself and return to the barn, but when he pushed to his feet, the girls protested.

"You aren't leaving us?"

"Please stay." Cora's tone revealed nothing. Did she want him to stay for her sake?

He'd stay only because she asked him.

The ladies remained for three hours, as if there was nothing more important in anyone's life than sitting in the shade.

Finally, Nancy, who seemed to be in charge, pushed to her feet. "It's time for us to leave. It's been so nice visiting with everyone."

Wyatt rose as soon as she moved and nodded to her and to the others as they left.

Only after they rumbled from the yard, calling more goodbyes, did he let his gaze go to the barn. It waited patiently for boards to be nailed into place.

Cora let out a long sigh. "Ma needs our help." The girls gathered up quilts, glasses and the remnants of the afternoon and traipsed indoors.

"Supper will be ready shortly." Cora paused to inform him, then disappeared inside.

Lonnie had already gone to see the pigs.

Wyatt jammed his hands in his pockets. What was he to do with himself? It hardly seemed worthwhile to climb the ladder. He wouldn't have time to fit a board into place.

He barely finished the thought before Cora called out, "Supper."

Wyatt aimed to get his brother, but he saw the boy was already headed for the house.

They joined the others.

The meal was rushed, as everyone seemed eager to do the work that had been neglected over the afternoon, but they still took time for Bible reading. Wyatt enjoyed this pool of calm at the end of the day.

Mr. Bell had barely said "amen" before Cora bolted to her feet.

"The cows are getting impatient to be milked."

He realized they had been calling softly and followed her outside. "Do you need help with the milking?"

Her eyes widened. "You can milk a cow? I didn't think cowboys considered the chore manly enough for their status in life."

"I heard that somewhere, too, but I milked cows once upon a time." Years ago, when his pa still had a prosperous farm, before he started selling off stock and moving around. "Don't suppose I've forgotten how."

They brought the two cows in from the pasture and left the dry one. Each one went to a stall in the shed.

"Well, let's see if you remember." Cora handed him a bucket and pointed him to the smaller cow. "You milk Maude, she's the gentler of the two."

He grabbed a stool, and he and Cora sat at the haunches of the cows. The *squish, squish* of milk going into the pail filled the silence. A motley-colored cat with a right-angle crook in its tail appeared, and Cora sent a stream of milk that it caught neatly.

"Where's Grub?" Seemed to Wyatt he should have been at the milking.

"He's mooching at the kitchen. Lilly will give him treats. Do you know she makes cookies for him?"

Wyatt snorted a laugh. "Cookies for a dog?"

"Not the kind you'd like. Believe me. I was once foolish enough to taste one. Ptooey. But Grub loves them."

She aimed another squirt of milk toward the cat. Wyatt made a smacking sound to get the cat's attention and sent a squirt its way. He laughed when it was right on target.

Cora stood, set the milk bucket to the side, let her cow out of the barn and returned to stand at his side. "Are you finished?"

He wasn't, but he wasted no time stripping the cow's udder of the last of the milk and turning her out with the other. He followed Cora to the house.

Lilly pulled what looked like cookies from the oven. He was thankful he'd been warned and wouldn't be sneaking any cookies from that tray.

Cora nudged him. "Milk goes in the workroom." He accompanied her there and poured the milk through the straining cloth.

"Could I offer you a cookie when we're done here?" Her innocent tone did not fool him.

He barked a laugh.

She grinned. "I guess you'll check every cookie carefully from now on before you bite into it."

"I'll make sure you take a bite first." He smiled at her.

The mischief in her eyes stirred his blood and made him wish for days and days of nothing but teasing and joy. His throat tightened. He couldn't stay, no matter how enticing the idea seemed. He must get far enough away that his past would never catch up with him, someplace where no one knew him or cared a fig about him.

Her hands stilled as the moment lengthened into something soft and alluring.

He sucked in warm air laden with the smell of fresh milk, cheese and a heartbeat of sweetness from the woman before him. His resolve threatened to crumble like dust.

"I need to take care of my horses." He bolted from the room, calling a hasty "Thank you and good night," and trotted to the campsite.

Lonnie thundered after him. "What's the hurry?"

Wyatt slowed his steps. "The day got away, what with company all afternoon."

"Didn't you enjoy it?"

"I wanted to get the roof built."

Lonnie shrugged. "We've got lots of time. Didn't you say it will be a month before Fanny and the foal can travel?"

"Yeah."

"So what's the harm in a little socializing?"

Wyatt stared at his brother. "Is this the same person who wanted to leave a few days ago?"

"That was two weeks ago. But now I got reason to stay."

"Like some young gal?"

Lonnie blushed. "I have to earn enough to buy two pigs. Remember?"

"Oh, right. That. You didn't get much done toward that today, what with all the socializing."

"I'll make up for it." Lonnie trotted on ahead.

Wyatt thought to warn the boy of the dangers they faced by staying. Not only to themselves but to the Bells and anyone else associated with them. They needed to put more distance between them and their past. But he couldn't ruin Lonnie's mood. It was the first time he'd seen him so content about staying and so ready to associate with others. Another reason to be grateful for the delay in their travels.

Before he caught up to Lonnie, alarm bells filled Wyatt's brain. Every delay increased the risk. But even worse was all this socializing. People would grow more demanding about his past. Lonnie might let something slip.

He'd simply have to excuse himself from any more of it.

It should be simple enough. From what he'd observed, it wasn't as though the Bells entertained a lot or visited others. He had no call to go to town on Saturday and could find some excuse to miss church.

How hard could it be?

The next morning, Cora put on her oldest dress and headed for the barn as soon as the chores were done. Wyatt and Lonnie had arrived a few minutes ago and were nailing boards to the rafters.

At her approach, Wyatt came down the ladder. "Cora, for my peace of mind, please stay off the roof."

The pleading look in his eyes caused her determination to waver. "But I have to help." Even to her own ears, she sounded less than convincing.

"It's far too dangerous with those long skirts."

She looked down at her dress. "I could borrow a pair of Pa's trousers."

Wyatt hooted. "Can I listen while you ask him?"

She grinned in acknowledgment. "Pa would have a fit, wouldn't he?"

"I expect so."

"That leaves me little choice, then." She took a step toward the ladder.

"Cora, please reconsider." He caught her arm, sending a jolt through her nerves and making it hard to remember why it mattered that she worked on the barn if he cared so much.

"Hey, Wyatt, I need another board," Lonnie called.

His words were all the reminder she needed. They were working to pay for feed for their horses and the meals the Bells provided. However, building the barn was not their responsibility. They'd be moving on. North somewhere. She'd be here with an unfinished barn if she didn't do her share.

"I'll see that the barn is built." She'd promised herself the day Pa fell from the ladder. She'd drive every nail by herself if she couldn't get help. "I thank God He sent you to help, but it's still my job."

"Why not trust Him to provide enough help that you don't need to take risks?"

She met his gaze. Was he asking her to trust God? Or him? She tried to read past the appeal in his dark eyes, but he had closed his thoughts to her probing. Disappointed, she turned away. How could she trust a man who shut himself off from her? As to trusting God… "I trust God to protect me." And give her strength.

Wyatt let out a long sigh as if she taxed his patience. He muttered something under his breath. Sounded as if he said, "How hard can it be to convince her?" Then his gaze slid by her and his eyes widened. "Looks as though you've got more company coming."

She turned to shade her eyes and watch three wagons approach. "What's going on?"

"I'll let you figure it out." He climbed up the ladder and started hammering furiously.

"Wyatt?" What was wrong? He should be happy that

more visitors had descended on them. Wouldn't it ensure she couldn't help?

The wagons drew closer. Ma and Pa and the twins lined up to watch.

"Why, Pastor Rawley," Pa said, stepping forward as the first wagon drew to a halt. "What brings you our way?"

Mrs. Rawley sat beside him in the wagon. Anna and two men rode in the back. The second wagon had four men in it, and the third two women and two men. Some of the people were from nearby farms; the rest were from town.

Cora could not think what they wanted.

Pastor Rawley jumped to the ground. "My Anna came home yesterday to say you were putting up a barn by yourselves. Now, we all know that isn't a job for a family to do alone. So we decided to do the neighborly thing. We've come to help."

The others stepped to the ground, each man carrying the tools they'd need.

Mrs. Rawley and the other women approached Ma. "Now, we know you weren't expecting a crew, so we brought along food for the noon meal."

"Bless you," Ma said. "Bless you all."

"I see you've done a great deal already," Pastor Rawley said.

The men moved to the barn and Wyatt slowly turned to greet them.

Cora couldn't figure him out. For a man who thought she should trust God to provide help to get the barn done, he certainly seemed reluctant when all this help appeared.

Anna caught Cora's hand and dragged her away. "Isn't this wonderful?"

"Indeed." Cora gave her friend a little squeeze. The barn would be finished in no time. Wonderful news.

So why did she feel as if she'd been robbed of something special?

She would not answer the question.

But as the sound of hammers on nails and saws through wood filled the air, she couldn't shake the feeling.

She helped move two tables under the trees and set out the food.

"Stop staring at him," Anna said.

Cora jerked her attention back to filling a dish with bread-and-butter pickles. "I'm watching the progress on the barn. I can't believe how fast it's going." The roof was almost finished.

"Uh-huh. But I have to say, he is worth taking a long look at."

"Who?" Though there was only one person to be considered.

"Why, your Wyatt Williams, of course."

"He's not my—"

Anna patted her arm. "If you say so."

Rose and Lilly joined them.

Cora hoped they were too late to overhear Anna's silly comments. But she forgot to hope Anna wouldn't repeat them.

"She's not staring at Wyatt," Anna said.

"Of course she is. Just like the rest of us."

"Rose." Cora couldn't believe her younger sister. "Have you no shame? If Ma heard your comments she'd confine you to your room."

Rose laughed. "Do you suppose she looked at Pa that way once upon a time?"

They all looked toward Pa. Ma sat with the other women, shelling peas as she watched the progress.

"I expect she did," Lilly said.

A little later, Ma called out for everyone to come eat. The men gathered around the table. Wyatt, Cora noted, came last.

Pastor Rawley said grace and then, one by one, the crowd filed past the table, filling their plates with a wide variety of food. The ladies must have planned this the previous evening, as they'd brought fried chicken and potato salad, along with several kinds of vegetables.

Lonnie made no secret of examining the array of desserts. "You sure there's going to be lots?"

One of the men said, "Not if I get there first."

Wyatt laughed along with the others.

Cora's heart beat more smoothly than it had all morning. Perhaps she'd only imagined that Wyatt objected to the visitors.

Everyone settled on the grass except Pa, who sat on a chair next to Ma.

Cora wanted nothing so much as to sit next to Wyatt, but it would be unseemly. When Anna whispered in her ear, "Let's sit over there," and pointed to a spot close to Wyatt, Cora shook her head. "I'm going to sit beside the twins."

Anna pouted a little but followed Cora.

After the food was put away, Cora looked longingly at the garden, but she could hardly turn her attention to hoeing while they had company. She suggested they go for a walk along the river, but Anna begged off.

"My shoes are too tight."

Cora silently groaned. "What do you want to do, then?"

"Sit here and watch. And don't tell me you don't want to do the same thing."

Cora quirked an eyebrow. "I guess there'd be no point if you have your mind set on believing otherwise."

"Exactly." She plopped down in a spot that allowed them a view of the men shingling one side of the barn. Of course, one of the men was Wyatt, Lonnie at his side.

Cora observed for several minutes and began to notice something. She sat up straighter so she could see better.

Anna nudged her and laughed.

Cora ignored her and kept her attention on Wyatt. The other men talked and laughed and called to each other. Wyatt did not.

Why had he withdrawn?

Chapter Fourteen

The barn stood with its roof finished. Apart from doors and the interior, it was done.

Wyatt admired the job along with the rest of the men. They filed past and shook his hand, and he thanked each one. They hadn't been helping him specifically, but he was grateful Cora wouldn't feel bound to climb up to the roof to help.

Their arrival had been a surprise—a mixed blessing, to be sure.

He'd meant to avoid meeting any more people and instead was surrounded by them. Friendly, inquisitive people who wanted to know everything about him. At first, he'd been able to answer without revealing anything of importance. The men liked to hear of his horses. When he said he was headed north, several offered suggestions for a good location.

But when the talk turned to the robberies occurring in town, he knew he'd better watch his every word.

The men loaded up their wagons and in short order they were driving their horses out of the yard. Wyatt had been aware of Cora's concerned looks all afternoon. As if she wondered at how he'd pulled away from the conversations around him. He'd seen the determination on her face and guessed she meant to question him. But he could not give her an answer. At least, not one he cared to share.

He decided the best thing would be to pass on supper and return to his camp, even though his stomach growled at the thought. Before he could escape, Cora appeared at his elbow.

"I expect you're relieved to see the barn done."

"Uh-huh. Aren't you?"

"Of course I am."

They were both talking to avoid saying what they really wanted to say. He wished with all his heart he could tell her the truth. Would she run away from him if he did? Or would she comfort him with words and touches?

At the thought, his mouth dried so much that he almost choked.

"Let's go for a walk," she said, and headed for the river.

He meant to say no. He knew a dozen reasons he should refuse. Instead, he walked at her side.

"It's nice that you have friends to help," he said. *Would you accept me as a friend if you knew the truth? Would they?*

"Both Stu Maples and Mr. Frank said no one would help because of the Caldwells. I guess they were wrong."

"It seems the Caldwells have less power than they think." These people were willing to stand up to the Caldwells. Would they be as ready to stick by the Bells if they were associated with a jailbird?

As they walked, Cora paused occasionally to caress wildflowers.

He glanced at the flowers, but they weren't as beautiful or beguiling as Cora. Had she thought him silly to say the Bell sisters were like a summer bouquet? A long-forgotten memory sprang to mind and it tumbled from his mouth before he could put the brakes on his words.

"These flowers remind me of a time when Lonnie was about three—which would make me eight. Our pa had just moved us to a new farm with his horses. Lonnie and I were out exploring and we found a whole meadow of flowers." He remembered the vivid colors. "Bluebells and purple spiky things and little red flat flowers and tiny white lacey ones." He smiled as he recalled the details of that day.

"Lonnie laughed and spun around like crazy in the flowers. Said they were as pretty as a rainbow. A butterfly flitted about and Lonnie tried to catch it. He called it a butter bee. You know, mixing up butterfly and bumble bee." He smiled clear to his socks as he thought of the joy of that moment.

"Of course, we picked an armload of flowers and took them home to Ma. She found a Mason jar and filled it and put it in the window. 'Now it's really our home,' she said."

His smile disappeared and his insides turned brittle. He did not want to remember what happened next.

Cora slipped to his side and rubbed her hand up and down his arm, easing some of the tension. "It sounds like a beautiful day."

He nodded. He kept his gaze focused on the horizon, knowing if he looked at her she would see his pain and he would pull her into his arms, seeking her comfort.

"Something happened to turn it into a bad memory, didn't it?" she asked quietly.

He sucked in air until his lungs could hold no more,

but it didn't release his heart to beat with normal regularity.

"Wyatt." Her voice was soft as the brush of butterfly wings. "What happened?"

A shudder shook him from head to toe.

Her arm pressed about his waist and steadied him.

"Pa was in a rage about something. I suppose he was angry he'd had to sell the old farm, though it was nothing to do with me. Or Lonnie." He swallowed hard. "He came in as Ma was arranging the flowers and grabbed me. Cuffed my ears for wasting Ma's time." His head had rung the rest of the day.

"I'm so sorry." She pressed her cheek to his arm.

"That wasn't the worst part."

She held on to him.

He knew he should hold himself tight, not let go of his emotions lest they drown him. But he raised his right arm, wrapped it around her shoulders and breathed deeply of wildflowers.

"He slapped Lonnie so hard—" His voice tightened. "So hard Lonnie fell to the floor screaming. Ma tried to stop him, but he pushed her aside and said if she ever interfered again he would boot her out on the road."

He'd forgotten that Pa had said that. Remembering it helped him understand why Ma never did anything to stop the beatings.

"Wyatt, I am so, so sorry for both of you. That isn't the way God meant for families to be."

"I know. I see how your family is. You're very fortunate to have them." He pressed his cheek to her head and let her comfort wash through him.

"Thank goodness you and Lonnie had each other. You take good care of your brother."

Wyatt released her. "Seems Lonnie thinks I'm like Pa. I'm not, you know. I'm not."

She caught his hand. "I think he knows it. He's just afraid to trust."

"I'm his brother. He should trust me." He couldn't disguise the pain in his voice. Didn't even try.

"I guess some hurts take a long time to heal."

"I guess so."

She tugged at his hand. "Wyatt?"

Slowly he brought his gaze to hers. In her eyes he found a store of comfort and understanding, and he allowed himself to soak it in.

"What about you?"

"Me? What *about* me?"

She smiled gently, chidingly. "What about your hurts?"

"My hurts?" At first he didn't understand, then he realized he'd let his barriers slip and she meant to step into forbidden territory. He pulled his hand away. "I'm fine. I'm older. Been away from home for a bit so I got over Pa's meanness." In prison he'd met people even more cruel than Pa and learned to stay out of their way, though he'd never stood by while they'd picked on someone smaller or weaker. Guess that grew out of his attempts to protect Lonnie from their pa. Jimmy Stone turned out to be more vindictive than Pa had even been.

She grabbed his shoulders and faced him squarely.

He settled his gaze on a lacy flower over her right shoulder.

"I don't know if you truly believe that or not. But I don't. Wyatt, I see before me a man with a whole lot of secrets and hurts. You need to let go of them and let people care about you."

His gaze met hers. Soft and inviting, full of comfort.

"Cora." The word grated from a tight throat. "You don't know what you're asking." No, that said too much. "You don't know what you're talking about." He stepped away, put enough distance between them so she couldn't reach for him. Heaven help him, if she wrapped her arms about him and asked the source of his hurt, he might well blurt out the whole ugly truth. *Would you still be so sure people should care about me?*

Would you care about me?

He couldn't live with the alternative—having her turn her back on him, knowing others judged her because of him.

"We need to get back." He waited for her to fall into step with him and made sure to keep a good, safe distance between them.

When they reached the house, Rose stepped outside.

"I was just about to come looking for you," she said. "Supper's ready."

"Thanks, but I need to check on Fanny. Make sure she's okay. Tell Lonnie there's no need to rush back." He strode away without a backward look, even when Cora called his name.

A can of cold beans and some jerky would have to suffice. At the least, it'd serve to remind him to guard his heart and his words more closely.

Saturday dawned with a festive feel in Cora's mind. The barn was almost finished. She sang as she milked the cows. Today they would go to town. She meant to steal a few minutes of Wyatt's time and take him around on her own. She planned to show him the house they used to live in, now occupied by another family. They'd go by the school and the little grove of trees in the back of it where she and Anna had spent many happy hours.

She hurried through her daily tasks so they could get away in good time. Yet part of her watched the trail that would bring Wyatt and Lonnie up from their camp. What was taking him so long? He usually arrived before she finished the chores, but today the milking was done, the milk put to cool, the wagon loaded with produce to take to town and still neither Wyatt nor Lonnie had appeared.

She was about to suggest that someone should check on them when a figure loped toward them. Lonnie. But where was Wyatt?

Lonnie reached the wagon. "Wyatt says he can't go to town. He says he's neglected the horses and wants to tend to their needs today."

"That's fine," Pa said. "Is there anything he wants me to pick up for him?"

"He didn't say." Lonnie shifted from one foot to the other.

"Did you want to come?" Pa asked.

"Can I?"

"Certainly. Unless Wyatt needs you."

"He said I could go if I wanted." Lonnie scrambled into the back of the wagon and sat beside Cora.

Cora smiled a welcome even though her heart felt as if it had been gouged with a handful of spikes. But perhaps this was another way to get through to Wyatt. She'd go through Lonnie.

But as soon as the thought came, she dismissed it. She would not use such devious methods. Instead, she joined in the general chatter with her sisters and Lonnie. All the while, more than half her brain and most of her heart lingered back at the farm.

If it wouldn't be inappropriate and forbidden by her parents, she would have asked to stay behind, as well. But all she could do was laugh and smile through the day. She did her best to do so, but a day in town had never felt so long.

Or so unwelcome.

They arrived back at the farm in time to prepare supper.

Ma said what Cora longed to hear. "Lonnie, bring your brother up for supper. I don't like to think of him eating on his own when we have such abundance."

Lonnie ran to do her bidding and Cora ducked her head over the salad she prepared lest anyone see the anticipation on her face.

But if she hoped for a chance to talk to Wyatt alone after supper, she was disappointed. The girls were full of news from town that they were eager to share with him. Neither of them appeared to notice the distance in the back of his eyes.

The evening flowed past until Ma and Pa announced bedtime, and still she hadn't had a moment alone with him.

She crawled into bed, pulled the covers to her chin and closed her eyes. *God, how can I help him deal with his inner hurts? Oh, I know I am powerless to help him in any way, but I do want to see him open up. Please help him, and if You can, please use me to help him.*

Tomorrow was Sunday. She prayed Pastor Rawley would have words to minister to the brokenhearted, meaning Wyatt. That Wyatt would have ears to hear the words and readiness to apply them to his life.

She sat straight up in bed. What if he refused to go?

The moonlight through the curtains revealed both girls looking at her.

"What's wrong?" Rose asked.

"What if Wyatt chooses not to attend church tomorrow?"

"Why would he do that?"

"Why didn't he go to town with us?" She didn't wait for an answer. "I get the feeling he's wanting to leave." Or at least distance himself from them—or her. She swallowed the thought as if it were bitter gall.

Lilly sat up. "Surely not. Fanny and Bell Flower aren't strong enough yet."

"You're right, of course." She lay down, not comforted in the least.

"I expect he'd come if you ask him nicely." Rose's innocent-sounding words didn't disguise the teasing.

"I agree," Lilly said. "Ask him."

She would.

And the next morning she did. And he agreed.

She smiled all the way to church.

Wyatt had meant to find an excuse for staying home Sunday. But when Cora came to the camp, looking like a pretty blue flower and asking him to accompany the family, he couldn't say no.

Nor did he regret it.

Pastor Rawley spoke about the prodigal son. "I know some of you have prodigal sons or daughters. Are you ready and willing to welcome them home? Perhaps some of you are prodigals. Return to those who love you. It is never too late or too early to start over again. To receive the love and acceptance offered you. Often the first step is the hardest. But I urge you, don't keep running. Isaiah

55:7 says, 'Let him return unto the Lord and he will have mercy upon him.'" The pastor then went on to admonish each one to be prepared to welcome and accept prodigals. "Make this church and community a place where repentant sinners and returning prodigals find a home."

Wyatt listened to every word, his heart hungry for such acceptance. Would he find it in this community if they knew the truth? He believed the pastor would live up to his words. But what about the others?

For the first time since his release from prison, he allowed hope to creep into his heart.

Hope rooted and grew throughout the day as the Bell family lazed about on a warm, sunny Sunday.

Cora suggested a walk and he readily agreed, wanting to talk to her about the sermon.

"I'm glad you came to church with us," she said as they wandered along the river.

"I am, too." They paused to watch a crow and a sparrow dueling in the air, amazed at the boldness of the smaller bird. Then they continued on until they reached a row of boulders and sat down.

"What did you think of the sermon today?" he asked.

"I agreed with every word. People should be accepted for who they are. Backgrounds shouldn't make any difference if the person is honorable and good."

His heart did a happy flip. "Even if the person carries a bad reputation?"

"If the person is ready to leave that behind, people should accept that and allow that person to start over." She turned to study him. "Are we talking about anyone in particular? You, perhaps?"

He took one step into dangerous territory. "The past can't be erased."

"It can't even be forgotten." She stared down at her hands twisting in her lap.

She had a loving family and belonged in a supportive community. He couldn't imagine she'd ever done anything she'd be ashamed or embarrassed about. "What's in your past you want to forget?"

Her posture pulled at his heart. Why should the subject distress her?

She looked at him with her brown eyes bleeding pain. "I want to forget that my papa left the three of us in the middle of the prairie and rode away, never to return."

As he stared at her, his heart drained of all feeling. With each beat it filled again—with shock, surprise and wrenching sorrow. He could not ignore her pain and sidled closer to wrap an arm about her shoulders and pull her against his side.

"Tell me what happened."

"I remember my mother. Before she died, she made me promise to take care of the twins. I remember a man. I guess he was my father. I am no longer sure of my memories, but in my mind I think I see a man lift us from a wagon to the dusty ground and then drive away. I do remember staring after the wagon until it disappeared. And standing on tiptoe watching for its return. We waited and waited. Lilly started crying and then Rose. They always cried at the same time. I assured them Papa would come back. After a few hours I quit saying it and told them I'd take care of them. I don't know how long we were there. I know we fell asleep holding each other. We woke with the sun on our faces and resumed our post watching for Papa. The Bells found us and took us home and adopted us."

Though her words were spoken with cold precision,

his heart threatened to burst from the pain he knew she tried to disguise.

"I was five. The twins were three." She shivered.

He pressed close, offering his strength.

She leaned into him, accepting it and reached for his hand.

"I refused to go with them at first. Said our papa would come back and find us gone and he wouldn't like it. But they persuaded us we could wait at their place. They lived in Bar Crossing at the time. For months, years in fact, I looked for Papa. One day I thought I saw him, and my heart almost leaped from my chest. I raced over to him and threw my arms about him, but when the man looked at me I knew it wasn't my father. I was eight years old by then, and that's when I knew he was never coming back. From then on, the Bells were my only family. I owe them my life and the twins' lives. They have been ideal parents."

The final words came out strong and bold, yet she held his hand with such force he knew fears and uncertainties lay beneath the surface.

He recalled how she'd said some hurts take a long time to heal. Maybe there were some hurts that never healed.

She let out a breath that seemed to come from her very depths. "There are people who think less of us because of our background."

"Why, that's plain stupid. It wasn't as if you were in any way responsible." Maybe the community wasn't as accepting as he hoped.

She nodded. "Pastor Rawley said exactly that in one sermon. Oh, he didn't mention us by name, but I'm pretty sure he had us in mind. 'Friends,' he said in his gentle way. 'Judge not that ye be not judged.' Then he told a story about a missionary who did such wonderful work and said many a society had rejected him because his father was in jail for beating a man."

Wyatt's insides tensed, though he gave no outward appearance. Had she guessed his secret? Reason prevailed. Of course she hadn't. But her words offered him hope.

Impossible hope, all things considered.

She chuckled. "I'll never forget his words. 'Do not judge a man by his past but by his future, not by his failures but by his dreams and possibilities.'"

Wyatt breathed in each word. "It's idealistic."

"Yes, it is, but it's far better to reach for the ideal than to wallow in the unchangeable. Our pasts cannot be changed. Our future is a blank slate. We choose what goes on it."

"So you're saying to forget the past and move forward?"

She shifted to face him squarely, their hands still entwined. "Maybe I can't forget the past. It hurts to think my real father would abandon us. But I'm determined to put it behind me and press on."

The intensity of her gaze burned through his resistance and threw open the locked doors of his heart. He longed to be able to live without the burden of his past weighing him down.

Was it possible?

He touched her cheek and smiled. "You make the future look bright and free."

She trailed her finger down his cheek. "It can be."

Could it? Could he face his past here, in this family, church and community? Could he find acceptance?

Or would such a choice invite more of what he'd experienced and worse, in that it would affect the Bell family?

He could not risk that.

Seemed he had no choice but to stick to his plans.

He got to his feet and pulled her up. She clung to his hand as they retraced their steps, and he didn't even try to slip from her grasp. He told himself it was only to comfort her after learning about how she and the twins were abandoned.

But how could he deny himself the same comfort?

He couldn't stay, but how would he make himself go? Dare he allow himself to hope his past would never catch up with him?

Chapter Fifteen

After breakfast the next morning, Ma said, "Mrs. Rawley informed me the chokecherries and serviceberries are plentiful in the hills."

"We're going berry picking?" The twins grinned.

Cora smiled at them. "It's work, you know."

"But fun work," Rose said.

They crowded for the door and pushed through in their hurry to prepare for the outing. And crashed right into Wyatt.

"Whoa." He steadied them. His hands felt warm and firm on Cora's shoulders, reminding her of the emotional upheaval she'd been through yesterday. She'd found such comfort and strength in his arms that she'd almost turned to his chest for more.

Even now, her heart ached to feel his arms around her. Instead, she struggled to keep her reaction hidden.

She'd never confessed to anyone how it hurt to be left by their papa, but yesterday, when he'd talked about leaving the past behind, the words had tumbled out as if she'd been waiting all her life to tell someone. When he'd offered his comfort and strength she knew this was the person she'd been waiting to tell.

His sympathy had helped her realize how little it mattered that her real father had proved untrustworthy. She had a wonderful life here with her sisters and Ma and Pa. The past had no claim on her.

Now all she could hope for was that he'd also choose to put his past behind him—whatever it was—and be willing to—

What?

She closed her eyes and admitted what she hoped for.

She wanted him to be willing to start over right here in the Bar Crossing area.

"What's all the excitement?" he asked, bringing her back to the present moment.

"We're going berry picking," the twins chorused. "And you and Lonnie are coming with us."

Cora could have hugged Rose for saying what she hesitated to say.

Lonnie grinned. "I ain't never been berry picking."

"You'll like it," Rose promised.

"I guess I will," Lonnie said.

Wyatt had looked ready to refuse the expedition, but at Lonnie's eagerness he relaxed. "It sounds like fun."

Pa brought the wagon to the house and the girls helped Ma bring out a box of food, jugs of water and every bucket and basket they could lay their hands on.

Lonnie looked doubtful. "You expect to pick a lot of berries."

"It's fun," Lilly assured him.

Grub wriggled about, begging to accompany them.

Lilly patted his head. "You stay here and guard the place."

Cora and Rose laughed.

"He's not a very good guard dog," Cora explained to Wyatt. "But we hope when people see him they think twice before causing trouble."

At that, she glanced about the farm and searched every inch of the horizon. No sign of any Caldwell cowboys. Maybe they were too busy to bother the place today while the Bells were away.

Dismissing the concern, she took the hand Wyatt offered and stepped into the wagon box. The others climbed aboard, pushing aside baskets to make room for a place to sit.

She sat with Wyatt pressed to her side. "It's a perfect day for picking berries," she said. "Sunshine, a little breeze and no sign of rain."

They trekked west toward the hills, following a faint trail left by others. They passed some berry bushes, but Pa said there'd be better picking further along. A few minutes later he pulled the wagon into a little clearing.

Before the wheels stopped turning everyone grabbed a bucket and scrambled from the wagon.

"Come along," Rose said to Lonnie. "I'll show you what to do."

Lilly followed them.

Wyatt grinned at Cora. "Guess you'll have to give me berry-picking lessons."

"I don't mind. Not in the least." She realized she just stood there smiling at him and told her feet to start walking. In a few minutes she found a place where the serviceberries were big and plentiful. "Pick the purple ones. I try to keep from putting leaves or other garbage in the pail. Makes it so much easier to sort and clean the berries for canning."

He started picking berries at her side. As they worked, she moved left and he moved right.

"I love canned serviceberries," she said.

"I haven't had any in a long time, but I remember having them with thick cream. I liked the nutty taste."

"It's an almond flavor."

He didn't reply. The only sound was the plink of berries in the bottom of her bucket, which ended as she added more and more berries.

"Did your ma can berries?" Would he tell her more about his past?

"She did some." A beat of silence. "But then she got pretty frail."

Cora moved to where she could see Wyatt's face and detected tension around his mouth. A horrible thought surfaced. "Did your pa beat her, too?"

Wyatt's hands grew still and he slowly brought his gaze to her.

At the dark despair she saw in his eyes, she grabbed a branch full of ripe berries to steady herself.

He swallowed hard. "He didn't beat her physically as far as I know. But she feared him and he used that to control her." He shrugged, but the gesture wasn't dismissive so much as it indicated how helpless he felt.

"I'm so sorry." How many times had she said that to him? "I'm sure you did everything you could to make it easier for her."

He jerked his attention to the berries on the branches before him and picked with a decided urgency. "I tried." The words rang with failure.

He'd left for a time. A year, had he said? He'd left both his mother and Lonnie to cope with an angry man.

Why had he done so? Where had he gone? "Where did you go when you left them alone?"

His hands grew still. The air pulsed with hope and possibility. Then he shuddered. "I wish I could tell you, but it involves other people who would be hurt if I told you the whole truth."

"I see." But she didn't. How could she trust him if he harbored secrets? She closed the distance between them and waited for him to meet her gaze. She hoped she conveyed both trust and a desire to help.

"Wyatt, don't you know you can trust me? You can tell me without fear of it going further."

Every heartbeat pounded behind her eyes as she looked deeply into his gaze.

She could almost hear his pulse beat, too, as he considered her words.

Hope flicked through his eyes. He opened his mouth. Then he snapped it shut and shook his head. "I'd like to tell you everything, but it's better if I don't."

"Better for who?" She wanted to shake her hands at the sky and demand answers.

"For Lonnie." His voice thickened. "For you."

"For me?"

He nodded, all misery and regret.

"How can that be?"

"Trust me. It's better you don't know." He sucked in a shuddering breath. "Do you still believe it's possible to start fresh? Put the past behind and forget it?"

She opened her mouth, then closed it again without saying anything. She wanted to say yes. But he had a past full of secrets. That was different. At least it was different for her. She didn't know if it was possible to build a future on the unknown.

"Maybe what I'm asking is—can you trust me without knowing the answer to your question?"

She could tell he tried to keep his voice neutral, as if her answer didn't matter, but she heard the yearning and knew he longed for her to say yes. The seconds rushed by as she considered her response. Would knowing the past change what she knew about him? She'd seen him being tender, gentle, noble, kind and comforting. He'd held her and made her past less hurtful.

Could she not do the same for him?

All she had to do was speak the words. All doubts fled as she realized how much she wanted to give him the gift of her trust.

She rested her hand on his arm, warm from the sunshine and as strong as the man himself. "Knowing your secret will not change who you are or how I feel about you."

He rested his hand on hers. "Thank you." His eyes filled with brightness.

They stood smiling at each other a moment as the distant voices of her sisters and Lonnie reached them. Birds chattered in the trees. A juvenile robin swooped in to enjoy the berries.

"The birds are going to eat them before we get our share," he observed.

They pulled apart and returned to picking.

The air shimmered with hope and trust and possibility.

They picked steadily. Twice they returned to the wagon to dump their buckets in a basket. The third time they got there along with Lonnie and Rose.

"The baskets are filling up fast." Cora's satisfaction came from more-than-successful berry picking.

Ma and Pa arrived with their buckets of berries, and all of them quickly grabbed a sandwich and a handful of cookies and ate before they returned to work.

Cora and Wyatt moved deeper into the bush where they found a patch with extralarge serviceberries and set to work. She moved quickly, wandering farther to her left, knowing that whatever they got today would provide a welcome addition to their meals during the winter months.

Her thoughts sang a happy song as she worked. Wyatt had asked her to trust him. Had asked if it was possible to start over. If he meant to stay in the area they could get to know each other better. There'd be time and opportunity for attending socials together. She wrinkled her nose. Nancy and Mary Ann would surely hover around seeking his attention. She grunted. But they wouldn't accompany Cora and Wyatt on long solitary walks or little picnics. Soon the summer busy season would end and she'd have time for such things. Wyatt and Lonnie could visit and play board games with Cora and her sisters. They could read to each other.

Her heart thrilled with what the future offered.

The leaves rustled to her right. "Wyatt?" She stepped around to see him. Perhaps she'd tell him all the things she hoped for.

Whoof.

A black bear rose up on his hind legs, as startled to see Cora as she was to see him, though she'd guarantee he wasn't a fraction as afraid.

"Wyatt!" She called his name without thinking whether or not it would anger or frighten the bear.

Whoof.

Wyatt stopped to listen. It sounded as though someone exhaled really hard. Had Cora fallen and had her breath knocked out of her? His heart kicked into a gallop. She might be hurt.

"Wyatt!" Her voice sounded strangled.

He dropped his pail to the ground and rushed toward the sound. But there were so many bushes in the way. How far had she gone?

"Cora, where are you?"

She didn't answer.

He met a wall of bushes. What direction to go? "Cora?" Still no answer.

He flung about to the right and the left. Where was she? He sucked in air and forced himself to slow down and think. The sound had come from the left. He held still, hoping to hear her. He didn't, but through the bushes he saw a bit of her straw hat and pushed past the berry-laden branches.

There she was. She was edging backward toward him.

He looked past her and saw a bear on his hind legs sniffing the air. His heart lunged to his throat and refused to work.

Cora was doing the right thing, retreating as quietly as possible, letting the bear know she was no threat and the animal was welcome to the area.

He held his breath and prayed as never before. Two more steps and he could pull her to safety.

Cora edged her foot back, caught it on a clump of wiry grass and started to go down. Her hat fell to her back and hung by its ribbons.

A silent scream tore at his throat. Clamping his teeth closed to keep from crying out, Wyatt forced himself to remain motionless. If the bear thought it was outnumbered, it would feel more threatened.

She caught herself, took one more step, and he grabbed

her and pulled her out of sight into the bushes. He didn't stop moving until they were a safe distance away, then he turned her into his arms and held her tight. He buried his face in her hair and struggled to regulate his breathing.

She clung to him, her arms around his waist as shuddering breath followed shuddering breath.

Slowly his heartbeat calmed and his lungs remembered how to work. He plunged his fingers into her hair and pressed her head to his chest, close to his heart where he could keep her safe.

"You gave me an awful fright." He didn't even try to hide the croak in his voice.

She shuddered and her arms tightened about him.

"You're okay now," he soothed. "I've got you. I won't let anything happen to you."

Would she be so willing to come into his arms if she knew the truth?

He closed his eyes and wished he could tell her everything, but first he must talk to Lonnie. But how could he be certain of her reaction? He did not want to lose this connection with her. Couldn't bear to see scorn and rejection in her eyes.

He'd asked her to trust him enough to not ask to know his secrets.

Did he trust her enough to tell them to her?

Slowly she relaxed, but she didn't pull away. Her head rested below his chin and she breathed calmly.

He made no move to end the hug, either. If they could stay this way, in this place—minus the bear—his past wouldn't matter. But time did not stand still. Life must be lived.

"We should warn the others about the bear," he murmured, reluctant to end the moment.

"Of course." She eased back and lifted her face to him. "Thank you."

It was he who should thank her, for offering to trust him. "You did everything right. Your pa will be proud of you."

"I was never so scared in all my life."

For him, it rivaled the moment he'd discovered Lonnie standing over their father, a bloodied shovel in his hand and the man beaten almost beyond recognition. He shook the image from his mind.

"Where did you leave your berries?" he asked her. "If you dropped your bucket near the bear, we are leaving it behind."

She chuckled. "I thought the bear was you."

"You think I look like a bear?"

"No, of course not, silly. I heard something in the bushes and thought it was you. I wasn't expecting it to be a bear. I left my bucket over there." She pointed.

He measured the distance with his eye. Was it far enough from the bear that it could be retrieved safely? He checked for signs of the animal and saw the furry hide farther up the hill. "You stay right here and I'll get it."

He retrieved it, then they returned to the spot where he'd left his and they returned to the wagon. Mr. and Mrs. Bell were there.

"Ma, Pa, I met a bear over there." She pointed.

"Are you okay?" Mrs. Bell grabbed her and ran her hands over her arms and back.

Mr. Bell stood very close, his eyes full of worry.

Wyatt smiled at their tender concern. "Your daughter handled it very well. She backed away quietly until she was out of sight."

"I remembered all the lessons you drilled into us, Pa."

"Good." Both parents shifted their attention to the bushes around them. "What about the others?"

"Our berry picking is over," Mr. Bell said. He cupped his hands and called the others.

Cora joined him in calling their names and Wyatt added his voice. They paused to listen.

"Coming," a distant voice answered, and in a few minutes the three of them broke into sight.

"We're done here." Mr. Bell took their pails and set them in the back. "Cora met a bear. We're going home while we're all safe." He helped his wife to the wagon seat and the others clambered into the box.

The twins each grabbed one of Cora's hands, peppering her with questions.

Cora told them the details of her bear encounter, all except the few precious moments she and Wyatt had held each other.

Lonnie stared at the three girls.

Wyatt wished he knew what the boy was thinking. Did he see the affection among the Bell family and want to be part of it?

Maybe they were safe here. Perhaps they could settle nearby and enjoy a life that included the Bells. Wouldn't it be nice to learn to live and love as they did?

Wouldn't it be sweet to spend more time with Cora?

He stared at the scenery drifting away as they followed the trail back to the farm and tried to convince himself he had nothing to fear from people in his past.

If anyone noticed his shudder, they'd likely put it down to the bear. But what scared him as much as seeing the bear facing Cora was knowing she would endure harsh comments and condemnation if anyone ever discovered he'd spent time in prison. Or even worse, Jimmy Stone if he ever discovered Wyatt's whereabouts.

Not too many people were willing to overlook that kind of a past.

Dare he hope no one would ever recognize him? He recalled his reaction to the man at the livery stables. The man in the shadows had looked so much like Jimmy Stone. Would he ever stop looking over his shoulder for the man who had vowed revenge? Jimmy was lazy. Maybe too lazy to follow Wyatt across the prairie. But he was not the sort of man to overlook a grudge.

Was Wyatt dreaming impossible dreams to think he could escape his past and Jimmy Stone?

Chapter Sixteen

The next day, Cora wanted to help Wyatt on the barn. He had the doors and stall partitions to install. But Ma needed all the help she could get sorting and preparing berries. Besides the serviceberries that were processed in syrup, the chokecherries had to be cooked. They'd put them through a sieve and then add sugar to the pulp before cooking the mixture into jam. It was hot, time-consuming work, but no one complained, knowing how delicious both would taste during the long winter months.

As much as possible, Cora sat outside the kitchen door, sorting berries where she could watch Wyatt and Lonnie work. Or if she had to be in the kitchen, she often glanced out the window.

"You can't keep your eyes off him," Rose teased.

"I feel I should be helping with the barn." It was a poor excuse and she knew everyone saw through it.

The twins had quizzed her last night about how Wyatt had rescued her. Fortunately it had been too dark for them to see the warmth that flooded her cheeks and stained them a telltale pink. All she'd said was that he dragged her away and then retrieved her pail of berries.

She was not prepared to reveal how tightly he'd held her. And how she'd held him just as tightly. Reaction to the scare explained only a portion of why they'd clung to each other.

She, for one, had welcomed the excuse to be in his arms, finding comfort and strength she'd ached for since—

Maybe since she'd told him about her papa. Or was it since he'd caught her as she about tumbled from the partly finished loft floor? Or maybe when they'd shared the awe of seeing a new foal. She couldn't say where it had started. Only that she was at home in his arms, his heart beating soundly beneath her ear.

But from the way the twins winked at each other and rolled their eyes each time they caught her looking toward the barn, she had to wonder if they guessed more than she meant to confess.

By the time the berries were done, it was late afternoon and the kitchen was so hot Cora feared Ma would have heatstroke.

"Let's eat outside," she suggested.

"Good idea," Rose said. "You set up a table for the food and we'll carry it out."

Pa helped with the sawhorses and planks that created a table.

Wyatt and Lonnie trotted over, their hair wet from soaking it in water they pumped from the well.

They gathered in a circle, holding hands.

"Let's sing the blessing, Pa," Lilly said.

So they sang the doxology. And if anyone noticed that Wyatt's voice was indeed more of a growl than a tune, they didn't mention it.

"How much did you get done on the stalls?" she asked Wyatt, who sat beside her on the warm, dry grass.

"One more good day should see them finished."

"Done already? I never thought to see it go so fast."

"Helps to have lots of hands."

She wasn't sure if he meant the work bee of a few days ago, or the help he and Lonnie provided.

"All the help has been an answer to prayer," Pa said.

"Amen," Ma added.

Cora insisted on helping finish the barn the next day. Not that Wyatt objected. His mind twisted and turned with possibilities. Could he discover how she'd feel about a man who had been in prison without implicating himself or Lonnie? Or was he building dreams on nothing but fluffy clouds of wishing?

They stopped for dinner and then hurried back to work. The sun had barely passed its zenith when they hung the last gate on the last stall.

"Done!" She clapped her hands as Lonnie put away the tools. She went to the door and smiled at the bright landscape. Her sisters worked in the garden. Her ma sat in the shade of the house, shelling peas. Noises from the work shed indicated where her pa was.

She called them all over. "Thanks to Wyatt and Lonnie and our friends from town, we have our barn. Isn't it great?" She walked them all through and took the twins up to the loft. Lonnie followed, but Wyatt remained on the ground with her folks.

"Ma, Pa," she called from the loft door, and they looked up at her. "This calls for a celebration. Let's go on a picnic."

Lonnie looked as eager as any of them.

Wyatt schooled his face not to reveal his own anticipation of the idea.

Mrs. Bell shook her head. "I'm too tired. But you
young people go ahead if you like. You all deserve a
break from the work."

"Can we take the wagon?"

Mr. Bell agreed they could. They decided to take a
picnic supper and go to Chester's Pond.

Cora explained to Wyatt. "It's a pond created by a
small landslide. It's a beautiful spot."

"Sounds nice." He thought the driest spot on the bald
prairie would be pleasant enough to thrill him.

"I'll get the wagon," Mr. Bell said, and Wyatt went
with him to hitch up.

By the time Wyatt drove up to the house, the girls
had a box full of food and several quilts ready to load.

He wondered if Lonnie would sit by him on the seat,
but he scrambled in beside Lilly and Rose, his arm on
the box of food as if he had to make sure it wouldn't
disappear.

"I'll ride with you," Cora said with a sweet smile.

He tucked the smile and her offer into his hopeful
thoughts. Starting over might be possible. His heart thud-
ded against his ribs in eager anticipation.

"Turn that way." As Cora pointed to her left, her arm
brushed his and optimism walloped into him. *Don't expect acceptance until you get it.* But the warning seemed
unnecessary. Hadn't she already said she trusted him?

They took a direction away from town, for which he
was grateful. Would he ever feel comfortable around others? Perhaps he'd always fear having his past revealed.
Wasn't that reason enough to confess it? But how could

he tell her the whole truth? It would mean condemning Lonnie, and he'd spent a year in prison to prevent that.

They followed the river for a few miles, then she pointed again. "There it is."

A grove of trees prevented him from seeing a pond, but no doubt she knew how to reach the water.

"Turn here, and then there's a trail that will take us through the trees."

He saw the tree-shrouded opening and followed it.

The twins and Lonnie crowded to his back.

As soon as the water came into sight, Lilly sighed. "This is one of my favorite spots."

"Me, too," Rose echoed.

Cora said nothing and Wyatt glanced at her. She caught his gaze and smiled so widely, so invitingly that he forgot about the water, the twins, Lonnie…everything but the joy of this moment, the anticipation of sharing the afternoon with her.

"Ahem," Rose said. "Did you forget we're here?"

He jerked away. "It's a very pretty place." What he meant was that any place was beautiful with Cora at his side, smiling so sweetly, so trustingly.

Would the truth steal it away?

He stopped the wagon and jumped down. The others scrambled from the back, but Cora waited for him to help her down. He didn't mean to hold her longer than he should, but his hands lingered at her waist as she lifted her face to him.

Perhaps she'd meant to thank him, but no words came from her mouth as their gazes caught and held, hers so deep and burning he felt as if the sun had seared his insides.

"Come on, you two," Lonnie called, and they slowly backed away from each other.

His hands lingered, reluctant to let her go.

"Look," Lonnie called.

Cora's smile seemed as regretful as he was. But they traipsed over to join the others.

Lonnie had found an arrowhead with a broken shaft attached. "Do you think there are Indians here?" He glanced around, a mixture of fear and excitement on his face.

Lilly pulled Rose close. "There aren't, are there?"

Wyatt wished he could reassure them all that they were safe. The government had recently established a reservation for the Natives and they had supposedly gone willingly, but only thirteen years ago, Colonel Custer had been badly beaten by Sitting Bull and his angry braves.

It was enough to make them all look intently into the trees searching for Indians.

Cora laughed nervously. "Even if they left the reservation, they'd be back in the hills where there's lots of game."

Lonnie squinted into the trees. "'Less they want revenge for us taking their land."

Wyatt groaned. "Thanks, Lonnie. That's reassuring. Let me see the arrow."

Lonnie reluctantly handed it to him. "I want it back."

Wyatt examined it. "This is old. Look at how the end of the shaft is rotting. It's likely been here a long time."

"Might be from Custer's last stand."

Wyatt didn't bother pointing out that the battle had taken place to the southeast, many miles away.

Cora let out a long breath. "Just the same. Maybe we should head back home."

The twins shook their heads. "There's nothing to be afraid of."

"I can't chance that."

The twins faced her, a wall of protest. "Stop worrying about us. We're all grown up now."

"You're only eighteen."

The twins looked at each other then back to her. "Most girls our age are married. We'll likely be old maids because no one is ever good enough for us."

Wyatt laughed at the sorrowfulness of their words. "What does she do? Stand at the end of the lane and beat suitors off with a stick?"

Lilly looked guilty. "No. But she doesn't need to. She just scowls at them and they turn tail and run."

"I'd say if they aren't prepared to fight a few battles, maybe confront opposition from your family or the community, they aren't worthy of you." His words swelled within his heart. Was he willing to face opposition in order to be with Cora? More important, would she face it to be with him?

Rose nodded. "That's true." She faced Cora. "We are staying and enjoying ourselves." She and Lilly marched away.

Cora scowled at him. "Don't be encouraging them to be foolhardy."

"I didn't mean to." Were they being reckless, or was she being overly cautious? Overly protective? That might be the flaw in his hopes. Cora might be willing to face his past, but it wasn't likely she'd let anything threaten her sisters' happiness and security.

"Come on." Cora grabbed his hand. "We're going to make sure no one is lurking in the trees."

He willingly allowed her to lead him into the bushes.

But she had serious searching on her mind. They looked behind every tree, parted the bushes to make sure no one hid in them, examined the ground in open areas for tracks. Crows flew from the treetops cawing their protest. A rabbit skittered away. But they saw nothing that meant a threat.

They returned to the edge of the pond. "Are you satisfied?" he asked, half amused.

"I guess so." The others circled the water, examining pebbles and bits of wood. Lonnie tried to skip rocks.

Cora sat on a fallen log and patted the spot beside her. "It's nice to see them enjoying themselves, isn't it?"

"Yup," he said, though he thought the Bell sisters always enjoyed life. It was Lonnie who had relaxed and grown happy here.

Reason enough, he decided, to risk telling Cora part of the truth and measure her response. He'd thought of several ways to broach the subject but none seemed to fit.

"Do you think you'll ever forgive your real father for leaving you?"

She continued to stare toward the others but her fingers clenched. "I don't think about him much at all. He didn't care about us when we needed him and we don't need him now, so it doesn't matter."

But it did matter. She hurt because of it and obviously hadn't forgiven him.

He realized his own fists were clenched and made an effort to loosen them. It didn't bode well for him that she didn't forgive her own father.

Why should she forgive Wyatt? Though he'd done nothing wrong. Except keep a potentially hurtful secret. But he'd only done it to protect them all.

"Maybe he had a good reason for leaving you. Maybe

he sincerely meant to return but couldn't through no fault of his own."

She fixed him with blinding accusation in her eyes. "Why are you defending him?"

He shrugged. "I'm not. I don't even know him. All I'm saying is there might be an explanation."

Her look challenged him to find one.

"Maybe he was in trouble with the law and had to run."

"A criminal as well as a man who abandons his children? I hardly find that comforting."

"What if he had been blamed for something he didn't do?"

"An honorable man would have made sure his family was safe. He'd put their needs ahead of his own."

He nodded. So that was his answer. He must put her needs, her sisters' needs and Lonnie's needs before his own selfish desires. So be it. He'd been doing so for years, so it wasn't anything new.

He took Cora's clenched hands and rubbed the backs of them. "You are absolutely right. I don't know why I thought I needed to bring it up. Guess I just like to find a sound reason for why people do things that leave us confused."

Her hands relaxed and turned palm to palm with his.

"That's very noble of you," she said, her eyes filled with sunshine. Sweetness filled the air. She so quickly put aside little annoyances, if not so readily the big things in life.

He entwined their fingers and smiled. This might be all he could have—a sunny afternoon, a few hours, memories of what might have been. He would make the most of them.

"Come join us," Rose called.

He pulled her to her feet and they walked along the edge of the pond to where the others were. Lonnie tagged Wyatt. "You're it."

Wyatt froze, and then a laugh rumbled from him. Lonnie wanted to play. Wyatt was more than ready to oblige.

The others joined in and they chased through the bushes and darted along the water's edge tagging one another and laughing.

Wyatt was it again. He had not managed to catch Cora. Each time he tried, she slipped away, dashing in a direction that left him to tag someone else. But this time he meant to catch her.

The direct route hadn't worked, so he tried another strategy. He pretended to chase Lonnie, who fled through the bushes. As soon as he was out of sight, Wyatt shifted direction and moved with as little sound as he could. To his left, Lonnie continued to batter through the trees, making a great deal of racket that served Wyatt's purpose well.

He paused to listen. Rose and Lilly whispered, giving away their position. He strained to catch any indication of where Cora might be. A rustle to his right. He moved in that direction.

She stood still, looking every which way. She tipped her head to listen.

He held his breath, but still she turned toward him.

Her eyes widened with surprise. She gave a yelp and took off with him on her heels.

"I've got you."

"No," she squealed, and slipped away. She glanced over her shoulder, which slowed her, and that was all he needed to catch up. He reached out for her but tripped on a root and couldn't stop his headlong flight.

His arms caught her in his path and he turned to take the brunt of the fall.

They went down with a thud that knocked the air from him. He forced his lungs to work. "Are you okay?" His voice whistled from his throat.

She didn't answer.

He turned. Her face was buried against his arm.

"I'm okay." Her words were muffled.

Between the weight of her in his arms and the struggle to catch his breath, he couldn't move.

She shifted, then sat up. "I guess you caught me."

He sucked in air and sat up facing her. "I almost killed you doing so. I'm sorry. You're sure you aren't hurt?"

She brushed her hands over her arms. "Well, my pride might be just a little wounded that you sneaked up on me like that."

He grinned. "You sure looked surprised when you saw me."

Her grin widened to match his. "I guess I didn't expect you to be so sneaky."

"Me, sneaky? Who is the one who runs so close to someone else I have to tag them?"

She shrugged. "Strategy, that's all." Her smile didn't falter a bit.

They pushed to their feet.

Grass and leaves were stuck in her hair. He plucked them out piece by piece, aware she'd lowered her eyelids, allowing him to see only the fan of her lashes against her cheeks. A strand of her hair caught on his finger and his movements slowed as he lingered on the feel of silk against his skin. He swallowed hard, wondered if she noticed and forced himself to continue. He grasped her chin and turned her head to check each side.

Her skin was warm and smooth.

"I think that's all." His husky words revealed how deeply he'd been affected.

"My turn." Did her voice sound as thick as his?

She plucked things from his hair, each touch of her fingers sending a jolt through his brain until he thought his head couldn't contain it.

"All done." She reached around him to pick up his hat where it had fallen.

Her eyes lifted to his, full of awareness and longing.

His own must brim with the same thing, he thought. He longed to hold her next to his heart. Tell her every secret of his life.

She lowered her gaze, but before he could find solid ground, she lifted them again.

He forgot every reasonable argument about his past, his present and his future.

A persistent idea knocked at the back of his brain. This couldn't last. She'd never overlook his past and all the risks it brought to her family's safe little place.

But all that mattered right now was this precious moment of time.

He'd risk everything for the joy of right now.

Chapter Seventeen

Cora saw the longing in his eyes as clearly as she felt it in her heart. The whole afternoon had been a prelude to this moment. Running from him when she wanted to run *to* him, sharing him with the others when she wanted him to herself… Everything had accumulated until she could think of nothing else but Wyatt. Touching his hair to remove the twigs and leaves had left her unable to remember any reason she should be cautious around him.

Secrets mattered not. All she cared about was what she saw and knew of him. She lowered her gaze to his mouth, touched his lips with her fingertips.

He caught her hand and pressed her palm to his cheek.

"Cora." Her name rang like a clarion call, making her like the sound of it as never before.

He cupped his hand to the back of her head. His eyes filled with promises and pleasure, and he bent his head.

Just before his lips touched hers, he paused.

Whether to change his mind or give her time to pull away, she couldn't tell. But she didn't intend that either should happen and she lifted her face to him.

Their lips touched. Sweetness like pure warm honey

poured through her and she knew she would never feel the same.

They clung to each other, though she couldn't have said if it was a long or short time.

With a satisfied sigh, he leaned back and smiled at her. "Cora, what would you think if I settled in this area?" He rushed on as if he needed to explain. "Lonnie is happier than I've seen him in a very long time. I think he's starting to put the past behind him."

She trailed her finger along his jawline. "I think it would be a lovely idea. But I hope Lonnie's not the only one putting his past behind him. Aren't you, as well?"

"If I can't start over here, I don't know if I ever can."

She smiled at how much his answer revealed. Her heart danced to think he'd found peace and belonging here. He hadn't said so, and perhaps it was too early to wish for it, but she hoped she'd played a large part in his decision. And would play an even larger part with the passing of each delicious day.

"Who's it?" Lonnie's voice came through the woods.

"I guess we better get back to the others." Wyatt sounded as reluctant as she felt. "I don't think I'll say anything to Lonnie about my decision just yet."

She nodded. "It will be easier for him that way." Once Wyatt could say to Lonnie, "This is where we're going to live," the boy would have something solid to hold on to.

They returned to the others. She ignored the teasing grins her sisters sent her way. The game ended and they gathered round in a circle to talk.

For the first time, Lonnie spoke of his past. "My ma was so different from yours. She was weak. Or maybe frail. I don't remember cookies or cakes since I was about five." He sent a questioning look to Wyatt. "Do you?"

He shook his head.

Cora edged closer, not caring what the others thought, and squeezed his hand. "We're very fortunate. Our ma spoils us with her cooking."

Wyatt relaxed and gave her a lazy smile. "Seems you all do your share to make your home happy and welcoming."

"And productive," Rose added.

They fell into a contemplative silence for two minutes.

Lonnie spoke again. "Did you girls like school?"

The three of them said they did.

Lonnie said he kind of did, too. For a while they discussed their favorite subjects.

Cora turned to Wyatt. "What was your favorite part of school?"

He considered the question a moment. "Singing." His face was so serious she almost believed him.

Then she burst out laughing. "Did the teacher give you a bucket to carry the tune in?"

He grinned. "She asked me to stand at the back and only pretend to sing."

The others laughed.

Cora turned to her sisters. They had always liked to sing together. They nodded in understanding and the three of them began their favorite songs. Lonnie joined in on the ones he knew.

Wyatt leaned back, listening.

Cora felt his gaze on her and tried to ignore it, but she couldn't and wondered why she even tried. This afternoon was to be lived to its fullest and enjoyed, hopefully as a prelude to many such days to follow. She turned to him and sang as if no one else was there, her heart bursting with music above and beyond the songs.

His look never faltered from hers, opening his heart and his thoughts to her.

The others might be there. They might be observing them but she didn't care. All that mattered was Wyatt's trusting look and her trusting heart.

And his plan to settle in the area.

The next day, Wyatt rode away intent on finding a place to live. She knew where he meant to go but said nothing. She wondered what explanation he'd given Lonnie, but the boy didn't seem concerned.

"I need to put in some more hours to pay for my pigs," Lonnie said.

So she put him to work hauling water to the garden.

Wyatt returned later in the afternoon. He gave a barely perceptible shake of his head. He hadn't found anyplace suitable. She smiled encouragement.

They walked along the river later that evening. "You'll find something," she assured him. "God will guide you."

"I pray so."

She hoped it would be close enough they could see each other regularly and often. The future beckoned with a thousand stars.

He walked her back to the house, but Lonnie and the girls were outside so he only said a gentle good-night, called for Lonnie to join him and left.

She stared after him, wishing they could kiss again. Not that she needed another kiss to remind her of all she'd felt last time.

Smiling, she went inside and prepared for bed. She kept her feelings to herself even when the twins teased her, wanting to know what she and Wyatt had done on their walk.

* * *

In the past few days, Wyatt had ridden every direction from the Bell farm and found no suitable land nearby. Heading out to try again, he dismounted on the trail and looked around, as if the right land would appear on the horizon.

Perhaps God meant to let him know this plan of his wasn't right. Wyatt had promised Cora he'd pray about finding a place. *God, guide me to where I should go.* He knew his open-ended prayer meant he might have to accept being led farther away than his dreams took him.

But God knew best. Even if it meant he couldn't live his dream, Wyatt would follow His lead.

A rider approached from the trail to the east, an older man with skin leathered from years of living and working outdoors. He was lean as a whip with deep blue eyes that studied Wyatt with interest.

"You lost, young man?"

"Just deciding." He didn't know what direction he should go today to look for land.

The older man swung down and walked to Wyatt with the peculiar bow-legged gait of a long-time cowboy. He introduced himself as Jack Henry. He stood beside Wyatt, studying the lay of the land. "While ya make up yer mind, why not ride along with me?"

It was an offer Wyatt didn't mind accepting. They both returned to horseback and ambled south.

"Where you from? Where you headed?" Jack asked.

"Been at the Bells'. Now I'm looking for a place to start ranching."

"Know the Bells. They's good people."

A short time later, Jack said, "This here is my place."

He indicated a low ranch house and a cluster of outbuildings half a mile off the road.

Wyatt had ridden by a couple of days ago and admired the yard, but it didn't have a for-sale sign posted so he'd gone on by.

"Why not light awhile and tell me more. Do the Caldwells still object to the Bells farming in the middle of their ranch land?"

Wyatt accepted the offer mostly because he didn't have the heart to push on. And he enjoyed the old man's company.

They rode into the yard. "Nice place." Sturdy buildings. Well maintained. He told how the Caldwell cowboys harassed the Bells in the hopes of persuading them to sell their bit of land. "The Bells have turned their few acres into a beautiful productive place. I don't blame them for refusing to sell it."

Jack nodded. "A man's roots can go down mighty deep. Take me, for instance. I been here since before the Caldwells. I brought my missus out with me. She died five years ago. We never did have the family we hoped for. Say, do you want to see around?"

Wyatt accepted the invitation out of curiosity and the hope of learning from a man who'd been in the area a long time.

They rode around the place, admiring the crop of calves the man's cows had.

"I should be moving on," Wyatt said as the afternoon lengthened. He longed to see Cora and be assured that she wanted him to stay in the area and that it wasn't just wishful thinking on his part.

Jack sat beside him, one leg bent over his saddle horn. "Son, take a look around you. Why, there ain't nothing

you can't grow here—cows, sheep, crops and gardens."
He paused. "And a family."

"I'm sorry you didn't have the family you dreamed
of."

"It's my only regret in life."

Wyatt waited for Jack to corral his thoughts.

"I'm getting too old for all this." He pointed to the
cows but Wyatt understood he meant the land and the
work, as well. "You say you'd like to settle in the area."
He nodded once as if coming to a conclusion. "You're
the sort of man who would benefit the community."

Wyatt stared at the man. How could he come to such
a verdict? One that could easily be proved wrong. He
silently prayed that God would keep the truth about his
past hidden.

Jack continued. "Like I say, I'm tired." He gave Wyatt
a direct blue-eyed look that made Wyatt feel as if the
man saw clear to the depths of his soul. "I'd be pleased
if you would join me. I'd make you part owner for now.
You do the work to earn your share. In time it would be
all yours."

"I'm honored you ask me." Wyatt could picture himself here raising a family. Maybe sharing his life with
more than Lonnie.

Hope burst forth like blossoms before the sun. "I accept your offer. How soon do you want me to join you?"

"Soon as you can. Bring those horses and let's get
the herd growing."

Wyatt laughed. "I can't believe this." Doubts erupted
in his brain. "Why would you ask me?"

Jack drew in a slow steady breath. "Son, just this
morning I was talking to God again. Said how much I
wanted to turn this place over to a younger man. And

seeing as God hadn't blessed us with children, I asked Him to send along someone who would take the place of mine. I saw you there at the side of the road and knew God had answered my prayer."

"But you know nothing about me."

"Know enough. Seems God led ya here for a purpose. One that benefits the both of us."

They shook hands on the agreement and Wyatt headed back to the Bell place.

And a future as bright as the sun overhead.

He resisted the urge to make his horse gallop all the way back, but by the time he rode into the yard, he was ready to burst with his news.

Mr. Bell waved a greeting as he approached.

Mrs. Bell's face appeared at the kitchen window and she raised her hand.

He realized he needed to take care of his horse before he told his news and turned to go to his campsite, where he unsaddled his horse, rubbed the animal down, and fed and watered him—all things he did on a regular basis so they were almost second nature. When had they ever before consumed so much time?

Finally, satisfied he'd done all he needed in that regard, he trotted up the hill.

"You're just in time for supper," Rose called.

Food seemed an intrusion at the moment, but through the open door, he saw Cora setting plates at the table. He'd not be getting a chance to talk to her until after the meal.

Lonnie bumped into him in his hurry to get to the food.

Resigned to the delay, Wyatt followed him inside and took his customary place at the table beside Cora.

When Mr. Bell held his hands out to grasp the hand of

the girl on each side of him, Wyatt eagerly took Cora's hand. Would she know by the strength of his grip that he'd found a place? One he hoped she'd appreciate?

The meal took a long time as the family discussed the trip to town earlier in the day. Seemed all the news was about the continued robberies and who might be responsible.

No one knew he was a jailbird, so fingers wouldn't be pointed his way. But if the news ever came out…well, he knew what to expect.

Was he doing the right thing, subjecting Cora to such risk?

He vowed he'd tell her where he'd spent the missing year and see if she still welcomed the idea of him settling in the area.

Finally the meal ended and the kitchen was cleaned.

"It's a lovely evening," Cora said. "Would you care to go for a walk?"

He'd thought the opportunity would never come and hurried to the door.

Lonnie and Lilly headed toward the pigpen.

"I have news," Wyatt said, and called Lonnie to join them.

Lonnie came with such reluctance, his boots scraped every step of the way. "I want to help Lilly feed the pigs."

"This won't take long." He led them toward the barn, thinking after he told Lonnie, he'd go on to their campsite where he and Cora could sit and discuss the future.

At the corner of the barn, Lonnie dug in his heels. "Wyatt, what do you want?" He glanced over his shoulder. "If it's about the horses, I'll tend them after I feed the pigs."

"Very well." He smiled at Cora, his heart bursting

with his news. From the way her eyes widened and filled with gladness, she guessed what he was about to report. "Lonnie, I have found a place for us. We move on Monday. It's—" But before he could say where it was, Lonnie interrupted.

"No," he shouted. "I don't want to go. I like it here just fine. No one will hurt me here."

Wyatt reached out to him. "No one will hurt you where we're going. I'll see to that."

Lonnie, breathing hard, stared at him. "I'm scared of you."

"Me?" Wyatt jerked back as if the boy had hit him. "I'd never hurt you. You should know that. After all—" He curbed what he was about to say. Now was not the time or place.

"I know you're mad at me that you went to jail." Lonnie's eyes were wild. He was unaware of what he said.

"Jail?" Cora said, the word sucked in on her breath. She stared at Wyatt with eyes as big as moons.

"I'll explain later," Wyatt said. First he had a brother to deal with.

"Lonnie, I am not mad at you. I've never been mad at you." *Please, God, help him believe me.*

"You went because of me."

"I would do it again." He didn't want to reveal that Lonnie had been the guilty one, but he had to reassure him. "Lonnie, it was far easier for me to be there then to think of you in that place." Lonnie would have found the threats and violence impossible to deal with.

"But it was me who did it." Agony drew each word into a wail.

Wyatt gripped the boy's shoulders. A shudder raced clear through Lonnie.

He had to make Lonnie understand. "I would do it again. I couldn't have lived free knowing you were in jail. It would have been torture." Far worse than jail had been.

Lonnie's eyes clung to Wyatt. "Was it very bad?" he whispered.

He didn't answer the question, couldn't. "What made it bearable was knowing you weren't in there."

Lonnie searched Wyatt's eyes and finally saw that Wyatt meant it.

"How can you not be mad at me?"

"Because you're my little brother." He pulled the boy closer, pleased when Lonnie didn't shy away.

"Are we really moving?"

"Yes."

"Not far away?"

"Not far at all."

Lonnie nodded. "Okay, then. Can I go now?"

"Go look after the pigs."

Lonnie galloped away.

Wyatt stared at the ground in front of him. He couldn't bring himself to look at Cora. He was as an ex-con, even though he'd gone to jail for Lonnie. Would it change how she saw him?

Chapter Eighteen

Cora's mind stalled. She couldn't process this information. "This was your big secret?"

He nodded, all misery and staring at the ground.

"You went to jail to protect Lonnie, but you didn't feel you could tell me this?" Pain shot through her heart. "Did you think I would judge you?" She wrapped her arms about her and held tight. "You asked me to trust you but you couldn't trust me. Why?" She wanted to shout the question but kept her voice low so as not to draw attention from the others.

He scuffed the toe of his boot in the dirt. "I didn't want people to learn the truth about Lonnie. I still don't. He needs to be able to get on with his life, not be judged for the past." Finally he brought his gaze to her. "And I wanted to protect you."

"From what?" Her pain and uncertainty was mirrored in his eyes.

"People look at me differently. They act differently when they know I'm an ex-con."

She caught her breath, then forced words from her tight lungs. "Did you think I would see you differently?"

He didn't have to answer. She saw the flicker of admission in his eyes. And her heart answered with a stabbing pain that reached every cell of her body.

But she swallowed it. Of course he was uncertain. A pa who beat him. A year in prison. Had he ever known the kind of love and certainty Ma and Pa and her sisters gave her?

Her heart softened like butter on a warm day. "Wyatt." She pressed her hands to his arms crossed tightly over his chest. "When you asked me to trust you without knowing your secrets, I said I would. I decided I would go by what I saw and knew of you."

His eyes flooded with such yearning she couldn't speak for the span of a heartbeat, two and then a third.

"I'd seen how kind you were, how protective of Lonnie. I knew you to be noble, hardworking and a man I could honor and trust."

The doubt in his eyes faded.

"Knowing the truth has not changed my mind in the least. If anything, it's made me see you as even more noble."

His arms relaxed. He drew Cora into the shadows of the barn, where he leaned against the wall and grasped both her hands.

She lifted her face to him and let him read the truth of her words.

"You don't care that I've been in prison?"

"Of course I care. I'm sure it was an awful place."

He shuddered. "It was."

"But you did nothing wrong. You have nothing to be ashamed of. You can move forward."

He nodded, his gaze searching her eyes, drifting along her cheek and coming to rest on her mouth.

Did he mean to kiss her again?

But he lifted his face to the sky. "I almost forgot. I found a place. Do you know Jack Henry?"

"Of course."

"He's asked me to become his partner and I said yes."

Her heart leaped for joy. He still planned to stay in the area. The Henry place was not far away. The future looked as rosy as the sunset painting the sky in deep pink.

She leaned into him, wrapped her arms about his waist and hugged him. "I'm so glad."

He pressed his palms to her back and held her close. His chest rose and fell with such regularity it filled her with sweet calmness. He was staying. The future lay before them to grasp and live and enjoy.

Wyatt and Lonnie talked late into the night, seated around their campfire. Lonnie wanted details about what it was like in jail. Wyatt told him of the tedious routine, the shuffling in line like a bunch of cattle, the tasteless meals. But he didn't tell him about the bullying, the cruelty or the fear. As Cora said, he wanted to put it behind him and face the future. Even more, he did not want Lonnie to carry a burden of guilt and regret.

The next morning was Sunday and he looked forward to attending church. Now that Cora knew his past, he felt free and open before her.

They arrived at church just before service started and slipped into a pew.

The young ladies glanced toward him and quickly averted their gazes. That was fine with him. He didn't care for their attention. Perhaps they saw him and Cora as a pair now and gave up their aspirations of drawing him into their social circle.

Several people turned in their direction, then bent to whisper to their neighbors.

Wyatt tried to think what caused their interest. He glanced around the congregation and saw no one new, no one from his past. Perhaps he was only being edgy because he'd told Cora his secret.

That must be it.

He turned his attention to the preacher as he rose to greet them and announce the first hymn.

Beside him, Cora sang with pleasure and he listened, her voice a melody in his heart. He couldn't sing a note but he sure could enjoy listening.

As soon as church was over and they had shared a meal with the family, he meant to ask her to walk with him. He'd tell her every detail about the ranch. Would she be eager to hear? Had she ever visited Jack Henry and seen his house? Did she like it? Jack had said they could live in the house with Lonnie and he'd move into the smaller cabin, which suited him better.

He mentally walked through the rooms. He'd glimpsed the two bedrooms through the open doors. The kitchen was big and well equipped, though it showed signs of neglect from the lack of a woman to keep things proper. He tried to see it through Cora's eyes but couldn't imagine what she'd think. She'd no doubt love the sitting room with its big burgundy sofa and two rocking chairs. A pot-bellied stove would drive away the chill on winter nights.

The preacher said, "Amen," and Wyatt realized he had let his thoughts wander throughout the entire sermon.

He hoped God would overlook it this time.

As the family exited, Mrs. Rawley greeted Mrs. Bell, but several other ladies marched past without speaking.

"What on earth?" Cora murmured. "They have something in their craw. I wonder what."

Wyatt's heart scraped along on the bottom of his boots. "Someone must have learned who I am."

"How is that possible?"

He shrugged. "I don't know, but how else do you explain this?" Several people threw them scolding, accusing looks.

Anna Rawley hustled to Cora's side. "They're saying Wyatt is a criminal. Why would anyone say such a cruel thing? It simply isn't true."

Seeing the glance between Cora and Wyatt, Anna looked shocked. "It's not, is it?"

Wyatt nodded. "I spent time in jail."

"For something he didn't do," Cora said heatedly.

Anna shook her head sadly. "They're saying he's responsible for all the robberies around here lately."

"I was afraid this would happen." Wyatt could barely get the words past a lump in his throat the size of the good preacher's Bible.

"But you've been at the farm the whole time," Cora said. "How can they accuse you?"

The owner of the lumber yard marched over. Stu Maples, if Wyatt remembered correctly. He confronted Wyatt. "Jailbirds are not welcome here." Several others came to the man's side, nodding.

Pastor Rawley heard him and joined the gathering crowd. "A man is innocent until proved guilty."

Wyatt knew the pastor meant to be fair, but his words were as condemning as any of the others.

"Once a jailbird, always a jailbird."

Wyatt didn't know the speaker. Why were people so willing to believe the worst about a man? Especially without cause.

Mr. Bell went to Cora and she whispered to him, no doubt telling him of Wyatt's past. Would the man be willing to believe him innocent as he claimed to be?

Mr. Bell stepped to Wyatt's side. "This man is my guest. I suggest he be treated civilly."

A murmur of dissent came from the people, but they kept any further accusations to themselves.

Cora stood close to Wyatt's side. Not touching him. Not smiling at him. But confronting his accusers with a fierce look. He could feel his admiration for her growing in his heart.

The three of them walked to the wagon and climbed aboard, joining Lonnie and the rest of the Bells, who sat in shocked silence.

As they left the yard, many townsfolk turned to them with angry expressions.

Rose and Lilly patted Wyatt's arms. "Lonnie told us," Rose said. "Those people have no reason to accuse you."

He noticed Cora held his hand in a tight grip. Or did he hold hers?

They meant to comfort him, but the accusations rang through his head. *Once a jailbird, always a jailbird.* Could he never be free of that stigma?

When they reached the farm, he held back. "We'll make our own dinner."

"Nonsense," the entire family said in unison.

Cora wound her arm through his and drew him into the house.

As they sat at the table, waiting for Mr. Bell to say grace, the man turned to each of them. "We've all heard

Wyatt's story. How he was in prison but he did no wrong. I think the less that is said about it, the better. Lonnie and Wyatt deserve a chance to start fresh and I, for one, would be honored if they chose to do it in our community."

Wyatt's smile was uncertain. "I'm not sure that's possible now." This morning had changed everything.

"Oh, but you already have a place picked out," Cora reminded him. She turned to her pa. "Jack Henry asked him to be his partner. Said he'd eventually turn the place over to him." She faced Wyatt. "And you gave your word."

"He might not be so welcoming now."

Mr. Bell chuckled. "Jack sees a man for what he is and isn't swayed by what others think."

"Say you'll stay," Cora begged.

"Yes, do," the twins chimed in.

Mr. and Mrs. Bell smiled at him and he felt as if he'd been given a special blessing.

"I want to." It was all he could promise at the moment.

That afternoon, he knew he'd been right not to promise more.

The sheriff rode into the yard and asked to speak to Wyatt.

"Come into the house," Mr. Bell said.

Sheriff Thomas looked ready to refuse, then nodded. "Very well." He stood to the side and waited for Wyatt to go ahead of him.

Lonnie started to follow but Wyatt waved him away. No reason everyone should hear this.

As he sat down across from the sheriff, Cora slipped in and sat beside him.

He dared not look at her. He did not want her implicated in any way. But he couldn't ask her to leave. Her presence strengthened him.

Not that she'd likely go even if he asked.

"Several people have come to me accusing you of certain crimes," the sheriff said. "At this time, I have no evidence, but I assure you, if you're responsible I will find out."

"I've done nothing wrong."

"He's been here the whole time," Cora said.

The sheriff narrowed his eyes. "You can vouch for him?"

"Of course."

"Twenty-four hours of the day?"

"Not at night." Shock filled her words.

"Most of the crimes have taken place after dark, so I'm afraid your assurances mean nothing." The sheriff fixed him with a hard look. "I understand you did time in jail."

"I can't deny it."

"I ain't got much use for jailbirds myself."

Cora sputtered a protest.

Mr. Bell held up a hand to silence her. "Sheriff, I suggest you deal with the facts and put your opinions aside."

The sheriff rose. "I intend to do just that. Good day."

Silence filled the room. Wyatt couldn't lift his gaze from the top of the well-worn wooden tabletop.

"Wyatt, you're innocent. People will soon see that," Mr. Bell assured him.

"I wish I could be so certain." How would he survive if he got thrown back into jail? How would Lonnie? He turned to Cora. "What about Lonnie? If something happens to me—"

"He'll have a home here, won't he, Pa?"

Mr. Bell nodded. "He'll be safe. But so will you. Despite his tough way of talking, Sheriff Thomas is a fair man."

It was small comfort for Wyatt. "So long as Lonnie is okay, I can handle whatever happens." He'd at least have sweet memories of time spent with Cora to comfort him this time.

Later, he returned to the campsite. Lonnie crawled into bed and fell asleep, his world safe with the Bells.

Wyatt sat up staring at the flickering coals of the fire. Would his innocence be proved? Would the truth about Lonnie be discovered? It would mark Lonnie just as much as jail time had marked Wyatt. Was he being fair in staying in the Bar Crossing area? Would his presence always be the cause of hurtful comments and sly accusations? Would Cora and her family be hurt by his presence?

God, show me the right thing to do. I want to stay. I want to spend more time with Cora. But I don't want her or any of the Bells to be hurt. What should I do?

Maybe a cup of tea would help him think through his questions.

He added more wood to the fire, filled the kettle and sat back to wait for the water to boil.

A branch nearby cracked. "Who's there?"

Two men stepped into the circle of light. He recognized them as men from town. Their hard expressions warned him they hadn't come on friendly business.

"Howdy. How can I help you?" He hoped Lonnie would stay asleep or, if he woke, have enough sense to be quiet and not alert the men to his presence.

"You aren't welcome around here."

"Says who?" He could have pointed out that the

Bells had welcomed him but knew it wouldn't be wise. It would likely invite trouble into their lives.

"Us. And we speak for most of the citizens of Bar Crossing."

"I see. Well, sorry to say, I have made plans to stay." He didn't know why he felt the need to provoke them. Except he did. They were bullies and he had no sympathy for such.

One of the men leaned forward. "You might find you don't like it here much." His laugh lacked mirth but carried a large dose of meanness.

The larger of the two grunted. "Well, don't say you weren't warned."

They stomped away.

Lonnie slipped over to join Wyatt. "Will they hurt us?"

"They'll try to make our lives miserable so we'll feel forced to leave." He'd say no more. He didn't want Lonnie to worry. Whatever happened, Wyatt would take care of them.

"Maybe we should leave. Didn't we mean to go to Canada?"

Wyatt stared at the flames. They could leave. Or they could stay. If they left, he'd be riding away from the best thing that had ever happened to him and Lonnie—the acceptance and warmth of Cora and her family. But if they stayed, would the Bells suffer?

Was the nighttime visit from those two men a sign from God to leave?

Or was it a challenge to face his past?

He turned to Lonnie. "I was wrong to think we can outrun our past. Running is not the answer."

"Then what is?"

"I don't know." He gave Lonnie a sideways hug. "Go to sleep. I'll figure out what we need to do." Tea forgotten, he dumped out the pot of water and stared at the fire until nothing remained but coals.

Finally, he crawled into his bedroll. He knew what he must do.

He'd confront his past head-on.

Chapter Nineteen

Wyatt's mind was clear the next morning, despite his lack of sleep. He washed and shaved. He'd recently had a haircut but he might be getting another one for free soon. Might have saved himself the two bits.

He pulled on clean trousers and a clean shirt. Might as well go looking his best.

Lonnie watched him. "What are you doing?"

"I'm going to face my past." He threw a saddle on his horse.

Lonnie jerked to his feet and clenched his fists at his sides. "You're going to turn me in?"

Wyatt grabbed the boy and hugged him tight. "Never. That crime has been paid for. You can forget it." He held his brother until a shuddering breath released his lungs and he relaxed.

"Then what are you doing?" Lonnie's face wrinkled with worry. "What will happen to me?"

"The Bells have promised you can stay with them." It was his one consolation. That and Cora's continued faith in him. "Let's go."

Lonnie held back. "Where are we going?"

Wyatt led his horse and Lonnie trotted after him. "You're going to the Bells and I'm going to deal with this."

He had no idea what he'd say to Cora, but when she faced him, her eyes wide with shock, he wished he'd thought of a way to explain what he meant to do. They escaped to the privacy of the orchard.

"Where are you going?" she asked.

"I can't stay unless I can lay this matter to rest."

"Can't stay?" She turned away from him to stare past the fruit trees.

He looked at the wizened green apples on the tree before him. Hadn't he once wondered if his ways could be grafted into the gentle ways of the Bell family? The question needed to be answered to his satisfaction before he would feel free of his past.

"I need to talk to Jack. Explain this turn of events. He might change his mind about wanting me for a partner."

"And then what?" She gave him a look that pierced to the depths of his soul—accusing, begging, promising all at once. "What if he says no? Will you ride away? And if he says yes, he still wants you to be his partner, is that enough to make you stay?" She grabbed his arms and shook him. "Wyatt, what is enough to make you stay?" She dropped her hands and stepped back. "I hoped I was." Her voice trailed off into despair.

"Cora, you are. But only if I can stay here without fighting my past." He wouldn't tell her any more. No point in filling her with false hope. He pulled her close, brushed her hair back from her forehead and kissed the spot his fingers had touched. "Pray for me." He forced himself to release her and hurried away before he changed his mind.

* * *

"Wyatt." She called his name. "Where are you going? What are you going to do?"

He strode on without turning. Without answering her questions.

"Wyatt!" she screamed, but still he hurried away.

She raced after him, but he swung into his saddle and rode off without a backward look.

Cora sank to the ground. He was gone.

The twins joined her, sitting on either side.

"Lonnie said he went to put his past behind him," Rose said. "What does that mean?"

"What's he going to do?" Lilly asked.

"I don't know," Cora replied. "He's going to see Jack. Says he's going to face his past." She pounded the ground. "Then what?"

The girls pulled her to her feet and led her to the house. Lonnie hovered in the shadows.

Cora had promised that Lonnie would always have a home with them, no matter what. "Come along," she called to him. "Let's see if Ma has tea and cookies." Did Ma have a special blend to fix broken hearts?

She joined the others at the table. Heard her parents say Wyatt would do what was right. All the while her thoughts circled madly.

What was right for Wyatt? If he thought leaving was the thing to do, he was wrong. She couldn't imagine life without him. She didn't care what anyone else said about him. If they accused him of things he hadn't done, she'd face them defiantly. If they tried to drive him away, she'd tell them to mind their own business.

And if he felt he had to leave the community, she would go with him.

She would stand by his side through good and bad because—

"I love him." She blurted out the words, then clamped her hand to her mouth.

Lonnie stared.

"Well, I do," she said, bringing her gaze to her ma. Would she scold Cora?

But Ma smiled gently. "Does he know?"

"I never told him."

Pa cleared his throat. "It might make a difference."

She nodded. "But what am I to do now?"

"I think you're the only one who can answer that," Pa said.

"I need to think and pray." She excused herself and hurried to the river, where she could be alone with the vast rolling plains and the majestic mountains and listen to the tumbling of the water.

"God, I love him. I thank You for bringing him into my life." She trusted Wyatt without reservation, but a thread of fear lingered. What if he left? Just like her papa. Just like Evan. She snorted. Wyatt was not Evan or her father. He was a man willing to face difficulties and do what was right. *Thank You, God, for bringing such a man into my life. He's shown me a man can be trusted.*

If God brought Wyatt to her, did He not have a plan for how to deal with this problem? What was her role in it?

"God, show me what to do. Help people see that Wyatt is innocent of any crime in the past or present."

That was it! The answer she needed. She would go to Sheriff Thomas and explain that Wyatt was innocent without implicating Lonnie.

She raced back to the house. "Pa, Pa, I need to go to town." She explained her plan.

"You do what you must do." Pa hitched the horse to the wagon. "Just don't do anything rash."

She waved as she drove the wagon forward. She'd do whatever she needed to prove to one and all that Wyatt was not only innocent but a good man they should welcome into the community.

Wyatt found Jack in the barn examining a harness.

"I been expecting you," the older man said. "Where's that brother of yours? I've been wanting to meet him."

"I didn't bring him. There've been some developments that might be cause enough for you to change your mind about wanting us to join you."

Jack grunted. "Sounds like something we should discuss over coffee. Come to the house."

Wyatt couldn't stop himself from looking around as they crossed the yard. He'd need more corrals if he meant to raise horses and break them. Maybe add a shed to the side of the barn for Lonnie's pigs.

His fists clenched as he forced his thoughts to stop. They might never move here.

"Whatever you got to say can wait until I pour coffee." The blackened, dented pot stood on the back of the stove. Jack threw a chunk of wood into the stove and pulled the pot forward.

Wyatt thought the man had made an attempt to tidy the place since Wyatt had seen it a couple of days ago. He tried to see it through Cora's eyes.

Why was he tormenting himself with such thoughts? Yes, he wanted to share his life with her, do everything in his power to make her happy. But she'd never said anything to make him think she felt the same, and he sure hadn't spoken the words buried deep in his heart. A couple of times he'd considered doing so, but now he was glad he hadn't.

Jack set two chipped cups on the table and poured in coffee so black Wyatt thought he might have to use a spoon to get it from the cup. No milk or sugar was offered.

Wyatt hoped he wouldn't choke on the stuff that Jack sucked back with obvious satisfaction.

Jack nursed his cup. "Now tell me what's bothering you."

Wyatt began with how his father had grown mean, meaner with every passing day. How Wyatt had tried to protect Lonnie from the abuse. "I guess I was more like a father to him than our pa."

The story poured forth, every detail revealed. "Lonnie didn't handle the beatings as well as I did. Inside, I told myself the old man could beat me to death but he could never touch me. Just my body. Lonnie was different. He let it hurt him inside. Until he couldn't take any more."

Jack nodded occasionally but never interrupted Wyatt's flow of words.

"One day I was away from home and Pa flew into a rage. Near as I can figure, he went after Lonnie with a shovel. Somehow Lonnie got it from him and turned on Pa. When I found them I had to pry the shovel from Lonnie's hands. Pa was unconscious and bleeding. Someone had heard the commotion and called the sheriff. They found me with the shovel in my hands. It was easy to say I did it."

"So you went to jail to protect your brother and now

everyone says you're a jailbird and a dangerous man? That about sum it up?"

"There's a little more. The people in town believe I'm responsible for the rash of thefts." He allowed himself a beat of silence before he added, "I'll understand if you withdraw your offer."

Jack fixed him with eyes that made Wyatt feel exposed. "Huh. So you going to turn tail and run?"

"Maybe. If that's what it takes."

Jack had been tipped back on two legs of his chair but now he crashed down. "Boy, tell me one thing. Do you want to throw in with me?"

"Almost as much as I want Cora to be part of our agreement."

"Fine. I'd say you got plenty of reason to stand and fight. If you have a mind to, that is."

Wyatt nodded. "I have a mind to, all right. But I don't know if it will do any good."

"Guess you won't know if you don't try."

"Guess I won't."

Jack slammed his cup to the table. "So why are you still here?"

It wasn't until Wyatt was on the road that he thought of the answer to Jack's question. Because he didn't have any idea what to do.

Somehow he found himself heading toward town. That seemed as good a place as any to start standing. He rode down the main street. Looking neither left nor the right, he made his way to the sheriff's office.

He tied his horse to the post and strode inside as if he knew exactly what he meant to do.

Sheriff Thomas sat behind his big wooden desk, sharpening a pencil with his pocketknife. He saw Wyatt, closed his knife, stuck it in his trousers pocket and put the pencil at the top of the blotter covering the desk in front of him.

"What can I do for you?"

"I haven't come to confess to anything, if that's what you're thinking."

"Can't say as I was thinking that, but okay."

Seemed the man wasn't going to invite Wyatt to sit, so Wyatt grabbed a chair and pulled it to the desk. "I've been in jail, just like everyone says. But I'm no criminal."

"Uh-huh." The man packed a lot of doubt into a couple of syllables. "Then why were you in jail?"

Wyatt stared at the sharpened pencil. How much could he tell without sounding like a whiner and without bringing censure down on Lonnie?

"Someone got beat up. And I went to jail, but I didn't do it."

"Let me guess. You're protecting someone?"

"I'd do it again if I had to."

The sheriff shoved his chair back. "They don't send innocent men to jail. You didn't answer my question."

"Is the penalty paid?"

"I guess it is."

"So no one will have to go to jail for it in the future?" He had to know in case the truth about Lonnie got out. He'd leave and ride clear to the Yukon with his brother if he thought the boy would end up in prison.

"Can't see it happening unless that person confesses."

That wasn't going to happen. If Lonnie ever got the notion in his head, Wyatt would point out he'd gone of his own free will, and his sacrifice would be wasted if Lonnie went, too.

"That's good to know. I hope you'll believe me when

I say I was innocent when I went to jail, and I'm innocent of these current crimes."

The sheriff tipped his chair back and considered Wyatt for a long moment. "You willing to prove that?"

"I'll do whatever it takes."

"Then make yourself comfortable in one of the cells while I investigate these robberies."

"You're locking me up?" He sprang to his feet. "What kind of justice is that?"

"Look at it from my side of the desk. If you are truly innocent, you'll hunker down and wait for me to complete my investigation. If you leave, what assurance do I have that you won't ride away? The thought tends to make me a little nervous."

Wyatt considered his options and finally nodded. "If that's what it will take to convince you." He followed the sheriff into the cell block with its two side-by-side cells. His nerves jangled in time to the keys the sheriff carried. He never thought he'd be back in jail. And of his own accord.

He turned his back as the sheriff clattered the door closed and locked it. He flung himself down on the hard, bare mattress and stared at the pocked ceiling. This might be the second hardest thing he'd ever done.

He'd done the first one to protect Lonnie. He did this for the hope of putting the past behind him and living in this community.

About all he could do at this point was wait and pray.

The street door opened and closed a number of times. Once he heard voices, then all was silent. Was he alone?

He stared at the cell door. Did he lie on the cot in vain?

While he hoped to be proved innocent, was the sheriff collecting evidence to prove him guilty?

Was this to turn into something he'd regret?

Chapter Twenty

Cora pulled the wagon to a halt in front of the sheriff's office and jumped to the ground.

Young Robert Patton ran along the boardwalks, the thump of his shoes echoing loudly. He skidded to a halt in front of Cora.

"Ya looking for the sheriff?"

"Why, yes I am."

"He ain't here."

She hadn't considered that possibility. "Do you know where I can find him?"

"Nope. Best you wait for him to come back."

"Okay." Wait? She didn't have the patience to wait. But what choice did she have? She glanced up and down the street, but she didn't want to visit with anyone or face questions as to why she was in town on a Monday afternoon.

A trio of ladies stepped from Frank's Hardware and Necessities. One looked in her direction then leaned over to speak to the others.

Cora turned and hurried away, not stopping until she reached the church. She tiptoed inside. The place was empty. She sat on the end of the nearest pew and let the quiet fill her senses.

God, I know Wyatt is innocent. Help me be able to make the sheriff and everyone in town see it.

She sat for some time as peace and assurance filled her soul. God would make the truth clear to everyone. She had to believe it. For she doubted Wyatt would stay if he had to live with daily accusations.

But either way, before he left, she would tell him how she felt.

And if he still left…

Well, she'd been left before and she'd survived. Her insides curled like dry autumn leaves. This time would be different. She couldn't imagine the agony. She'd told herself she'd leave with him, but would he ask her? Could she ride away from Ma and Pa and the twins? If she must, she would. She would do whatever was necessary to be with Wyatt.

She sprang to her feet. She must convince the sheriff Wyatt was innocent.

Her racing feet carried her back to the sheriff's office and she burst inside. Sheriff Thomas sat behind the desk but leaped to his feet at her rushed entrance.

"Miss Cora, to what do I owe this honor?"

She hurried to the chair across the desk from him and perched on the edge. "I've come about Wyatt. Wyatt Williams. I know people are saying all sorts of things about him but they aren't true. He simply can't have robbed anyone."

"What proof do you have?"

"I know it in here." She pressed her hand to her heart.

The sheriff smiled gently. "And you consider that proof?"

"Sheriff, I love him. I know without a doubt that he's a good and noble man. What you need to understand is he is so noble he would go to jail for another person."

The sheriff nodded, his look thoughtful. "Miss Cora, I value your opinion, since you are such an upright citizen, but to prove anything, I need good, solid evidence. Do you have that?"

She thought for a moment. He'd helped on the barn. He'd taken good care of his horses. He was tender and gentle with Lonnie. He'd kissed her. Without thought, she pressed her fingers to her lips and then, realizing what she did, she jerked them away. All of those things and many more proved his innocence to her satisfaction. But they weren't the sort of thing the sheriff meant. She shook her head. "I don't suppose I could prove it to you."

"I see."

Dare she tell him why Wyatt had been in prison? But wouldn't revealing the truth about Lonnie invalidate the year Wyatt had served to protect him? She couldn't share that bit of information.

"Sheriff, I beg you to get to the bottom of these robberies. If you do, you'll certainly discover that Wyatt is innocent." She pushed to her feet. "Now, if you'll excuse me, I have someplace I need to be."

She meant to tell Wyatt she loved him no matter what.

But first she had to find him. Wyatt had said he'd go see Jack Henry. She'd go there in the hopes of finding him.

She strode from the sheriff's office and was almost trampled by two men dragging a third, who fought and cursed.

She squinted at the man being dragged. She'd seen him before. Where?

What did it matter? She had more important things to be concerned about.

"You got the wrong man," he shouted. "It's that jail-bird Wyatt Williams you should be dragging here."

Those words stopped her dead. She knew where she'd seen that man before. By the livery barn. And Wyatt had stared at him as if he recognized him.

Somehow the two were connected, and she meant to find out how. She followed them into the sheriff's office.

They pushed the struggling man against the desk.

"This fella had all sorts of things stashed under his mattress." The speaker dumped coins, jewelry and paper money on the sheriff's desk.

"It's been planted," the man insisted. "It wasn't there when I left this morning."

"Uh-huh." The sheriff crossed his arms and gave the man a hard look. "So who would plant it?"

"Wyatt Williams, I've no doubt."

"Who are you and how do you know Wyatt Williams?"

"Name's Jimmy Stone and I knew Wyatt when he wasn't pretending to be such an upright citizen."

"In jail, you mean?"

"That's right." Then, realizing he'd put himself where he wanted everyone to believe Wyatt belonged, he hastened to add, "Not that I was there myself, you understand."

"If you say so." The sheriff sighed heavily. "Might interest you to know Wyatt couldn't have planted the evidence."

"Huh. Suppose he told you some wild story about being innocent and you believed him."

"I'm inclined to believe his story, seeing as he's been

locked in my jail for the past few hours, and before that he was with Jack Henry. So you see, I have all the evidence I need to believe him."

Cora was grateful for the chair near the door when her legs started wobbling. She sat down before she fell on the floor.

"He's here?" she squeaked.

"Yup." The sheriff drawled the word. He tossed a set of keys to one of the men. "Unlock him and put this man in there. You," he said to Jimmy Stone, "will be tried. Best you be prepared to return to jail."

The man struggled all the way through the door at the back of the office.

Cora stared at the cells beyond. Wyatt was there? He'd been there all along? She wanted to run to him, but her legs refused to work.

Before she could even stand, Wyatt came out, followed by the two men who had assisted the sheriff.

"Thanks, boys." The sheriff waved to them as they went outside.

Sheriff Thomas leaned against the desk. "It appears to me you two have some unfinished business. I'll leave you to deal with it. Wyatt, when you're done, your horse is out back." He headed for the door then paused. "I believe the truth about Wyatt's innocence has been revealed. I suggest the two of you make the truth about your feelings just as clear." He slipped out and closed the door quietly behind him.

Cora stared at Wyatt. Did he seem older, more drawn, than when she'd seen him this morning? Then a smile touched the corners of his mouth and he looked just right. She couldn't ask for better.

His smile didn't go any further. Was he upset at her for getting involved with Sheriff Thomas?

"I had to come," she said. "I had to make the sheriff see the truth. Though I guess he was looking for it all along."

"I heard you."

For a moment she was confused by his reply, then its meaning hit her. He'd heard her say she loved him? "Every word?" she asked, her mouth suddenly dry.

"Every word." The smile that toyed with his mouth now filled his eyes, widened his lips and lit his face. "Every sweet, telling word." He pulled her to her feet.

Her gaze clung to his. Now was her chance to say the words she'd vowed to say, directly to the man himself.

But when she opened her mouth to speak, he pressed a fingertip to her lips.

"I have something to say first." He studied every feature of her face until she felt as if her skin would bloom like summer flowers.

He brought his gaze back to her eyes. "I couldn't tell you this before my name was cleared, but, Cora Bell, I love you and I want to share the rest of my life with you. Now, I know there will still be people who judge me because I've been in jail, so maybe it's not fair to ask you to share that—"

She pressed her fingertips to his mouth. "Shh. It's my turn to speak. Wyatt Williams, I love you now and forever. I don't care what others say. I know what kind of man you are."

"What kind is that?" His voice thickened.

"A noble, kind, giving, honorable, loving, protective man. One who I know will never fail me, never abandon me, never intentionally hurt me."

He swallowed hard. "That's a lot to live up to. I'm bound to fail."

"As am I. But what counts is moving forward. We'll forgive each other when we fail and we'll grow better and stronger together." She ducked her head. Had she rushed him into more than he meant to give? "If you want it that way...."

He tipped her head so they looked full into each other's eyes. "Cora Bell, would you marry me and make me the happiest man on the face of the earth?"

"Do I have the power to do that?" she asked through her smile. "To make you happy? It seems like a tall order."

He chuckled. "Your love makes me happy. Like I've never been before."

"Your love makes me so happy I feel as if I'm going to burst. Yes, I'll marry you."

"I never knew love could feel this way." He looked awestruck, then blinked and bent his head to hers.

She wound her arms about his waist, pressed her palms to his back and lifted her face to him. Her heart beat a steady rhythm against her chest. She felt his heart's answering beat, and then their lips touched and nothing else mattered but this man and their love.

Epilogue

Three weeks later

Cora stood inside the back room of the church and smoothed the front of her ivory-colored wedding dress. At first, she'd demurred at the idea of a new dress that she would only wear once, but the twins had begged her to go ahead.

"We'll help make it," Rose had said.

"Maybe someday we'll wear it." Lilly had gotten dreamy eyed. "Wouldn't it be special if we all wore the same dress for our weddings?"

So Cora had agreed. They'd picked a simple style with a full satin skirt, leg-of-mutton sleeves and lacy accents at the shoulders.

Rose arranged the back of the skirt to her liking. "It's a beautiful gown."

Cora agreed. "I feel like a princess."

"About to marry her prince."

Cora smiled so wide it almost hurt, but there was no room in her heart for anything painful. "I'm so happy."

Somehow her sisters managed to hug her without mussing her hair or her dress.

"You deserve to be happy," Rose said.

Cora nodded. "I'm glad we'll be living close enough that I can make sure you two are okay."

The twins exchanged looks and a secret flickered through their eyes.

"What is it you're not telling me?" Cora asked. She caught each of them by the hand. "I don't want you to feel like you can't share all your secrets with me anymore."

Rose patted Cora's hand. "We know you feel responsible for us."

"You don't need to," Lilly added.

"We're grown up now. It's time for you to move on and think about your own happiness instead of ours."

"They're the same thing. My happiness would never be complete if I thought either of you was unhappy."

"We're both happy and we don't want you to worry about us," Rose said. "Promise us you'll do that."

Cora nodded, her throat tight. "I promise." She leaned over and kissed them each on the cheek. "I'll miss you."

Rose chuckled. "We'll see each other so often you won't have a chance."

"If you need any more help getting your place into shape, just let us know and we'll come," Lilly offered. She and Rose had accompanied Cora, Wyatt and Lonnie to Jack Henry's place for several days. They'd helped Jack clean out his things from the house and move them to the little cabin where he and his wife had first lived.

At first, Cora had demurred. "We'll take the cabin," she'd said. "I've no wish to displace you."

Jack had chuckled long and hard at that. "You're doing me a favor. All I need is a bed, a table and a stove. All this—" he'd waved around the room of the house where they stood "—is too much work for me."

So Cora had continued to clean the house. Her sisters had helped her wash the walls and cupboards. They'd made the wooden floors gleam. Jack had insisted he didn't need all the kitchen things, so they'd washed every pot, pan and dish, and arranged them in the clean cupboards.

Cora had let the twins help clean the smaller bedroom where Lonnie would sleep, but she'd insisted she alone would arrange the furniture of the bedroom she and Wyatt would share.

As she made the bed and hung new curtains, her heart rejoiced. When the room was done to her satisfaction, awaiting their marriage, she'd knelt by the side of the bed to thank God for their love and for the bright future ahead of them. *Bless us with happiness and a large family.*

Organ music began to play in the sanctuary of the church, pulling Cora from thoughts of her new home. Anna had insisted on playing for the ceremony.

When wedding plans had been discussed initially, Wyatt had suggested they get married at the farm with just family present. "I'm not sure the community is ready to accept me."

Cora had, at that moment, decided she wanted a big church wedding. "No more will we hide from what people think. This is our community. There are people here who accept us without reservation. The rest will soon learn that they are wrong."

Pastor and Mrs. Rawley had been thrilled at their decision to get married in the church.

"May I have the honor of providing tea after the ceremony?" Mrs. Rawley had asked.

Ma had agreed to accept her help.

Cora could hardly wait any longer for her wedding. And she didn't have to.

"It's time," the twins said, taking her hands.

They each kissed her, then slipped through the door.

Cora peeked out to watch her sisters follow each other up the aisle. Then she got her first glimpse of her groom.

Wyatt stood at the front, so handsome, so strong and noble that her heart swelled with joy.

Lonnie stood beside him. He pulled at the collar of his shirt and then stood at attention.

Beside Lonnie stood Jack Henry. He cut a striking figure in his suit. She'd grown fond of the old man in the past few weeks.

She glanced around the church, saw a goodly number of people in attendance and smiled. Just as she'd hoped, people were accepting Wyatt. *Thank You, God.*

"Are you ready?"

She turned to Pa. "I'm ready." She drank in his familiar, comforting face. "Pa, I owe you a world of thanks. You've been the best father I could ever ask for. I love you." She leaned over and kissed his cheek.

Pa squeezed her shoulder. She understood he would have hugged her, except he didn't want to disturb her dress. "I love you, too, daughter. You have been a true gift and a blessing from God." His words grew thick and he swallowed hard. "Best not to keep Wyatt waiting any longer."

They stepped to the aisle and all faces turned toward her.

Wyatt's gaze met hers and the rest of the world slipped

away. She drew closer to him, feeling as though she was walking on air, and took his arm. As if from a distance, she heard the preacher's words and repeated her vows as prompted, but the only part of the ceremony that seemed real was Wyatt's kiss.

"I present to you Mr. and Mrs. Wyatt Williams," the preacher announced.

They marched down the aisle and outside to where the side yard was festooned with streaming crepe paper and flowers. She ate the tiny sandwiches and cake handed to her, clinging to Wyatt's hand to keep herself grounded.

Many people from the church and the town filed by to congratulate them and welcome Wyatt to the community. Many brought gifts, and with Wyatt's help she opened them, almost overcome with emotion at their generosity.

Finally they were able to slip away and head toward their new home, where they could finally be alone.

Lonnie would be staying with Ma and Pa for a few days, and Jack would be camping. He'd said he could hardly wait to ride into the hills without worrying about how things were at home.

Wyatt lifted her from the wagon and carried her into the house. "Here we are."

Cora clung to his shoulders. "Our future begins now."

He nodded. "No looking back." He claimed her mouth in a sweet, gentle kiss, then set her on the floor. "Cora Williams, I love you."

"I love you." She wrapped her arms about his neck and kissed him again.

He held her close. "I never thought I'd see the day when I would know such love."

She laughed with pure joy. "Our love will grow richer

and sweeter every day." She'd do her best to see her words came true.

He kissed her again and she forgot everything but this wonderful man God had brought into her life.

* * * * *

BIG SKY DADDY

He brought me up also out of an horrible pit,
out of the miry clay, and set my feet upon a rock,
and established my goings.
—*Psalms* 40:2

My father taught me many things: how to shoot a gun, how to drive a car, how to find fossils in a gravel bed, how to recognize the constellations in the sky, but most of all, through his example, he taught me how a noble, kind man should act. This book is dedicated to his memory.

Chapter One

~

Bar Crossing, Montana
Fall 1889

Did he hear gunshots? Caleb Craig jerked toward the window. "Listen." He held up his hand, trying to cut short the storekeeper's detailed description about the young woman who had stepped out of the store as Caleb and his son, Teddy, went in.

"Lilly Bell," the storekeeper had said. Twin sister to Rose, the two were the least alike, though to be sure, both were sweet and generous and loyal. Their parents were elderly, but that didn't mean they were feeble. Oh, far from it.

A series of pops convinced Caleb someone had set off firecrackers. They were not as deadly as gunshots, but they were enough to start a dangerous chain reaction.

Before he reached the window, Caleb knew it had already started. Several women screamed. A deeper voice called out. The rattle and creak of wood and harnesses signaled frantic horses.

"You stay here," he ordered five-year-old Teddy, and then raced through the door.

The young woman, whose virtues the storekeeper expounded on even as Caleb hustled out of the shop, wrestled with a rearing horse hitched to a swaying wagon. Packages and sacks tumbled out the back. A redheaded woman raced toward the struggling gal. *That must be the twin sister, Rose.* An older man hobbled across the street toward them while other people huddled on the sidewalks, watching but doing nothing.

Caleb saw it all in one glance as he jumped to Lilly's side and grabbed the harness, his hand right next to hers.

"Steady there," he ordered, his voice stern yet kind—something animals understood.

Breathing raggedly, the horse allowed Caleb to pull his head down. Still holding tight to the animal, as was she, Caleb turned to the young woman. The name Lilly suited her. Blond hair, unblemished skin, blue eyes flashing like lightning.

She was understandably upset.

"What idiot set off firecrackers?" he demanded.

She snorted. "That Caldwell cowboy."

Ebner? His boss? Caleb glanced about but saw no sign of the Caldwell foreman. "Is anyone hurt?"

The redhead rushed to their side. "Lilly, are you okay?" She rubbed her hands over the young woman's arms. "I saw the whole thing." She jammed her fists to her hips. "I can't believe anyone would do such a stupid thing. Not even a Caldwell."

Caleb's neck tensed. He'd been working at the Caldwell ranch a couple of weeks now. Ebner was tough, allowing no slacking and objecting to Caleb keeping Teddy with him as he worked. Caleb had reminded Ebner several times it had been part of the agreement before Caleb had taken the job.

Mr. Caldwell was away on some errand, leaving Ebner in charge. The foreman ran the place with efficiency. Caleb had certainly seen no sign of such wanton disregard for the safety of man and beast.

"I'm fine," Lilly said. She sucked in air as if to calm her nerves and faced Caleb. "Thank you for your help. I saw you at the store, didn't I?"

"Yes, ma'am." He gave his name.

"Pleased to make your acquaintance." The smile she gave him could have changed rain to sunshine.

"Papa." Teddy's trembling voice made them all turn toward his son. Both ladies murmured, "Ah," as they saw Teddy.

Caleb understood how the boy would pull at one's heart. Big blue eyes, tousled hair that refused to be tamed, a look of innocence, though it was impossible there could be any innocence left after what the boy had been through. Teddy leaned on his crutches, his right leg not touching the floor.

"Son, I asked you to stay inside."

"I know, Papa. But what if something happened to you?"

Lilly's attention flickered between Caleb and Teddy. Rose's lingered on the boy.

"I don't intend for anything to happen to me."

Teddy nodded, his expression more worried than relieved.

"You stay there while I help these ladies collect their packages."

"Yes, Papa."

"That's my boy."

An older man approached them. "Are you girls okay?"

"We're fine, Pa," the pair chorused.

So this was Mr. Bell. Caleb introduced himself. In turn, Mr. Bell introduced his daughters.

The horse had settled down. Caleb left Mr. Bell holding him and strode to the back of the wagon to gather up parcels and return them to the box.

Lilly scurried around to pick up things as well. "I hope nothing was damaged."

Teddy hobbled along the sidewalk to see better what Caleb was doing.

Lilly lifted a sack and paused to watch the boy. There was no mistaking the question in her eyes. She was wondering why the boy wasn't walking.

If only someone could provide that answer.

"Caleb." Ebner rode toward the wagon. "Leave them people to gather up their own stuff. You get our wagon on home now. Hear?"

"Yes, boss."

Lilly glowered at Ebner as he rode away laughing. Then she turned toward Caleb. "You work for them?" She grabbed the package from his hands and shook it as if his mere touch had somehow soiled it.

"Yes, ma'am. 'Fraid I do." And if he wanted to keep his job, he needed to do as the boss said. "Glad no one was hurt."

She snorted. "I'm sure your boss won't agree."

If only he could explain. But what could he say? His job with the Caldwells was too important to risk losing over a few packages in the dirt. He needed the money to take Teddy to a new doctor down east. Perhaps this special doctor would be able to say why Teddy still wasn't using his leg though it had healed up. At least on the outside. The several doctors he'd already seen suggested there was nerve damage. Or something. They had all been vague and none had helped in any way.

"Goodbye." He included the sister and father in his nod and joined Teddy on the sidewalk. "Let's get going."

The walk toward the wagon couldn't be hurried even though Teddy had gotten good at walking with his crutches over the past few months. At the wagon, he scooped Teddy up and set him on the seat. "Now don't you be driving off without me."

Teddy laughed. "You know I can't drive a wagon." He leaned forward as if to take the reins. "Unless you let me."

Caleb climbed up and sat beside his son. "Seems to me it's about time you learned." He pulled the boy to his lap and let him hold the reins, his big hands firmly on Teddy's small ones.

Teddy turned his face up to Caleb and gave him a smile as wide as the sky.

Caleb's heart caught the smile and clung to it, determined not to let the past steal the joy of this precious moment or any others yet to come with his son.

If only he could go back and undo the past. But he couldn't. He couldn't bring back his wife, nor could he stop the thugs from breaking in and taking her life. He'd discovered them and shot them, but in the gunfight Teddy had been injured. Caleb's throat constricted with the same mire of emotions he'd experienced when he found his son, his leg bloody, his little face filled with terror.

Caleb swallowed hard and forced air into his lungs. He'd never know if he had been the one who fired the shot that hit Teddy. He lived for only one thing—to see Teddy's fears end and the boy walk normally again.

If that required him to work for the Caldwells knowing Ebner could stoop to such dastardly deeds, well, that wasn't his concern now, was it?

As if suspecting Caleb might be having second thoughts, Ebner rode up beside him.

"You've got to understand something. The Caldwells don't get along with the Bells. We've been feuding ever since the Bells had the gall to file claim to a piece of land right plumb in the middle of Caldwell land. Seems some ignorant file clerk made a mistake. But will the Bells do the right thing and go farm somewhere else? Nope. They've got to keep on causing trouble. No one who works for the Caldwells can figure on being friends with the Bells. Understand?"

Caleb nodded. "Don't see I've got any cause to have truck with them."

"See that you don't." Ebner rode away, leaving Caleb to muse about his words.

"Papa, that man at the store, Mr. Frank, he said the Bells were nice people."

"Uh-huh. I expect they are." The way Rose and Mr. Bell had clustered around Lilly to make sure she wasn't hurt sure made him think so. It'd been a long time since he'd seen such care and devotion. Or rather since he'd experienced it. Amanda had been an efficient housekeeper and a good mother to Teddy, but she'd been distant and critical when it came to Caleb. He stilled his thoughts. One didn't speak evil of the dead even in his mind.

They rumbled down the road toward the Caldwell ranch, Teddy so focused on handling the horse that he never lifted his eyes from the animal.

Something in the bushes to the side of the road caught Caleb's attention. At first he thought someone had discarded a cow hide and wondered if there were rustlers about, but then he made out a nose and ears. A pup. Dead by the look of it.

He didn't want Teddy to notice, so he leaned over the boy. "Remember, you must always hold the reins as if something could startle your horse. Never get so relaxed he could get away from you."

Teddy pulled his hands from Caleb's and straightened, leaning hard into Caleb's shoulder as he turned to look to the side. "Papa, it's a dog."

"Don't you want to drive the wagon still?"

Teddy patted Caleb's shoulder. "He's hurt."

"Son, we have to get back." *Please, Teddy. Let it go. You don't want to see any more suffering and death.*

"Papa, he needs our help."

When Caleb continued onward, Teddy pounded his shoulder. "Papa, you can't leave him. You can't. He's hurt. You have to help. Stop. Please stop." Tears mingled with Teddy's demands.

Caleb pulled the wagon to a stop and held Teddy by the shoulders. "Son, he's dead and I don't want you to see it."

Teddy flung his father's hands off his shoulders. "You don't know that. What if he's only hurt?" He pursed his lips and gave Caleb a narrow-eyed look. "You ain't gonna just leave him there to die, are you?"

"He's already dead." How could such a small body hold so much stubbornness?

"Then we need to bury him."

Caleb would have protected his son from ever again seeing blood and death and burial, but the boy seemed to have other thoughts on the matter. "Very well." He jumped down, lifted Teddy to the ground, handed him his crutches and grabbed a shovel out of the wagon. He followed his son to the dog.

A pair of eyes opened and followed their approach.

"Papa, he's alive."

Caleb knelt by the dog. It had been slashed, and whimpered as if in pain. He saw it was a female. "Teddy, she's barely alive and she's hurting." He pushed to his feet. "I want you to come back to the wagon." He waited for the boy to obey, but Teddy only looked at him in puzzlement.

"Why, Papa?"

"Just do as I say." Caleb's feet felt heavy as rocks as he went back to the wagon and reached under the seat. He had to do what he had to do. *It will be a kindness. The poor animal shouldn't be allowed to suffer.*

Teddy hobbled after him, saw Caleb reach for the rifle and screamed. "No. You can't shoot my dog." He scrambled to the animal so fast Caleb held his breath for fear he'd fall and further injure himself.

"She's my dog." Teddy huddled forward. "Ain't nobody ever gonna hurt her."

"Son, she isn't going to live."

"You're wrong."

He tried every argument to convince Teddy of the futility of trying to save the dog, but his son would not relent. Though Caleb saw nothing ahead but sorrow and regret, he couldn't stay at the side of the road any longer. He wrapped the injured dog in a gunny sack and carried her gingerly to the wagon. "We'll take her home and stay with her so she doesn't die alone." He made the animal as comfortable as possible.

"I'll stay with her."

Knowing when to concede defeat, Caleb lifted Teddy in beside the dog and continued on his way. At the ranch he pulled up to the storage shed and unloaded the supplies. Thankfully Ebner wasn't around to demand he explain why it had taken so long to get back. It also saved Caleb from confronting the man about how he'd treated the Bells.

His task done, he carried the dog over to the covered wagon he shared with Teddy. He could have joined the others in the bunkhouse, but it wasn't the sort of atmosphere he wanted Teddy exposed to. It would soon get too cold to sleep in the wagon—he counted on having enough money to head east before then.

"You know what Mr. Frank said?" Teddy sat beside the dog, rubbing a spot behind the animal's ear.

"He said a lot of things." The man had seemed bent on informing Caleb about the "beautiful Bell girls." He'd overlooked one tiny detail—the Bells and the Caldwells didn't get along.

"He said that pretty lady you helped knew how to fix things."

"Things?" Was she a blacksmith? He couldn't imagine it, but he'd encountered stranger things in the West.

"Hurt things." Teddy must have thought he needed to explain her abilities more. "Mr. Frank said she helps people, too, and all kinds of animals."

Caleb smiled at his son's enthusiasm. "Hurt people, too, huh?" He wondered if she could help him. He silently laughed in derision. It was those around him who would need her help. People who got close to him tended to get hurt.

"But especially hurt dogs." Teddy gave Caleb a wide-eyed, pleading look that brought a smile to Caleb's lips. How long had it been since Teddy had cared enough about something to use that special look of his?

"What are you saying, son?" As if he didn't know. But he dared not give the boy any encouragement. The dog looked beyond saving.

"We could ask her to help my dog."

"It might not do any good." But what harm would it do? Perhaps Lilly *could* help. Perhaps Caleb could protect his son from more pain.

"Couldn't we try, please?"

Lilly put the last of the packages into the wagon and then stared after Caleb and his son. Poor little fellow was limited by having to use crutches. Had he broken his leg? Perhaps he had a severe cut. She hoped, whatever the cause, the injury was temporary. *God, please help the little fellow get better.*

Caleb was so tender with the lad. He had lifted him to the wagon seat and laughed at him, and then had taken him on his lap as they drove away, little Teddy almost bursting with pride as he gripped the reins.

There was a time she'd hoped she'd have a little boy or girl of her own. But thanks to one Karl Mueller, she'd given up such dreams.

Tightness weaved around her spine. How could she have let herself care so deeply? And in hindsight, so foolishly? She could put it down to age. She had been a mere sixteen years old when she'd been thrilled and somewhat surprised at the attention he'd paid her. After all, he had been handsome and so grown-up at eighteen. So attentive. He'd made her feel important when he tipped his head to listen to her talk. She'd told him her dreams and her fears. He'd assured her he understood. They'd agreed that when Lilly turned eighteen they would marry. And she'd trusted him. Sometimes she wondered if Karl really believed the things he'd promised, or if they'd fallen off his tongue simply because he thought they would please her. One thing Karl liked was to know people were happy with him.

Karl had saved his announcement for her eighteenth birthday, as if it might have been a reason for celebration. He'd revealed he had other plans. He'd been employed by Mr. Fry at the hardware store for a year. Mr. Fry said how much he appreciated Karl's work and asked him to go to Oregon to take over the operation of another Fry store. Karl's chest had expanded three sizes as he told Lilly this.

Karl had never once suggested she accompany him. His words made it very clear that it wasn't part of his plan. "My time and attention must be on this business. I intend to make this the most successful store Mr. Fry has. He'll be so pleased he'll make me a partner." Karl fairly glowed with self-satisfaction. He'd never expressed a word of sorrow over ending their plans so abruptly. Never suggested they keep in contact. Never even—she sucked in air heated by her anger—asked if she'd like to join him once he'd settled into his new job.

She'd finally learned her lesson, one she should have learned at a very young age. She and her sisters had been abandoned by their birth father after their mother's death, and had been left alone on the prairie to find their own way in life when the twins were three and Cora was five. It had set the tone for Lilly's relationships. Easy come, easier go.

Ever since Karl had left her, she had guarded her heart. That meant no man of her own. No child of her own. But never mind. She had Ma and Pa and her sisters and the many animals she took care of. That was enough for any woman.

Rose nudged her. "Stop staring at him. Have you forgotten he's a Caldwell cowboy?"

"I haven't forgotten. At least he had the decency to help us." She and Rose climbed to the seat of the wagon and Pa got wearily into the back. He had mentioned several times how the cold hurt his bones and it was only October. When they got home, she'd ask Ma to give him a tonic.

She guided the wagon out of town. "I wonder what's wrong with his boy."

Rose turned to face her squarely. "Don't you go getting all interested in them."

Lilly snorted. "I don't intend to." She glanced back. Pa had stretched out, his head resting on one of the sacks, and fallen asleep. "I haven't forgotten Karl, you know."

"He wasn't the right man for you. He only cared about himself."

Lilly tried to remember what it was that had attracted her, but after a moment's thought she realized a couple of things. Although Karl had let her talk about her dreams, he had done far more talking than listening, and more importantly, her insides no longer wrenched at the sound of his name. She'd finally been able to push the sharp pain of his leaving from her mind.

She didn't intend to ever again give someone the right to hurt her like Karl had. "He certainly didn't think I was right for him. Good thing I found it out when I did."

"Karl is completely forgettable."

"Guess it goes both ways." Lilly's thoughts turned back to the events in front of the store. "I don't think he knew Ebner threw the firecrackers." Caleb had seemed somewhat surprised.

Rose chuckled. "I don't think we're talking about Karl anymore."

Lilly laughed. "He's forgettable, remember?" Though she wouldn't so readily forget how it had felt to watch him walk away with barely a wave.

Rose giggled. "He certainly jumped to obey when Ebner ordered him to stop helping you."

Lilly knew Rose was back to talking about Caleb.

"I almost expected him to pull his hat off and bow a little," Rose added.

Lilly chuckled, though she didn't find it all that amusing. She'd been surprised and not a little disappointed to realize he worked for the Caldwells and was eager to obey Ebner, the man who had been responsible for so much of the damage inflicted on the Bell farm. Though he was smart enough and cautious enough to always make it look like an accident.

"How can a man with any integrity work for that crew?" Lilly asked. "Wouldn't he have to take part in some of their activities?" Her voice hardened. "Like driving the sheep into the river. I'm not apt to quickly forget that one of the lambs died as a result of it." Not once but twice, the Caldwell cowboys had shepherded the sheep into the river while the Bells were away.

Rose squeezed her hand. "We both know the Caldwells are a bad bunch."

There was no need for Lilly to reply. They all knew the truth about the Caldwells. They insisted it was a mistake made by some inexperienced clerk that a quarter section of land right next to the river had been left off the Caldwells' land title. The Bells should have realized that was the case, Mr. Caldwell insisted, and not taken advantage of the mistake. The Caldwell cowboys had done their best to drive them off before Pa could prove up on the homestead. They'd failed. Even then they hadn't given up.

She realized she was clenching her teeth—something she did every time the Caldwell name came up. Why couldn't they leave the Bells alone? They had thousands of acres. The quarter section Pa owned shouldn't matter.

Over the years, she'd decided the Caldwell quest had nothing to do with reason. Some people weren't happy unless they had everything.

They approached the farm and Lilly allowed herself to study the place with pride. She and her sisters had a hand in developing the few acres into a Garden of Eden along the river despite the Caldwells' objections to their presence. She studied the place hard. The sheep were grazing placidly in their pasture. The milk cows looked up at their approach but didn't move, contentedly chewing their cuds. The hay was safely in the barn, and the oats were harvested and the grain stored for winter use. The garden was almost done as well—only the root vegetables were left to be brought in.

She let out a sigh of relief. "Everything looks the way it should."

"For now." Rose sounded dubious. But then they all knew it was only a matter of time before the Caldwells struck again.

"I hope Ma's all right." Lilly passed the new barn. "It's not like her not to go to town with us."

"She said she was tired."

Lilly glanced back at Pa, who was still asleep. "So is he."

"I think they're missing Cora." Their older sister had married a few weeks ago and moved with her husband, Wyatt, to a nearby ranch.

"Pa thinks he has to take over Cora's chores." Lilly tried to persuade him that she and Rose could manage without his help, but he still offered it constantly. "The cold bothers him. I'm going to ask Ma to give him a tonic. Maybe I'll suggest she take it, too." They drew up before the house. Ma watched from the window.

Pa woke and eased from the wagon. Rose and Lilly hopped down and scurried around to get the packages before Pa could do it.

"Did you sell all the produce?" Ma asked as they entered the kitchen. They took garden produce and medicinals to town each Saturday.

"Every bit of it," Rose assured her.

"Did you see Mrs. Andrews? How is she feeling?"

Lilly answered Ma's question. "She's much improved. I gave her some more cough syrup and I looked at little Andy. He's got a bad case of thrush."

Pa sat at the end of the table and sorted through the mail—mostly newspapers and a farm magazine.

Ma scurried about to make tea and they all sat down to enjoy it. "What's new in town? Did you see Mrs. Rawley?" Ma was speaking about her dear friend the pastor's wife.

"She asked after you," Lilly said.

Rose plunked her teacup on the table. "Ebner threw firecrackers under the horse."

"Goodness." Ma glanced around the table. "Is everyone okay?"

Rose chuckled. "A very handsome cowboy came and helped us."

Lilly squinted at her sister, knowing Rose meant to tease her. "I could have managed on my own."

Rose gave a dismissive shrug. "I didn't see you telling him to leave you alone." She turned to Ma. "Lilly could hardly tear her eyes off the man."

Ma studied each of the girls. "Is this a nice man? Should we invite him to join us for Sunday dinner?"

The skin on Lilly's face grew tight. "Ma, no."

Between them, the two sisters related the events. "The boy doesn't use his right leg," Lilly told her. "He walks with crutches. But Caleb—Mr. Craig—is very patient and tender with him."

"He's a Caldwell cowboy." For Rose that was all that mattered. She, of all the Bells, bore the most resentment toward their neighbors. Probably because Duke Caldwell, the son and heir, had teased Rose throughout school.

Ma held up her hand. "You can't judge a man solely because he works for the Caldwells. A man should be judged by his actions and his choices."

Rose grunted. "He chooses to work for the Caldwells. Guess that says a lot about him."

"Nevertheless," Pa said, with final authority. "We will be fair and give the man the benefit of the doubt until we have reason to think otherwise."

Rose pursed her lips.

Lilly knew her twin didn't think anything good could come from the Caldwell ranch. But finally Rose lowered her challenging gaze from Pa's patient one. "Yes, Pa."

Pa turned to Lilly. "We'll give him the benefit of the doubt, won't we?"

Lilly nodded. "Yes, Pa." She agreed readily enough. For one thing, she'd like to know why Teddy didn't walk.

Maybe she or Ma could help. She'd also like to know how a man who obviously had tender feelings could work for the Caldwells. Or perhaps his feelings were for Teddy and no one and nothing else.

There was one thing she would be clear about. She would not let her interest in the pair go beyond surface curiosity and concern.

Not that she expected she'd see them again unless they happened to bump into each other in town. So guarding her feelings shouldn't be a problem.

A few minutes later she went to the barn to start feeding the animals. She smiled as she stepped into the interior. The barn was cozy and warm and solid. The animals were safe in there.

If she could turn her heart into a solid barn she could keep her feelings safe and warm, too. She chuckled at the silly thought.

When she was done with the feeding, she stepped back outside and blinked as a wagon approached with Caleb in the seat. Teddy peered out from behind his father.

She stared. "What are you doing here?" Her words sounded rude, though she didn't mean them to.

But what was a Caldwell cowboy doing on Bell land?

Chapter Two

Teddy nudged Caleb. "Papa, tell her about my dog."

Caleb's heart swelled as he took in the pretty little farm—the decent-sized, new-looking barn, the outbuildings, the house surrounded by yellow flowers, the garden with pale cornstalks and orange pumpkins still on the vine. Once, he'd had a little ranch similar to this with a herd of cows that had increased in number each year. It was all he'd ever wanted.

His dream of settling down and raising cows and children had vanished the day Amanda had died and Teddy had gotten injured. After that, he couldn't abide the place. He'd taken care of Teddy as his leg healed, and then he'd begun looking for a doctor who could fix his son so he could walk.

"Papa." Teddy's voice brought him back to his task.

He wondered if she would welcome him or ask him to get off their property simply because he worked for the Caldwells. But surely she'd be moved by the needs of an animal and a small boy. He didn't expect or welcome any sympathy regarding his own losses.

He cleared his thoughts and spoke to the woman who

was waiting patiently in front of him, her expression rife with caution. "We got us an injured dog. Mr. Frank told us you help injured animals."

Lilly nodded. "I do my best. Where's the dog?"

He jumped down and went to the back of the wagon to gingerly lift the limp dog out of it. The poor animal whimpered. "Hang on, buddy. We'll help you."

Lilly hovered by his side, her attention on the pup in his arms.

"What happened to it?" Her nearness rattled his insides. He'd vowed to never again think of sharing his life with a woman, but sometimes it was hard to remember that. Like now, as she tenderly ran her fingers over the furry dog. When her arm brushed his, his mouth went dry. He drew in a strengthening breath and righted his thoughts.

"This animal has been neglected." She fired a hot look at him, as if to silently accuse him.

"We found her by the road." He wanted to make it clear he wasn't responsible for the condition of the animal.

"Can you make her better?" Teddy asked.

Thankfully she shifted her powerful gaze to Teddy, and Caleb pulled his thoughts back to where they belonged—finding help for the dog, finding help for his son and preventing any woman from entering his life.

She smiled at Teddy. "I'll certainly do my best."

Her gaze returned to Caleb, warm with a compassion that slowly cooled as she looked at him. He understood her kindness was aimed at Teddy and likely this unfortunate pup. Toward him, she seemed accusatory.

Well, it wasn't like he wasn't used to accusations, mostly from his own thoughts. At twenty-five years of age, he had a number of failures to his name. Likely more than a man twice his age ought to have. He'd failed to protect his wife. He'd failed to help his son with his problems. Letting this dog die in his arms was not another failure he meant to endure. "Can you help?" His question rang with more harshness than he felt. She had no way of knowing he only wanted to make this turn out right.

"Follow me." She hurried toward the barn, seeming to expect him to follow.

He didn't move. He couldn't carry the dog and help Teddy down, too.

"I'll wait," Teddy said.

"See that you do." Caleb gave him a look that ought to have pinned him to the wagon box, but Teddy's eyes lingered on the dog.

Caleb hustled after Lilly. The woman moved like a whirlwind. By the time he caught up she was already inside the barn, a scrap of old blanket on the floor in front of her.

"Put her here. Gently," she urged as if she thought he'd drop the dog.

It was on the tip of his tongue to point out he'd rescued the dog and brought her here for the animal's good and he wasn't about to do anything to make things worse. Instead he knelt and eased the dog to the mat.

She examined the poor critter with gentle fingers. The dog moaned and opened her eyes briefly.

"What do you think?" Sure looked to him like the pup was about to draw her last breath.

"She's very weak. There are a number of cuts on her. She's got some nasty bruises. And she's been badly neglected." Her voice grew harder with each word. "Who would do this to a dog?"

"Same sort who would hurt a woman or child." He heard the strangled sound of his voice but hoped it wasn't noticeable to Lilly. He kept his attention on the suffering animal as a thousand pictures flashed through his mind. Amanda's blood pooling on the floor. Teddy's pale face as Caleb cradled Amanda and tended to his son's wounds.

Lilly nodded her head in decision. "Let's get to work."

"You're gonna save her, aren't you? She's my dog. I want her to live."

They both jerked toward Teddy, who stood in the doorway. Without waiting for an answer, he hobbled toward them.

Lilly's eyes filled with pity.

Caleb stiffened. Pity would not do Teddy any good. The specialist down east had promised to fit the boy with a brace that would teach the leg to work again. Or so the man had claimed. Caleb had long since lost his faith in doctors. "Let's get started."

Lilly bent over the dog, but her hands didn't move. He wondered what she thought about it all—Teddy, the dog, him. Well, he already knew what she thought of him. He worked for the Caldwells. That made him part of the wrong side in a land feud. Good thing she didn't know his past or she'd have reason to think even more poorly of him.

"You want me to get water?" he asked.

She let out a gust of air and nodded. "There's a bucket by the door and the pump is toward the house."

Caleb scrambled to his feet and then hesitated.

She glanced up, a question in her eyes.

"Is it all right if I leave him here?" He gestured with his head toward Teddy.

She looked at his son and her mouth curved into a smile as warm as the morning sun on the horizon.

His breath caught partway up his throat at her gentle, sweet regard for his boy, who had been hurt so badly. He closed his eyes against the rushing memories. The boy was without a mother because Caleb had been unable to save Amanda. He'd been away from home when the cowboys had entered, set on punishing him for interfering after he'd caught them tormenting the young man running his father's store. If Caleb hadn't come along, the pair would have helped themselves to whatever they liked from the shelves without paying. In hindsight, he should have known they were the sort who would want revenge, but he thought the incident was over with when he rode away. Later he'd arrived home and come face-to-face with their blazing guns. He'd shot the two men in self-defense after they'd murdered his wife, and he lived with the agony that he might have been the one who shot the bullet that injured Teddy. His hope, his prayer, was that he could make up for it by getting Teddy the best of care. *God, let this doctor be one who can really help.*

He strode out to get water. He pumped with such vigor the water splashed out of the bucket, and he realized he was angry. What was the use of anger anyway? His energies would be better spent getting help for Teddy. And if that meant working for the Caldwells while seeking Lilly Bell's care for the dog that Teddy had claimed as his own, well, so be it.

He wouldn't let a feud that meant nothing to him stand in the way.

Lilly smoothed the dog's fur across the top of her head, which was about the only place that wasn't soiled with dirt and blood. "Poor puppy. You'll be okay now." She'd do her best to make sure that was true.

Teddy scooted closer and leaned over to put his face close to the dog's. "You're my dog and you ain't gonna die. You hear?"

The dog stuck out her tongue. It touched the tip of Teddy's nose and the little boy laughed.

Lilly wanted to pull both of them close and shelter them in her arms. Seemed life had been unfair and cruel to the pair. "I'll do my best to make sure she gets better."

Teddy studied her so intently her lips twitched with a smile.

"The man in town said you had a special way with sick animals. Do you?"

She laughed. "If taking care of them means I do, then yes."

"But nothing special?"

She studied him carefully. He was such a sweet-looking child. What had happened to his leg? She'd ask his father the first chance she got. If she or Ma could do anything to help… "I just use the skills my Ma taught me."

Caleb returned and set the bucket down. He squatted next to his son.

She turned from the pair, dipped a rag in the cold water and began to sponge away the dirt and blood from the pup.

"Can I help wash her?" Teddy asked.

"If it's okay with your papa."

After a moment of consideration, Caleb gently said, "It's okay."

She handed Teddy a wet rag and showed him a place where it appeared only dirt had smudged the fur.

"After all," Teddy said as he dabbed at the spot, "she's

my dog. I should take care of her." Teddy sounded so serious she ducked to hide her smile.

"Teddy." Caleb's voice held warning. "You just found her. And she's in pretty bad shape."

"But Miss Lilly can fix her. Can't you? That man in town said you could."

She caught his hands and held them until he met her eyes. "Teddy, we will do our very best. Sometimes the best thing we can do is love our friend."

"I love her."

She felt the depth of his yearning in the pit of her stomach. He needed this dog. She prayed the injuries weren't too bad and she'd survive. *God, give me hands to heal and words to strengthen.* She meant both the dog and his young owner.

Grub padded in at that moment. The silly dog never noticed people coming, and usually barked a warning upon their going. But the big, clumsy, lop-eared dog was dearly loved by the entire family. Grub saw Caleb and Teddy and gave a halfhearted *woof.* He noticed the injured dog and ambled over to smell it. He then sat two feet away and watched.

"This is Grub. He's our dog." She'd never tell a stranger how useless he was.

Caleb snorted. "Johnny-come-lately, I'd say."

Lilly let the comment pass. "What's your dog's name?" she asked Teddy.

"She's a girl, right?"

"Yes."

"A girl might not like being with two boys."

"Two boys?" Was there another one hiding in the wagon?

"Me and Papa."

Caleb made a noise like he was holding back a laugh.

Lilly dared not look at him for fear of revealing her own amusement and offending Teddy. "Oh, I see. I don't think a girl dog will mind."

"That's good. You know any good girls' names?"

"Well, let me think." She continued to wash the dog as she talked, thankful she'd discovered nothing but cuts so far, though some of them were deep enough to make infection a real possibility. "My sisters are named Cora and Rose, but those aren't very good names for a dog. The girls I know have names like Nancy and Katie. I know a little girl called Blossom."

Teddy nodded and smiled. "I like Blossom. It sounds like a pretty flower and my dog is as pretty as a flower. You like it, Papa?"

"I like it fine." He knelt beside Teddy and patted Blossom's head gently, earning him a grateful swipe of the dog's tongue.

Lilly studied the man. He had dark brown hair, curly and tangled like it hadn't seen a brush in several days. His dark brown eyes set off a face full of determination. She felt a flash of sympathy. No doubt he worried about his son. It was on the tip of her tongue to ask where Teddy's mother was, but it didn't matter to her except where it concerned the boy.

Caleb met her gaze. "Blossom is a fine name for a dog who looks to be half collie and half bulldog, or something equally—"

Afraid he'd say "ugly," she quickly inserted her own word. "Strong."

He nodded and grinned.

She blinked. My, how his eyes did darken and flood with warmth when he smiled. His whole face underwent such a transformation she was almost tempted to say he was handsome. Which had been her first thought when she'd seen him at the store. Good thing Rose hadn't been there to take note of the way her cheeks had warmed as he brushed past with an apology.

She thought about how strong and kind he had been when he'd helped her calm the horse. Her feelings had been struck again with awareness of tenderness and strength when he took his son on his knee and drove from town.

Despite all those wonderful virtues, he had so much working against him. He was obviously married, even if she'd seen no evidence of a wife. He worked for the Caldwells, which put a barrier as big as the Rocky Mountains between them. Not that any of that mattered, because she had no intention of ever again getting close to anyone outside her family.

If you get close to people, you will just suffer more losses down the road.

She'd help the dog. She'd even help Teddy if Caleb let her and if she could. But she would not let her heart be drawn to either one of them.

She'd keep on repeating her vow every day if necessary.

Chapter Three

Blossom! Caleb had almost laughed at the name. The animal looked more like trash than a flower, but he would respect Teddy's devotion and hope the boy wouldn't end up with a broken heart.

Lilly bent over a cut on the pup to examine it more closely, and then let out a sigh. "It's not deep."

"Blossom sure likes me washing her." Teddy wiped at the fur. Indeed, the dog opened her eyes and focused on Teddy, who leaned closer. "You're so pretty. Prettier than any other dog I ever seen."

Caleb chuckled. The dog would likely grow into a good-sized animal with long silky hair like a collie. Her face, on the other hand, would probably look like she'd run into a train. "Beauty is certainly in the eye of the beholder."

Lilly made a sound—half grunt, half sigh. "Seems to be true on many levels."

Caleb considered her at length. It sounded like she had personal experience with the old saying, but it couldn't be on her own behalf. She was quite the most beautiful woman he'd ever seen. "I met your twin this morning. What about your other sister? Is she older or younger?"

"Cora. She's two years older. She got married a short time ago and she and her husband, Wyatt, live on a small ranch not far from here."

"How old are you?" Teddy asked, the question so out of the blue and so inappropriate it shocked Caleb.

"Son, we don't ask personal questions." He needed to give the boy some lessons on how to carry on a conversation with a woman. Not that he would mind knowing the answer. There was something about Lilly that made it impossible to guess her age. She had a twinkle in her eyes and a freshness about her that spoke of young innocence, but several times he'd glimpsed wisdom lurking in the depths of her gaze.

Lilly chuckled. "It's a perfectly natural question. I'm eighteen."

Teddy considered it a moment. "Mr. Frank said you and that girl you were with are twins. So your sister is eighteen, too?"

"That's correct."

"I'm five."

Caleb ducked his head to hide his smile at how Teddy delivered his announcement. As if it carried a huge amount of importance.

"My pa is twenty-five. Isn't that right, Papa?"

Caleb didn't know whether to laugh at his son's audacity or to scold it. The boy had developed a sudden need to tell Lilly everything. Everything? He hoped not. He did not want Teddy informing Lilly that his mama had been murdered and his papa had shot two men. And worst of all, that his papa might have been the one to injure his leg. Perhaps he could distract the boy. "Blossom is watching you."

Teddy smiled at his dog and patted her back. "My mama was twenty-four when she died." Teddy cocked his head as if thinking about Amanda's death.

Caleb held his breath. Teddy had refused to say a thing about the day of her murder ever since it happened. *Please don't start talking about it now. Not in front of a stranger.* How would Caleb deal with the press of regrets and the weight of sorrow if he had to confront his past before this beautiful woman? He swallowed hard and gritted his teeth. He would not let his emotions escape into the open.

"Papa, does that mean she's still twenty-four?"

His lungs relaxed and released the pent-up air. "I suppose it does." Forever twenty-four. For some odd reason the notion gave him a measure of comfort.

Lilly touched Teddy's head. "I'm sorry about your mama." She shifted her gaze to Caleb. It was soft, gentle, full of compassion. He tightened his jaw. Her expression would have shifted to horror if she'd known the details. Lilly rubbed Teddy's back. "I'm so sorry, Teddy. I lost my own mama and papa when I was three."

He looked at her. "You did? I thought that man was your pa." He was referring to Mr. Bell.

"He is. He and my ma found us and adopted us."

Teddy studied her unblinkingly.

Lilly met his look with a kind smile.

Finally Teddy spoke. "I've never known anyone who was adopted. I found Blossom." He turned to Caleb. "Can I adopt her?"

Caleb chuckled. "I don't think it's called that when it's an animal." Teddy already had his heart set on keeping the dog. The animal wasn't as sorry looking as she had been when they'd found her, but she still looked mighty poor. "How is she?" He directed his question at Lilly.

She continued examining the dog. "There are some serious cuts, but nothing is broken that I can tell. She's awfully tender over her ribs, though, so it could be some of them are broken. They're certainly bruised. I'll get some ointment to apply to the cuts. She needs to rest and get some proper food in her."

"Lilly, you have guests. I didn't notice anyone drive up." The sound of a new voice drew Caleb's attention. Mr. Bell stood in the doorway.

"Hi, Pa. You remember Mr. Caleb Craig and his son, Teddy? They found this dog and brought her to me for some care."

"Of course, the Caldwell cowboy."

The man's voice revealed no emotion, but Caleb felt condemned by the statement.

Mr. Bell rumpled Teddy's hair. He knelt by the dog and ran his fingers through her fur. "Found her where?"

Caleb answered the man. "Down the road about three miles."

Mr. Bell grunted. "Close to where the Bixbys live. He's a man with no regard for God's creation. Lets his animals suffer. Uses his land unwisely. What's your verdict?" He asked the latter to Lilly and she repeated what she had told Caleb.

Mr. Bell nodded. "He might benefit from Ma's tonic. She gave me a shot of the stuff and I feel better already." He chuckled. "Might be the nap and a hot drink of tea helped, too."

"I was going to ask her for some."

Mr. Bell planted a hand on Lilly's shoulder. She

smiled up at him. Their love was obvious. It seemed neither of them regretted finding the other.

A found family full of tenderness and love. It was almost enough to give a man hope—

He jerked his thoughts away from that trail.

Mr. Bell headed for the open barn door and then paused. "Lilly, you need any help with the dog?"

"I think I can manage on my own."

"Then I'll be in my shop." The man disappeared through the door.

Lilly went to the neat room in the corner and returned with a jar and a roll of bandage. She looked from Caleb to Teddy.

He felt her hesitation and wondered what she wanted. He didn't have to wait long to find out.

She knelt in front of Teddy and commanded his attention. "I am going to fix Blossom's cuts." She explained how the ointment would help the wounds heal. "Now Blossom might not like me touching them." She let the information settle in Teddy's brain.

"Sometimes you gotta do what's best, even if it's hard." The words seemed to come from a dark place inside Teddy.

Feelings of pride and pain warred inside Caleb.

Lilly squeezed Teddy's hand. "You are exactly right. And very wise."

Teddy beamed.

"Now here's where you have to make a choice. Do you want to stay even if you have to see Blossom crying, or do you want to have your papa take you outside and wait until I'm done?"

Caleb jerked forward. "May I speak to you?" He indicated that they should retreat to the tack room.

She rose slowly. Leaving her supplies behind, she joined him, though she hovered just inside the door as if ready to take flight.

"I don't think he should have any choice in this. I'll take him to the wagon or over to the pump for a cold drink of water."

She refused to meet his eyes. "I'm sorry I spoke out of turn. But I've already given him the choice." She shot him a look of defiance.

"Papa, Miss Lilly, I've made up my mind."

Caleb knew he wasn't mistaken in thinking Lilly was relieved about the interruption. Maybe he was, too. He had no desire to engage in an argument with her about what was and was not appropriate for his son. All he wanted was assurance the dog Teddy had adopted on sight would live.

Teddy sat up, his expression eager.

"Son," Caleb began, intending to warn the boy that they were leaving the barn, but Teddy had already started to talk.

"I decided. Blossom is my dog. She wants me to stay."

Caleb jerked back. How could he disagree with that kind of conviction? "Very well. But you must be brave."

Teddy looked so determined that Caleb stifled a chuckle.

"I can. I remember how. Mama told me."

Caleb stared. In the past nine months, Teddy had steadily refused to talk about Amanda's death. Many had suggested it might help the boy if he did. Seems finding this dog had done something for Teddy that Caleb, the doctors and even Amanda's parents had not been able to do.

Lilly squeezed Teddy's shoulder. "Blossom will be much happier with you here."

Teddy beamed.

Another thought surfaced. Maybe Lilly had played a role as well, with her gentle kindness and direct way of talking to Teddy. If she and Blossom combined forces, could they help his son? He didn't expect the pair could figure out what Teddy needed in order to walk again, but it seemed at least they might help him come to grips with Amanda's death. That would be worth something.

Would she agree to spend more time with his son? But even if she did, how could he ask her without risking his job at the Caldwells'? Ebner made no secret of his antagonism toward the Bells.

Lilly knelt beside the dog, her knuckles white as she held the jar and supplies she'd brought.

Caleb's heart went out to her. She had a difficult job to do, applying ointment and dressings to the wounds. It would be doubly difficult with Teddy watching. Maybe she regretted allowing Teddy to stay. "Teddy, it's not too late to change your mind," he said.

"No. I gotta do this. Big boys don't let hard things stop them from doing what they have to."

He narrowed his eyes at the boy. Where had Teddy heard those words? Had Caleb spoken them to his son? He didn't remember doing so, but then a person can say a lot of things carelessly that a listener might take seriously. He'd best watch his words in the future. He didn't want to make the boy feel he had to take on a load too big for his little shoulders.

Lilly gave the boy a gentle smile. "Then let's get it done."

"Is this when she cries?" Teddy's voice was clogged with sadness.

She sat back to study him. "You don't have to stay."

He blinked back tears. "I can be brave."

"Very well."

Caleb sat behind the boy and held him close. "You won't be alone."

Lilly studied him. He wished he could read her expression. Did she see his care for Teddy and approve of it? Or was she able to see past all that to his pain and guilt? He was getting plumb foolish. Of course she couldn't see anything of the sort.

She ducked her head and set to work. She screwed the lid off the jar and dipped her finger into a thick yellowish ointment and applied it to the first wound.

As expected, Blossom yipped.

Grub ambled over to investigate. He shoved his nose into Lilly's neck as if to inform her she'd hurt the other dog. She elbowed him aside. "Grub, go lie down. Everything is just fine here."

Grub padded back to his spot in the patch of sunlight pouring through the open door.

As Blossom whined, Teddy smoothed the fur on her head and whispered, "It's okay, little one. We're going to make you better."

Lilly kept her attention on her task. She applied the ointment to many of the wounds, flinching when Blossom cried. Some of the cuts she left open to the air, and a few she wrapped with bandages. When she was done, she sat back. "That's the best I can do for now. I'll get her some of Ma's tonic. But first, I'll bring her water."

Teddy looked at her with eager eyes. "I'll take good care of her."

"I know you will." She shifted her gaze to Caleb. "I

really think she needs to stay here a few days so I can watch for infection."

Teddy let out a small cry. "She has to come with us."

Lilly caught his hand. "Teddy, I promise I'll take really good care of her for you."

"No. No." Teddy shook his head. "I'm not leaving her." He turned to Caleb, his eyes wide. He plucked at Caleb's shirt front. "Don't make me leave her. Please, Papa."

Lilly closed the ointment jar and tidied up the bandages. She took them back to the tack room and then stood at the doorway. "Caleb, may I speak to you in private? Teddy, will you watch Blossom carefully while I get her some water?"

Caleb took Teddy's hands and waited for the boy to look him in the eye. "I'll be right back. You hear?"

Teddy nodded. His eyes remained too large. His pulse beat frantically in the veins of his neck.

Caleb followed Lilly outside to the pump, where she already had a pail full of water.

She faced him. "I know this might seem presumptuous, but why not leave Teddy here? I can make sure Blossom doesn't get infected and he can be with his dog."

Caleb stared. This was what he wanted, wasn't it? But he couldn't leave Teddy alone.

Nor could he afford to lose his job by risking Ebner's ire.

What was he to do?

Lilly almost choked the words of invitation out. Not because she didn't welcome Teddy's company or think it would do him good to be with his dog.

But because she knew it would inevitably mean seeing more of Caleb, and there was something about him that made her heart pull at its moorings. A dead wife. A son who, for whatever reason, needed crutches to walk. Yet rather than seeing a man wallowing in self-pity she'd seen numerous glimpses of a tenderhearted man. She'd seen it in the way he'd held Teddy as she ministered to the dog. She'd seen it in the way his eyes filled with concern that Teddy might be upset by watching her work. And she saw it now in the way his expression went from surprise to interest to doubt and finally to decision.

"I couldn't leave him. He's not been away from me since…"

She waited, but he didn't seem about to explain further. "I understand. But the dog…"

He looked past her to the horizon. "Yes, the dog. It'll upset him some to leave her."

She nodded. But there was little more she could offer. "If you leave Teddy here, perhaps Ma and I could help with his leg."

Interest flared in his eyes and then faded. "I've been to a dozen doctors and they've not helped." Doubt and hope seemed to cling to his words.

"Do you mind telling me what happened? Is his leg broken?"

Caleb turned so she saw only his profile—he swallowed hard and sucked his lips in. "His ma was murdered."

A gasp tore from her throat. "I'm sorry."

He nodded but continued to stare at something far off. "I found two intruders. They came at me with guns. I used mine." He sounded as if he were working hard to grate his voice from his throat. "When it was over they were dead. Amanda was already dead—murdered by the pair."

"And Teddy?" she whispered, hardly able to take it in.

"Amanda must have seen the intruders coming and made him hide in the closet. When I found him, he'd been shot in the leg."

"Oh, no." Pain and sorrow twisted through her with such vengeance she couldn't breathe. "How awful." Caleb's face contorted and she knew he was reliving the horror. The only comfort she could offer was the one thing Ma had taught her. Sometimes all a person could give another person in pain was presence and touch. She pressed her hand to his arm. "Caleb, I am so sorry. It's too dreadful for words."

A shudder shook him hard. He turned to face her, his eyes dark as a summer storm, his mouth a white line.

She too shuddered at the frank agony she saw.

"That's not the worst part." His voice was a hoarse whisper. "I'll never know if I was the one who fired the shot that hurt him."

She nodded, understanding this feeling of guilt must edge every thought, every glance at his son. What comfort could she offer him? Only the truth.

"You have no way of knowing it didn't come from some other gun, either."

He nodded, but she could tell the words had not gone farther than his ears.

"How long ago did all this happen?"

"Nine months. Almost ten."

That long and the boy's injury still remained? There had to be something wrong, likely an infection. One that long-standing was unusual and—she shuddered—usually life threatening.

"Has the wound not healed?"

"It's healed, but he can't use the leg. And I have no

idea why. No doctor has been able to help me." He told
her about the many trips he and Teddy had taken to
find help. "I have to get him to a doctor down east." He
stepped away as if he were already on his way. "I can't
leave him here. I need the job at the Caldwells in order
to pay the special doctor."

She nodded. She and Ma used only common sense and
old-fashioned remedies, along with herbs and poultices.
Surely a special doctor would have newer things to offer.
But if the infection had gone to the bone…

She shivered. If she could do anything to help, she
would. She opened her mouth to ask him to reconsider
taking Teddy away for the night.

Caleb turned on his heel and strode toward the barn
before she could utter the words.

She rumbled her breath out. She'd been about to suggest he stay, too.

How had she so quickly forgotten that he was a
Caldwell cowboy? Rose would be shocked.

Worse, she'd shocked herself by how much she'd been
drawn to this man and his pain.

She could see Teddy through the open barn door, leaning over his dog, crooning words of comfort when he
himself needed those same words. Likely some of Ma's
medicinals wouldn't do his leg any harm, especially if
infection had gone deep inside, but that type of deep infection usually resulted in severe pain, and the boy didn't
appear to be suffering.

She or Ma could at least provide comfort measures to
Teddy until Caleb took him to the special doctor.

Never mind that his father worked for the Caldwells.

Halfway across the yard, Caleb's feet slowed and he

slowly came about to face her. With measured steps he returned to her, his expression full of determination.

"Tomorrow is Sunday. I don't have to be at the Caldwells'. If your invitation is still open, I accept for the day."

One day! What could she hope to do for Teddy or Blossom in one day?

"Unless you've changed your mind. Perhaps your family wouldn't welcome a Caldwell cowboy." He had clearly mistaken her hesitation.

Rose would have concerns, but she'd voice them in private. Ma and Pa would take a wait-and-see approach. As for Lilly, she'd make the most of the limited time, grateful in a way he'd not be there longer. The locked doors around her heart shuddered every time she thought of what he'd been through. "The invitation is still open."

Caleb gave a quick nod. "I'll deal with the consequences when I get back."

"I'm not trying to discourage you, but are you sure about this? From what I've seen of Ebner and the others, they won't be happy to know you're consorting with the enemy, so to speak. Only the Caldwells view the disagreement in such terms. We only want to be left in peace to farm our little bit of land."

"I only want to do what's right for Teddy. I'm sure I can make Ebner understand that." His words rang and his dark eyes flashed.

Lilly had her doubts, but she'd never before let the Caldwells stop her from doing what she thought was right.

She certainly wasn't about to let them stop her now.

Chapter Four

Caleb hadn't decided how he'd deal with Ebner should the man object, but he felt he should be able to do as he chose on a Sunday and return to his work at the Caldwells' on Sunday night without questions being asked.

He was a free man, after all.

He tried to dismiss the doubts cluttering his mind. At the moment, staying seemed the right thing to do.

Lilly's invitation had sounded sincere, but her eyes were now shadowed by second thoughts. Was she concerned about how the Caldwells would react? Or her family? Then she smiled and drove away every bit of darkness. "Let's make Blossom comfortable. Then I'd like Ma to look at Teddy's leg, if you don't mind."

He wouldn't have minded if he'd thought there was any chance they could help, but—

"He's been prodded and poked. Some of the suggestions for helping him have been absurd. And too many of them cruel. Hang him in a harness until he uses his leg. Use some kind of noxious rub that would burn a hole in the hide of a cow. Poke his legs to stimulate the nerves. Seems everyone had a cure. Too bad none of them worked." He sucked in air. "No more torture."

Her hand brushed his arm and stilled his rush of words. Her touch when he'd been almost overwhelmed by his memories had soothed him. He had noted, too, how she'd touched Teddy to calm him. He didn't know if he should object to the touch or thank her for it. But he couldn't pull words from his brain, so he simply stood there as she spoke.

"Caleb, I promise you neither my ma nor I will do anything to hurt Teddy." She held his gaze unblinkingly until he nodded.

"Very well."

Satisfied, she said, "I'll let you tell Teddy." She carried the water to the barn.

Teddy turned to them as they entered, his expression tight as if he expected Caleb to insist they had to leave.

Caleb's insides warmed at his ability to give his son one small gift—a yes to his request to stay. He squatted in front of him. "Teddy, I've decided we can stay until tomorrow evening. Then I'll have to go back to work and you'll have to come with me."

"One day?"

"I'm afraid that's all we have."

Teddy sighed softly. "Then God will have to make Blossom better in one day."

Caleb blinked. How could his son have any faith left after all the praying that had been done over him to no avail? But he would not rob his son of it. *Please, God, honor the faith of this little one.*

"I brought water." Lilly had poured some into a little dish.

"Can I give it to her?" Teddy reached for the dish.

"Of course you can. In fact, I think she might prefer it."

She helped him place the dish close to Blossom's nose.

Grub came over and lapped at the water. Lilly pulled him close to her. "I'll fill your dish in a minute. Let me help this little girl first."

Grub plunked down at her side and watched. "Good dog."

Caleb had his doubts about Grub's qualifications as a guard dog, but he certainly passed with flying colors as a friendly, obedient pet.

Teddy leaned over Blossom, patting her head. "Come on, Blossom. You have to drink so you can get better. We don't want you fading away to a shadow, do we?"

Lilly choked back a chuckle.

Teddy was repeating something Caleb had said often when Teddy was mending and didn't want to eat. "At least he listened to some of what I said."

She laughed. "I expect he takes in everything you say and do."

Caleb nodded, smiling at his son, filling with pure pleasure. With a jolt he realized he'd been so focused on getting help for Teddy's injured leg he had almost forgotten the joy that came from simply spending time with him. He opened his mouth, about to thank Lilly, for he knew it was because of her calmness in dealing with Teddy and Blossom that some of his tension had disappeared.

He closed his mouth again. How could he possibly hope to explain this feeling?

He studied Lilly out of the corner of his eye. She bent over Blossom, murmuring encouragement to the dog.

She touched Teddy's head to encourage him as well. Grub pressed to her side.

It hit him like a sledgehammer.

This was a woman made for giving and receiving love. Not that he should care. But for her sake he was glad he would only be there one day, lest she begin to care for him more than she should. He did not want to think he would bring sorrow or heartache into her life, as he'd done to others'.

He could list a whole lot of times people had been hurt because of him. Most of the events he hadn't thought of until after Amanda's murder, and then the memory of them had returned with a vengeance, as if to reprimand him for having forgotten them.

The time he lied about taking eggs to one of Ma's customers, instead having broken them while chasing a gopher. The customer had berated Ma publicly and Ma had gone home crying.

Then there was the time at school when he'd pulled a chair out when his friend Toby had gone to sit down and Toby had banged his head. Caleb had laughed until he realized Toby had taken a long time to bounce up again.

He would not continue to list his guilty deeds. Suffice it to say Caleb knew he was bad news to those who happened to have the misfortune of hanging around him.

He'd be extra careful while at the Bells so they wouldn't pay a price for helping him. Though it was Teddy they meant to help.

Blossom lapped the water a few times and then ignored it.

"That's a real good start." Lilly patted Teddy on the head and pushed to her feet. "I'll go to the house and get

Ma's tonic." She had only made it to the barn door when Rose came out of the house and trotted toward them, carrying a dish. "Pa told us about the injured dog. I made that gruel you like."

She handed Lilly the dish and the bottle of tonic. Her look blared a challenge.

Lilly knew exactly what she was wondering. *Why is a Caldwell cowboy here and why are you helping him?* She backed up so Rose could step into the barn.

"Rose, you remember Caleb Craig and his son, Teddy?"

Rose snorted so softly Lilly hoped she was the only one to hear it. "The Caldwell cowboy from town. I'm not likely to forget." Her piercing look said, *But it seems you are.*

Caleb set Teddy behind him and got to his feet to face Lilly and Rose. "Sorry to intrude on your fight about the Caldwells, but we found this dog and my son instantly claimed him. Your sister kindly offered to help."

Rose met his gaze. Neither of them blinked as Lilly held her breath, wondering who would relent first.

Caleb spoke again. "She's even offered to let us stay the night so Blossom here can rest."

Oh, no. Now Rose would blurt out how much she disliked the Caldwells.

Rose blinked. "Blossom?"

"The dog."

"Overnight?" She glared at Lilly.

Lilly smiled, not at all deterred by her sister's shock. Rose would soon realize that Teddy and Blossom needed their help.

Caleb shifted his gaze to Lilly and gave her a smile full of gratitude. "Your sister is very generous." Beyond the smile, Lilly glimpsed an ocean's depth of sorrow.

She couldn't look away. This man had every reason in the world to have a furrowed forehead. She shivered at the thought of everything that had happened to him.

If it had been possible, she would have applied one of Ma's healing balms to this man's heart.

"Oh, fine," Rose grumbled, and moved toward Blossom and Teddy. "So this is the dog you found."

"She's mine," Teddy said.

"Then I'd say she is very fortunate."

Lilly smiled. Rose might have been one to fight and sputter, but she didn't have an unkind bone in her body.

Caleb looked at the thin mixture Rose had made— oats cooked with meat broth—and shuddered. "I sure hope you mean that for Blossom."

The twins laughed, though Rose did so with more abandon than Lilly, as if enjoying his suspicion.

"Yes, it's for the dog," Lilly murmured and knelt beside Teddy. Together they managed to get Blossom to lick up some of the concoction. Then she uncapped the tonic. "Teddy, I need to give her these drops. Think you can help?"

He nodded eagerly.

"That's good. You hold her head while I put the drops in her mouth."

Teddy did as instructed and Blossom swallowed the drops and drank more water. Wearily, the dog closed her eyes.

Teddy glanced from the dog to Lilly to Caleb and then did it again.

"Papa?"

"What is it?"

"Wasn't that stuff supposed to make her better? She's still just lying here."

Lilly touched Teddy's head and smiled at him, her heart brimming with sorrow and tenderness at his question. How many times had this child been promised something would make him better and then been disappointed? She pushed her lips together as Caleb's words echoed in her head. The treatments the poor boy had endured. And his father along with him.

"Healing takes time. It can't be rushed."

Teddy gave Lilly a look of frank admiration. "You sure do know a lot about taking care of sick animals."

Rose laughed again. "She's had lots of experience. When we lived in town she rescued all sorts of dogs, cats, birds, chickens and even mice, and she nursed them. We were ten when we moved to this farm and she's collected all sorts of critters since."

"Like what?"

"Well, she raises sheep and pigs. People bring her animals that are doing poorly. Mostly she fixes them up and sends them back home, but sometimes we keep them. That's how we got our horse, and we have a motley collection of cats she's rescued. You should see this place at milking time. Say, I think you will. Lilly, when are you bringing in the cows?"

Ignoring the reminder of chores to be done, Lilly glowered at her sister. "Rose, please don't tell them everything you know about me."

Rose's smile widened. "Only the interesting stuff."

Lilly gave her a hard look. "That would be everything."

Rose opened her mouth as if to argue and instead burst out laughing. "You almost had me that time. One of these days you are going to convince me with that deadpan way of yours." Her expression grew thoughtful. "Maybe our first pa was a gambler. You might have learned that from him."

Lilly shook her head. "You've had him be everything from a wild horse wrangler to a traveling preacher. And now a gambler."

"I'm just curious, you know?"

"No, I don't. Seems to me what's in the past is best left in the past." They had loving parents in the way of Ma and Pa Bell. That was enough for Lilly.

But it had never been enough for Rose. She constantly tried to discover something about their birth parents.

Lilly dismissed the direction of the discussion.

"I'll bring in the cows," she said. Rose left the barn to do her own chores.

"Can I go with you?" Teddy asked. Then he sagged. "I guess I should stay with Blossom."

The dog was sleeping peacefully. "There's not much to do for her right now but let her rest. You're welcome to accompany me," Lilly said. "Both of you."

Teddy scrambled to get his crutches and hurried to her side. Caleb followed after.

Lilly didn't know whether to be grateful for his company or annoyed he probably didn't trust her alone with his son. Then again, she had invited him. And it really didn't matter either way—her only interest was in seeing Blossom get better and helping Teddy if that was possible.

Lilly led the way past the house. Out of habit, she scanned the pasture and fields. The cows waited patiently. Beyond them, the white sheep dotted the faded green pasture. The yellow and gold leaves on the fruit trees and bushes flapped in the wind. The garden lay peaceful.

Everything seemed in order. She allowed her breath to ease out even though it was only a matter of time until the Caldwells would do something.

"Is anything wrong?"

She startled at Caleb's question. "Just checking."

"For what? Are you expecting some sort of trouble?"

She snorted. "You might say that."

"Like what?" He squinted at her and edged closer to Teddy as if to protect him.

"Nothing to concern you. At least not directly." She shouldn't have said anything, but now that she had, perhaps it was best she told him the truth. Perhaps he had been unaware of how dangerous the Caldwells could be. "You should understand who you work for. The Caldwells are always up to mischief." Aware Teddy could hear every word, though he seemed more interested in watching the cows press toward the fence, she kept her words low and benign while frustration raged through her. Why couldn't they leave the Bells alone?

He nodded. "You're right. It's nothing to do with me. I need the job and who they choose to feud with is not my concern."

She wanted to argue. But what could she say? That a man of honor would not work for people like the Caldwells? But why did it matter one way or the other if he was honorable or otherwise? Yet somehow it did. For Teddy's sake, she reasoned, it mattered.

They reached the gate and she opened it. "Come on, girls. Milking time." Two dough-faced Jerseys cows lifted their heads. "Come, Bossy. Come, Maude," she called.

"Look, Papa, they come when she calls them."

She led the animals to the barn with Teddy and Caleb at her side. She scooped oats into the manger for each.

"Are you going to milk them now?" Teddy asked.

"I like to get it done before supper."

"Papa, Mama used to milk a cow, didn't she?"

"She sure did. She insisted you have milk so I got her a decent milk cow."

"She used to take me with her." Teddy's sad voice scraped Lilly's nerves raw. She'd lost her birth parents when she was three—one to death and one to abandonment—and had only a fleeting recollection of them. Or were they memories the girls had created over the years? She didn't know. Perhaps it would have been better to not have any memories of her birth parents at all—they only made her sad.

Teddy brightened. "I used to give the cow oats just like Miss Lilly did."

Lilly pulled a three-legged stool close to the first cow. "This is Maude. She's gentle as a lamb."

"Can I pet her?"

"Best wait until I'm done milking." *Squirt, squirt.* The milk drummed into the bucket.

Meowing cats exploded from everywhere. A couple, seeing strangers, hissed.

"Mind your manners," Lilly scolded, shooting streams of milk at each cat in turn.

Teddy's eyes were round. His mouth gaped open.

Caleb laughed. "Guess you never saw so many cats at one time."

"I want to pet them." Teddy dropped his crutches and sat down amid the melee.

Seeing the concern in Caleb's face, Lilly reassured him. "It's okay. None of them will hurt him." She smiled at the pleasure in Teddy's face as the cats rubbed against him.

She might only have one day, but she'd do all she could to see he enjoyed every minute spent on the farm.

Caleb felt as if he had stepped back in time to a gentler, sweeter place where life followed familiar routines and his son enjoyed normal pursuits.

Two cats crawled into Teddy's lap, purring loudly. Teddy laughed. The purest laugh Caleb had heard from him in many months.

Caleb's eyes misted, no doubt irritated by the dust the cats were kicking up and nothing more.

Now satisfied with their drink, several cats hissed at Blossom. She opened one eye and closed it again but otherwise paid them no heed.

Grub cocked his head and watched the scene with a puzzled expression.

"Why do you have so many cats?" Teddy asked.

"Mostly because we had three batches of kittens this year."

"And you get to keep 'em all?"

"For a while. Usually once cold weather sets in and mice move indoors, people come and ask for a cat to keep the mice population down."

"Guess you don't have any mice around here."

"Not many."

"Would have to be an awfully brave mouse to come here." Teddy laughed so hard at his joke that tears trickled from his eyes.

Caleb watched in pure and natural pleasure.

Lilly chuckled as she finished with Maude. Then she stood at Caleb's side, a foamy pail of milk in one hand, and watched Teddy. "If that isn't the sweetest sound in the world, I don't what is."

He looked at her. She looked at him. And for a moment they shared something. Something he had not shared with anyone since Amanda died. A common delight in his son. It was temporary, he warned himself. But for now, he allowed himself to enjoy the moment. "His laughter is better than Sunday music."

She laughed. "Tons better than Sunday music if you happen to sit next to Harry Simmons, who sings like a hoarse bullfrog." She croaked out a few words of a song, then broke off and covered her mouth with her hand. "Oh, I'm so sorry. I should not be mocking anyone." Pink flared up her cheeks.

He'd laughed at her imitation of the poor Harry Simmons, whoever he was, but his laughter stalled in the back of his throat when he looked at her. The woman could go from straight-faced teasing, to lighthearted imitations, to apologies so fast it left him dizzy.

And more than a little intrigued.

Her eyes widened and then she ducked her head.

Oh glory, he'd been staring long enough to make her uncomfortable.

He bent over Teddy and stroked one of the cats. Lilly hurried over to the other cow and started milking.

"What's her name?" Teddy asked.

"This is Bossy."

Did Caleb detect a note of relief in her voice, as if she were happy to be talking about cows again?

Teddy seemed to consider the name for a moment. "Is that 'cause she's mean?"

"No, she just likes to do things the same way and if I try to change anything, she insists otherwise."

Teddy brightened. "That's like Papa."

Caleb stared at his son. "Me? Why would you say that?"

"You always put your boots in the exact spot every night. Once I moved them 'cause I wanted something and you made me put them back. You always make me sleep on the same side of you even when I want to sleep on the other side. And every morning, you stare at the fire until the coffee is ready. And you tell me not to talk until you have your coffee."

It was all true. "That doesn't mean I'm like Bossy. I can change if I want." He stole a glance at Lilly. She had her head pressed to the cow's flank, but—he narrowed his eyes—her shoulders were shaking. "You find this funny?"

She nodded without lifting her head.

He crossed his arms and considered the two of them. Teddy innocently petting a lap full of cats. Lilly trying to hide her amusement.

So his son considered him inflexible. Stuck in a routine. As for the coffee, he simply had to get his first cup before his brain started to perk. It didn't mean he was bossy or stuck in a rut.

Lilly gasped, tipped her head back and laughed aloud. She held up a hand to indicate she wanted to say something as soon as she could speak.

He waited, none too patiently. Did the woman intend to spend the rest of the day laughing?

She swiped her hand across her eyes. "I'm sorry. I shouldn't laugh, but if you could see your expression…" She chuckled some more and then tried to press back her amusement, but it showed clearly in her eyes.

From a deep well within, one that felt rusty with disuse, a trickle of laughter escaped. It grew in volume and intensity. He laughed. And laughed. And continued to laugh until his insides felt washed with freshwater. Until his stomach hurt. Until he realized Lilly and Teddy were watching him with wide smiles.

He sobered and drew in a deep breath. "I guess it is funny to realize a five-year-old has been taking note of my habits."

She grinned. "It's kind of sweet if you think about it."

He couldn't seem to break from her warm gaze. It was as if she approved of him. No. That wasn't it at all. Really, it was as if she approved of the way he and Teddy were together.

Bossy tossed her head.

"Okay. Okay." Lilly turned her attention to the cow. "I'm done. I'll let you go."

If Caleb had a lick of good sense left, he'd be done, too. He'd be on his way before his brain got any more affected by this woman.

Only he couldn't break the promise he'd made to Teddy. He'd stay the night, enjoy one day of being part of a normal family. Then he'd return to the Caldwells and his job with his resolve renewed and his face set to reach his goal.

He'd dare not linger overlong at the Bell place and risk losing his job with the Caldwells.

Not that he was tempted. Not at all.

Chapter Five

Lilly turned the cows out. "I'll take the milk to the house and let Ma know you're staying overnight. She'll expect you to join us for supper."

"That's not necessary," Caleb said. "We have supplies in our wagon. But could I turn the horse in to the pasture?"

"By all means." She wanted to kick herself for not suggesting it the moment Caleb had said he'd stay.

She would have accepted his refusal to join them for supper, but Ma would have had a fit if she didn't bring them.

"Ma's a very good cook."

Teddy got a look on his face that could only be described as hungry. "Papa, she's a good cook."

Caleb chuckled. "Are you saying I'm not?"

"I like your food." He sounded so uncertain that Lilly smiled.

Teddy brightened. "But it might be nice to try someone else's for a change."

Caleb gave his son such a loving, amused look that tears stung Lilly's eyes. She almost envied the boy such devotion, which was plumb foolish. Ma and Pa loved her every bit as much as Caleb loved his son. But oh, to see such a look meant especially for her. She shook her head hard, trying to clear her brain of such confusing thoughts.

Caleb and Teddy had followed Lilly as she put the cows in the pen for the night. He turned his horse in to the pasture, and then they returned to the barn.

"Look, Papa," Teddy chirped. "Blossom wagged her tail. Isn't that good? Means she's getting stronger." Teddy eased himself down beside the dog and petted her, murmuring encouragement. "You're safe here. Don't be afraid. No one will hurt you now."

Caleb pressed a fist to his chest as if, inside, his heart were hurting.

Lilly touched his arm. "He's safe, too."

Caleb nodded, but his eyes did not show relief. "I wish—" He shook his head.

She patted him twice. "I'll ask Ma to look at his leg after supper."

"Thanks."

"I'll leave you two with Blossom." She hurried to the house to strain the milk. As she passed through the kitchen, she stopped to speak to Ma.

"How's the pup?" Ma asked.

"She's a fighter. I think she'll be okay. Ma, I asked them to stay overnight so they could be with the dog."

Ma nodded. "Sounds sensible. Did you ask them to come for supper?"

"Yes. Ma, the little boy has something wrong with his leg." She repeated what Caleb had said. "I said we'd do what we could to help. Can you look at the leg after supper?"

"Certainly." She stirred a pot on the stove.

"Caleb was afraid we might torture his son." She told Ma the things Caleb had said.

Ma dried her hands on a towel and looked out the window toward the barn. "That poor little boy and that poor father. I hope you assured him we'd be very gentle with the lad."

"I did, but I warn you, he's very protective of his son."

"As well he should be." Ma returned to the stove and her meal preparation, her lips tight.

Lilly stared. Was she thinking of her three daughters? She had never said much about the circumstances of their adoption. She had only assured the girls over and over that they were loved, that they were a blessing from God to a childless couple. But no doubt she wondered what had happened to the girls' birth parents. Or more accurately, their father. Cora could remember their mother had died. Lilly figured it must have been something horrible that caused their father to abandon three little girls in the middle of the prairie. She went to Ma's side and brushed her hair off her forehead. "You're the best ma," she said. When had Ma's hair gotten so gray? Both her parents were in their seventies, but she didn't like the thought that they were getting old.

"I'm glad you think so. Now you get on with your chores so you'll be done in time for supper," Ma said. "It will be ready soon."

"Yes, Ma." Lilly went to the workroom, strained the milk and set it to cool. Pa would take the cans to the river after supper and hang them in the water, where the cold would keep the milk fresh and sweet for days. Soon that wouldn't be necessary. The workroom would be cold enough once winter set in. Many days it was so cold the milk froze. Lilly smiled. She loved spooning the crystalline milk from her cup. It was almost as good as ice cream, a rare treat they only enjoyed at community gatherings.

Although done, Lilly lingered. She didn't want to rush back to the barn and give anyone reason to think she was being overly curious or concerned about Caleb and his son. Though, of course, she had Blossom to check on, and she had said she and Ma would do what they could to help Teddy. It would be nice to have more than one day on which to help. But she'd tell them Ma would look at Teddy's leg after supper.

She turned, her reasons for returning firmly established. But still she hesitated. There was something about Caleb that upset her equilibrium. She might have said it was concern and sympathy over Teddy's plight, but it was more than that.

She might have said it was compassion because Caleb's wife had been murdered. Or she might have said it was because they had shared a good old-fashioned belly laugh at Teddy's description of his father's routine.

It was all of those things. But still more. Something about the man touched a tender, expectant spot deep inside that she hadn't been aware of before this day.

And that frightened her. She didn't like surprises, and this unexpected feeling left her off balance.

But why let it bother her? He'd soon be gone. He'd made that very clear.

Rose stepped into the room. "I can't believe you asked him to stay."

There was no mistaking the challenge in her sister's voice. "Only for one night, so Blossom has time to rest."

Rose made a dismissive sound. "Never thought I'd

see the day you'd hang about a Caldwell cowboy." She didn't give Lilly a chance to answer before she grinned and spoke again. "Though he is rather handsome, and seems a decent sort of man." She grew glum again. "For a Caldwell cowboy."

Lilly shrugged. "Hard to judge a man after only a few hours, but I'm glad he's staying long enough for Ma and me to look at Teddy's leg and see why he doesn't use it." She explained yet again what had happened to the boy.

"Oh, that's terrible. I wouldn't wish that kind of disaster even on a man who works for the Caldwells."

Lilly chuckled. "Nice to know."

Rose studied Lilly long enough to make her squirm inside, but outwardly she returned the look, hoping she was managing to keep hidden every hint of her confusion about her feelings for Caleb and Teddy.

Rose's expression softened as if satisfied with what she saw.

Lilly might demand to know what exactly Rose thought that was, but she didn't care to encourage Rose's curiosity about the Caldwell cowboy and Lilly's choice to open their home to him.

"I came to tell you supper is ready," Rose said. "Will you let the others know?"

"Certainly." Lilly left the house and stopped at Pa's shop to tell him, and then made her way to the barn. She paused outside the door. Why hadn't Rose informed everyone of supper herself? Lilly narrowed her eyes. Was she purposely avoiding contact with Caleb and Teddy simply because Caleb worked for the Caldwells? His reasons were noble—to earn enough money to take Teddy to a special doctor. She'd have to tell Rose that and set the record straight.

Caleb was sitting near Teddy and Blossom, his back against a post, his legs stretched out halfway across the alley. He'd perched his hat on a nearby nail. He was watching his son, an affectionate smile curling his mouth. She drew in a breath at the depth of his devotion. Many men would simply accept the fact their son would only walk with crutches and get on with their lives. But not Caleb. It seemed he meant to move Heaven and earth to help his son. It was truly admirable and brought a sting of emotion to the back of her eyes.

Teddy fussed with the dog, petting her head and talking to her, urging her to eat more.

Neither of them had noticed Lilly in the doorway until Grub padded toward her.

She stepped inside. "Supper is ready."

Caleb tugged on the lobe of his ear. "We don't want to be a bother."

"It's no bother."

Slowly he rose. "If you're quite certain?"

"I most certainly am." More than anything, she wanted them to join the family for a meal. She wanted more time to observe them.... She meant, observe Teddy.

"Then we will come." He signaled for Teddy to join him and the pair fell in step with Lilly as she crossed the yard.

Teddy grinned up at his father. "I was afraid you would say no."

"Why would you think that?"

"'Cause sometimes you are so stubborn."

Lilly choked back laughter. Young Teddy must have really kept Caleb on his toes.

"Son, must you point out all my flaws and perceived failings in front of Miss Bell?" His voice deepened.

She couldn't say if it was from amusement or annoyance or perhaps a combination of both. "Please, call me Lilly." He'd used her Christian name several times already—perhaps not aware he was doing so. She certainly didn't want to revert to a more formal way of address.

"Lilly and Caleb it is, then."

She realized she, too, had easily used his Christian name even without permission. Maybe working together over an injured pup erased some of the normal polite restraints.

"Papa, I only say what I see."

Lilly could not contain her amusement at Teddy's directness and burst out laughing.

Caleb rocked his head back and forth in dismay, but she understood it was only pretend because his eyes brimmed with mirth, and in a moment he chuckled.

Teddy grinned, pleased with himself for making them both laugh.

Ma and Pa would enjoy a young boy's presence at supper. Even Rose would see Caleb was a nice man.

She realized her smile might have appeared too bright as she entered the house, so she forced a bit of seriousness into her expression.

Still chuckling, Caleb followed Lilly to the house. Teddy had not once complained about the simple food they ate, but perhaps the meals, although adequate, were lacking in imagination.

He was willing to give his son a good meal tonight. Then it was back to their regular fare after tomorrow.

Lilly led him into the house.

The scent of roast pork, turnips and apples brought a flood of saliva to his mouth. The meals he'd had over the past few months certainly didn't carry such tantalizing aromas.

"Papa, it smells awfully good," Teddy whispered.

"It does indeed." Caleb glanced about. It was a usual-looking kitchen—cupboards to one side, a big stove belting out heat, a wooden table. But there were touches that revealed the family, too. A rocking chair with a basket of mending. A spinning wheel and a basket of carded wool. A stack of papers teetering on a side table. And on the cupboard, four golden brown loaves of bread were cooling beside jars of applesauce and jars of dark blue-purple jam. He could almost taste the jam on the bread.

He and Teddy seldom had bread. A man on his own didn't have time to make bread, even if he knew how. They ate biscuits unless they found bread to purchase in one of the many towns he'd visited in his search for a doctor who could help Teddy.

The woman by the stove turned at their entrance.

Lilly pulled them forward. "Ma, this is Caleb Craig and his son, Teddy." Lilly and her mother's love for each other was evident in the way they each smiled. "Caleb, my mother."

Both Teddy and Caleb offered their hands and Ma shook them. "Pleased to meet you."

Mrs. Bell indicated two chairs at the table and he and Teddy sat down.

The others took their places. Rose and Lilly sat across from him and Mr. Bell sat at the end, facing his wife.

Caleb glanced around the table, but his gaze stalled when it landed on Lilly. She smiled as if to assure him they were welcome.

"Papa." Teddy tugged at his sleeve to get his attention. "This is like we used to have."

Caleb nodded. "Yes, son." They'd once known family. Though Amanda admitted she didn't love him and had married him only to get away from her overly strict upbringing. He'd tried to love her as a man should love his wife, but she had rebuffed every attempt, so they had lived together in peaceful coexistence, both committed to providing their son with a pleasant home.

But that home had never felt as warm and welcoming as this one did already.

Mr. Bell cleared his throat. "Welcome to our guests. I'll give thanks." He reached for Rose's hand on one side and Caleb's on the other. Seeing what Mr. Bell meant for them to do, Teddy reached for Ma's and Caleb's hands.

Caleb hesitated. Regret, refusal, confusion and pain all flashed through his brain. Being invited so intimately into this family circle had set his nerves to jangling. He had vowed to distance himself from people after Amanda's murder. Or maybe it had begun long before that, during the years when Amanda had remained cold to his love. Slowly, over time, he had closed his heart in order to protect it. Now he was grateful he had done that. It kept him from overreacting to this current family situation. He'd only be here one day. He sucked in air and allowed Mr. Bell to take his hand.

He sought Lilly with his eyes. She smiled and gave him a tiny nod. Confused by the way his heart tipped sideways at her gesture, he bowed his head as Mr. Bell asked the blessing. A question blared through his mind. Why had he looked to Lilly for reassurance? He didn't need or want assurance from anyone. And yet his insides felt soft and mellow knowing she was sitting across from him, and she cared enough to take note of his hesitation.

He jerked his thoughts to a halt. If he kept going in

that direction he would lose sight of his every goal. He was only there to get a dog tended to, his son looked at and a savory meal or two eaten. Then he would return to the Caldwell ranch.

All that mattered was getting Teddy to that doctor down east.

"Amen," Mr. Bell said, and the word echoed around the table.

Throughout the meal Teddy raved about the food. He turned often to Mrs. Bell to ask questions.

Mrs. Bell helped him cut his meat and butter his bread. She filled his cup with milk three times. "You can have as much milk as you like," she said. "We have lots of it. Milk is good for strong bones."

"Would it make my leg work again?" Teddy latched his trusting, begging gaze on Lilly's ma.

She didn't answer at first. "It might depend on what's wrong with it, but it can't hurt."

"Then can I have some more?" He downed the contents of his cup and pushed it forward for a refill.

"Son, remember your manners." Caleb spoke softly, not wanting to spoil Teddy's enjoyment of this family meal, but needing him to be polite.

"Please," Teddy said. As Mrs. Bell filled his cup again, he added, "Thank you so much." He drawled the words to make sure Mrs. Bell understood he was terribly, terribly grateful.

Lilly and her sister glanced at each other and ducked their heads to hide their amusement.

Mr. Bell smiled at Teddy. "A young boy with a healthy appetite is a good thing to see."

Caleb murmured his thanks. He had no objection to

the kindness and attention this family seemed prepared to heap on his son.

Mrs. Bell patted Teddy's hand. "You'll go far."

Lilly watched Teddy. She swiped at her eyes and glanced at Caleb. Then she ducked, as if uncomfortable that Caleb had seen her tears. Rose also swiped tears from her eyes.

The tenderness of this family's behavior toward his son stirred Caleb's heart. Perhaps the boy would find something here he hadn't had since his mother's death—the loving care of a mother figure. Only in this case, two mother figures, a grandma figure and a grandpa-type man.

Too bad he could only spend a day with them. No. He didn't want more time. He clanged shut the doors guarding his heart, doors he'd built with steel and sealed with rock. His future did not include a loving family and a warm home. He had Teddy. That was enough.

When the meal ended, Mr. Bell spoke. "We'll have our Bible reading now." He lifted the Bible from a nearby shelf and opened it.

"Papa," Teddy said, "you used to read the Bible every night. How come you quit?"

Caleb shrugged. "Things change." It hadn't been intentional. At first he'd been in shock. Then his energies had been bound up in caring for Teddy. Then the two of them had been on the move, going from one doctor to another.

Mr. Bell turned pages. "God changes not."

Caleb nodded. "For which I am grateful."

"Tonight's reading is from Job, chapter thirteen." He glanced about the table, giving each person a moment's attention. "May we each be blessed by the hearing of

God's word." He read the chapter until he reached a verse that he emphasized. "'Though He slay me, yet will I trust in Him.' We'll stop there. Job, a man like us, faced troubles and trials most of us will never know, thank God, yet he chose to trust God through them all. Shall we pray?" He again reached out for the hands on either side of him and prayed that each be blessed, and each have a good night's sleep. "May we honor You in all we say and do. Amen."

Teddy clung to Caleb's hand even when the others started to push back from the table. He pulled at Caleb to draw his attention. Caleb leaned toward the child. "What is it?"

Tears flooded Teddy's eyes.

Caleb groaned inwardly. What had upset the boy so much? "Do you miss Mama?"

He nodded. "But that's not why I'm sad."

"Then what's wrong?"

The room had grown quiet. Caleb glanced up and met Lilly's gaze. Her lips lifted at the corner—it was not quite a smile, but there was no mistaking that she meant to encourage him. He nodded and turned back to Teddy.

"What is it?"

"He asked God to bless me."

"Yes. Mr. Bell asked God to bless each of us." He didn't understand why that had made Teddy cry.

"Can God make my leg better?"

Lilly hurried around the table and knelt beside Teddy. She touched his head and looked at Caleb. He felt her concern clear through to the bottom of his heart.

"Can He, Papa?"

Caleb pushed his chair back and pulled the boy to his lap. "God made you. I expect He can fix you."

Lilly hovered close. "God can do anything. Do you want my pa to pray for you?"

Teddy sniffed. "Would he?"

Mr. Bell had already moved to Lilly's side and placed his hand on Teddy's head. Rose scurried around to stand behind Teddy's chair and Mrs. Bell stood behind Caleb, her hand warm on his shoulder.

Mr. Bell prayed. "God of all mercies and love, look upon this little child of Yours and make his leg strong and well again that he might run and play like other little boys, and most of all, that he might love and adore You all his life. Amen."

For a moment no one moved, and then Mrs. Bell squeezed Caleb's shoulder and stepped back.

Teddy beamed up at Mr. Bell. "You know God real well, don't you?"

Mr. Bell chuckled. "I've known Him a long time."

Lilly leaned over and kissed the top of Teddy's head.

Caleb rubbed the bridge of his nose and kept his gaze on Teddy until the rush of emotions passed. He'd beseeched God to heal his boy, but he'd never felt as blessed and supported by the prayers of others as he did here in the Bell house.

Would God choose to heal Teddy?

For good measure he added a silent prayer. *Help me earn enough money this fall to take Teddy down east.*

As soon as he thought the words, he regretted them. A doubting man would not receive anything from God.

Would his prayer, expressing doubt as it did, be the reason Teddy's didn't heal?

A familiar sense of failure caught at his thoughts.

Chapter Six

Ma signaled to Lilly to join her. "God will do His part. Now let us do ours."

Lilly nodded. "Caleb, would you let my ma examine Teddy's leg and see what she thinks?"

Caleb pushed to his feet and handed the crutches to his son. "Where do you want him?"

"The cot." She indicated the narrow bed at the far side of the room.

Teddy remained beside the table. "You're not gonna hurt me, are you?"

Lilly sat on Caleb's chair and faced Teddy. "Did I hurt Blossom?"

"A little, maybe."

"But she had open cuts. Do you?"

He shook his head and leaned close to whisper to Lilly. "Will you look at my leg instead of your mama?"

"My ma knows more about such things."

"Nonsense," Ma said. "You are every bit as good as I any day of the week." She smiled at Teddy. "Certainly she will look at your leg. Do you mind if I watch her?"

"That's okay." Teddy hobbled toward the cot. "Do you want me to lie down?"

Lilly knelt before him. "First, can you pull your pant leg up and show me where you were hurt?"

He did so.

Caleb stood at Lilly's shoulder, his presence making her nervous. And yet she didn't want him to move away.

She saw the boy's scar, the skin pink and uneven. She checked the underside. The bullet had gone in and out, leaving two roundish scars in the fleshy part of the leg just above the knee.

She probed the area, watching Teddy for signs of pain or tenderness or evidence of the bone being injured. He never once flinched. There was no heat in the area, which was a good thing.

She cupped her hand under the knee. "Can you swing the leg in and out?"

He did so.

"Does it hurt anywhere?"

"No."

"You can lie down now, Teddy."

Once he was comfortable, she lifted his leg, put it through a range of motions, felt the muscles for any lack of mobility and again, watched for signs of pain. "Thank you, Teddy. I'm finished." She turned to consult with Ma. "I detected no infection. Every muscle is working, as far as I can tell."

Ma nodded. "I agree."

There might be nerve damage, but from the placement of the wound, it seemed unlikely. "Teddy, what do you think is wrong with your leg?" Sometimes people had an intuition about their own bodies.

"It's forgotten how to walk."

She smiled. "I think you're right." She turned to Caleb. "I think it needs a little help remembering."

"What kind of help?"

"Well, if he was to remain here a few days I would try some warm poultices to stimulate the muscles and I'd do some exercises to help the muscles remember how to work."

He shook his head, but she didn't give him a chance to voice his explanation again.

"I can teach you what to do and you can do it yourself."

"I appreciate that."

Teddy pushed his pant leg down and sat up. "Are you going to make my leg work again?"

"I'm going to help if I can. But it will be you and God that make it work again."

Teddy stole a glance at Pa, who was sitting at the end of the table while Rose cleaned up the kitchen. Teddy signaled for Lilly to lean close. "Can you ask your papa to talk to God about my leg again tomorrow?"

Lilly tousled Teddy's hair, which wasn't hard to do. The little guy had three cowlicks that gave his hair a permanently rumpled look. "Would you like me to ask my pa to pray for your leg every day until it's better?"

Teddy nodded eagerly.

Lilly turned to Pa and repeated the request.

Pa smiled. "Young man, it would be my privilege. You can ask Him, too, though. God likes to hear young boys pray."

"I'll ask Him when I say my bedtime prayers."

Lilly allowed herself to look at Caleb. She saw hope and despair in his gaze, as if he wanted to believe but was afraid to. She'd like to ask him why he couldn't let himself believe. But he wasn't going to be around long enough for her to ask those sorts of questions.

"I'd like to try a cowslip poultice."

Ma nodded. "I'll get it from the shed." Ma's medicinals were kept in the gardening shed, where she sorted, prepared and stored everything. She brought the tinctures that would freeze into the house for the winter.

Ma returned with a little jar. "The root is most effective, especially in cases like this."

Lilly knew she meant in cases of mild paralysis. Lilly had learned most of the remedies and herbs by heart, though Rose had begun a project to record all of Ma's medicinals. "For after she's gone," Rose had said. The words had brought a protest from Lilly. She did not want to think of that happening, but Rose was right. The remedies should be written down so others could use them.

"Thanks, Ma." Lilly went to the cupboard. "Caleb, I'll teach you what to do."

Caleb stood at her elbow as she spread a small amount of the ground root on a piece of brown paper and folded it to seal the edges. "We put that on Teddy's leg, cover it with a warm, wet cloth and leave it for about half an hour."

They went to the cot and she did as she had described, and then she looked about. Now what? How was she to amuse them for half an hour?

Pa put down the paper he'd been drawing on. He was always working on some kind of invention. Some had been successful. Others, less so. "Caleb," Pa asked, "where do you hail from?"

Caleb pulled a chair to the side of the cot and sat down. "I was raised in Nebraska. After I married I had

a little farm there. I was increasing my cow herd…."
His voice trailed off.

Lilly wanted to pat his arm to comfort him, but
pressed her hands to her knees and sat stiffly in a chair
by the table. Teddy lay on the cot, Caleb sitting at his
side. They were so alone, while the Bell family was clustered together near the table. It didn't feel right.

Pa cleared his throat. "I heard of your misfortune. I'm sorry. Tell me about your family—parents,
brothers, sister…"

Teddy perched up. "I have a grandmother and grandfather in 'Delphia."

Caleb smiled. "Philadelphia. Teddy's maternal
grandparents. My own parents and brother are still in
Nebraska."

"Philadelphia!" Rose snorted. "I suppose you heard
that Douglas Caldwell has been there and is on his way
home. I expect Philadelphia has had enough of him."

"Rose," Ma scolded without saying anything more.
Rose hung her head, but Lilly knew she wasn't sorry
for what she had said. Rose and Duke, as everyone else
called Douglas Caldwell, the son of the Caldwell Ranch
owner, had never gotten along.

"I've not heard a thing about Douglas Caldwell,"
Caleb said.

Lilly didn't want Rose to continue that topic of conversation. She went to Teddy's side and lifted the poultice. "How does it feel?"

"Nice and warm," Teddy said, straining upward to
check on what she was doing.

"Good. A little longer and then you're done."

"I'll be all better?"

She chuckled. "It might take a little time."

Pa began to talk about the plans for Montana to achieve statehood and the time passed quickly.

She removed the poultice. "The skin is pink and warm." She showed Caleb. "Now I'll do some exercises." She did them while Caleb observed. "Sometimes it's hard to remember everything, so you do them now and I'll watch."

Caleb gently lifted Teddy's leg and bent it.

"You need to keep the leg properly aligned." Lilly placed her hands on Caleb's, her arms crossing his as she guided the movement. It was almost like a hug. Rather than think like that, she concentrated on the exercise. Caleb's arm muscles flexed. Strong arms that held a little boy, that lifted heavy sacks of feed as she'd seen him do in town and that felt warm and steady underneath her own.

Her cheeks grew hot enough to make her wish she could hide her face. Could she hope no one else would notice? Even Rose, who watched her every move?

"I think I've got it," Caleb said, and she jerked her hands away and stepped back.

"Good. I'll go through the instructions about the poultice again in the morning."

"How often you think this should be done?" He waved at Teddy's leg to indicate he meant the poultices and exercises.

"Best if it's done three times a day, wouldn't you say, Ma?"

"That's what I would recommend."

"I see." He helped Teddy sit up and then turned to Pa. "Lilly invited us to stay overnight so Blossom could rest. I trust that meets with your approval?"

"By all means. Stay as long as you like. Do you need a bed? The cot is narrow, but you're welcome to it."

"No, no. We're fine. We've got the wagon all set up." He gestured to Teddy and they went toward the door.

Teddy stopped. "Aren't you coming to see Blossom?" he asked Lilly.

"I haven't forgotten." Her first thought was to rush out the door with them, but she forced herself to wait, practicing her intention of guarding her heart against intimacy. "Shall I go with you now?"

"Yes, please."

She could hardly refuse a request like that.

"Rose, go with your sister," Pa said.

Lilly smiled at Rose, though she wished to go without Rose observing everything she did and said. How foolish. There'd be nothing for her to notice. All Lilly meant to do was give Blossom some more tonic, make sure the dog was comfortable, and then bid Caleb and Teddy good-night.

Caleb watched Lilly and Rose until they entered the house and closed the door behind them. They'd helped Teddy tend the dog and then left. He lifted Teddy into the wagon. The poor boy was exhausted. It had been a long day. They had gotten up early so Caleb could feed Teddy before doing chores, then they had made the trip to town. Teddy had been so excited by it that he'd bounced up and down on the wagon seat and talked nonstop. Then they'd found Blossom.

Caleb smiled. He'd had a dog growing up, both he and his brother, Ezra, claiming it as their own. They used to have contests to see which one of them the dog would go to, both boys using every imaginable treat to tempt the dog. Bacon had certainly worked well.

Teddy touched Caleb's cheeks. "You're smiling."

"I guess I am."

"You liked having supper with the Bells, didn't you? I sure did."

"It was awfully nice. Sorry I haven't been making better meals for you."

Teddy patted Caleb's cheeks. "You do the best you can. No one can ask more than that."

Caleb chuckled. Teddy sure had a way of picking up wisdom from others. "How does your leg feel? Any different?"

"Not yet. Miss Lilly said it might take a while. Maybe in the morning it will be better."

"Maybe, but it might take longer than that." He didn't want Teddy to get his hopes up, but without hope what did the boy have? The possibility of finding something that would help kept Caleb going day after day. That and his determination to see his son walking on both legs again.

He helped Teddy remove his boots and trousers and put them on the trunk that held Teddy's things. Exactly where he always put them. He chuckled.

"What's so funny?" Teddy asked.

"I always put your things in the same place, don't I?"

"Uh-huh." Teddy pulled on his flannel nightshirt and sat cross-legged on the bedroll spread in the wagon box. "I want to pray like Mr. Bell does."

Caleb closed his eyes and sucked in a deep breath. Bedtime prayers were one more thing that he had neglected. No wonder God wasn't listening to his desperate pleas. Caleb had neglected his duty as a father. His sense of failure made his shoulders sag.

But there was no time like the present to change things. "Then let's pray."

Teddy knelt on the bedroll, his hands clasped before him, and squeezed his eyes tightly shut. "Dear God, I don't know You like Mr. Bell does, but I know You are strong and You can make me better. So will You, please?" He paused as if listening for a reply. "It's nice to be with the Bells. They're a good family. Bless them." He named each one. "And bless my papa. Help him to get better, too. Amen." He crawled between the covers and pulled them to his chin.

Caleb shook his head. "Son, I'm not sick or injured."

"But you're sad. I almost never hear you laugh anymore." Teddy sat up, surprise widening his eyes. "Until today. You laughed a lot today."

"I suppose I did." Lilly had a way of making him see and enjoy the humor in things.

Teddy twisted the covers in his hands. "Papa, are you mad at me?"

"Mad at you? How could you think such a thing?" He pulled Teddy to his lap and wrapped his arms about him. "I could never be mad at you."

"Even if I broke something like your knife that Uncle Ezra gave you?"

Caleb chuckled. "Well, I might be mad for a few minutes, but I couldn't stay mad for very long because I love you so much." He held the boy close. This child was all he had left of his family and his dreams.

"That's good." Teddy yawned.

"It's time you went to sleep." He tucked the boy in and kissed his forehead. "I'll just be outside." It was too early for him to go to bed, and he needed time to think. He slipped from the wagon, sat with his back to the wheel and stared at the star-studded sky.

His gaze went to the little house, where he could see golden light glowing from the window. Mrs. Bell crossed the room. Mr. Bell sat at the table. He couldn't see the twins, but he knew they were near their parents.

Hadn't he longed for such a home since the day he and Amanda married? A home filled with love and faith. He still did, but now he knew it wasn't possible. He carried too much pain and failure in his knapsack to ever again hope for such a home.

Mr. Bell had spoken about how Job had lost everything, yet still had vowed to continue trusting God. Caleb could do that as well.

"Papa. Papa." Teddy's screams rent the air and brought Caleb to his feet in one swift movement. He rushed into the wagon and scooped Teddy into his arms.

"It's okay. I'm here. You're safe. Shh. Shh."

Teddy sobbed and clung to Caleb. Finally he calmed enough to shudder out a few words. "I saw him again. He had a big knife." His crying intensified.

Caleb knew he meant one of the men who had invaded their home and murdered Amanda. He rocked Teddy and murmured comfort. Caleb's insides filled with bile. These nightmares occurred every night. If only he could erase the terror from Teddy's mind.

Teddy leaned back and looked at Caleb. "I wouldn't be scared if you brought Blossom in to sleep with me."

Caleb closed his eyes a moment and wished for patience. They were crowded enough in the wagon without sharing the space with a dog. Despite that, he knew he wouldn't be able to say no. But tonight was not a good idea. "Blossom is hurting too much to be moved right now."

He felt Teddy slouch. "I guess so. Maybe tomorrow?"

"Maybe." They'd be back at the Caldwells then. Blossom would have to sleep somewhere, and he kind of guessed Ebner wouldn't be all that welcoming of an injured dog.

"You won't go away, will you?"

"I'll never be where I can't hear you if you need me."

"Okay." Teddy allowed Caleb to tuck him back under the covers. "We'll take good care of Blossom, won't we?" Already he sounded half-asleep.

Caleb waited until Teddy's breathing deepened. "I'll take good care of her, but I'll take even better care of you. I promise."

This was one aspect of his life where he couldn't allow himself to fail.

Chapter Seven

Ma and Pa retired to their bedroom and Lilly and Rose went to the room they shared. In companionable silence they prepared for bed. Both read a portion from their Bibles. They prayed silently and turned out the lamp.

Then, as they always did, they talked.

Lilly propped herself up on one elbow and turned to her sister. She could see her in the dim light of the moon. "I can't help feel the Bell family can help Teddy, but he's only going to be here one day. What can we hope to accomplish in that time?"

Rose studied Lilly for a moment. "You sure it's just Teddy you're interested in?"

Lilly bristled. "Of course. And Blossom, too."

"And perhaps the Caldwell cowboy? I noticed he couldn't keep his eyes off you during supper. And you pretended not to notice, but I know you did."

"He's had a lot to deal with. I certainly feel sorry for him. But that's all." She only partly believed it. But yet, something deep inside called out to him at every turn, every word, every sign of distress he hid admirably well.

"Well, don't feel so sorry for him that you forget he works for the Caldwells."

"Honestly, Rose. I fail to see what that has to do with it. He's a fellow human being. Shouldn't that count for something?"

"Don't you think it's rather convenient for Ebner to have someone visit us? Perhaps inform him as to where he could do the most damage?"

"It's not like that at all. Caleb is worried Ebner will find out he's here and fire him."

"So he says. Just be careful."

Lilly lay down and stared at the ceiling. The same ceiling she'd stared at for almost eight years. Ever since they had left Bar Crossing and Pa had built the house on this bit of land.

Rose spoke, slowly at first. "I think you feel a connection to Teddy because he's lost his mother. Just like we lost our parents. But don't let it cloud your judgment."

"Oh, Rose, can't you let it go? Cora says she remembers a wagon riding away with our father in it."

"She remembers that our mother was dead." Rose jerked up and stared at Lilly. "What if she'd been murdered? Maybe in an Indian attack."

Lilly shuddered. "You're always imagining something, and every time it gets worse. I wish you'd stop. Like I've said a hundred times, it might be better not to know what happened."

"More like a thousand times you've said that." Rose chuckled, as if to make sure Lilly knew she was teasing. Suddenly she sat up and stared at Lilly. "But that's what Teddy is dealing with. Poor little boy. I don't blame you for wanting to help him."

Lilly's insides twisted into a knot. "I can't imagine the horror. We must pray that Teddy's leg gets better."

Lilly sat up and reached for Rose's hands. They each prayed for Teddy's leg.

But Rose didn't immediately crawl under her covers again. "I wonder what Caleb does with Teddy while he's working."

Lilly had wondered the same thing, but knew whatever he did, Caleb would not let Teddy out of his sight.

"He'll return to his job tomorrow and that will be the end of it." Lilly knew it was for the best and said so.

"He might be okay if he didn't work for the Caldwells."

Lilly smiled. Coming from Rose, that was a big sign of approval. Her sister had grown quiet and Lilly turned to a more comfortable position. Tomorrow was all she had, and she meant to use it wisely.

The next morning, Lilly braided her hair more carefully than usual and considered winding the braids about her head like the girls in town often did. Then out of need to prove to herself she wasn't doing it because they had company, she tossed the braids down her back, and as she left to do the morning chores, she pulled on the oldest, rattiest straw hat she could find.

Rose, helping Ma prepare breakfast, stared at the hat and covered a giggle.

"What?" Lilly demanded.

"Did you have to fight the mice for that hat?"

She tipped her nose and sniffed. "My cats keep the mice down." Recalling Teddy's amusement at how brave a mouse would have to be to live around here, she chuckled as she crossed the yard toward the barn.

She drew abreast of the wagon and stopped. The wagon's rocking indicated someone was inside, but she heard no voices.

Then Teddy peeked out through the front opening.

"Good morning," she said.

He glanced over his shoulder. "Don't talk to Papa until he can make some coffee."

Lilly grinned. "Is he truly so cross before coffee?"

Teddy nodded, eyes round. "Like an old bear."

"I can hear you, son." Caleb's growly voice came from the wagon.

"Sorry, Papa." Teddy mouthed the words, "I told ya."

Lilly's grin widened and she raised her voice slightly. "Pa has coffee ready in the house if you care to join him."

"Well, why didn't you say so?" Caleb picked up Teddy and jumped out the back. His expression was grim as he looked toward the house. He strode past her, carrying his son and the crutches as if waiting for Teddy to cross the yard under his own steam would take too much time.

"Ma's expecting you for breakfast, too."

Caleb didn't slow a bit until he disappeared into the house.

Lilly turned back to her chores, a smile upon her lips.

And if she cared to notice and admit it, a song in her heart at seeing this amusing side of Caleb.

She went first to Blossom to get her to drink. The dog was weak and limp. "Girl, don't you dare die." She examined the dog again. The cuts showed no sign of infection.

She sat back on her heels. "You are in no shape to travel." But that afternoon, Caleb would take the dog and leave. *God, please don't let Blossom die. Poor Teddy has had enough death and pain to deal with already.*

She fed the pigs and chickens, milked the cows and returned to the house.

Caleb sat at the table with a cup of coffee between his palms, his back to her.

Teddy turned to look at her as she stepped into the kitchen. "He's okay now. You can talk to him."

She chuckled. "What happens if you run out of coffee?"

Caleb shuddered. "Perish the thought."

"We did once. Remember that, Papa?"

"Better'n I care to."

"What happened?" Lilly expected Teddy would be full of details.

"Son, some things are just between you and me."

Teddy paid no heed. "Pa hitched the wagon up real quick and ran the horse all the way to the first farm we came to. He bought a few beans off the lady for a whole lot of money."

"She drove a hard bargain," Caleb grumbled.

Every one of the Bells laughed.

Teddy grinned, pleased at the response he had gotten.

Caleb grunted. "There is no such thing as a secret with a five-year-old watching everything I do."

"And that's a good thing," Pa said, filling Caleb's cup again. "We learn to speak and act more wisely because of them."

Caleb nodded. "One thing I've learned…"

Lilly stopped pouring milk into a jug to listen.

He continued. "Always keep a good supply of coffee on hand."

His unexpected words brought another round of chuckles from the family.

Lilly saw Pa give Caleb a look of approval and her insides felt warm and sweet.

"Breakfast is ready," Ma announced, and they gathered round the table.

Teddy enjoyed breakfast with as much enthusiasm as he had his supper.

"I never tasted such good food," he managed to say between mouthfuls.

Caleb planted his hands on either side of his plate, a fork and knife clutched tight. He looked at Teddy with raised eyebrows. "The way you talk makes it sound like we eat poorly."

"You do the best you can," Teddy said. "But we don't eat anything like this."

Lilly pressed her lips together to stifle a laugh.

Caleb favored her with a scowl, though she saw amusement in his eyes and realized he enjoyed his son's comments as much as anyone. "What about Mama's cooking? Didn't you enjoy that?"

Teddy's fork paused halfway to his mouth. He looked thoughtful. "I guess it was okay, but only 'cause I hadn't eaten food as good as Mrs. Bell's." He gave Ma an adoring look.

Why, the little scamp was deliberately flattering her.

Ma smiled. "Thank you, Teddy. That's very generous of you. It's easy to prepare nice meals if there is lots of good food, and we have that here on our farm." She leaned closer as if speaking for Teddy's ears only. "But no need to pour on the praise. I'll feed you all you want as long as you and your papa care to stay."

"Well, young man," Caleb said. "Does that teach you anything?"

Teddy gave his papa a dismissive look. "Yes. Good cooks are generous and kind."

Caleb sent Lilly a look full of surprise and pleasure. "What am I supposed to do with him?"

Did he mean the question for her? Or maybe Ma or Pa? But his gaze rested on her as if he wanted her opinion.

"Seems to me you should keep doing whatever you've been doing. The results are rather pleasant," Lilly said. She meant Teddy. Didn't she? Though he and Caleb made a very nice package together.

He smiled, relief, gratitude and something more in his eyes. "Thank you."

Rose made a soft sound as if to inform Lilly she'd seen something as well.

Lilly ducked her head and wiped her plate clean with the last bite of her bread.

"Thank you for another wonderful meal," Caleb said, when they had all finished.

Teddy rubbed his tummy. "Thank you very, very, very much. I shall enjoy the memory of this meal when we eat something cooked over an open fire." He sounded so sad and regretful.

"You'll do just fine," Caleb said. He brought his attention to Lilly. "Would you show me again how to make the poultice and do the exercises?"

"Gladly." She pushed away from the table.

Caleb had rehearsed every step during the night. Spread the stuff Mrs. Bell supplied, fold the paper, cover it with a warm, wet cloth. It was fairly simple. He cut a piece of paper.

"It's a little small," Lilly said, peering over his shoulder. "But it will do."

He spread the mixture.

Lilly stepped forward. "That much would burn his skin. Use a very thin layer." She showed him. "There you go." She moved aside and let him fold the paper. She'd made it look so easy, but his effort resulted in a lumpy mess.

"Like this." She flipped and rolled until the poultice was smooth and flat. She handed it to him.

He realized she was waiting for him to take over and went toward the cot.

"You'll need a warm, wet cloth." She nodded toward the cloth sitting not more than four inches from where he'd been working.

"I went over every step during the night," he grumbled. "Now I can't remember anything."

"It will come with practice."

He didn't point out that there was little time for practice. He had to learn in a hurry.

He dampened the cloth and let her test it.

She nodded her approval. "You don't want it too hot."

Caleb was beginning to think there was far more to this whole procedure than he had thought. It had seemed so simple when he'd watched her the night before.

Teddy waited on the cot, his pant leg pulled up, and Caleb applied the poultice. Now to wait the half hour.

"Today is Sunday," Mr. Bell said. "We go to church in Bar Crossing."

Caleb hadn't attended church since his arrival at the Caldwells', and he thought longingly of sitting in a service with the likes of the Bell family. But perhaps they wouldn't want to be seen in public with a man who worked for the people on the other side of the feud.

"It would be nice if you came with us," Mr. Bell said, eliminating that possibility and leaving Caleb with another. Would the Caldwells object to him attending with the Bells? He would not let their opinion sway him except for one reason—he needed the job.

On the other hand, Ebner had not attended church since Caleb had started work and somehow Caleb didn't think it was something the man practiced. And Mr. Caldwell and his wife were away. Didn't seem as if there'd be anyone to object.

"I'd like that."

Teddy grabbed his hand. "We're going to church? Like we used to?"

"Yes, son." How many times had he deprived the boy of things he enjoyed or accepted as part of normal family life simply because he was on the move, or tired, or discouraged?

"Last time we went to church was for Mama's—what do you call it?"

"Her funeral." Caleb forced the words past the restriction in his throat.

Teddy nodded. "Mama would be glad we are going."

"Yes, she would be." Amanda had been rigid in her church attendance.

"Do you think God will talk to me?" Teddy asked, delivering a shock to Caleb's midsection. He didn't know how to answer the boy.

"What do you want to hear?" he asked.

Teddy glanced around the table and whispered, "I can't say."

Mrs. Bell took Teddy's hands and looked deep into his eyes. "Teddy, I believe God will tell you what you need to know."

Teddy held her gaze for a moment and then nodded.

Caleb's heart was so tight he didn't dare look at Lilly

for fear it would burst open, but he heard her sigh and guessed she'd been as moved by the exchange as he.

Mr. Bell cleared his throat. "We leave in forty-five minutes."

"That's plenty of time to do Teddy's exercises," Lilly said. "We'll give the poultice a few more minutes." They waited a bit then she let him remove it. "Let's see how well you remember them."

"Not very well, I'm afraid."

"We'll do them together." She guided his hands. His arm cradled hers in many of the movements as he followed her lead. Would he ever remember how to do all these without her guidance? He must, of course. But her sure, steady hands and her calm words reached into his heart and strengthened him in a way he hadn't known since…he wasn't sure he'd ever felt so confident.

He tightened his jaw muscles. Had he forgotten his many failures? His hand faltered. She steadied it and smiled, thinking perhaps he had forgotten what he was doing.

But he'd remembered. *Don't let people get close to you. They'll get hurt.*

"That's enough for this morning," she said, and stepped back.

Little did she know how true her words were.

"Papa, can we go see Blossom now?"

"I tended her this morning," Lilly said.

Teddy grabbed his crutches. "Is she all better?"

"Not yet, I'm afraid."

"Oh." The word dripped with disappointment. Then Teddy brightened. "Good thing we're going to church. I can ask God to make her better."

"You can, indeed," Mr. Bell said. "But you don't need to wait for church. You can talk to God anytime."

Teddy nodded. "But it's better in church."

No one argued with his five-year-old wisdom as he headed out the door, Caleb and Lilly on his heels.

Lilly hung back and indicated she wanted to talk to Caleb.

He fell in at her side.

"I didn't see any improvement in her this morning. I'm sorry."

"Are you saying—" He couldn't imagine how Teddy would respond if the dog died. "I thought…I hoped." He stopped talking. What was there to say? She could only do so much. Isn't that what a dozen doctors had said to him about Teddy? Such futile, hopeless words.

She touched his elbow. "Don't give up hope. I haven't."

He nodded. Easy for her to say. It wasn't her son, her life. He shook away the troubling thoughts. She was doing her best. A person couldn't ask for more.

They followed Teddy into the barn. The dog lay limp and motionless until Teddy called her.

Then her head came up and her tail wagged.

"Look at that," Lilly said, her voice round with surprise. "It's like she'd been waiting for him."

Caleb grinned at the pleasure in Teddy's face. He only hoped Blossom wasn't saving the last of her strength for Teddy as a goodbye gesture.

But Blossom drank some water, ate the gruel Lilly had prepared and took the drops. She licked Teddy's hand then closed her eyes and went to sleep.

Caleb watched, praying the dog wouldn't die. Blossom's chest rose and fell in regular rhythm and the tension eased from Caleb's body.

"She's doing fine," Lilly said, brushing his arm. "Now I must get ready for church."

He realized he could do with some cleaning up, too, as could Teddy, and they headed for the wagon.

They each had one good set of clothes and he pulled Teddy's from his trunk first. His shirt and trousers needed to have a flatiron applied, but Caleb didn't have the means to do so.

"You bought me these for Mama's funeral," Teddy said as he donned his nearly new clothes. "Look, my pants are almost too short." Teddy grinned, smoothing his trouser legs.

"Why, I believe you've grown three inches this summer. Guess the food I serve you can't be so bad after all."

Teddy's hands stilled. He looked up. "I didn't mean it was bad."

Caleb chucked him under the chin and laughed. "I know you didn't. Now, if you want to wait outside and give me room to change, that would be nice."

Teddy lowered himself to the ground and leaned on his crutches. "You gonna wear the suit you bought for Mama's funeral?"

He looked at the items in his trunk. "It's the only good clothing I have."

"You looked very handsome in it."

"Did I, now?" He'd have thought Teddy would be so consumed by shock and pain that he wouldn't notice or remember any details from that day. "I'm surprised you noticed."

"Well, I didn't," he mumbled, studying the ground at his toes. "But I heard some ladies talking and they said you were handsome."

"Hmm."

"One of them said something really strange."

"Really?" He couldn't imagine what.

"She said you were a good catch. Papa, what does that mean? I thought you caught fish. You're not a fish." He giggled.

Caleb pulled out his newish shirt and slipped into it. He removed his well-worn denim pants and pulled on the black trousers. For the last occasion he'd donned this outfit, he'd worn a Western bow tie with tails that hung down several inches. Now he chose it again and pulled on his black suit jacket. He brushed his hair back and took a clean black cowboy hat from the hatbox where he had stored it. He brushed the dust from it and planted it on his head. He grabbed a damp rag to clean his boots with and then jumped down to face Teddy.

"What do you think?"

Teddy studied him with narrowed eyes. "I guess you look handsome."

Caleb chuckled. "So do you."

Mr. Bell came out to hitch the horse to their wagon.

"I better get our horse, too," he said, but Mr. Bell heard him.

"No need to take two wagons to town. You can ride with us."

Caleb hesitated. Not that he minded riding with the Bells, but he didn't want for him and Teddy to become a nuisance. Besides, there was this feud with the Caldwells. Apart from his job at the Caldwells', though, this disagreement between neighbors had nothing to do with him, so why should he let it influence him? He realized he wanted to ride with the Bells, be part of the family, observe Lilly with her sister…. He cut the rambling, traitorous thoughts short. "Thank you. I appreciate it."

"Jump aboard."

At Mr. Bell's command, Caleb lifted Teddy to the back of the wagon and climbed in beside him. The elder man drove to the door.

Mrs. Bell came out wearing a dark blue dress and matching bonnet with a black shawl pulled around her shoulders.

Rose came next, her red hair coiled back and covered with a pale gray bonnet. Then Lilly stepped out and Caleb was glad he'd worn his suit. Lilly looked like a lovely flower in a cornflower-blue dress, her hair a golden halo framing her face, her eyes bright as the Montana sky.

Rose looked at him and then nudged Lilly.

He hoped it meant he had passed inspection. He had only Teddy's word that he looked his finest.

He assisted the girls into the back of the wagon, where they sat on quilts their father had put on the box to protect their clothing.

They arrived at the church and Caleb jumped down to help the ladies. But when he reached for Teddy, the boy held back. "Pa, will people laugh at me 'cause I use a crutch?"

His insides crackled like old paper. If they did—well, he didn't want to think how he'd react.

Lilly answered Teddy. "No one will think anything of it."

Teddy nodded, pressed close to Caleb's side and gave Lilly a beseeching glance. "Will you stay with me?"

Lilly looked startled and looked toward her parents.

Caleb's jaw clenched. Did she object to escorting them? Was it because he worked for the Caldwells? Or did she have a beau who might object? Why hadn't he considered that? Of course she would. The young men of the community were probably lined up six deep hoping for a chance to court her.

Mrs. Bell smiled at her. "A little reassurance goes a long way."

Lilly nodded and stayed next to Teddy as the three of them followed the others inside.

Lilly crowded close as they walked down the aisle. Just like a regular family, Caleb thought. But then he hardened his heart. He would never again have a family.

They sat down, Teddy between Caleb and Lilly, and glanced about. There was something familiar and comforting about the place. It might have been the grinding of the pump organ, the greetings between friends and neighbors. Or maybe it was the sense of coming home. He hadn't attended church much since Amanda's funeral, but before that he'd missed it only in emergency situations.

He scanned the congregation and didn't notice any young men looking in Lilly's direction. Odd. He must have missed it. Or seeing him at her side, they'd guarded their interest.

The preacher stood behind the pulpit.

Teddy leaned forward, as if intent on hearing from God.

Caleb hoped he'd find what he sought.

They sang familiar hymns. Lilly and Caleb held the hymnal in front of Teddy. Although he could not read, he looked from Caleb to Lilly and wriggled with excitement. Oh, to be so eager to hear from God. He and Lilly shared a smile over the boy's head. Seemed to him they'd often shared pleasure regarding him. Caleb liked the feeling.

Pastor Rawley opened his Bible and Teddy fixed his eyes on the man. "When God speaks, do you listen?"

Teddy nodded vigorously.

Caleb stared. Had someone told the pastor of Teddy's desire to hear from God? No, that wasn't possible.

The pastor continued. "I expect most of you are saying you do. But is it true? Do you listen and obey when He says, 'Forgive others as I have forgiven you'? When He says, 'Fear not, I am with you'? Or when He says, 'Seek Me with all your heart and I will be found of you'?"

Teddy's mouth hung open. He turned to Caleb and indicated he wanted to whisper in his ear. Caleb knew such behavior was inappropriate, but he made an exception. "I knew God would talk to me," he whispered, his voice filled with awe.

Caleb patted Teddy's back and smiled. What exactly had God said to him? He listened intently to the sermon, hoping to understand. The words burrowed into his heart. Having faith, seeking God, forgiving others. What about forgiving oneself? The thought burned a path through his brain. He'd never thought of having to forgive himself. But Pastor Rawley pointed out that if God had forgiven a person, shouldn't the person also forgive his own failings or mistakes or sins or whatever lay like a burden on his shoulders?

He ended with a prayer while Caleb's thoughts churned with hope and possibility.

Teddy's face glowed. "I heard God."

"I'm glad for you."

They joined the others exiting the church. Lilly introduced him to Pastor Rawley and his daughter and several other young ladies. Caleb shook hands and continued on his way to the wagon. Several young men passed by and nodded a greeting, but he felt slightly smug when Lilly kept her attention on Caleb and Teddy without showing any interest in the possible beaus.

As he helped Teddy and the ladies into the wagon and climbed up to join them, his thoughts returned to the service. He felt as if he might have heard from God, too, but he wasn't sure he was ready to forgive himself. His failures were a heavy chain about his neck.

Lilly found the service refreshing despite her awareness of Teddy and Caleb at her side. She watched Teddy as he listened to the sermon. The little boy longed so much to hear from God. *Please, God, honor Teddy's desire.*

After the service, the town girls had whispered as they clustered around her, demanding to know who the good-looking cowboy was. She'd introduced them so they could find out for themselves, but they'd wilted at his lack of encouragement.

Cora and her husband, Wyatt, as well as Wyatt's sixteen-year-old brother, Lonnie, joined them. They had slipped in too late for any of the Bells to speak to them before church started.

Now Lilly introduced them to Caleb and Teddy.

Cora's eyes went from Caleb to Lilly and back again several times.

Lilly pretended not to notice, but she inwardly groaned. Cora would demand to know every detail. Not that Lilly had any reason to object. He was just a cowboy looking for help for his son and a pup. A Caldwell cowboy.

"Do you girls want to ride with us?" Cora asked.

Lilly hesitated. It seemed rude to leave Caleb on his

own, but if Rose went and she didn't, who knew what kind of picture Rose would paint.

"I'll ride with Ma and Pa if you don't mind," Lonnie said. He'd claimed Lilly's parents as his own after Cora and Wyatt married.

Taking everyone's acceptance as a given, Lonnie trotted over to the Bell wagon and climbed up beside Caleb and Teddy. He spoke to Pa, who nodded and waved goodbye.

Lilly waved back, her gaze on Caleb and Teddy.

Rose climbed into Wyatt's wagon. "Now we can bring you up to date on all the news."

Oh, great. Lilly could hardly wait to hear Rose's interpretation of the previous day's events. She climbed up beside Rose and Cora, leaving Wyatt to drive the horses and listen to everything the girls had to say. Not that she minded. Wyatt had proven to be fair and noble. He might even be led to correct some of Rose's wild imaginations.

Rose had the good grace to wait until they left the churchyard behind before she started. "I tell you, he is every bit as good-looking as Wyatt."

Wyatt looked over his shoulder, a grin splitting his face. "I see your taste is as good as Cora's," he said.

Annoyed at being left out, Lilly said, "I think you're good-looking, too. But—"

Rose chortled and cut off Lilly's words. "Not as good-looking as Caleb? Is that what you were going to say?"

"No. I was going to say a little boyish."

Wyatt looked startled and then whooped with laughter, while the other girls grinned.

"Boyish?" Wyatt said. "So this Caleb is an old man?"

"A handsome old man?" Cora probed. "Does Pa approve?"

"He's not old." She'd asked him. "He's twenty-five. And why would I need Pa's permission to help his son? And care for his injured dog?"

"A dog?" Cora's eyebrows headed for her hairline. "You never said anything about a dog."

"He brought an injured pup for some doctoring." She explained about Blossom, causing Cora to chuckle several times at little Teddy's behavior.

"You know, that's very interesting." Cora's grin grew wider and wider.

Rose wore a look of triumph as she nodded and nodded.

"You're going to hurt your neck," Lilly warned. Then she squinted at Cora. "What's so interesting about an injured pup? More than anything, it's a pity that people would purposely or carelessly hurt an animal. There ought to be a law against it." She ran out of protests and glared at her sisters, who continued to smile as if they shared some superior knowledge.

"Let's see," Cora began. "Wyatt shows up with a horse that needs to rest and a brother who is afraid. Caleb shows up with an injured dog and an injured son. Seems to be a pattern here."

"Lots of people come for Ma's help," Lilly protested. "That's nothing new. Besides, what no one has mentioned is he's a Caldwell cowboy."

Cora's amusement died. She stared at Lilly for three heartbeats and then turned to Rose. "Is that true?"

Rose nodded. "It is." She spoke as if she'd lost her best friend.

"What's he doing at the farm? Are Ma and Pa in danger?" She pressed to Wyatt's back, peering down the trail to where the Bell wagon was rattling homeward.

Lilly let out a long-suffering sigh and explained yet again that Caleb worked for the Caldwells because he needed money to take Teddy to a special doctor. "In the meantime, Ma and I are teaching Caleb to spread a poultice, and to do exercises to stimulate Teddy's leg and maybe get it to work."

"You're teaching him?" Cora sounded incredulous.

"Yes. He'll have to do it himself when he gets back to the Caldwell ranch tonight."

Cora sank back. "My goodness. I barely get married and things go awry at the farm."

Lilly rumbled her lips. "Everything is fine. None of us is in danger. You can continue to be a happily married woman and we'll manage just fine."

Wyatt turned around and grinned at her. "I don't think Cora is about to change her mind about being married, are you, dear?"

Color flooded Cora's cheeks. "I'm quite happy where I am."

Wyatt gave Cora such a loving smile that Lilly turned away, feeling she had intruded on a private moment.

She stared at the passing scenery, seeing nothing.

She had closed her heart to the possibility of ever having a love like the one Cora and Wyatt shared. The knowledge brought her pain when she considered it, but she ignored the burning in the depths of her heart and reminded herself that being left behind hurt even more.

A door in some far corner of her heart cracked open slightly, but the fear of pain and rejection was too strong and she slammed it shut.

Love was too great a risk.

Chapter Eight

"I wanted to go with Lilly." Teddy watched the wagon following them, carrying the three sisters and Wyatt. He made it sound like he was riding by himself in the Bells' wagon, but Lonnie and Caleb were with him.

"She wanted to be with her sister." Caleb, too, watched the wagon. No doubt they would tell Cora about him and Teddy. What would they say? How he'd like to be a little mouse in the corner and overhear that conversation.

One thing he knew: Rose would make sure none of them forgot Caleb worked for the Caldwells.

What would Lilly say? Would she talk about the injured dog? Would she explain how Teddy's leg had gotten injured? Or would she mention how she and Caleb had laughed together at Teddy's antics?

"Cora misses her sisters," Lonnie said. "Except she mostly thinks about Wyatt. A body could get tired of it. Wyatt this and Wyatt that." His mouth drew down to a frown and then he laughed. "It's not much better when I'm with Wyatt, except it's Cora this and Cora that." The young man sobered, grew morose. "Sure hope I never fall in love like that."

Caleb nodded and smiled. He let Lonnie think he shared the feeling, but to him falling in love seemed the best possible thing that could happen to a man.

His smile flattened. His teeth clenched. That sort of relationship was out of the realm of possibility for him.

Lonnie didn't seem to care if Caleb contributed to the conversation or not. He spoke of the older man who was Wyatt's partner—Jack Henry. "He says Cora and Wyatt put him in mind of the way he was when his missus was alive."

Lonnie spoke about coming to the Bell farm. "One of our mares was ready to foal so we couldn't keep going. Wyatt and I were looking to start our own place." He looked past Wyatt to a distant spot. "We were running from our past." He brightened. "But Cora helped us see we didn't have to keep running."

Teddy turned to Lonnie. "What were you running from?"

Caleb touched his son's shoulder. "It's not proper to ask personal questions."

"Oh, that's okay." Lonnie said. "We went through kind of a rough spot. I don't like to talk about it. I'll tell you this, though. My pa was nothing like Mr. Bell." His adoring glance rested on the older man driving the wagon. "Mr. Bell is a good, kind man."

"He is, indeed," Caleb agreed.

They arrived at the Bell farm and entered the house. A leaf was put in the table to extend it. The girls soon had it set and Mrs. Bell brought from the oven a roast surrounded by vegetables.

Wyatt, Cora and Lonnie sat beside Rose on one side of the table. Lilly sat between Teddy and Mrs. Bell to Caleb's left. Teddy grinned as if he'd been highly rewarded. Caleb had been busy guarding his heart. Maybe he should have been guarding Teddy's, as well. The boy looked ready to move in and settle down permanently.

Any hope of such would end this afternoon. They'd head back to the Caldwell ranch. End of story.

The conversation around the table was lively as the Bells told Caleb about the different people they'd spoken to at church. He didn't know if they were watching how they were talking about their friends and neighbors because Teddy was listening, or if they always spoke kindly, but he figured it to be the latter.

Lilly turned to help Teddy with his food. She poured him several cups of milk.

Caleb chuckled. "I think I'm going to have to find a milk cow." He meant it jokingly. A man headed down east didn't take a cow with him. The thought soured his insides. "If I ever put down stakes somewhere again, that is." He concentrated on his food, not wanting anyone to think he was feeling sorry for himself.

Cora laughed softly. "Wyatt had moving on his mind, too, until I made him see the folly of the notion."

Wyatt grinned. "Now I can't imagine why I thought it was a good idea."

Caleb noted the way Cora's eyes softened. He liked this couple. Cora had a mother-hen attitude toward her sisters and he guessed she'd felt responsible for them all her life. Wyatt had a brash, bold look that seemed to say he'd face whatever life placed in his path and deal with it. Even though Lonnie had hinted at a spot of trouble, Caleb thought it likely Wyatt's life hadn't tossed anything hard his way, or he might not have been quite so cheerful.

After dinner, Mrs. Bell served up generous portions of

stewed fruit. She passed fresh cream so thick he spooned a dollop onto the delicious fruit mixture.

Everything about the meal and the company was pleasant. But Caleb couldn't fully enjoy it. So many things were roiling inside him. Uppermost was worry about Teddy. Would he ever again walk on both legs?

Beyond that, deep inside, so deep it hid in blackness, lay his unacknowledged, impossible longing to share his life with a woman who loved him. A woman to whom he could freely express his love. Someone who would stand at his side in creating a family like the one the Bells had.

Thankfully the meal ended before his thoughts grew more hopelessly hopeful.

Lilly turned to Caleb. "I suggest we wait to take care of Teddy's leg until the kitchen is clean and the others have gone outside."

"I agree." He did not wish to have the others see his bumbling ways, nor did he want Teddy to have to endure curious stares, no matter how kind they were.

Besides, he wanted to be able to enjoy Lilly at his side without so many pairs of watchful eyes. He ignored the irony of wanting something he'd vowed to deny himself.

"Of course, you'll have to help with dishes." Lilly tossed him a tea towel and a challenging look and then plunged her hands into the hot, soapy dishwater.

He felt the others watching. "I've been known to dry a dish or two." He stood beside her.

"My papa makes me help with dishes when we're living in our wagon."

Caleb grunted. His son was turning into a real chatterbox. "You dirty half of them, so it seems you should wash and dry half of them."

"See?" Teddy crowed, as if Caleb had confessed to

some terrible deed. Then he squinted at Caleb. "But he won't let me cook over the fire."

The girls giggled. Wyatt and Lonnie grinned widely.

Lonnie patted Teddy's shoulder. "I know exactly how you feel, kid. Wyatt here always treated me like I couldn't take care of myself."

Wyatt gave his brother a long, measuring look. "I was only trying to protect you."

Finding someone on his side, Caleb met Wyatt's look. They considered each other a moment and each gave a little nod. Nothing had been said. No signal had been given. But Caleb knew they somehow shared a common bond of caring for a younger one—in Wyatt's case, a brother, in Caleb's, a son.

"I know." Lonnie grinned. "And I 'spect that's what your papa is doing, too."

Teddy nodded.

Lilly planted a wet dish in Caleb's hands and he brought his attention back to the task at hand.

Amid laughing and good-natured teasing, the dishes got washed and the kitchen got cleaned. Lilly shooed the others outdoors. Her parents said they were going to nap and disappeared into their bedroom.

"Now, let's see what you can do." She stood to one side and observed as Caleb prepared a poultice. "I couldn't do better myself," she said as he put it on Teddy's leg.

He concentrated on each step. He had to remember how to do it without supervision so he could continue the treatment back at the Caldwells'.

She pulled two chairs close to the cot and they sat side by side. "Sundays are my favorite day," she said.

He could see why that might be, but he wanted to hear her reasons, so he asked.

"So many reasons. For now, it means Cora and Wyatt and Lonnie can be with us for the day. I guess it won't be that way once the cold weather and snow set in." She brightened again. "Most of all I like the familiar routine of it." She ducked her head. "I don't like things to change."

He could understand that, too. "You have a nice family and a nice home."

"I know."

"Papa, how can you run away from the past?" Teddy's question halted their conversation.

Caleb explained to Lilly what Lonnie had said. "I don't know if you can, son. The past is always a part of us. Guess we can only learn how to accept it." Likely the boy was referring to the horrible events that had occurred in their once peaceful home—though it had lacked the warmth and joy the Bell home had. He wanted Teddy to learn to confine the horror of that day to a small corner of his mind and not let it rule his life.

Lilly leaned over Teddy and stroked his forehead. Her tenderness with his child made the back of Caleb's nose sting.

"Teddy," she said, "my ma once told me if I want to get rid of a bad picture in my mind, I have to replace it with a good one."

Teddy clung to her gaze. "How?"

"What's your favorite thing?"

"Blossom."

Caleb saw her flinch ever so slightly and knew she had the same awful thought he did—what if Blossom didn't make it?

She continued. "What you do when the bad picture

comes is pretend to turn around so your back is to the picture and you think of the good thing instead."

"Did you do that?"

She nodded. "I used to wake up crying. I was so afraid I didn't want to go to bed. After Ma talked to me, I would think of one of my favorite things." She laughed. "Strangely enough it was much like you and Blossom. I loved a furry little kitten I called Puff."

Teddy nodded. "Did your mama let you take Puff to bed with you?"

"Ma doesn't like cats in the house, but she did let me keep Puff in my bed a couple of times when I was especially afraid."

Caleb was again struck by the loving kindness in this family.

Teddy turned to Caleb. "See, I need Blossom with me."

Caleb laughed. Teddy certainly had a way of working things to get what he wanted.

"I suppose Blossom will have to sleep somewhere." It was time to remove the poultice and he did so.

Lilly checked Teddy's skin. "It's important to make sure we don't burn him."

We? Caleb would not acknowledge how good that sounded because there would be no 'we.' There would be only him. "I'll see if I can remember the exercises on my own."

He regretted his words immediately as Lilly stepped back and allowed him to manage on his own. Only twice did she correct him with verbal instructions. He could do this, he congratulated himself. On his own.

That particular victory fell flat.

* * *

Lilly watched Caleb's growing confidence with a mixture of pleasure and regret. If he meant to take care of Teddy on his own, he was proving capable. In the back of her mind she'd unwillingly harbored a hope he could struggle and decide Teddy needed to stay with the Bells. Wouldn't he then have to stay, too? Why would she think such a thing? Of course he wouldn't stay. He had a job and needed the money to take Teddy for treatment. Unless, of course, she and Ma could help Teddy, and then he wouldn't need to work for the Caldwells. Nor go east to see a doctor.

She jerked her gaze from Caleb, but she saw nothing except a twirl of confusion that came from inside her head. All that mattered was taking care of Teddy's leg using the best of the skills Ma had taught her. Where and when Caleb went afterward was of no concern to her. Hadn't she learned her lesson? *Don't get close to people. Don't care too much. It'll just be one more loss down the road.* The road she walked with Caleb and Teddy was to be just one day long.

She sucked in air and held it until her brain hammered for oxygen. She released her breath slowly, in firm control of her wayward thoughts.

The others returned to wait for Lilly to join them.

Their usual Sunday activity included wandering around the farm, letting Cora catch up with any changes and generally sharing the latest news each had. Soon the cold and snow would make them unable to get together on Sundays. Lilly did not welcome the thought. She enjoyed seeing Cora every week.

"Ask him to come along," Rose whispered, and Cora nodded.

"Yes, do."

She shook her head at her sisters' suggestion. Hadn't she only moments ago talked herself into keeping a distance from Caleb? Asking him to join them would put him squarely into her life, where she did not want him. "He'll want to stay with Teddy."

Ma stepped from the bedroom, patting her hair and then trying to hide a yawn. She headed for the stove to make herself some tea.

"Ask Ma to watch him," Cora said. "You know Ma would be glad to."

Ma noticed their conspiring. "What are you girls up to now?"

They turned as one.

Cora answered. "We wondered if Caleb would like to join us on our walk."

Lilly watched Caleb. His face lighted as if the thought pleased him, but guilt quickly replaced the pleasure. He lifted a hand toward Teddy. "I have to keep an eye on my boy."

Relief, along with a twinge of sadness, filled Lilly. For a moment she'd thought he would agree.

"Tsk. You don't have to spend the afternoon indoors," Ma said. "It'd be my pleasure to watch him."

He thanked Ma. "In that case, I'd love to go for a walk with all of you."

Lilly turned toward the outdoors, not wanting anyone to see her smile.

Rose hurried ahead, calling Grub to her side, Cora and Wyatt following arm in arm. Lilly glanced about for Lonnie, but he hung over the fence at the pig pen, watching his favorite animals.

That left Lilly no option but to fall in at Caleb's side

and traipse after the others. She twisted her hands into a knot. Why did it matter if they walked together? It meant nothing to either of them. But something about caring for Teddy and seeing Caleb's tenderness toward his son had awakened a desire she had tried to bury a mile deep, where it would never surface.

However, if Caleb walked at her side, it would give her a chance to talk about Teddy, though she wasn't sure what she needed to say. Caleb could handle the poultice and exercises fine on his own. And she said so.

"It would be an answer to a prayer if this works," she said.

"I confess I move between hope and despair. I would dearly love to see him walk without having to endure any more pain and discomfort. I know God could heal him, if He so chooses. But is my faith enough?" He shrugged.

"I suppose it depends what you have faith in."

"Why, in God, of course."

"Oh." She purposely looked puzzled. "Didn't I hear you say you wondered if your faith was enough? Seems that means you're trusting in what you can do."

He stopped stock-still and turned to stare at her, surprise filling his eyes. "I never thought of it that way. Of course I don't think it depends on me." He considered it a moment and shook his head. "At least I don't mean to." He turned to follow after the others again. "You've given me food for thought."

She couldn't tell if he appreciated it or not. "I hope you didn't think me harsh or judgmental. I spoke without thinking."

"No, no." He strode on, his hands stuffed into his pockets.

In the lead, Rose guided the group toward the sheep

pasture. They lined up along the fence and watched the animals grazing peacefully. Glad to be rescued from the uncomfortable conversation, Lilly counted her flock.

It grated at her nerves that one of the lambs had been drowned by the Caldwell cowboys.

Rose sidled up to her. "Those horrible Caldwells," she murmured, and cast an accusing look past Lilly to Caleb.

If Caleb heard the comment, he gave no indication.

"My little flock is expanding." She hoped to divert Rose from the attack she sensed was coming. "I'll spin this spring's wool as soon as the snow falls."

Cora explained to Caleb. "She makes sweaters and mittens from her wool and sells them. She always has a ready sale for them. Settlers and ranchers stop at the store and admire her things and soon all her handiwork is gone."

"It sounds like a lot of work," Caleb said.

"I enjoy it." She especially enjoyed knowing people received a quality product in everything she made.

"Work isn't difficult if you enjoy it." Wyatt pulled Cora closer and planted a kiss on her forehead. "Or if you do it for the one you love."

Lilly rejoiced for the love her sister had found. But even so her heart ached. She couldn't pinpoint the exact cause. Was it regret over how things had changed? How Cora now had a life that didn't include her twin sisters? Or was it something more—longing to experience the same thing?

She shook her head. A love like the one Cora and Wyatt shared was nice to see, but was it worth the pain and risk it carried in its arms?

"Let's see how Pa's trees have fared." Cora turned toward the orchard.

As they walked by the various fruit and berry bushes, Lilly explained how Pa had tried to produce fruit trees hardy enough for the Montana climate. A few scrawny apples remained on the trees, pockmarked by hungry birds. "Pa always leaves some fruit for the birds and deer."

Caleb smiled. "I like that."

They continued on their way, going toward the garden shed.

Rose turned to Cora. "I've made good progress in getting Ma's medicinals and remedies on paper."

"Rose is the family diary keeper," Lilly said by way of explanation.

"Someday you will thank me for making sure they are written down."

"You're doing a good job," Lilly admitted. "Cora, you should see the beautiful leather notebook she is writing in." She'd only started the new notebook a few days ago. Before that she'd written her notes in a plain booklet.

Rose grinned. "Why, thank you, dear sister. For that compliment I promise not to tease you for the rest of the day."

Cora and Lilly grinned at each other.

"Do you believe her?" Cora asked.

Lilly chuckled. "Not for a minute. She can no more resist teasing me than she can stop breathing."

Rose flounced away. "Don't say I didn't offer."

Wyatt laughed and turned to Caleb. "They sound like they mean it, but be warned, don't ever try to come between any of them. They'd turn on you so fast you couldn't escape without bruises."

Cora gave him a playful shove. "You make us sound vicious and we never are."

Wyatt pulled her to him. "You're far more subtle, aren't you? But I'm not fooled." He planted a kiss on her nose.

Lilly's throat clenched and she turned her attention to the landscape. The sun was warm, the sky almost cloudless. Dry leaves crackled underfoot. The breeze off the river carried a chill, warning people not to grow complacent and forget about the approaching winter.

"There's snow on the mountains," Wyatt said.

Cora pressed her cheek to his shoulder. "You'll be warm and dry in our little home this winter."

He nodded and smiled down at her. "I shall enjoy every minute of it." He leaned over as if to kiss her nose again.

"Enough of that." Rose shepherded them along the riverbank amid laughing protests from Wyatt and Cora.

They wandered for a spell until they reached a grassy slope, a favorite spot for Lilly and her sisters, and they sat down. Autumn leaves rustled in the nearby trees. Birds chattered noisily.

"Look," Lilly said, pointing to the prairie across the river. "A herd of antelope moving south for the winter."

They watched the animals for a few minutes and then settled back to enjoy the rest of the afternoon. Apparently done with the pigs, Lonnie jogged over to join them. The conversation went round various topics, especially plans for the coming winter. For the girls, that included spinning, knitting and quilting. The men discussed Wyatt's livestock.

Throughout the conversation Lilly noticed that Caleb kept looking toward the house. She was about to suggest they return when the topic shifted, as it seemed to always do, to the Caldwells.

"We haven't seen any of their cowboys around in days," Rose said, glancing about, as did the others, to make certain today wasn't the day they showed up to do their mischief.

"Has anyone heard if Duke has returned yet?" Cora asked.

"Douglas." Rose refused to call the Caldwell son by the nickname everyone else used. "Maybe he got lost or changed his mind about returning. Philadelphia might suit him better than Montana."

"You know you're just dying for him to get back. You miss him so much." Lilly grinned at Caleb to invite him in on the family joke.

Rose spun toward Lilly. "I most certainly do not."

Her reaction drew a chuckle from the other sisters.

"But he so admires your red hair," Lilly teased.

"He mocks it." She turned to Caleb. "He used to chant 'redhead, redhead, fire in the woodshed.' I know what he meant." She tapped the side of her head and rolled her eyes. "As if having red hair means there's something wrong with my mind. *Phewt.* I could live quite happily never seeing him again."

Caleb's eyes sparkled, but he looked sincere as he leaned toward Rose. "I expect he's jealous of your beautiful hair."

His compliment brought a rush of pink to Rose's cheeks and more laughter from the others.

"Of course, Rose didn't take his teasing without retaliation," Lilly added.

"I would be surprised if she did." Caleb looked from one to the other. "What did she do?"

"She punched him in the stomach so hard he could hardly walk afterward." Lilly had been proud of her sister's actions, but at the same time she'd been a little afraid of what Ma and Pa would say.

"Ma and Pa made me write a letter of apology." Rose still grumbled at the idea. "I wrote it, but I never meant a word I said."

Caleb studied the three girls each in turn, his gaze resting finally on Lilly. "It sounds to me like things could get interesting when this Duke fella comes back."

"Douglas," Rose corrected. "And if he tries anything, he'll soon discover we aren't helpless little girls anymore."

"Tell me you won't do anything foolish," Cora begged.

"Depends what you call foolish." Rose looked away, silently informing them she would not reveal any plans she might have. She jumped to her feet. "Look, something's caught in the river."

They all hurried to the bank. Bright red and blue flashed in the water.

"They look like ribbons," Cora said. "Oh, I'd love some more ribbon."

Wyatt waded into the water and caught one strand as it fluttered by, a blue ribbon he gave to Cora. She rewarded him with a kiss full on his mouth.

The other ribbons drifted by but got caught on a rock. "Let's get them," Lilly called, running downstream.

"Let me." Caleb strode in and retrieved another length of ribbon, this one red. "It's for you." He handed it to Lilly.

"Thank you." She smiled, lowering her head and smoothing the wet ribbon. She might never wear it, but she'd cherish it as a keepsake.

She couldn't meet Caleb's eyes. But as she glanced

past him, a bit of blue caught her attention. "The other ribbon is caught."

Caleb trotted to the river, waded in and rescued the yard of ribbon. He handed it to Rose. "One each. How fortunate."

Rose's eyes widened and then narrowed. Lilly wondered if she would accept a gift from a Caldwell cowboy.

Lilly released her breath when Rose took the ribbon and said, "Thank you very much."

Hopefully Caleb wouldn't be offended by her less-than-enthusiastic response.

He glanced down at his wet trousers. "I best go change. Then it's time I got back to Teddy." His gaze went toward the house. "He might be getting worried."

Lilly's attention was riveted on Caleb's face. The depth of devotion she saw there struck at her heart.

Was it possible a man could remain faithful in spite of challenges that would rock even the strongest person?

Chapter Nine

The afternoon had passed with lightning speed for Caleb. He'd enjoyed spending time with the Bell sisters, Wyatt and Lonnie, and he had found himself relaxing and feeling unburdened in their company.

Now his chest muscles tightened. Forgetting his responsibilities was not a good thing. He had a son who required his full time and attention.

Despite his mental warning, he smiled as he remembered the way Rose and Lilly had teased each other—all without rancor. His smile disappeared as quickly as it came when he flashed to Rose's struggle to accept the ribbon from him. He understood it was because he worked for the Caldwells.

And if he wanted to keep that job, he'd better pack up and get back there.

"It's time for me to leave," he said to the others.

They rose and followed him across the yard.

He hurried into the house, expecting to find an anxious Teddy. Instead, Teddy was sitting at the table with a glass of milk, an empty plate with some crumbs on it and Mr. and Mrs. Bell huddled close. They were listening intently as his son told them stories.

What stories had Teddy told?

Caleb's heart twisted. There were far too many sad, bitter tales in the boy's life.

Teddy didn't even glance up at Caleb as he continued regaling the elder Bells.

"Papa told me I catched the biggest fish any little boy ever caught." He saw Caleb. "Didn't I, Papa?"

"You did, indeed." The memory came with surprising joy. A lively little stream ran through his ranch. Caleb often caught a fish or two for the next meal. Teddy had started talking about fishing when he could barely walk. Despite Amanda's protests that the boy was too young for such adventures, Caleb had started taking him fishing as soon as he could toddle. He couldn't have been more than three when he caught his first fish. "I'm surprised you remember."

"I 'member real good," Teddy said. "Mama cooked the fish for breakfast."

Caleb remembered, too. It was a good memory. One where he had accomplished what he had hoped to, instead of failing his son.

"Son, we need to go. Say 'thank you' to the Bells."

Teddy did so and hobbled over to Caleb. "Blossom is coming, isn't she?"

"We'll load her in the wagon." He thanked them all for their hospitality.

Mrs. Bell handed him a jar of ingredients for making poultices. "Maybe you can come visit us again. We've really enjoyed your company." Her gaze rested on Teddy as she spoke.

Teddy turned his big blue eyes to Caleb. "Can we, Papa?"

"We work at the Caldwells." That said it all. Ebner would not look kindly at him consorting with the Bells.

The others hadn't followed him indoors. Although Rose was the only one who made her suspicions clear, the others likely shared her opinion.

He insisted on paying Mrs. Bell for the medicine she had given him, and made sure the amount indicated his appreciation for everything, including the hospitality they had offered to him and Teddy.

After another round of goodbyes and thank-yous, he managed to shepherd Teddy out the door and toward the barn. Cora, Wyatt and Lonnie were standing at the fence, watching the pigs and talking. Rose ducked into the garden shed. He saw no sign of Lilly.

Not that it mattered, except he wanted to thank her for her help.

He and Teddy stepped into the barn and he smiled. Lilly was kneeling beside Blossom, giving her some more tonic.

"I'm glad to see you before we leave."

Her eyes snapped toward him.

Had he sounded too eager? He hastened to explain. "I wanted to be sure to thank you for all you've done for Blossom and Teddy." More than that, she'd given him hope that there was something he could do to help his son, but he couldn't say that.

"It was my joy to help them both." Her gaze connected with his. A smile curved her lips and made him wish he could stay longer. Then she jerked her attention to the dog. "Blossom needs lots of rest and good food. You can take these drops with you. Give them to her three times a day. I'm sending along some ointment, too. Apply it every night to prevent infection." She handed him the items. Her fingers brushed his palm and he felt an incredible urge to curl his hand around hers.

Instead he thanked her and stuffed the things in his pocket. "I'll hitch the horse to the wagon and get Blossom. Teddy, you stay here." He rushed out. He couldn't wait to get away while he still had his wits about him.

He hitched the horse and then drove close to the barn, hopped down and hurried in to get the dog and his son.

Lilly followed as he lifted the Blossom into the back of the wagon. "Don't hesitate to bring her back if you suspect infection. I can help you with that."

"I'm sure we'll be fine." They had to be. He had a job to protect and a boy to take care of.

And now an injured dog to tend.

Everything would have to fit in around his work. He didn't mean to give Ebner reason to fire him.

With that thought uppermost in his mind, he thanked Lilly again and bid her goodbye.

Teddy waved at her until he could no longer see her. "I like Lilly. Will we see her again?"

Not willing to give the boy reason to be sad, Caleb simply answered, "It's hard to say."

As he expected, Ebner was none too happy to discover Caleb had an injured dog with him. "A gimpy boy and now a half-dead dog. Have you forgotten you're here to work?"

Caleb silently objected to the way Ebner described his son, but he kept his thoughts to himself. He'd heard worse and so had Teddy. The world had more than its fair share of cruel people. "I haven't forgotten. I'll do my work as usual."

"Well, don't think you can waste time looking after that sorry mutt."

Caleb nodded, directing a steady look at his boss to inform him Caleb was his own man, even if he had to take orders from Ebner. "I'll give you no cause for complaint."

"Huh." Ebner stalked away.

Teddy glowered at Ebner's back. "Papa, I don't li—"

Caleb held up a hand to silence the boy. "He's my boss. No bad-mouthing him."

"Yes, Papa."

Caleb settled Blossom and Teddy, leaving them in the wagon, and then hurried to do the evening chores. It was late by the time he finished and turned his attention to making supper for them.

Teddy sighed softly when he saw it was to be beans, stale biscuits and peaches.

"I know I'm not the cook Mrs. Bell is, but I don't have time to make a proper meal."

"It's okay, Papa." Teddy's voice lacked even a hint of enthusiasm.

Caleb hurried through the meal knowing he still had both Teddy and the dog to take care of. He made the poultice and left it on Teddy's leg while he applied ointment to Blossom's wounds and got her to take the drops and some food. Then he did Teddy's exercises. It hit him how much time was involved in doing everything.

There was only one way to accomplish it without upsetting Ebner.

The next morning he rose before any men or animals had stirred and slipped from the wagon. He paused a moment and looked back at his sleeping son. *Don't wake up while I'm gone.* Teddy would panic if he found himself all alone.

Caleb glanced at the cold coffeepot. He took a step toward the place where he built a fire to make their meals then forced himself to turn away. He could wait for coffee. He'd ignore the pounding that entered his head at the thought.

He hurried to the barn and surprised the horses, who were still sleeping. They shuffled and stomped as he rationed out oats and hay for each of them. Then he grabbed the fork and cleaned the pens and alley. Satisfied that should give him enough time to take care of Teddy and Blossom, he trotted back toward the wagon.

Cowboys staggered from the bunkhouse, scratching and groaning. Caleb overheard grumbling about the horses waking early, but he didn't say anything about his part in it.

He jogged back to the wagon, anxious to drink coffee and take care of his son. Perhaps he could hope to have the first cup before Teddy stirred. At the wagon, he peeked inside to assure himself all was right.

At the sight greeting him, his heart fell like a stone.

Teddy was curled up beside Blossom, one hand pressed to the dog's head, the thumb of the other hand in his mouth. His eyes were wide as twin moons.

"Teddy, what's wrong? Did you have another nightmare?" Caleb jumped up and pulled the boy to his knee, holding and rocking him.

Teddy clutched at Caleb's jacket and burst into tears.

Caleb rocked back and forth and rubbed Teddy's back. He should have never left the child. But if he meant to do the things Lilly had suggested, he had no choice.

"I thought you'd gone," Teddy managed to say around his sobs.

Caleb tipped Teddy's face up toward him. "I will never leave you."

"Something bad might happen to you. Like it did to Mama."

Caleb pulled his son to his chest. He couldn't promise that nothing bad would ever happen to him. There simply weren't any guarantees in life. "I will do everything I can to make sure nothing happens to me, but if—God forbid—it does, you let Grandma and Grandpa know." Amanda's folks would come and get him.

"How?"

"Well." He shifted so he could reach the satchel containing letters and other important papers. "Everything you need to know is in here."

"Papa, I can't read." Teddy sounded like he couldn't believe Caleb had forgotten that little detail.

"You take this to some adult you trust and let them read it."

Teddy nodded vigorously. "Like Miss Lilly."

"Miss Lilly would be a very good choice."

Teddy sighed and curled against Caleb's chest. "I like Miss Lilly, but I don't want anything to happen to you."

Amen to that. No one must be allowed into Caleb's life who would turn one ounce of his attention from this precious little boy of his.

"Now I better make us some breakfast so I can get to work."

He hustled over to start the fire and set the coffeepot to boil.

Teddy watched his every move. "You ain't had coffee yet?"

"Haven't." He corrected Teddy automatically, his mind counting down the seconds until the coffee would have developed enough kick for his satisfaction.

Teddy sat back on the bed and bent over Blossom's head. "He hasn't had coffee yet. And he didn't even growl at me."

Caleb grinned to himself. *See,* he wanted to say to someone, *I can change. I'm not a creature of habit.* But there was only one person he cared to tell. And she was back with her parents and sister at the Bell farm.

The coffeepot hissed and spat. He poured a cupful and sucked back the hot liquid, gasping when it burnt his tongue.

From inside the wagon, he heard a little giggle and smiled again. He let the liquid cool a bit and then drained the cup. He quickly threw some sausage and potatoes into a skillet and set it over the rocks he used as a stove.

"Now, young man, let's get this poultice done." He put Blossom on the ground to do her business. Teddy had gotten into his clothes and sat with his pant leg rolled back.

That done, Caleb stirred the contents of the skillet and then tended Blossom. Next he broke six eggs into the skillet and stirred the mixture. While he did Teddy's exercises, the eggs set. "Good enough," he declared. He had no time to waste. He dished the food out and gulped his down. He had barely finished when the cowboys started to pour out of the cookhouse. The majority of them saddled up and rode away.

Ebner headed toward Caleb. Caleb grabbed his hat and rose to his feet. No time to do dishes. "Teddy—"

"Papa, can I stay here with Blossom?" Teddy whispered.

Caleb gave it a moment's consideration. From where he'd be in the yard, he would be able to see Teddy. Truth was, he could accomplish his work a lot faster if he didn't have a tagalong.

"Okay, but don't go anywhere." He hurried toward Ebner, who immediately barked orders at him.

"Get the barn chores done, then—"

"They're already done, boss."

Ebner's only sign of acknowledgement was a narrowing of his eyes. "Good, because it's too late in the season to be mollycoddling a hired man just 'cause he's got a gimpy kid. I want the big corral ready for use. When yer done that we need about half a dozen gates built. Then—" By the time Ebner finished, Caleb had enough work for most of the week. Did Ebner mean for him to do it all today? He didn't ask because he didn't want to know the answer.

With a quick glance over his shoulder to check on Teddy, Caleb hustled to begin his tasks.

He worked steadily all morning and then trotted back to the wagon to throw together some food, do the poultice and exercises and tend Blossom.

Ebner dogged Caleb's trail all afternoon. The minute one job was finished, he ordered him to do another.

Throughout the day, Caleb barely had time to glance at Teddy, let alone go over and see if the boy was doing all right. From what he could see, Teddy wandered about the wagon and sat next to Blossom most of the time.

This was no life for a child. But what choice did either of them have?

He finished his chores. Ebner had disappeared into the cookhouse, allowing Caleb to escape being assigned any more tasks. He rushed over and threw some food together for supper. Teddy needed to be fed better. No doubt he was thinking longingly of the meals at the Bells', even as Caleb was. But Caleb had plumb run out of time and was getting a little low on energy, too.

It was dark before he finished tending Teddy and Blossom and cleaned up the dishes from three meals.

He lay beside Teddy in the wagon, too weary to do anything but seek the bliss of forgetfulness in sleep.

This was the way things would be now. He'd manage somehow.

But after two more days of rising early, two mornings of ignoring the complaints of those who'd had their sleep disturbed by the horses thumping about before dawn and two days of work that could keep two men busy, Caleb came to a conclusion.

He couldn't do everything and be everywhere, and Teddy was the one suffering.

As suppertime and the end of the day approached on Wednesday, Caleb found Ebner. "Boss, we need to talk."

Ebner crossed his arms and faced Caleb. "So talk."

"I can't manage taking care of Teddy and doing the amount of work you expect."

Ebner had been saying so since Day One, and now he wore a gloating look. "You quitting?"

"No, sir." The man would have to fire him to get rid of him. Although he hoped Lilly's methods would help Teddy, he wasn't prepared to cancel his plans to go east to see that doctor Amanda's folks had found. He needed this job to accomplish that. "But if I get someone to look after Teddy during the day it would sure help me."

Ebner studied him intently a moment and nodded. "You do that." He strode away without asking who Caleb meant to ask, and Caleb wasn't about to tell him.

He jogged back to the wagon, hurriedly tossed his belongings aboard and lifted Blossom and Teddy into the back.

"Papa, are we leaving?"

"Son, I'm taking you where you can be properly looked after while I work."

Teddy's face drained of color. "You're leaving me behind?"

"I think you'll like what I have in mind. Now, wait here while I get the horse." When he returned, Teddy sat on the bench, grinning at Caleb.

"I know what you're planning," he said.

Caleb climbed up beside him and smiled at his son's joy. "Let's see if you're right."

"Company coming." Pa, about to come in for supper, paused at the doorway.

Lilly stirred the pot of stew that simmered on the stove and then joined Pa in the doorway. It was a covered wagon. She knew of only one person in the area who traveled about in such a fashion.

Caleb.

"It might be someone passing through," she said, as much in explanation to herself as to her pa.

"Could be," Pa agreed.

Rose and Ma emerged from the garden shed where they had been the past two hours, as Rose continued to catalogue Ma's herbs and remedies.

Rose shot an accusing glance at Lilly.

Lilly shrugged. If it was Caleb, she had nothing to do with his return. When he'd left Sunday night, she thought it would likely be the last she saw of the Craigs and their dog.

The wagon drew closer and she could see it was Teddy and Caleb. Teddy waved and grinned.

She lifted her hand to return the greeting. Then curled her fingers and lowered her arm, pressing it to her stomach. Her initial curiosity had bounced to gladness to see them again, but just as quickly she'd quelled the feeling. After all, he hadn't come to see her.

Why had he come?

The wagon passed the barn and drew up before the house.

"Evening," Pa said.

"Evening." Caleb nodded and continued to sit beside Teddy.

He'd come all this way to say that? Lilly almost laughed.

"What can we do for you?" Pa asked as Rose and Ma joined Lilly.

Lilly realized she was holding her breath, and she eased it out slowly and quietly so Rose wouldn't notice.

Caleb got off the wagon and came to face Pa. He clutched his hat in his hands. "Sir, Mrs. Bell, ladies." He nodded to each of them. "I have a very large request to make." He sucked in a breath. "I find I can't take care of Blossom, do Teddy's extra care and keep up with my chores." The hat twisted round and round. "Lilly said to come back if I needed anything." He swallowed hard.

Lilly suspected he wanted to ask for help, but the Bells waited, letting him do it in his time and his way.

"I'm here to ask if I can pay you to look after Teddy for me while I work." His gaze caught and held Lilly's, as if he meant the question solely for her.

Ma and Pa looked at each other and then Pa said,

"Why, of course we'll help with your son and the little dog. Bring them in."

"Thank you." He planted his hat on his head but didn't move. "Shall I put Blossom in the barn?"

Ma turned to Lilly. "What do you think?"

"Do you plan to leave Teddy here overnight?" Lilly asked, thinking Blossom might provide Teddy with comfort if that were the case.

The hat came off again and twisted round and round. Caleb's mouth pulled up at one corner. "I don't want to, but what choice do I have?" Agony tightened each word. "How can I bring him here each morning and get back to work then come get him each evening after work? It wouldn't take much to convince Ebner to fire me and I simply can't have that."

Lilly reached out a hand to him and then she pulled it back. Her sympathy must be contained, for if she expressed it as deeply as she felt it, she would squeeze his arm and smile reassuringly. Rose would object on the sole basis he worked for the Caldwells. Ma and Pa would warn her to be more circumspect. Instead of following her instincts, she slipped to Ma's side. "We can make sure he's safe and happy, can't we, Ma?"

"To the best of our ability. Bring them both inside."

Caleb again put his slightly battered hat on his head and turned to Teddy. "You want to visit the Bells for a while?"

Teddy nodded and grinned and then almost leapt into his father's arms. As soon as Caleb set him on the ground, Teddy put the crutches in place and headed for the house. "I knowed he'd bring me here."

Lilly went to the back of the wagon, from which Caleb

lifted Blossom. The dog raised her head and licked Caleb's hands.

"She's looking better," Lilly said.

Caleb grinned. "Must be all the loving she gets from Teddy."

"I expect you've done your part by tending her wounds." Even a quick glance revealed they were clean.

"There's been no change in Teddy's leg."

"I'm sorry. But it's only been a few days."

Caleb held the dog, his gaze on Lilly as if seeking something from her. Was he discouraged? Perhaps he felt he'd failed.

"It's a lot of work to take care of an injured dog and a boy needing special attention." She hoped he'd find her words reassuring.

He nodded. His eyes darkened, and then he shifted his gaze to Blossom. "Where do you want me to put her?"

"I suppose Teddy will sleep on the cot, so why don't you put her on the floor beside it?"

"Good. She'll keep him company."

They went indoors and settled the dog. Lilly brought water and food for her and grinned at how eagerly Blossom took both. "It's good to see her gaining strength."

Teddy hurried over and sat on the floor beside her. Blossom wriggled from nose to tail. Teddy patted her head. "She's going to be better soon, so then she can run and play with me."

Caleb slowly brought his gaze up to meet Lilly's. She read the despair there, knew he was wondering if Teddy would ever be able to run and play again.

Ma observed them. "Love and proper care work wonders. Have you had your supper?"

Teddy answered immediately. "Pa's been awfully busy. Says there's no time for cooking."

Caleb groaned.

"It's okay, Papa. I'm not 'plaining."

Caleb rolled his eyes.

"We were about to eat," Ma said. "Please join us."

Teddy was on his feet headed for the chair he'd formerly occupied before Ma finished her sentence.

Even Rose chuckled at his eagerness.

Soon they were gathered around the table. Pa held out his hands and Caleb took the one on his side.

As Lilly took the hands of Rose and Ma, she thought how Caleb and Teddy fit right in, how the family seemed livelier with them there. And how glad she was to see him across the table.

Thankfully, Pa said grace at that moment, preventing her from examining the thought.

After the meal, Caleb grabbed a towel and helped dry the dishes.

"Just like Wyatt used to do," Rose murmured.

What did she mean by that? But she couldn't ask and get an answer in front of everyone else.

After the kitchen was clean, Lilly helped Caleb prepare the poultice. They took care of Blossom and then she supervised Teddy's exercises.

"You're doing good."

He smiled, but it did not reach his eyes. "If I didn't need…"

She understood what he didn't say—if he didn't need the money, if he didn't need the job, he would make different choices. He'd take care of Teddy himself. But wishing didn't change anything. If it did, she could wish for a man to love her like she wanted. She could hope for a family of her own. But she knew the folly of wanting those things. She'd never forget the disappointment and pain of opening herself up to those dreams, only to have them snatched from her.

Caleb finished Teddy's exercises and stepped back. "I'll bring Teddy's things in."

Lilly glanced around. Pa was reading. Ma was knitting. Rose was writing in her book of cures. That left her to accompany Caleb. "I'll come with you." She sensed how difficult it was for him to consider leaving Teddy.

They went outside to the wagon. Caleb reached into the back for a small trunk, groaned and stepped back. "I don't want to leave him. I'm all he has."

She rubbed his arm. "He has Blossom. We'll take good care of them both."

"I have no doubt of that, or I wouldn't even have considered this. But he's just a small guy who has lost his mother. I don't want him to think I'm leaving him, too."

"You can make him understand."

"I'll put him to bed before I leave." He hoisted the trunk and returned indoors with Lilly following.

She couldn't imagine how hard this was for both of them. If only she could do something to make it easier.

Caleb put the trunk at the end of the cot. "I'll help you get ready for bed, Teddy."

Teddy stood at Pa's side, looking at something Pa had drawn. At his father's word, he went to Caleb.

"Am I going to sleep here?"

"Is that okay?" Caleb asked.

He nodded. "Blossom will want me to stay close." He slipped into his nightshirt and Caleb folded his clothes neatly and put them on top of the trunk.

Teddy sat on the bed with an expectant look on his

face. He signaled for Caleb to move closer so he could whisper something.

Caleb nodded. "I'll ask." He turned to Lilly. "Teddy wants to know if you will listen to his prayers."

"Me?" The request slammed her in the middle of the chest and then the feeling eased, leaving her insides quivering with yearning and pleasure. She could love this boy. If she let herself.

"Please," Teddy begged.

She'd stood lost in contemplation long enough to make him think she'd refuse. "I'd be honored." She sat on the bed and Teddy crawled into her lap and closed his eyes.

She closed hers as well, more to contain the bittersweet joy of being near this child than to prepare for prayer.

Teddy prayed for his father, Blossom and each one in the Bell family, and then he asked God to make his leg remember how to work. "Amen."

A still quiet filled the room.

Lilly slowly turned her gaze to Caleb. His dark eyes were filled with hope and despair. She knew her own eyes must have shown her feelings of joy and pleasure, because she could not contain nor control them. He smiled as if he were correctly reading the tender feelings his son brought to her heart.

He turned away. His expression softened as he studied Teddy. "I'll tuck you in."

Lilly scurried out of his way.

Teddy crawled under the covers. "Cozy," he said, his voice soft with contentment.

Caleb tucked the blankets tight and bent over to kiss him on the forehead. His hand lingered, brushing Teddy's hair back, wiping an imaginary spot of dirt from his son's face. He sucked in air and straightened. "Good night, Teddy. I'll be back tomorrow evening. Be a good boy." He wheeled around and headed for the door.

Teddy sat bolt upright in bed, the cozy covers tossed aside. "Papa, you're going?"

"Yes, I thought you understood that. But I'll be back."

"No, Papa. You said you'd always be close enough to hear me. You can't go. You can't." Tears and sobs intermingled with Teddy's anguished words.

Caleb hesitated at the doorway.

Lilly held her breath. Would he leave? What choice did he have? Her heart echoed Teddy's cries. Her birth father had left her and Rose and Cora. Wasn't he supposed to stay close and take care of them? She pushed her fist into the pit of her stomach in an attempt to stop the pain. Was she so unimportant, so unlovable, so forgettable that even her own father could walk away?

She wanted to pull Teddy into her arms and shelter him from such fear, but she was riveted to the spot as firmly as if someone had driven nails through her shoes.

Chapter Ten

Caleb stood in the doorway, Teddy's cries tearing wide wounds through his heart. He had promised Teddy he would never leave him, he would always be close.

But he had to work.

Who would comfort his son when he cried in the night?

"Papa, Papa, don't go," Teddy sobbed.

Caleb closed his eyes as pain seared from the soles of his boots to the top of his head. He couldn't do it. He couldn't leave his son. Somehow he had to work things out. He turned slowly and faced the Bells. "I can't leave him."

Mr. and Mrs. Bell nodded. "We understand."

Teddy's sobs shuddered to a stop. He swiped at his tears.

Lilly jumped to her feet. "Ma, Pa, why can't Caleb stay?" She flung about to face Teddy. "If your papa stayed here overnight, would you be happy to stay with us during the day?"

Caleb shook his head. "My job—"

"You can ride back and forth. It's not far on horse-

back. Go back in the morning. Come here after work."
She turned to her parents. "Don't you think that would
be good?"

The older couple looked at each other, stayed silent
for a moment and then nodded at the same time. Mr. Bell
answered. "You're welcome to stay and leave Teddy here
during the day."

It sounded like a good idea, but Caleb shifted his attention to Teddy. His son would have to approve. "What
do you think, Teddy?"

"Could Blossom stay with me?"

Lilly answered his question. "She certainly could."

"And you'd come here every night?" he asked Caleb.

"Every night."

"Then I guess it's all right."

"Good. I'll park the wagon and come back and get
Teddy." He meant to sleep in the wagon as they had
done previously.

Mr. Bell waved away Caleb's plan. "No need for that.
Teddy is already settled. You can sleep with him if you
don't mind being crowded, or better yet, bring your bedroll in and sleep on the floor beside him. Unless you object to sleeping on the floor."

Caleb laughed as much with relief as with amusement.
"No objection at all. Teddy, I need to take care of the
horse and wagon and then I'll be back. Okay?"

Teddy nodded. "I'll wait for you."

He almost told the boy to go to sleep, but he understood Teddy would not settle until he saw Caleb ready to
sleep beside him. "I'll be back in a few minutes."

Lilly followed him to the door. "I'll get your horse
some feed." Caleb left the wagon parked beside the barn

and then led the horse inside, where Lilly put out a bit of grain and some hay.

She leaned on the pitchfork handle, her chin resting on her clasped hands. "Caleb, I hope I haven't put you in an awkward position."

He brushed the horse down. "How's that?"

She made a sound, half snort, half laugh. "I can't see the Caldwells being happy about you riding over here every evening."

He turned the horse into the manger for its feed, using the time to consider his reply. Ebner most certainly would raise a ruckus if he knew where Teddy was staying. "What is good for Teddy is more important to me than what Ebner thinks."

"Very noble. But you might lose your job." She cleaned up a bit of scattered hay, making it impossible for Caleb to see her expression. Did she approve of his decision or consider him foolish?

He felt he needed to explain his behavior to her. "I promised Teddy I would always be close enough that he could call me."

She studied him with a look of confusion. "But you won't be here in the daytime."

"He's okay during the day. Night is when he gets scared and has frightening nightmares. I can't imagine what he'd do if I wasn't there to hold him and tell him he was safe." Memory of the horrors that plagued his son gripped Caleb so hard he struggled to breathe. "I can't leave him." He choked out the words.

She stood beside him and rubbed his arm.

He could not deny himself this bit of comfort. He covered her hand with his and pressed it tight to his forearm.

"No father should ever leave his children."

Her words sounded as if her throat were as tight as his. Her mouth twisted.

"I will never leave him. It's a promise I made to both myself and him."

"I didn't mean to suggest you would, but not every child is so fortunate. Thank God for people like Ma and Pa who took us in."

If he wasn't mistaken, her words conveyed regret as much as gratitude. He curled his fingers about her hand where it lay on his forearm. "Lilly, what happened to your parents?"

A jolt shook her and he held her hand tighter, narrowing the distance between them to only a couple of inches. Whatever had happened, it still had the power to shatter her world.

"My mama died. My papa left us in the middle of the prairie and rode away."

Did she realize when she spoke of them she still sounded like a little girl? He ached to pull her into his arms and comfort her as he would have Teddy.

"We never saw him again. Don't know what happened to him or why he left us." She shook herself a little, pulled her hand away and squared her shoulders. "So you see, I know that not all fathers promise to never leave their children, and even fewer keep that promise."

He stood silent and waiting, hoping she would open her past a bit more. Somehow he knew, though he couldn't explain how, that inside she had a room full of sorrow she needed to empty.

But she placed the pitchfork in the tack room, dusted her hands off and faced him, her expression serene, as if all her thoughts were joyful and peaceful.

He knew otherwise.

"Are you ready to go back to the house?" she asked.

He nodded. "Teddy will be anxious."

They stepped into the dusky evening and closed the barn door behind them. A cat slipped inside just before the door shut. Grub sat waiting for them and almost fell over his own feet in his rush to get to their side.

Caleb chuckled. "Don't suppose he'll teach Blossom his ways, do you?"

She laughed. "Are you suggesting that would be a bad thing?"

"Hmm. Let me think." He rubbed his chin. "I guess it depends on whether I want a big clumsy animal or a dog who will protect my son."

She stopped and rubbed her chin, imitating his contemplative action. "I'd think the answer would be obvious. Isn't it your job to protect Teddy?" She didn't wait for him to answer. Not that he needed to. The question had been purely rhetorical. "So it seems what Teddy needs from Blossom is a playmate. Besides, Grub isn't clumsy. He's just…" She pressed her lips together to search for a word she liked. "Overeager."

"If you say so."

Grub, sensing they were talking about him, turned around in an excited circle and ended up on his back with a silly grin on his face.

Caleb chuckled as Lilly patted the dog.

"You're a good old dog, no matter what he thinks."

Grub scrambled out from underfoot and they continued on their way to the house.

"How do you know what I think?" he asked.

"You've made it plain you think our dog is useless."

"Only as a guard dog," he said. "He's very good at…

other things." He purposely made the words vague, matching his voice.

"Yes, he is."

When they reached the door, Grub flopped down beside the house and Caleb and Lilly stepped inside.

Teddy sat with Rose beside him looking through a book. Mrs. and Mr. Bell had pulled chairs close to the cot and were looking at the pictures along with them.

Caleb ground to a halt. He'd once dreamed of such a homey scene.

He and Amanda had loved this child. Her murder had robbed Teddy of this sort of attention. Was he doing the boy a disfavor by letting him enjoy it here with the Bells, knowing it would be temporary? He answered his own question. He couldn't deny him the joy, nor could he take the boy back to the Caldwells' knowing he would have to neglect the poultices and exercises if he meant to keep his job.

Mr. and Mrs. Bell pushed their chairs back to the table. "Girls, it's time for bed," Mr. Bell said. "This little fellow needs his sleep, and we'll need to rise early in order to get breakfast ready for Caleb before he leaves."

"Oh, no need to put yourselves out." The last thing Caleb wanted was to become a burden to them. "I'll take care of my own needs." He had supplies in the wagon and had cooked his breakfast almost every morning since that awful day.

"Nonsense," Mrs. Bell said. "That would be plumb foolish when we have an abundance to spare."

"Besides." Lilly spoke softly, as if she didn't want Teddy to hear her. "Don't you think you should make sure Teddy is okay before you leave?"

He squinted at her. She knew it was an argument he

couldn't ignore, but why would she use it? Did she want him to stay for breakfast? Or was she only thinking of Teddy and how it felt to have a father leave you behind? He studied her gentle smile a moment, but she revealed nothing in her gaze.

For Teddy's sake, he would accept their invitation. "It's most generous of you." He would pay these people for their kindness.

Rose and Lilly went to one room. Mrs. Bell pushed the kettle to the back of the stove and fussed about tucking Teddy in again.

"I'll leave you that lamp." Mr. Bell nodded toward the one in the middle of the table, lit another and then headed for the bedroom.

"Good night," Caleb said. Mr. and Mrs. Bell said good-night before they closed their door and two voices called good-night from the other bedroom. He stretched out on his bedroll, his hands clasped behind his head. The sound of those friendly good-nights lingered in his head like a sweet melody.

"Papa?"

"Yes, Teddy."

"This is the nicest we've had it since Mama died." He sighed contentedly.

"Yes, it is." He never thought he would again feel the pleasures of home. A warning signal jolted up his spine. He jerked his hands to his side and closed his eyes tight. He felt like he was walking on a very thin board high above a raging storm with the Bell family following him. One misstep would send them all plunging into the turbulent waters below. Why should he feel this way? He accepted their hospitality with no intention of prolonging his visit beyond what was necessary. It was the best way to take care of Teddy.

Sooner or later, Ebner would discover what he was up to.

The tension in his spine increased. Surely Ebner wouldn't punish the Bells for helping him. Still, he couldn't shake the feeling of disaster.

His thoughts darkened. He'd brought pain into too many lives already.

God in Heaven, protect these people from any harm.

It was all he could do at the moment. He needed their help until he finished the job at the Caldwells' and took Teddy down east.

Rose turned out the lamp and darkness folded in on Lilly.

She tried to calm her thoughts, but they went round and round, faster and faster. Why had she told Caleb about their birth father abandoning them? It wasn't like she usually gave it any stock or let it fill her thoughts. Not like Rose did. No, she liked things exactly the way they were.

Her heart kicked up a protest.

Okay, there were things she might wish for, but she'd realized how foolish it was to have dreams that depended on other people.

Caleb would never leave his son. He was a father his boy could count on.

That did not, she warned herself, mean he was a man another person could count on.

"Lilly, why did you get so upset when Teddy cried?" Rose asked.

Lilly sat up and stared at her sister, though in the darkness she saw little but the shape of her in bed. "Didn't you?"

The shape moved and sat upright. "Of course I felt badly. But you acted like Caleb was leaving. Lilly, you haven't fallen in love with him, have you?"

She snorted. "Me? I think I can live without the risk of falling in love."

"What risk do you mean? Why are you afraid of falling in love?"

Lilly wasn't sure how honest she wanted to be. "Well, first there is what happened with Karl—"

"He doesn't count. We both agree he wasn't the sort of man you want."

Lilly didn't remember agreeing to that, but she knew it to be true. Karl had been more interested in Karl than in a life with Lilly.

Rose pressed her. "What if you found a man like Wyatt?"

"I don't think Cora would be willing to share him." Lilly's laugh sounded false, even to herself.

"You know what I mean. What's to be afraid of?"

"What are you afraid of?"

Rose grunted. "I'm not afraid. I'm just waiting for someone to come along who sees my value. What are you waiting for?"

Lilly sighed. How could she explain it to her sister? What better way than with her motto? "You get close to people, it'll just be one more loss down the road."

"I don't think you are talking about Karl."

Surprisingly, she wasn't.

"Now I see it." Rose's voice rang with victory.

"It's dark. How can you see anything?"

"You saw yourself in Teddy. You felt his fear that his

father would leave him. And all this time you say you don't think about our past, don't want to try and find out who our birth parents were. You say you like things just the way they are—"

"And so I do."

"But don't you see the past is controlling you? It isn't Karl's leaving you that has you afraid. It's our father riding off and leaving us. You're afraid another man might do the same thing. Maybe that's why you pretended you cared about Karl. You knew he would live up to your expectation of eventually deserting you."

"Girls." Pa's voice was coming from the other room. "Some people would like to sleep."

"Yes, Pa," the twins chorused and lay back down.

"I'm right," Rose whispered. "And I think you know it."

Lilly didn't answer. Whether or not Rose was right didn't change a thing. Either way, she had no intention of opening her heart to more loss.

Though it might be too late in Teddy's case. She cared far more deeply for him than she knew was wise. Her heart would bleed more than a little when they left.

And Teddy's father?

She wasn't that foolish. All she felt for him was sympathy.

Within minutes she fell asleep, but sometime later, a sound startled her awake and she jerked up in bed.

Rose sat up, too, barely visible in the dark of night. "What was that?"

"Teddy's crying," Lilly murmured. She was grateful the darkness hid the sheen of tears in her eyes. In her mind a memory flashed, so sharp and painful she almost moaned. She had only been three at the time, but she remembered the fear that had threatened to rip her heart from her as she stood holding Cora's hand, looking down a long, empty road.

Teddy's sobs grew muffled and the low rumble of Caleb's voice calming him eased the tension from Lilly's spine. She lay back, her own painful memory fading into the night.

She woke the next morning to the sound of Pa starting the fire in the stove and Ma splashing water into the kettle, and she bounded from her bed.

Would Caleb have left already?

She was in her clothes and out of the room before Rose had even brushed her hair.

"Good morning," Ma said.

Lilly answered without looking at her, her attention elsewhere. Caleb sat at the table with a cup of coffee between his palms, his eyebrows knotted together in concentration.

Pa held the coffeepot and filled his own cup.

Teddy sat on the floor next to Blossom.

Caleb hadn't left. And he hadn't had his first cup of coffee. A grin tugged at Lilly's lips. "Good morning, Caleb."

He grunted.

Teddy held a finger to his lips. "He hasn't had his coffee yet."

She nodded. "I kind of thought that." Unable to resist the urge to tease him, she sat down across from Caleb. "Is it too hot to drink?" she asked in her most innocent voice.

He glowered at her and gulped a mouthful, gasping and waving his hand at his mouth to cool his burnt tongue.

She pressed her lips together to keep from laughing, but she knew he could see the amusement that made her eyes smile.

"Lilly, leave the man in peace," Pa said. He turned to Caleb. "Forgive her. She's not a coffee drinker, so she doesn't understand."

Lilly chuckled. "I can't help but feel a little sorry for Teddy. How does he put up with this day after day?"

Caleb cautiously swallowed more coffee. His eyes slowly softened, and he sighed. "With a great deal more kindness than you've shown."

She grinned. "Sorry."

"You are not."

"You're right. I'm not. Like Pa says, I don't need coffee to make me cheerful in the morning." Was the man unreasonable if he didn't get that first drink?

"Papa didn't have coffee right away for the past few days," Teddy said. "He got up early and hurried to do the chores before everyone else was up. And he didn't even get mad at me."

Lilly widened her eyes. "Wow, I'm impressed."

Caleb quirked his eyebrows. "I'm really quite noble, you know."

Rose joined them. "Don't see how a noble person could work for the likes of the Caldwells."

Caleb shrugged. "They pay well, and besides, I didn't know I'd stepped into a feud."

"I suppose not," Rose acknowledged. "And maybe having you there will mean we will get some warning when they plan to do something."

Caleb's expression grew dark. "You're asking me to spy?"

"She is not." Lilly jerked to her feet. "Rose, how could you?"

Rose leaned close and spoke so quietly Lilly doubted anyone else could hear. "Don't be so naive. Don't you wonder if he is spying for the Caldwells?"

Lilly could only gape. It wasn't possible.

Rose continued, more loudly. "Besides, are you going to say that if you knew ahead of time they planned to chase your sheep into the river you wouldn't have stayed home to protect them?"

"Well, of course I would have," Lilly said. She sank back to her chair. "I would have done anything to save my lamb."

Caleb sat back. "They did that?"

She nodded.

"And worse," Rose added.

"I wish I'd known before I took the job, but now—" He shrugged.

"Girls," Ma said. "This isn't appropriate table conversation."

"Yes, Ma," they chorused.

Pa refilled Caleb's cup. "We don't hold you responsible for what the Caldwells have done, do we, girls?"

Lilly answered quickly. "Of course not."

Rose mumbled something. Lilly knew she wasn't willing to overlook the fact that Caleb worked for the Caldwells.

Lilly set the table and Rose helped Ma prepare the food. Soon a hearty meal was on the table. Caleb ate hurriedly, glancing frequently at the window. As soon as he was done, he pushed away from the table. "I must be on my way." He knelt at Teddy's chair. "You be a good boy. I'll be back tonight."

"We'll expect you for supper," Ma said.

He hesitated a moment and then nodded. "Thank you. For everything. I'll certainly pay you."

Pa waved away his offer. "We'll see."

Lilly grabbed her shawl. "I'll show him the cross-country trail. It's much shorter."

They left the house. Caleb's long legs ate up the distance, forcing Lilly to trot to keep up.

He lifted a saddle from his wagon and tossed it on the horse. She pointed out the trail.

He swung into the saddle and paused to look down at her.

She patted his leg. "I'll take good care of Teddy. We all will."

"He has a special fondness for you."

The words melted her heart. "And I for him."

Caleb touched her hand and rode away. He lifted his hat at the crest of the hill and waved to her. She waved back and stood watching until he was out of sight.

He would return tonight, just as he said.

Because of Teddy, she reminded herself. Not because of her. She turned and retraced her steps as the truth of her words settled into her heart.

She would not expect any man to return to her. That led only to disappointment and pain. As Rose had pointed out, she'd learned that lesson at a very young age and she'd had it reinforced throughout her life.

Unless she'd simply trusted the wrong people. Or like Rose suggested, chose the sort of person she knew would leave her simply to prove her point. The thought felt so wrong she couldn't accept it.

No. It was in looking for and longing for what she didn't have that she found disappointment. She was more than content living on the farm with her family, tending the garden and the animals. But she'd accept the company and care of Teddy and his father for a short time, even knowing it couldn't last.

The pain would be worth the joy of the moment.

Chapter Eleven

Caleb kept his horse at a steady pace as he rode toward the Caldwell ranch. He reached the yard just as the other cowboys headed out from the cookhouse. Good timing. Ebner would have no cause for complaint.

He tended his horses and set to work on the barn chores. He had almost completed them when Ebner stepped in.

"Good to see you back at work."

"Did you think I would leave?"

Ebner grunted. "Then who would muck out the barn?" His tone conveyed the message that only Caleb would be desperate enough to take the job.

Caleb shrugged. He couldn't deny it was the sort of job he might have once shunned. Now all that mattered was doing all he could to pick up the pay.

Ebner listed a number of chores that would keep a man hopping all day. Caleb didn't care. He'd do them and leave. He smiled as he thought of the welcome he would receive at the end of the day. Teddy's smile, a hot meal and—

Would Lilly be gladder to see him than the others would?

He jabbed the fork into the muck so hard the shock jolted up his arm. It wasn't a thought—or rather, a hope—he could allow himself.

He worked hard all day, finished the list of assigned chores and then washed up at the pump.

Ebner hurried over. "You figure on leaving?"

Ignoring the challenging tone, Caleb answered. "I finished my day's work. I don't think you'll find any reason to complain about how well the chores were done. Now I've got a boy to take care of."

Ebner jammed his fists to his hips and scowled. If he could find a reason to order Caleb to stay at the ranch, he would, but Caleb only worked there. Neither Ebner nor the Caldwells owned him.

His horse stood saddled and ready and he took up the reins. "I'll return in the morning." He swung into the saddle and rode away before Ebner could find any reason to make him stay.

Not that Caleb could have been persuaded on any grounds. He meant to get back to Teddy and the Bells. And even if he only pictured Lilly when he thought of the Bells, he wasn't about to admit that.

Teddy was in the yard when Caleb rode in and waved and yelled. Blossom was huddled at Teddy's side. Lilly stood nearby, a basket of carrots in her arms.

A sense of peace and contentment came over Caleb.

"Papa, guess what?"

Caleb dropped to the ground and swept Teddy into his arms.

"Guess what?" Teddy demanded again.

Caleb set his son on the ground. "Let me see if I can

guess." He studied him slowly. "I don't think you've grown since this morning." He turned Teddy's head from side to side. "Still just two ears."

Teddy giggled.

Caleb lifted his hands into the air. "I give up. What?"

"I got to help Lilly in the garden."

"Is that a fact?" So far he had avoided looking directly at her hovering by Teddy's side, but now he raised his gaze to hers. "So what did you do?" he asked the boy. "Dig carrots?"

"No, I couldn't with one foot, 'member?"

As if he could forget.

"I helped pick them up and then Lilly took them to their root cellar." He pointed to a dugout door. "She won't let me go in there. Says there are too many spiders. I'm not afraid of spiders, am I, Papa?"

Caleb's gaze held Lilly's. She tried to hide a shudder, and he chuckled. "Maybe Miss Lilly is afraid of them."

She gave a firm shake of her head. "Not afraid. I just don't like them." She let herself shudder visibly this time. "Creepy, crawly things. Ugh."

"Are you headed there now?" He indicated the basket full of carrots.

"Yes, I'm about to take in these carrots."

"Let me take them to the cellar for you." He reached for the basket.

Lilly eagerly accepted his offer and led the way.

Rose crossed the yard with another basket, this one full of potatoes. She laughed. "She's just a tiny bit afraid of spiders."

Lilly frowned at her sister. "So are you."

"Not like you. I'd never let it deter me from doing anything."

"I took my fair share of loads into the cellar."

Caleb leaned close to Rose. "Hang on a minute. There's something in your hair."

"A spider?" She practically screeched the word.

He laughed and flicked something away. "Just a leaf."

She jammed her hands on to her hips. "You did that on purpose."

Lilly crowed with laughter. "He called your bluff. Serves you right." She patted Caleb's shoulder. "Good job."

They looked at each other. He felt as if he could almost lose himself in her smiling, approving eyes.

Grinning, satisfaction warming his insides, he entered the dark, dank cellar and poured the carrots into the bin built against one wall. It held a goodly supply of carrots. More than he figured a family of four could eat in five winters.

He left the cellar, dusting his clothes to make sure no spiders came with him. "You planning to feed an army?"

Lilly chuckled. "We need lots to sell and give away."

"Who do you give them to?"

"Anyone who needs them."

He puzzled that a moment. "If you give them away, who buys them?"

"People we don't like." There was no mistaking the anger in Rose's voice.

"Rose, that's not true," Lilly protested. "We sell them at the store in town."

Caleb knew who Rose had been talking about, but he decided to let that particular conversation slip by without comment. "Do you want me to dump your potatoes?" He held a hand out to Rose.

"Thanks." She handed him her basket. Likely she didn't care to risk encountering any spiders.

He stepped in again and dumped the potatoes. That bin was only about half full—there were likely lots left in the garden still. If he had the time to spare away from his job at the Caldwells', he would help dig them. He stood admiring the bounty and shared in the sense of satisfaction, even though he wouldn't be one of those who benefitted from the Bells' garden. Seeing a root cellar full in preparation for winter brought to mind so many things he had lost—home, hope and dreams. He sighed and went outside again.

The twins were waiting for him, Teddy at their side.

"That's all for today," Lilly said.

Rose's eyes widened and she pointed to Lilly. "There's something in your hair."

Lilly shook her head. "I'm not falling for that trick just because you did."

"No, really." Rose backed away and shuddered. "Caleb, look. There's something there."

Lilly scowled. "You're not funny, you know?"

"Caleb, please," Rose begged.

He moved closer and leaned over. She smelled outdoorsy, like freshly turned soil and spicy fall leaves. He shoved his thoughts into proper order and squinted at her. A fat spider clung to her hair, a black intruder against the strands of blond.

"Don't move." He kept his voice calm.

She stiffened. "Do you see a spider?"

He caught the insect between his thumb and forefinger and pulled it off her. Stilling his own revulsion against spiders, he squeezed it and wiped his finger on his pants. "It's gone now."

She shuddered enough to shake her whole body. "Agh. I hate spiders." She rubbed her hands over her hair, wiped her skirt down and stomped a few times just in case.

Teddy had watched the entire proceedings with interest, his expression serious, but now he started to giggle.

Lilly stopped her anxious flitting about, planted her hands on her hips and stared at him. "So you think it's funny, do you?"

He nodded. "You're a grown-up," he managed around his giggling. "You aren't supposed to be afraid of things."

"Who says?"

He sobered and looked a little confused. "Everybody knows that."

She snorted. "Well, everybody is wrong. Everyone is scared of something, even grown-ups."

"Not my Papa," chirped Teddy.

Caleb almost crowed. Having his son's high regard was just fine by him.

Lilly turned slowly to face Caleb. "Is that so?"

Uncertain how to interpret the challenging look in her face, he instinctively backed up a step.

"See that? I think he's afraid of me. Why, I think if Rose were to join me, we could make him very afraid."

Rose seemed to know what Lilly had in mind and came to her side.

Caleb looked from one to the other. Both wore challenging looks, but he riveted his attention on Lilly. He had no idea what they had in mind. Retreat seemed the wisest plan, so he backed up. For every step he took away, they took a step toward him.

"Papa, you're not afraid, are you?"

His son has interpreted his caution as fear. "Teddy, I assure you I'm not afraid. But I don't like the looks on their faces." He took another step backward. "Son, it's like this. You can never be too careful about how you act around women."

"Is that a fact?" Lilly drew her brows together. "Rose, what do you think?"

In tandem they stepped closer, forcing him to back up still more. That's when he discovered a wheelbarrow behind him. He landed backward in the bucket, his feet pointed skyward.

Laughing, Rose and Lilly grabbed the handles and pushed him on a mad ride.

He clung to the sides, afraid they would dump him out.

Teddy hobbled after them. "Don't hurt my papa."

Lilly called over her shoulder. "We'll let him go as soon as he admits he's afraid."

"I admit it," Caleb said, willing to do almost anything to get his feet back on the ground and restore his dignity.

The girls let the contraption come to a rest.

Lilly held out her hand to help him up. He scrambled to his feet.

"You two are a menace."

"Only to prideful men," Rose said.

"I'm not prideful."

"Nope," Lilly agreed. "I think we cured you of that."

The two of them laughed at him.

Caleb shook his head in mock disbelief, but their enjoyment of life and each other, and Lilly's sparkling gaze catching and holding his, caused a flower to blossom in his heart. He choked back a snort. What kind of cowboy thought frilly things like that?

The answer rose within him. A cowboy surrounded by beautiful, cheerful women. He'd defy any man—cowboy or clerk—to resist the joy the pair provided with their good-natured teasing and mutual love.

What would it be like to be included in that love the way Wyatt was?

Wyatt seemed to like it well enough.

But then Wyatt had no reason not to eagerly join that happy family circle. Caleb could think of at least two reasons it wouldn't be possible for him. Teddy and the need to get his leg fixed. And Caleb's own fear of failing at love.

It was a good thing Lilly didn't know of his deepest fear, though what difference would it make?

He'd given her no reason to expect anything from him and he certainly wasn't about to give himself one.

But still the question lingered.

What would it be like to be part of a loving family circle? To enjoy the love of a strong woman?

Lilly sensed Caleb's withdrawal and instantly regretted the way she and Rose had mercilessly teased him. "I'm sorry. We sometimes get carried away."

"We do not," Rose defended them both. "It was all in good fun."

Caleb waved his hand dismissively. "No harm done." He turned to his son. "Teddy, how are you doing?"

Teddy swung to his father's side so fast, Lilly reached out to catch him. But he didn't need her help. Caleb caught him up in his arms.

"I knew you weren't afraid." Teddy patted Caleb's cheeks. "You only said it to make them happy."

Caleb chuckled, a deep and pleasing sound.

"Sure, that was it," Caleb said.

Lilly and Rose looked at each other. Rose rolled her

eyes and Lilly delivered their decision. "For Teddy's sake, we'll let him believe he's right."

"You are too generous."

"I know." Shaking her head, Rose headed toward the house.

"Tell me about your day." Lilly assumed he meant the question for Teddy, even though he looked at her as he spoke.

Teddy rattled off the many things he'd done. Help Rose get the eggs. Feed the milk cows. "Just like Mama let me do." Sort bolts for Mr. Bell. Help Mrs. Bell make cookies.

"You didn't help Lilly do anything?"

"No, but she took me to the river and showed me where there are fishes. She said you should take me fishing. Will you, Papa?"

Caleb's warm gaze held Lilly's. Did he mean to thank her for helping his little boy enjoy the day? His gaze went on and on, as if looking for things hidden deep in her heart—truths she only sensed in some vague way. As he searched her thoughts, the truth grew stronger, almost clear enough for her to understand.

"I'll take you if Lilly agrees to come."

Teddy grabbed her arm. "Say you will, please."

"Of course." She knew her heart would pay a price when this connection came to an end, but she hoped the pleasure would be worth the pain.

"Now I have to warn you both," Caleb said. "You'll have to wait until I can get away from my job."

"That's okay," Teddy said. "Isn't it?" He directed his question to Lilly.

"Of course." Though she would be counting the days

until it happened. A blaze of doubt flashed through her mind. Unless he was giving the promise carelessly.

But surely he wouldn't promise Teddy something and not follow through on it.

Because the cows were already milked, Caleb helped put away the baskets and tools used to gather the garden produce. By then supper was ready and they went inside.

After the meal, Caleb grabbed a tea towel and dried the dishes without being asked. He handed Teddy a towel as well and insisted he help. Not that Teddy minded.

Later, she helped do the poultice and exercises for Teddy. She could see no change in Teddy's leg and understood that Caleb was disappointed. It would take time. Something they had very little of. If Teddy didn't start to use his leg, Caleb meant to go down east with him. *God, help Teddy's leg get better.* If that meant they must leave, so be it. She'd never expected anything else. But if the poultices and exercises worked, wouldn't they be able to stay?

Why was she letting her hopes be raised? They would only be dashed.

She thought of what Rose had said about Lilly only letting herself care about people she knew would leave.

She shook her head. It wasn't so. Rose was getting far too fanciful.

She helped get Teddy ready for bed, marveling over his little boy smell and his father's strong arms as he tenderly washed Teddy's face and hands.

Blossom whined to be in bed with Teddy and she lifted the dog to Teddy's side. She glanced at Ma to see if she might disapprove, but the gentle smile on Ma's face said it all. Whatever this little boy needed to make him happy, Ma would gladly do it.

Teddy said, "I'm not sleepy. Can Lilly read to me?"

"Why, of course," she replied. "I'd love to if it's okay with your papa."

Caleb nodded and pulled a chair close. "Mind if I listen?"

"Not a bit." She felt her cheeks grow warm and hoped they hadn't turned pink. But the thought of sitting together caring for this little boy triggered longings that she didn't want to admit.

"Do you have storybooks?" Teddy asked, bringing her back to reality.

"I do somewhere, but I have an idea. Instead of reading a book, why don't we make up a story?"

"You and me?" He sounded excited and cautious at the same time.

"Do you think it would be fun? Shall we write it down?"

He nodded. "Then I can always have it."

She found paper and pencil and sat beside Teddy. "Do you have any ideas?"

"No. Do you?"

"Let's do a story about a dog."

"Like Blossom?"

"That's a very good idea."

Teddy snuggled close as she drew a dog somewhat like Blossom.

"What's the dog's name?"

"How about...Tiny?"

"Tiny, it is." She wrote the name across the top. "Let's get to know Tiny. Where does she live?"

She continued on with questions and drawings to match his answers. Who was in Tiny's family? What was her favorite food? What games did she like to play? Then she asked, "What's Tiny afraid of?"

Teddy sat back and stared at the page. "Tiny," he whispered, "is scared of bad men."

Lilly glanced at Caleb, noting his sudden alertness. She had no doubt the boy was referring to the bad men who had hurt his mama. But she continued. "What do bad men do to Tiny?"

Teddy wrapped his arms around Blossom's neck. "They do bad things. They hurt Tiny's family."

Lilly stared at the page. "I'm not sure what to draw."

He asked for the paper and pencil and scribbled dark, harsh lines. Then he gave it back. "I can't draw it."

She turned to a new page, wanting to shift the story to something happier. "Let's play a game with Tiny." She drew a ball with stripes. The ball was almost as big as Tiny. "What's she going to do?"

Teddy giggled. "Try to catch it."

Lilly did her best to draw the puppy tumbling over the too-big ball while Teddy continued to giggle. "She's happy now."

She drew Tiny on a bed. "Who is going to sleep with Tiny?"

"A little boy."

She wasn't good at drawing people, but she did her best to make a little boy who looked like Teddy.

Teddy nodded. "He's not scared anymore."

"That's good. I think Teddy and Blossom should go to sleep now, safe and sound in the Bells' house." She tucked the covers about him and kissed his forehead. She patted Blossom's head.

Teddy's eyes closed, a smile on his lips.

Caleb rose to stand next to Lilly. "Thank you," he whispered.

They moved away from the cot. Lilly wanted to talk about the experience, but only with Caleb. "Ma, Pa, I'm going to check on the sheep." Would Caleb want to accompany her? She toyed with the idea of asking him, but hoped he would offer on his own.

"I'll keep her company," Caleb said to her parents.

She turned to pull a warm sweater from the row of coats and such, hiding her pleased smile from her family.

Caleb planted his hat on his head and took his own jacket. They stepped out into the cool evening air.

They walked toward the pasture, both of them silent. Lilly's heart was full of things she wanted to say, but the words didn't come.

Caleb sighed deeply. "That was a good idea to use a dog and child to help Teddy tell us how he feels."

"It seems clear that he's talking about his life, don't you think?" They reached the fence and stopped. She ran a quick glance at the sheep, who were resting peacefully in the shelter of the trees.

"Sure seems that way to me." He shuddered. "Except it's Teddy who is afraid, not the dog."

"It's easier to talk about it through the eyes of someone safe."

"Like a pretend pet?"

"Exactly." She turned to study his face in the dusky light, looking for clues as to how Teddy's confession of fear had affected him. His jaw muscles were clenched. His brow was furrowed, which didn't tell her if he was worried or determined, or fighting pain and fear of his own. She figured it was a combination of all those things.

He must have felt so helpless at his wife's murder and

his child's injury. She understood helplessness at another's actions. Having no control yet bearing the consequence.

"I know how horrible tragedies can leave a person feeling like there is no safe bottom to the life they live, no security for the future. For if these things happened once, what's to stop them from happening again?"

He brought his gaze to her, his eyes slowly focusing on her face as if he was bringing his thoughts back from a far distance.

"My abandonment was a small thing compared to what you and Teddy experienced." She took his hand, wanting him to see the truth that had freed her from her fears and uncertainties. Mostly freed her, she amended, for there remained certain fears about change. "I used to be so afraid any time someone in the family was gone. When Cora started school, it was very hard for me to understand. I was afraid she was leaving us."

He nodded. "You feared abandonment. With just cause in your case."

"But that's it. I'd been abandoned once for whatever reason. That didn't mean I should expect it again. Ma taught me a verse in Psalm 23. 'Yea, though I walk through the valley of the shadow of death, I will fear no evil: for Thy rod and staff they comfort me.' God's comfort and His promise to always be with us—surely that means something." Her conscience condemned her. Here she was telling Caleb how to find peace and comfort, letting him think she'd been successful in finding it for herself. Up until a few days ago, she believed she had.

Yet meeting Caleb and Teddy had brought all her fears and concerns back to life.

But if she could help Caleb and Teddy, she would do

so. Her own fears she would also put to rest. She would be wiser when it came to choosing who to care about in the future, and she would not pick people who were leaving.

She ignored the fact she was doing exactly that at this moment.

Caleb shifted his gaze to a point somewhere in the distance. "If you can help Teddy find this same assurance, I'd be grateful."

"I pray you find it, too."

His gaze came back to her and a smile slowly creased his face. "You are such an encourager. You almost make me believe I can go back to the simple faith of my youth." He shook his head. "But life is so much more complicated than I once believed."

She chuckled. "You make it sound like you are a weary old man." She sobered. "I don't think you can go back to a simple faith so much as a stronger faith. One that has been tested and tried and comes forth like pure gold."

His eyes widened as if he'd never before considered the idea. "Huh? A golden cowboy. That'd be something to see."

She smiled gently, amused but aware of the depth of their words. "Fortunately for you, the gold would be in your heart, unseen to gold hunters who would otherwise hammer away bits and pieces of you."

He chuckled. He lifted his hand to her cheek and cupped his warm palm to her skin. "I think I might end up coal, not gold."

She pressed her hand to his, holding it against her face. Her heart beat like a drum. "Coal has its purposes, too."

His eyes darkened. He studied her intently, but she did not lower her eyes as his look went on and on. Slowly, his expression changed from one of discouragement to one of hope. His thumb brushed her lips. Would he kiss her?

She swallowed hard. She hoped so.

Then he withdrew his hand. She liked to think he did so reluctantly.

"You've given me much to think about." He stuck his hands in his back pockets. "But it's getting late. We need to get back before your pa comes looking for you."

She tucked this information into her heart. Caleb was only being noble and concerned about her. Both admirable qualities. But a kiss would have been nicer, even though it would only have made it more painful when he left.

She'd allowed herself to go this far in caring about him and his son. There was no retreating now. Whatever was to happen to her in the future would be dealt with then.

She'd take each day as it came and accept whatever it brought. Even as she told herself so, her heart clenched like a fist inside her chest.

Was her heart about to be torn asunder?

Chapter Twelve

The Bells went to their rooms and Caleb spread his bed-roll beside Teddy's cot. As he lay staring into the darkness, he relived the events of the evening, lingering on the words Lilly had spoken. Coal or gold? Which would he end up being? Did he have any choice or would it simply happen? He didn't care for the idea that he had no say in the matter, though his life so far had revealed just how little control he had over anything. But hadn't she been talking about God's work? God had control. Surely, He would use the events in Caleb's life for good. He liked the idea of turning into gold—a golden cowboy, as he'd said to Lilly. Had she thought him foolish or had she understood what he'd meant?

Something about Lilly touched the corners of his heart like rain on barren ground, slowly causing his life to bloom. It was temporary, but why should he not enjoy the springtime of his soul while it lasted?

He left early again the next morning, eager to get to the Caldwells' so he could get his work done and get back to Teddy. *And Lilly?* his inner voice asked.

Maybe. After all, she was working with Teddy.

If Teddy would only start to use his leg again, there would be no need to go east. No need to leave.

He cut these thoughts short. Hadn't he decided to keep people at arm's length to protect them? And to protect himself from pain and guilt, he acknowledged.

Throughout the day, he often found himself smiling for no other reason than recalling the pleasure of the time spent with Lilly and her family.

He finished his assigned chores so early Ebner stopped him as he saddled his horse.

"Where do you think you're going?"

"I've done the work you laid out and I'm going to see my son."

"Huh. Guess I'm getting slack at assigning chores."

Caleb faced him squarely. "I worked double time to get done early. No other man would have worked so quickly, and you know it. I don't expect to have my load increased as a reward." He gave Ebner a look that said there'd be no compromise on the matter. Caleb meant to spend time with Teddy. And if Lilly was there, too, so much the better.

When he arrived at the Bells' farm he found them all in the garden digging the last of the potatoes. Teddy sat in the dirt, sorting them according to some system that had been explained to him.

Lilly stood up and smiled as Caleb approached. The others called a greeting but didn't stop working.

"Pa says there's a change coming in the weather. Says we have to get the potatoes in before it gets here," Lilly explained.

"I'll help. Let me take the baskets to the root cellar."

"You sure? I know you've worked all day."

This wouldn't seem like work. "I don't mind."

"Very well. The smaller potatoes go in one bin, the larger ones in another."

"Got it." He grabbed the full basket at the end of the row and headed for the root cellar. Back and forth he went—they filled baskets as fast as he could empty them.

Once he caught up, he grabbed a fork and started digging.

Lilly smiled at him. "Thank you." She turned to the side so the others couldn't hear. "We've been trying to get Ma and Pa to let us finish, but they insist they will stay until the end."

"Then let's get this done as quickly as possible." He'd been putting out all afternoon, but he kept up a steady pace until the last potato was out of the ground. He emptied the final basket in the cellar and stepped out, a sense of satisfaction easing through him. He liked helping the Bells.

With a grateful smile in Caleb's direction, Lilly turned to her parents. "Teddy's tired and hungry, Ma. You take him to the house while we clean up the tools. Pa, why don't you make a pot of coffee for Caleb? I expect he's in dire need of such."

"Sounds good," Caleb said, and he smiled as the elderly couple headed to the house with Teddy at their side.

"I can't thank you enough," Lilly said.

"Nor I," Rose added. "You're not half-bad for a Caldwell cowboy."

Caleb laughed as he helped put away the baskets and tools.

He paused to wait for Lilly to come alongside him. "Not half-bad for a Caldwell cowboy? Coming from Rose, that's high praise." He wondered what Lilly thought. Not half-bad? Real good? A golden cowboy? He almost hooted aloud at his foolish thoughts.

She patted his arm, a gesture he was enjoying more and more each day. "You're all right, Caleb Craig."

His chest swelled and his smile widened. All right! He liked that.

A few minutes later they trooped into the house for supper. Everyone ate with gusto. Made him wonder how long they'd been out in the garden without a break.

The main part of the meal over, Mrs. Bell said, "Who's ready for cookies?"

"Me. Me." Teddy practically bounced from his chair and Caleb didn't have the heart to scold him. He much preferred concern about the boy's manners over the continual worry about his leg.

Mrs. Bell gave Teddy four cookies and filled his cup with milk. Teddy took a bite of cookie and closed his eyes. "Good." He ate two and drank half the milk before he came up for air. He rubbed his tummy.

"Mrs. Bell, you are the best grandma in the world."

The woman's smile flattened and her hand flew to her chest.

"Teddy," Caleb warned. But it was too late to pull the words back.

Mrs. Bell's smile returned. "I don't have any grandchildren yet." She spared the girls an accusing look. "But I'd be honored if you'd call me Grandma." She squeezed Teddy's hand.

Teddy grew very still and slowly faced Caleb. "Can I, Papa?"

What could he say? If he refused, it would appear rude, even churlish. But if he agreed, wouldn't Teddy be hurt when they had to say goodbye to his chosen grandma?

He made up his mind. "So long as you remember it's only until we leave."

Teddy continued to stare at him, as if silently accusing him of robbing him of a perfectly good grandma.

"That's just fine," Mrs. Bell said. "And maybe someday you'll visit again."

"Would you make me ginger cookies if we did?"

"I'd be honored."

"Thank you, Grandma." Teddy couldn't have been more pleased, but Caleb was uneasy. Somehow he knew this wasn't going to end well, no matter what he did.

He sought Lilly's gaze. What did she think of this arrangement? She wore a cautious look, as if she shared the same wariness. Then she smiled and gave a little shrug.

He shrugged, too. There didn't seem to be any way he could renege at this point.

Mr. Bell took up his Bible. "Our root cellar is full. We have plenty to spare. God has blessed us abundantly and we give Him praise. But let us never lose sight of the fact that adverse circumstances do not mean God loves us any less. I want to read two verses from Habakkuk, chapter three." The Bible easily fell open to the pages as if Mr. Bell often read the passage. "Here we are. 'Although the fig tree shall not blossom, neither shall fruit be in the vines; the labor of the olive shall fail, and the fields shall yield no meat; the flock shall be cut off from the fold, and there shall be no herd in the stalls: Yet I will rejoice in the Lord, I will joy in the God of my salvation.'" He reverently closed the Good Book. "No matter what happens, God cares for each of us, and whether there are good or bad things in our lives, we are loved."

As Mr. Bell prayed, the words went round and round in Caleb's head. He had never considered that God loved him in such a special way. Thinking about it made the sorrow of his life fade in significance.

The next morning he rode away with a light heart, but he also did so reluctantly. He would have liked to spend Saturday with the Bells, but Ebner had not given him the full day off, though he couldn't deny him the half day off he'd given to all the other cowboys on the ranch.

The chores the foreman had laid out for him kept him busy until past noon. By the time he finished, he was impatient as a kid on Christmas.

The Bells went to town on Saturdays to do their shopping and sell their produce. Would they be back yet?

He strained to find some clue as he approached the farm. When he saw Teddy and Blossom alone in the yard, he sank back in his saddle. Then he saw Lilly nearby and smiled.

"Hello," he called, and they both waved.

"Grandma and Grandpa and Rose went to town," Teddy said as soon as Caleb was close enough to hear.

"You didn't go?" he addressed Lilly.

She shrugged. "Teddy and I decided to stay home." Because she lowered her eyes, he couldn't gain any insight into why.

"Lilly thought we should wait for you," Teddy said.

"Is that a fact?" The idea pleased him clear to the soles of his feet. "Do you want to go now? I could hitch up the wagon."

She lifted one shoulder in a small shrug. "I've been to town plenty of times. Unless you want to go?"

"I've got no need to go to town." A strong wind tore

at his hat and he grabbed it before it could blow away. "Besides, it's getting a mite cold."

"It's the change in weather Pa said was coming." She glanced down the road. "They should be home soon." She watched for a few seconds and then shivered. "We better go inside."

"I'll be along as soon as I take care of my horse."

A few minutes later he joined them in the house. She'd made coffee and poured milk for herself and Teddy. As usual, there were cookies to enjoy with the coffee.

She smiled at Teddy's enjoyment of the snack.

The boy finished and asked to be excused. He and Blossom went to the far corner of the room. Teddy pulled a handful of objects from his pocket and showed them to the eager pup. Soon they were engrossed in their own little world.

Lilly watched, a gentle smile on her lips. "Tell me what Teddy was like as a baby."

Lilly shifted her attention to Caleb when she asked about Teddy. He smiled and got a distant look on his face, as if falling into his memories. Hopefully, to a place that was pleasant for him.

"He said 'papa' before he said 'mama.' Amanda teasingly complained about that." Caleb chuckled. "I said it was because he knew that when he saw me it meant we were going to play. My, he did like to be tickled." He sighed. "No doubt you've heard it before, but babies grow up far too quickly. Especially when there aren't more little ones to replace them."

Lilly concentrated on the swirl of milk at the bottom of her glass. Would she ever know the joy of a baby? Not unless she found someone willing to settle for her, willing to stay long enough to see what Rose called her 'finer qualities.' This topic of conversation brought hard edges to her innards. But before she could think of something else to talk about, lightning flashed, filling the room with blinding light.

She jolted to her feet, her heart climbing to the back of her throat. The hair on her neck stood up, as her skin prickled. "I hate storms," she murmured, her words almost drowned out by the thunder that seemed to go on forever, rolling down from the mountains and echoing over the plains. Wind rattled the shingles and banged at the door. "I have to shut in the chickens." If she hadn't been distracted by Caleb's arrival she would have already done it. Now she had to go out in the storm.

She grabbed a slicker Pa wore in wet weather and shrugged into it. Never mind that it was miles too big and almost dragged on the ground. It would protect her from the rain that would surely come. Not to mention that wearing it, she felt safer, as if Pa's arms were about her. A floppy wide-brimmed hat completed her outfit.

Caleb followed her to the door. "Let me go. You stay here."

It was awfully tempting to agree. "Thanks, but someone needs to stay with Teddy, and I know what to do outside."

He stood at the door. "You'll be safe?"

A large portion of tension seeped away at the concern in his voice. "I'll be fine. You make sure Teddy is safe, too."

"I will." Still he did not open the door or step away so she could get out. She met his dark eyes, full of concern and maybe even regret, though she couldn't guess what he might regret. His gaze held hers as her heart settled into her chest with a sigh and then swelled with longing.

Lightning flashed again and seconds later, thunder rattled the glass in the windows.

She broke from his intense stare. "I must go."

Finally he held the door open and stood watching as she slipped loose the latch on the chicken pen. Lightning and thunder continued, but they seemed less frightening knowing Caleb was watching. She shooed the chickens inside and closed the door.

The barn door stood open. She needed to close it to keep the cows warm.

A glance at the house revealed Caleb still standing in the doorway. Then rain slashed down and he closed the door.

She couldn't remember feeling so alone before. But she had to take care of the necessary chores. Ducking her head against the wind and rain, she trotted to the barn.

She caught Caleb's horse and led it inside. Then she heard the loft door banging. It would not stay shut unless she threw the bar in place.

She stared at the ladder, trying to summon the courage to climb closer to the turbulent sky. She chanted Rose's words. "Just as safe up there as standing in the middle of a field." It didn't matter how true the words were. Fear didn't listen to reason, and Lilly had a huge fear of thunderstorms. However, she had to keep the barn dry for the sake of the animals. She'd do it for them. She let the huge slicker flap behind her as she planted one hand and then the other on a ladder rung. Gritting her teeth, she forced her feet to follow.

She found the length of wood Pa used to hold the door closed. Swallowing back a lump the size of a prize potato, she waited for the door to bang against the frame and then she caught it. Quickly she dropped the bar into place.

Lightning flashed and thunder sounded at almost the same time. Her scalp tingled. The smell of gunpowder filled the air. It had struck very close. She wanted to huddle in some safe corner, or rush back to the house and find comfort in Caleb's presence, but she could do neither. Her sheep would naturally seek shelter under the trees in the corner of their pasture. It was the most dangerous place they could be in a thunderstorm.

She must herd them to safety.

She clambered down the ladder and looked around to see if she could tell where the lightning had struck. She saw nothing damaged and no sign of fire, so she hastened onward to the sheep pasture. In her frenzied haste, she slipped on the wet ground, going down on one knee. She straightened and hurried on until she reached the gate of the pasture. What if lightning struck the moment she touched the wire? She'd be killed. Or at least thrown to the ground, her hair burned from her head.

She swallowed back a lump as large as a soup bowl. No one else would take care of her sheep. Ignoring the trembling of her limbs, she grabbed the gate, unhooked it and threw it back.

"Mammy," she called. The old ewe would be the only one to heed Lilly's call. "Mammy." Lightning flashed, allowing Lilly to look around her. There they were, huddled in the trees just as she suspected. "You silly sheep. You haven't got the sense to stay away from danger." She ran the length of the field, skidding and slipping. "Come, girls. Come, Boss." Maybe the ram would show his courage and follow her.

They bleated, but they didn't move. She grabbed a couple and shoved them in the right direction. They simply turned back to the shelter. "Mammy?" She located the ewe at the back of the flock and went to her side. "You're my only hope. Come with me and the others might follow. Please follow."

More lightning. More thunder. The sound crashed inside her chest each time. But she needed to get these sheep to safety.

She wrapped her arms about Mammy's neck. "You'll come with me, won't you?"

The ewe baaed.

Lilly took it as a sign of agreement. "Come along." She clung to Mammy's neck, hoping the ewe would cooperate. They took a step. Two. Three. Mammy baaed again and Boss came running to investigate. She kept Mammy going forward, one step at a time. "Come on, you sheep. Come, come. I'll put you where you'll be safe and dry." Would they follow?

One of the younger ewes rubbed against Lilly's legs.

She wanted to look back and see if the others were coming, but she had her hands full keeping Mammy headed for the gate. They were as nervous as she, jumping at every crack, every rumble.

They were almost at the gate when a blinding flash and a thundering boom shook the ground. Balls of fire ran along the wire of the fence and into the ground. She cried out as fear exploded inside her.

Caleb stared out the window. The lightning was so close he could feel the electricity in the air and could smell sulfur. Lilly had been gone far too long. Where was she? Had she been hurt? Struck by a bolt? He shuddered and strode to the door. He needed to make sure she was safe. But did he dare leave Teddy? He returned to the window, staring into the darkness. In the continuing flashes he could make out the barn, his wagon and the other outbuildings, but he couldn't see Lilly. Had she taken shelter in the barn, meaning to stay there until the storm passed?

Perhaps she had welcomed a reason to avoid his company.

But how could he be certain she was safe?

He studied Teddy. Blossom watched the boy's every move.

He stared at the door. He had to find Lilly. But if both of them were out in the storm, if both of them encountered trouble… What would happen to Teddy?

He looked back and forth between the door and his son, running his fingers through his hair until it grew so tangled his fingers caught.

She should have been back by now.

He made up his mind. He could not sit here wondering if she needed help. "Teddy, I have to go find Lilly. You stay here and don't go outside for any reason. I'll be back in a few minutes."

"Okay, Papa."

Still Caleb hesitated, torn between making sure his son was safe and making sure Lilly was. His chest tightened until it hurt to breathe.

He made up his mind. At the moment Lilly's needs were more urgent. "Blossom, you stay with Teddy."

The dog looked at him as if she understood what Caleb wanted of her.

Caleb grabbed his hat and stepped outside, immediately pelted by the slashing rain. He clamped his hat more firmly to his head and strode toward the barn. Lightning flashed. A bit of white to his right caught his attention. He turned and squinted, waiting for the next flash to illuminate the area. It came and he saw sheep gathered in a tight knot. What were they doing here?

Then he saw a black center amid the white. Another flash and he could make out the figure of Lilly. She was trying to get those silly animals to shelter.

But at least she was safe. He was so relieved he grinned as he jogged to her side. "Where are you taking them?" he called close to her ear.

"The shed on the side of the barn."

"Let's do it." He went behind the little flock and pushed at them as she led the way. They reached the barn, lightning flares showing the way to the shed. One by one, they managed to get the sheep inside, and then they closed the door.

It was quieter in there, and drier. He shivered in his damp clothes.

She made her way to his side. "Thank you. I couldn't get them to cooperate. Silly things. Especially after a bolt of lightning came within inches of us. You should have seen the fireball."

"Are you okay?"

"I'm fine." A blaze of light allowed her to see him clearly. "You're soaking wet."

"Yup. Might have been raining out there."

She snorted. "It's coming down in buckets."

"Is everything battened down?"

"As best I could."

"Then let's get back to the house." He took her arm. There was no way he would let her slip away and disappear into the storm for any reason.

"Teddy's alone?"

"Blossom is with him."

He pushed open the door, pulled her to his side and then, after making sure the door was firmly latched behind them, they dashed across the yard. They splashed through puddles they couldn't see, not realizing they were there, until the water slopped about them. They reached the house and Caleb pulled Lilly inside.

Blossom woofed gently, a greeting rather than a warning.

Lilly took off her slicker and hung it by the door. Caleb shook his hat and put it on the nearby cupboard to dry, and then stood there dripping.

She eyed him up and down. "You're certainly wet. What provoked you to go out in the storm without protection?"

"You."

"Me? But I wasn't even here."

"Exactly. Didn't you realize how close the storm was? A couple of times the thunder sounded at the same time as the lightning hit." He was cold and wet and more than a little annoyed at the way she was regarding him, as if he'd acted foolishly. "You were gone far too long. I thought I might have to rescue you."

Her eyes softened. "From what?"

"The storm, of course." He'd worried in vain, it appeared. But remnants of his concern filled his mind. He caught her by the arms. "You could have been struck by lightning."

She shuddered. Stark fear filled her eyes. "I had to take care of the animals."

He pulled her close and then remembered he was wet,

and held her inches away. "They're all safe and sound, and so are you."

She nodded, beginning to relax, and stepped back. "You must be cold. Come to the stove." When she kicked off her wet footwear, he did the same. He tipped his boots over the slop bucket to drain, and then padded after her.

She tossed wood into the stove and filled the kettle. "I'll make some of Ma's special tea. It will prevent you from getting a chill. She says it helps ward off a cold. It tastes just fine with a spoonful of honey. It's good for you."

Why was she rattling on at such a rate? Did his concern make her nervous? He watched her for a sign of what she was thinking, but she banged about in the cupboards, pulling out a tin of tea leaves and a small brown teapot.

Finally she looked at him, but only long enough to sigh at his wet state. "Here. Sit down." She pulled a chair close to the stove and then dashed into one of the rooms off the kitchen, returning with a thick gray woolen blanket. She draped it about his shoulders and patted it into place. "You really should take those wet things off." Her cheeks flamed bright red at her words.

"I'll be fine. I've been wetter than this and survived." Without anyone fussing over him. Not that he minded. Her touch on his shoulder, her concern about his well-being warmed him more thoroughly than did the fire.

She stared at the kettle and then shifted her attention to the window. "I believe the storm is moving away."

He listened. "I believe you are correct." Lightning still flashed, but the thunder sounded distant. And the rain settled down to a faint patter. It had been a brief storm. It had come and gone in minutes, though it had felt much longer.

She brought her attention back to him and he smiled.

"You don't like storms much, do you?" he said.

She shuddered. "About as much as cats like water." The kettle boiled and she bustled about making tea that she let seep for several minutes. She poured them each a cupful and stirred in generous spoonfuls of honey. "Here, try it."

The blanket slipped from his shoulders as he took the cup and she rearranged it, tucking it about his neck so he could drink and not lose the warmth.

He sipped the hot drink. "It's good." He meant more than the tea, but he wasn't about to confess that aloud. "I've never tasted anything quite like it. Dare I ask what's in it, or will that ruin it for me?"

She chuckled. "Depends how fussy you are." She waited for him to answer.

"If you stop to consider that for months I've been making my own meals, mostly over a campfire, you'll understand I'm not the least bit fussy."

"Okay, then, I'll tell you. The main ingredients are rose hips. I'm afraid I can't tell you the other things Ma puts in it or she'd have my hide for revealing her secrets."

It was his turn to chuckle. "Wouldn't want that."

She grinned at him, her eyes sparkling so much it seemed as if the skies had cleared and the sun had come out. "Let me assure you it wouldn't be pretty."

He sucked back another mouthful of tea and almost choked in his haste to dismiss his fanciful notions. "Has your Ma always been a healer?"

"A healer? Why that's a very nice way of describing her. Much kinder than some descriptions I've heard."

"Really. Like what?"

She studied her cup, from which she had yet to take a drink. "A lot of people consider her odd. Actually, they consider both my parents odd." She looked past him. "I've even heard it said that they stole us or somehow caused us to suddenly appear out of nowhere so they could have children. Some have said awful things about Ma and Pa and about us." She grew fierce. "People can be so cruel." Her gaze returned to him, full of sorrow and regret. "I'm sorry. I guess you know that better than most."

His fingers tightened around the cup. He knew he must have appeared angry. She'd take it to be about Amanda's murder, and it was. But distress raged through him at the way people had treated Lilly and her parents. "Do people still act that way toward you?"

She shrugged. "Mostly they accept us. People have come to value Ma's medicinals."

Blossom sat up and barked, looking toward the door.

Both Lilly and Caleb hurried to the window to see an approaching wagon, Mr. Bell guiding the family home through the gloomy dusk.

Lilly hurried to the door. "You're back safe and sound." Pa helped Ma to the ground and Rose scurried from the back.

"It was a cold, wet journey home," Rose moaned.

"You appear to be dry."

"'Cause Pa saw fit to bring along some canvas. He's the only one who is wet. Pa, get inside and get warm."

Lilly stuck her feet into her boots and dashed outside. "Yes, Pa. Rose take Ma inside. I'll tend the horse."

Rose hustled their parents inside while Lilly led the horse away. A few minutes later, she hurried back to the house and went right to her father's side. He was sitting before the stove, now in dry clothes. Rose poured him a cup of the hot tea.

"I hope you don't get a chill," Lilly said.

Pa waved away her concern. "I'm right as rain."

She grunted. "Not sure how right the rain was." She told her family about the lightning on the fence as she had been trying to get the sheep to safety.

Rose hustled to her side. "Lilly, you might have been killed."

"Guess it wasn't my time."

"God protected you," Pa said. "I pray He will always protect my girls and now Wyatt."

"What about me?" Teddy sounded hurt.

Pa patted his head. "Well, that goes without saying, doesn't it? I will always pray for you and your papa."

Teddy nodded and settled back, his new pet resting her head on his knee. The boy had a look of such contentment on his face, Caleb was tempted to forget about the crutches at his son's side.

Could Teddy learn to be happy and productive with only one good leg?

Caleb ducked his head, hoping no one would notice the way his jaw had clenched and his lips had pulled down.

How could he think of staying here with Teddy in his present state? He stole a glance at Lilly, who hovered by her father's side.

It had been a purely selfish thought because he liked the idea of becoming a permanent part of this family.

He drove the admission away as quickly as it had come. Hadn't he failed enough people already? Hadn't he vowed to never let himself care for another person?

It would only give him another chance to prove his inability to protect them.

Despite his vow, despite his fear and caution, Lilly had cracked open his tightly locked heart.

He would leave except he needed the job and he needed the Bells to help with Teddy. Surely there was no harm in enjoying Lilly's company and the comfort of her family for a few days.

What could possibly go wrong?

Chapter Thirteen

The rain stopped before they went to bed, and the next morning the sun was warm. By the time they left for church, all but a few puddles were dried up and the day promised to be glorious.

Lilly sat in the back of the wagon with Rose, Caleb and Teddy. The youngster bounced up and down, peering ahead. "Are we almost there?"

She'd never known a child so eager to attend church, though it was all she could do not to bounce up and down as well for an entirely different reason. Ever since the storm yesterday, her nerves had twitched with an awareness of Caleb. Glibly she put it down to coming so close to being struck by lightning. But she knew it was more than that.

It had begun when he'd come looking for her, concerned about her safety. The feeling had grown more intense when he'd pulled her close, stopping just short of holding her against his chest. She understood it had been because of his wet clothes, but she wouldn't have cared if she got a little wet. Well aware that she was treading perilously close to the dangerous precipice of caring more deeply for him than she should, she had covered him with a blanket, her fingers lingering one second longer than was necessary to secure the wrap.

Seeing him across the table, helping him with Teddy's care, observing the way he tenderly dealt with his son, had all added one hot coal after another to her feelings. Finally she wondered if she could contain—let alone control—them any longer.

They entered Bar Crossing at that point, so thankfully her thoughts were diverted. She watched the familiar buildings pass.

Church would give her something to think about besides Caleb. She'd concentrate on the sermon and that would make her forget everything else.

But she soon realized that was easier said than done. Again, Teddy made sure she walked in beside him and his father and he sat between them. He turned to whisper to her, "I like this church."

"Me, too," she whispered back. "Pastor Rawley is a very kind man. Mrs. Rawley is Ma's best friend."

His smile lit up his face. "I like them, too."

Lilly stifled a chuckle. In Teddy's mind, any friend of Ma's and Pa's was a friend of his. She glanced up at Caleb, seeing by the way he grinned at her that he'd heard the conversation and come to the same conclusion.

Their gazes locked long enough that Rose jabbed her in the ribs and whispered, "Stop making eyes at that man. Have you forgotten you're in church?"

Heat raced up Lilly's neck and she ducked her head as if needing to smooth her gloves. She could only hope Caleb hadn't heard Rose. But her sister was right, and she again vowed to concentrate on the service. Thankfully, at that moment Pastor Rawley went to the pulpit and announced the first hymn.

Lilly turned to share Rose's hymnal, but Rose had already offered it to Lonnie on her other side. That left her no choice but to share the book Caleb was holding toward her.

Their fingertips brushed under the cover. Her throat tightened so much she squeaked out the first note, but she cleared her throat and continued. She had always enjoyed singing, especially with her sisters. Wyatt couldn't carry a note in a bucket, but Caleb's deep voice echoed in her ears in perfect harmony. She could go on singing with him all morning.

But after two more hymns, the song service ended and Pastor Rawley announced the text. She'd brought her Bible, as had her sisters and Ma and Pa, and she shared the Book with Caleb.

It was smaller than the hymnal and his fingers didn't just brush hers, they maintained contact throughout the reading. For the life of her, she couldn't concentrate on the words.

What was wrong with her? She had never felt this way before. Certainly not around Karl. Why, the few times he had sat beside her in church, he'd kept his hands on his thighs and shaken his head when she'd offered to share the Bible or hymnal. It had always made her feel isolated, as if he had built a wall around himself that he didn't want her to breach.

There had been moments when she'd minded, but on the whole she'd welcomed the distance between them.

Not so with Caleb. Unfamiliar feelings bubbled inside her. A longing to touch and to be touched, to be held, to have no barriers between them. Those longings were exciting but at the same time, frightening. She knew the pain of being left behind. The feeling of not being enough to make people stay or have any regard for her feelings. Blame always came from her heart—she must have done something to drive them away. And she always vowed to do better, be better.

Most of all she promised herself to never again care so much.

She'd broken that promise. She cared about Caleb and his son so much it hurt. And it would hurt a thousand times more when he left. She pressed her fingers to her lips. Let anyone who noticed think she was moved by the sermon, though she couldn't have repeated a single word of it.

All she really heard was the final "Amen."

She rose and followed the others out, answering Teddy's questions, responding to the comments offered to her. But inside, she concentrated on telling herself how things would be. She'd allowed herself to care for both Teddy and Caleb, but no one would ever know to what depth.

After dinner at home, with Cora, Wyatt and Lonnie also in attendance, her older sister edged forward on her chair. "I'd really like to go to Chester's Pond this afternoon. It's such a lovely day, and who knows how many more chances we'll get. What do you think?" She looked at Pa for permission.

Pa nodded. "It's a nice afternoon for an outing. Ma and I can have a long lovely nap while you young people enjoy the day."

Caleb looked uncertain, as if he didn't expect to be included in the invitation.

"You, too, of course," Cora said to him.

"How far is it?"

"Take the wagon," Pa said.

Lilly and her sisters made short work of the dishes and packed a little snack. "It's tradition," Lilly explained to Caleb and Teddy. "We always have a picnic of sorts."

Teddy grew so excited he was in danger of falling facedown as he swung back and forth on his crutches.

Cora and Wyatt went to get the wagon, while Rose and Lilly gathered everything they'd need for an outing. In a few minutes they were loaded in the wagon and on their way.

Wyatt drove with Cora beside him. They followed the river for a few miles.

"You two rode together the last time we went," Lilly pointed out.

"Last time we were there, I kissed Cora." Wyatt's voice was husky.

Cora shook her head. "I thought I kissed you."

They laughed together.

Lonnie shook his head with mock disapproval over the way his brother adored Cora. "Well, I found an arrowhead."

"Papa, maybe I'll find one, too. Will you help me look?" Teddy's eyes widened with excitement.

"We'll all help you look," Lilly promised. "We're almost there."

A trail led through a grove of trees to the body of water. The twins sat up and watched as they drove closer.

Lilly sighed. "This is one of my favorite spots."

"Me, too," Rose echoed.

"October is my favorite month, when every leaf is a flower," Lilly said. And now she'd have even more reason to like the month.

With a start, she realized there were only a few more days in the month. She shivered. Would Caleb leave in November, making that month her least favorite?

She quickly dismissed the notion. She would not let such thoughts ruin this day.

Caleb jumped from the wagon as soon as it stopped and held out a hand to help her to the ground.

She placed her fingers in his strong palm. Warmth raced up her arms and pooled in her cheeks. She kept her head lowered as she stepped down. Only after she'd swallowed hard and adjusted her skirt did she glance up and thank him.

He nodded, a smile clinging to his eyes, and then he turned to lift Teddy to the ground.

"Where did you find the arrowhead?" he asked Lonnie. The pair headed to the shoreline.

They all followed, splitting off in various directions.

Cora and Wyatt disappeared into the trees.

Lilly stared after them. Was that where they had kissed? When had they known they loved each other? How had Cora been sure her heart would be safe with him?

She didn't have the answers, nor would she ask the questions. Whatever happened between Cora and Wyatt was particular to them. Neither she nor Rose could hope to copy it.

Caleb walked by her side. "It would be nice to find an arrowhead for Teddy."

"There's bound to be something around here." They traipsed about the pond for half an hour and saw nothing of interest, so they turned back.

When Lilly caught her shoe on a rock and stumbled, Caleb caught her before she fell. "Are you okay?"

She clung to him as she found her balance. And if she held his hand longer than was necessary, he didn't seem to object. Rose watched them from a few yards away and Lilly slowly withdrew, but her gaze remained locked with his.

Their look went on and on as if time had no end. Her heart unfolded like a flower before the morning sun. Thoughts that she'd kept hidden all her life took flight and flew upward. She longed to share each of them with Caleb, but now was not the time or the place.

She lowered her gaze. "I'm fine. Thank you for saving me from that fall." There would never be a time or place. Not with him leaving.

She pushed the secret thoughts back to the dark recesses of her mind. She'd never felt safe enough with anyone to open her heart fully. Although she found she had to remind herself of that fact on a frequent basis when in Caleb's presence.

The rock that had almost tripped her lay overturned at her feet. "Look." When she had kicked it, she had by chance uncovered an arrowhead. "Let's call Teddy and let him find it."

Caleb's warm smile thanked her more than words could.

She slid her eyes away from him. "Teddy," she called. "Come and see what we found."

"An arrowhead?" he called, hopping so fast over the rocks that her breath caught partway up her throat. If he fell…

"Teddy, slow down." Caleb's firm words did not completely disguise the fear in his voice.

Teddy slowed marginally. Lonnie stayed close to him, one arm outstretched, prepared to catch him if he stumbled.

Teddy's crutch caught on a rock.

Lilly gasped, expecting to see him hit the ground.

Caleb sprang forward, but Teddy righted himself and got the crutch safely back in place.

Lilly's breath whooshed out. Her heart continued to beat double time. She'd envisioned him crashing to the ground, further injuring himself.

How had he prevented the fall? She replayed the scenario in her head. Had he used his injured leg to catch himself? She stared at him, his leg now hanging limply. Was she mistaken? But she didn't see how else he could have stopped the fall. Was his leg able to do more than he thought?

She'd add a few things to his exercises and see if his leg could bear any weight.

He and Lonnie reached them.

"I think I saw something special on the ground here." Caleb pointed at the ground.

"What? What?" Teddy got on his hands and knees. "I don't see it."

"Maybe it's on this side of the rock," Caleb said.

Teddy saw the perfectly formed black arrowhead. He scooped it up. "Look, Papa. Look, Lonnie. Lilly, see what I found."

She squatted beside him. "It's very nice."

Lonnie looked over Teddy's shoulder. "It's a better one than mine."

Teddy fairly glowed with pleasure.

Lilly turned to Caleb. At the tightness in his expression she straightened. He looked about ready to break in two. She touched his arm gently. "Caleb?"

He shook his head and moved toward the water's edge.

She followed. "What's wrong?"

"Everything." He scrubbed at his neck.

"I thought you'd be happy that Teddy found an arrowhead."

"I am." He turned to face her, his eyes full of dark torment. "But don't you see? This is everything I ever wanted for him—people who care about him, enjoyment in life, a home, a family—" He broke off and shook his head. "And he has none of it. No family. No home. And how can he enjoy life to the fullest when he can't walk without crutches?"

His grief twisted her insides into a cruel knot. She reached for him, wanting to offer comfort and encouragement, but he shook his head.

"You've made me want to have and be what I can't."

She dropped her hand to her side. "And what is that?"

Rather than answer, he turned to stare at the water. "Life here is so simple. So…so…" He shrugged. "For want of a better word, sweet."

"And you object to that? Seems to me it's something a person would want."

"Wanting and having are two different things."

"I don't understand."

Slowly he brought his gaze back to her. She guessed he was trying to hide his feelings, but she saw the dark sorrow that filled his eyes.

"I can't have those things. I tried once and failed. Now it's just me and Teddy."

She thought of how she suspected Teddy had caught himself using his injured leg—the one that had forgotten to work. "What if Teddy's leg gets better without the help of a doctor? Then would you allow yourself those things? A home, a family, a sense of belonging?" *Love?*

The darkness in his eyes deepened. "I don't know. What if I fail again?"

He wasn't making sense. "How did you fail?"

His jaw muscles clenched, and the skin about his eyes pinched into harsh wrinkles. "My wife is dead. My son is injured. And you can ask how I failed?"

She backed away a step. He must have loved Amanda a great deal to mourn her so deeply, feel her loss so keenly. She could never hope for that depth of love. Especially from Caleb. But her heart went out to him, lost as he was in all that pain. "Caleb, you must not give up hope. I believe Teddy will walk normally again. Just as your heart will someday heal." She wanted so much more for him. "Someday you will find joy in your present life, hope in your future and forgiveness for your past. I pray the day will be soon."

He looked right at her, an unhurried, gentle melting coming through his eyes until they flashed what she could only interpret as the hope she had asked for. A slow, powerful smile caught his lips and her heart.

"Lilly Bell, if I could borrow just a fraction of your attitude I might see life as the joyful gift you believe it to be."

"You can have the same attitude I have. It's free to everyone. It's a matter of choice."

"Choice, huh? Sounds too easy."

"It is and it isn't."

His eyes crinkled with amusement. "How do you explain that?"

She tried to focus on what she meant to say, but she was distracted by the smile in his eyes. "Our doubts and failures get in the way of believing."

He nodded, his expression serious, as if he understood what she meant.

But did he only understand the difficulties? She pressed the point. "Do we believe the possibilities or the failures?" Perhaps she meant herself as well as him. Could she believe in a future that held the things she wanted while guarding her heart against them?

"Lilly, Caleb," Cora called. "Come have tea."

"Coming," she responded, but she wished she'd had a few more minutes with Caleb to see him choose to start life over again.

On second thought, perhaps she should be grateful. Cora's call had pulled her back from the dangerous territory she had been venturing into—a place that beckoned with all the things she yearned for but feared to believe were possible.

Wait. She reminded herself she longed for nothing more than what she already had—her parents and sisters and animals. Only it got harder and harder to believe it.

Caleb stole glances at Lilly as they sat around on logs, ate cookies and drank warm, sweet tea brought in jars. Teddy talked incessantly about the arrowhead he'd found.

Caleb was content to listen to the hum of conversation around him as he mulled over his discussion with Lilly. She wanted him to believe in life—and love? She hadn't said so, but her words had seemed to indicate it.

Did he dare believe he could have family and love again? Or was he looking for things beyond his grasp? Was he asking for another dose of pain and failure?

He knew he should listen to the warning words inside his head, but he couldn't keep himself from wishing he could have the very things he'd wanted for as long as he could remember.

Was it possible, if only temporarily? Was temporary enough? And why not? Why not enjoy the present, with Lilly filling it as she was with joy? He could relish the moment and let the future take care of itself.

Satisfied with his decision, he settled back to listen to the others talk.

Rose spoke. "I still think we should try to find out who our birth parents were."

Cora sighed. "I really don't see what we could do. Our mother is dead, and our father didn't want us when we were little. We don't need him now. We have our Ma and Pa, and each other. And now I have Wyatt."

Rose swirled the contents of her cup around. "I understand our mother died. But there must be some good reason for our father to have left us in the middle of nowhere for two days and a night."

Caleb jerked forward. "You were left alone? Overnight? You must have been terrified." He glanced at Teddy, who had gone back with Lonnie to search through the rocks along the edge of the water. He couldn't imagine leaving his son alone for any length of time.

"Exactly," Cora said. "I don't think we want to know what kind of man would do that to his children."

Caleb looked at Lilly, who had so far not joined this conversation about her birth parents. "That's dreadful. I can see why Rose would like to find out what had happened. There must be an explanation for such callous behavior. It's just not normal."

Lilly gave him a look fit to stall every thought he had. "I don't want to know. We have a perfectly good life here and now. Why complicate it with things we might not want to know?"

He opened his mouth to protest and then closed it again without speaking. How could he say anything about her running from her past when he had done the same thing? It was no wonder she clung to the security of her family, but somehow it seemed wrong when she did it.

Likely she would say the same about him. Just when he'd thought there was a bridge across the gulf between them, the gulf had widened.

But did he have to let that happen? Maybe it was time both of them stopped running. And what better place than here? And what better time than now?

Cora turned the conversation to other things—plans for the fall, things the girls wanted to make during the winter.

He sat back and watched them. Lilly came alive when she talked about her sheep and all the wool she would card that winter. She really did have the power to forget the past and enjoy the present.

What else had she said? Hope for the future.

For the first time in many months he allowed himself to think of doing the same, thanks to her.

The afternoon cooled and they headed back.

A soft breeze blew from the southwest as they returned. Grub and Blossom waited in front of the house. Blossom got stiffly to her feet and trotted over to greet Teddy, while Grub twirled about in excited circles, making them all chuckle.

In the garden, the dry cornstalks swayed and rustled. Cora looked in that direction and sighed. Rose and Lilly exchanged knowing looks.

He wondered what they were thinking.

Teddy hurried as fast as he could to the house, calling, "Grandma, Grandpa, look what I found." He stepped inside to show off his arrowhead.

Caleb went with Wyatt to put away the horse and wagon and the rest of them followed Teddy indoors.

"How's the boy doing?" Wyatt asked.

"He's the happiest he's been in ages, but he still doesn't use his leg."

Wyatt clapped him on the back. "Don't be in a hurry to give up on what Ma and Lilly can accomplish. This place sure helped Lonnie and me."

"How's that?"

"You haven't heard my story?"

"Just that you and Cora married and moved to a little ranch with Jack Henry." A simple life.

"We were running from our past. You see, I spent a year in jail before I came here."

"What? How can that be?" So much for assuming the man had led a simple life.

"Our pa was mean as a rattler. Sometimes a person can only take so much before they snap. I got charged with assaulting him."

The two men studied each other and something in Wyatt's face let Caleb know Wyatt wasn't telling him everything.

"When I got out, my pa was dead. My ma lived only long enough to see me set free and then we buried her, too."

"I'm sorry." This man had seen more than his share of trouble.

"We were on our way out of the country, trying to get away from all the people talking about my time in jail, when we landed here with a mare too heavy in foal to continue. I'd say God brought us here to help us. I'd say He brought you here for the same reason."

"Huh? What reason would that be?" He'd never been in jail or beat a man. Though he'd shot the two intruders in self-defense.

"Why, to find a reason to start over."

Lilly had said much the same thing. Was it possible to forget the past and start over? "I need to take Teddy to the special doctor."

"Like I said, don't be in a rush to leave. Now, shall we join the others?"

Caleb didn't move. "Did you really beat your father so badly you were sent to jail?"

Wyatt's eyes hardened. "He was fortunate he didn't die. Like I said, you can only push a man so far before he strikes back."

He thought of all he knew of Wyatt and Lonnie and all he'd observed of their relationship. "I'm guessing the man you said was being pushed around wasn't you."

Wyatt shrugged. "It's water under the bridge. Now I have Cora and a beautiful future."

"That's nice." Caleb would not say anything about their past. They deserved the chance at happiness.

Maybe he did, too.

He accompanied Wyatt to the house, where Teddy was still talking a mile a minute to Mr. and Mrs. Bell, with Lonnie adding details to the story.

The three sisters were preparing supper, glancing often to the four at the table, exchanging smiles of approval at how Teddy and Lonnie were entertaining their parents.

Caleb allowed himself to enjoy the scene. Home. Family. Belonging. Was it possible to put his failures and disappointments behind him?

Or was he foolishly begging for more trouble?

Chapter Fourteen

Lilly watched the play of emotions on Caleb's face. Her heart leapt within her. Did his contented expression mean he was thinking about staying? She stilled her eager thoughts.

If she had a lick of sense, she'd not be pinning her hopes on such.

She turned to stir the pot of soup Ma had started.

Cora was staring out the window toward the garden. Wyatt went to her side and wrapped his arm around her. "What is it, dear?"

She smiled up at him. "It's nothing, really. I'm just remembering how we used to enjoy running through the dry cornstalks trying to scare each other." She shrugged. "But I suppose I'm too old for that now."

He chuckled. "Yes, you are such an old lady."

Cora gave him a playful shove.

Lilly watched them together, her heart almost bursting with a long-buried longing. Oh, how she ached to be loved like that. She stole a glance at Caleb and saw he was watching the pair, too.

Did they want the same thing? A family, a home, a

forever love? But he'd had already it and lost it. That's probably what he was thinking.

Wyatt turned to the others. "Who'd like to run through the cornstalks?"

Lonnie and Teddy answered in unison. "Me."

Lilly and Rose waited.

Cora sighed. "Thank you for offering, but it's only fun if we do it at dusk, and we need to be on our way home as soon as we have supper." She grinned at the twins. "Remember how I used to scare you."

Lilly laughed. "She was so sneaky. She'd hide and not make a rustle and then jump out to frighten us."

"Sounds like fun," Lonnie said. Both he and Teddy looked disappointed that they wouldn't be able to play the game.

Wyatt rubbed his chin. "Well, let's see now. I think I'd like to be part of this fun. There's no reason we can't travel home after dark."

"Really?" Cora smiled up at him. "You'd do that for me?"

Wyatt nodded, looking at her in such a way that Lilly wondered if he even remembered the rest of them were in the room.

"Hello," Lonnie said. "We're still here, you know. Hey, can Teddy play, too? You know, with his crutches and all?"

Teddy gave Caleb a pleading look. "I can, can't I, Papa? I'll be careful. Besides, even if I fall I won't hurt myself." He sat up straight and looked around importantly. "I've fallen lots of times and I'm okay."

Caleb raised his eyebrows and met Lilly's glance. Of course, he wasn't okay, but that wasn't because he'd fallen. "I guess you can join in on the fun."

"Then let's get supper done." Rose set the table while Cora sliced a loaf of bread and Lilly dished soup into each bowl.

Teddy sat between her and Caleb and it felt exactly as it should. The family around the table. Even if Caleb and Teddy weren't truly a part of the family. But she'd enjoy the evening without worrying about what tomorrow might bring.

By the time the meal ended and the dishes were done, the sun filled the sky with streaks of red and pink and orange.

"Let's go," Cora said, and all but Ma and Pa hurried outside to the corn patch.

Cora and Wyatt disappeared into the rustling stalks.

"You'll have to stop giggling," Lilly called. "Or we'll know where you are."

Rose slipped away as silently as a shadow.

Lonnie went with Teddy, the clump of moving crutches letting everyone know which direction they were headed.

Lilly and Caleb glanced at each other and then Lilly slipped away. At first the rustle of leaves signaled her path, but then she drew back out of sight, stilling her breathing so she could listen. To her right she detected a movement and she jumped out. "Boo!"

It was Rose she frightened, and they giggled and tiptoed away in opposite directions.

A few minutes later she did the same to Lonnie and Teddy, who screamed. Next, she leapt out at Cora, and giggling, the two collapsed into each other's arm. Then Cora went off to stalk Wyatt through the corn plants.

Lilly stood still. Where was Caleb? She hadn't heard him since they'd entered the corn patch. She tipped her head to the left. Did she detect a noise? It had to be Caleb since she knew where the others were, so she eased in that direction. She was an expert at this game. She'd sneak up on him and give him a fright.

At the thought she pressed her hand to her mouth to silence her laughter.

Inch by inch she moved forward, guided by a faint rustle, her own noise so muffled she hoped he wouldn't hear her. To her right, the sound of the others laughing and screaming and crashing through the plants helped cover her approach.

Then the guiding sound stopped. She held perfectly still, holding her breath. Where was he? Something tickled her ear. A spider? She shuddered and brushed at the side of her head.

The tickle moved to her other ear. She shuddered. Had she walked into a nest of spiders? Were they crawling all over her? How she abhorred the creepy crawly creatures.

She couldn't stand it any longer. Not caring who heard her, she pushed away from the nearest plant and turned around to see what she'd run into.

"Boo."

Her heart crashed against her ribs. Her lungs refused to work. "Caleb. I thought you were a spider." Her voice trembled, revealing just how much he'd frightened her.

"Gotcha good."

Her heart and lungs and emotions released in a whoosh. "You scared me." She shoved him hard.

"Whoa." He stumbled backward, clinging to her arms to keep from falling, but to no avail. He went down like a ton of potatoes, taking her with him.

She lay sprawled across his chest, looking into his

eyes, made twice as dark by the fading light. "You are one awfully big spider," she managed.

He brushed her hair back.

"Please tell me there isn't a spider in my hair."

"Only me." He trailed his finger along her cheek to her chin and let it linger there.

Her heart fought for the next beat and the one after that, as if it had gotten lost in the warmth and tenderness of his touch. She wanted to feel him stroke her face again. Wanted to turn her face into his palm and kiss it. Wanted to—

"I can't get up until you do." His words cut off her fantasies.

"Of course." She scrambled to her feet, her mind in total disarray. What had she been thinking?

Only that she wanted him to hold her. Only that she longed to open her heart and soul to him and let him see every fear, every hesitation, every ache of longing.

He pushed to his feet. "That's better." He caught her upper arms and pulled her to his chest. "When I kiss a girl, I prefer to do it standing on my two feet."

"Kiss a girl?"

"I mean you." He caught her chin and lifted her face toward him. "Unless you object."

"Object?" She could think of no reason she wouldn't want his kiss. In fact, she'd been wanting it for a long time. Maybe all her life. "No, I've no objection."

"Good." He lowered his head slowly, as if savoring the anticipation as much as she was.

She closed her eyes and breathed in his scent, his nearness. And then his lips caught hers, firm, full of today and tomorrow. And forever? Never mind silly questions right now. All that mattered was this moment, when time stopped to allow them to give and take of this kiss.

She wrapped her arms about his waist and pressed her palms to his back, reveling in the power and warmth she was feeling.

And then it ended. He broke off, but he didn't move away. She stayed safe and secure in the shelter of his arms. Their foreheads touched and they breathed in unison, as if their entire beings had found union in the kiss.

"Lilly," he murmured.

"Yes, Caleb?" His name was sweet nectar on her tongue.

"I shouldn't have done that, but I can't say I'm sorry."

"Nor can I." She and Karl had kissed, but it had been a mere brushing of their lips. Cold and lifeless. In no way comparable to this.

"Papa." Teddy's call jerked them apart. "I can't find you." The corn plants rustled nearby.

Caleb brushed his knuckles along her jawline. "I have to say I really like playing in the cornfield. I'll never forget it." He lowered his hand slowly and then responded to Teddy.

"I'm over here. Come find me." He eased away from Lilly, leaving as silently as he'd come.

She stood rooted to the spot until Teddy and Lonnie came crashing through the plants. Then she slipped away, not wanting to see anyone until she had her senses about her again.

Would that ever happen?

She felt as if Caleb's kiss had forever changed her.

Caleb stepped into the dark cornstalks. He needed to consider what he'd done.

He'd kissed Lilly. Likely he shouldn't have, but he

sure didn't regret it. She'd come readily enough into his arms and lifted her face for the kiss.

He closed his eyes and made himself take slow, easy breaths, though they did nothing to still the racing of his heart. He'd kissed a woman before. After all, he'd been married for more than six years. But he couldn't recall a kiss that had claimed him so completely that he could barely recall his name.

A rustling nearby signaled someone's approach. He held his breath, not ready to desert his thoughts. Rose tiptoed past, unaware of his presence, and he let a fraction of tension ease from his limbs.

His name? Right. He was Caleb Craig. A widower with a five-year-old son who had a leg that didn't work. He was in the employ of the Caldwells, feuding neighbors of the Bells. He had to keep the job to earn enough money to take Teddy to a special doctor.

He recited the long list of reasons he could not let one kiss influence his thoughts. But all the reasons failed to quench the longings the kiss had awakened. It had the power to erase every rational thought from his mind. He wanted a new beginning and a love to fill his life with passion and meaning.

He shook his head. What he wanted and what he could have were not the same.

His nerves tensed as the cornstalks behind him rustled and Lonnie and Teddy jumped out yelling, "Boo."

Teddy giggled madly. "We scared you, didn't we?"

"You sure did." He scooped Teddy into his arms and tickled him as the boy squirmed and laughed. This was all that mattered. Taking care of his son. He could not allow anything to make him forget that. Especially the yearnings of his foolish heart.

The play continued for a bit longer and then Wyatt yelled out. "It's time for us Williamses to head home."

Caleb called out, too. "It's time for little boys to go to bed."

"Aww," Teddy answered.

Caleb met the boy at the end of the corn patch and together they headed for the house.

As Caleb prepared the poultice for Teddy's leg, his thoughts continued to war inside his head. He could imagine himself and Teddy living here. If not for the fact Teddy needed to see a special doctor, Caleb might consider staying in the area.

But some things would remain the same. He would still have to deal with his failure to protect those he loved.

Rose and Lilly entered the house a short time later as Caleb prepared to remove the poultice from Teddy's leg.

Lilly hurried to his side. "How is it?"

He looked into her gaze as she bent close. The air between them grew still. A longing as fierce as a winter storm gripped his heart at the blue welcome he saw in her eyes. The kiss had changed him. Perhaps it had changed her, too. But there were barriers he couldn't ignore. He tried to remember what they were, but the details eluded him at the moment. He knew he would recall them later and wonder how they could have slipped his mind.

She looked at Teddy's leg. "I'd like to try some different exercises tonight if you have no objections."

"None at all," Caleb said. She could have asked him to dance a jig in the middle of the room and he'd have had no objections. Thankfully, she didn't, for he really had no wish to make a fool of himself. He'd come perilously close to doing so as he'd stood there in the cornstalks all moon-eyed.

He blinked and focused on what she was doing.

She had Teddy sit on the side of the bed and press his foot to the floor. "Does that hurt?"

Teddy shook his head and patted Blossom.

She pushed on his ankle. "Try and keep me from moving your leg."

He pushed back.

She did it in every direction. "Very good."

She had him lie back and then she did the original exercises. "All done. Good job."

Mrs. Bell watched from her chair. "I see progress."

Lilly nodded. "I do, as well."

Caleb wanted to ask what they saw, but he didn't care to discuss it in front of Teddy. "Son, it's time to get ready for bed." It was past bedtime, but he wouldn't have robbed his son of the pleasure of that particular evening.

A smile tugged at Caleb's lips. Had Teddy had as much fun as his papa had? He hardly thought it possible.

"Can Lilly do Tiny's story with me tonight?" Teddy asked.

"'Fraid not, son. It's much too late."

"Ahh."

"We'll do it again tomorrow," Lilly promised, smiling at them both.

"Okay." Teddy settled into bed.

As soon as Teddy had prayed and bid good-night to all the Bells, Caleb turned to Mr. Bell.

"Sir, may I walk outside with Lilly? I'd like to ask her about—" He tipped his head toward Teddy.

Mr. Bell nodded. "'Tis a fine evening for a stroll."

Lilly hurried over to get a shawl.

Rose cleared her throat. "Don't suppose you'd like company?"

Caleb hesitated. He could hardly say no.

Lilly pulled the shawl close and didn't answer immediately. Then she nodded. "You're more than welcome to join us."

Rose laughed. "No, thanks. I was only teasing."

Lilly gave her sister a tight smile. "One of these days your teasing will get you into a heap of trouble."

"Not a chance." Rose grinned as Lilly and Caleb stepped into the night.

A gibbous moon lit the yard, gilding every leaf and branch in silver.

"It's a beautiful evening," Lilly said.

"I like your game of playing in the cornstalks." His voice rumbled in his chest, deepened by his memory of the other game he and Lilly had played in the corn patch.

They walked along the path that led to the barn and beyond.

"Do you mean the game of chasing and scaring each other?" Her voice was deceptively innocent. "Or were you referring to another game?"

"Both." He caught her hand and turned her about to face him, placing his hands on her upper arms. He resisted the urge to pull her into his arms and kiss her again. There were things that needed to be said. In the moonlight he could not read her eyes, so he was unable to see if she was longing for the same things he was. "I can't promise you anything but the here and now."

She nodded. "It's all I've ever had."

The words troubled him. Her pessimistic attitude was in such contrast to her assurance that a person could choose to live life to the fullest. Or was it? Perhaps she was simply being realistic and forging ahead despite the challenges of life.

"I'm sorry I can't offer more, but Teddy—well, Teddy has needs that must come above everything else."

"Of course they must. But his leg is improving."

His grip on her arms tightened. "What do you mean?"

"Those new exercises required he use his muscles and he did." She flashed a smile. "The muscles are responding to the treatments we've been doing." She planted her hands on his arms and squeezed. "Isn't that great?"

Hope leapt within his heart. Could it be possible? The flame of hope died as suddenly as it had sparked. Doctors had suggested that they'd seen positive changes before, but Teddy still didn't walk on that leg. He wasn't about to see Lilly's observation as a cure just yet.

He patted Lilly's shoulders. "It's a real good start." He needed still to keep his sights set on his goal of taking Teddy to the special doctor.

It was time to end the evening, so he turned back to the house, tucking Lilly in at his side.

He paused at the door. "It's been a lovely evening. Thank you."

"And thank you, too." They stood inches away from each other.

He wanted to kiss her again, but he feared doing so would make him lose all sense of his priorities. Still he ached to hold her and claim her lips. Feel again the depth of emotion that had rocked his world.

No, he must remain guarded, keep his head on straight. Not be led from his path by his heart.

"Good night, then." She opened the door and stepped inside, and he followed.

He'd waited too long, argued with himself until she'd taken the choice from him. He should have been relieved. Not filled with stinging disappointment as he was.

Chapter Fifteen

Lilly hurried into the bedroom, where Rose had already prepared for the night.

"How was your moonlight walk?" Rose asked, smiling as she teased her sister.

"We discussed Teddy. Did you see how the strength is coming back to his leg?"

"Don't get your hopes up."

Lilly didn't know if Rose was referring to Teddy's leg or to the possibility Caleb would see the improvement in his son and decide to stay. She took her time hanging her dress and pulling her nightie over her head. She didn't want to discuss the evening with anyone. It seemed Caleb only meant to enjoy a quick kiss and move on. He had even dismissed the notion that Teddy's leg was getting better, as if he needed to cling to that excuse for leaving.

Well, she should be relieved. At least he was being honest about not offering her anything more. And he was honorable enough not to kiss her again.

To her dismay, she wished he had. Even knowing he meant to move on. Even knowing her heart would break in a thousand pieces when he rode away.

Rose sat up on one elbow and watched Lilly. "I just don't want to see you get hurt."

Lilly purposely misunderstood her. "How would I be hurt if Teddy's leg doesn't fix itself? I never offered any assurance to Caleb or myself."

"You know I'm not talking about that."

"How could I know that?"

Rose chuckled. "Because we know each other so well. I meant Caleb, and you know that."

Lilly wouldn't give Rose the satisfaction of admitting it.

Rose sighed. "I see the way things are between you two and I'm afraid. You've been hurt before."

"I thought we'd decided Karl didn't matter."

Rose gave her a hard look. "You always say you're happy with things the way they are. You don't want to change for fear life could get worse."

"Uh-huh. So?" She crawled between the covers and picked up her Bible, hoping Rose would take the hint and drop this subject.

"It's just your way of avoiding dealing with something painful. You hide from it."

She opened her Bible. "I got over Karl a long time ago."

"But why did you pick him in the first place? Anyone could see you were only a convenient person for him to spend time with. His ambitions far outweighed any consideration he had for you. That's the very reason you accepted his courting, though it could hardly be called that."

Lilly stared at her sister. "Why would I do that?" Sometimes Rose pretended to understand a great deal more than was possible.

"To reinforce your belief that no one will ever stay with you. I guess you think it proves you aren't worth it."

"Huh. That's stupid." But the words edged into her heart and scraped away a protective scab. Her birth father had left her—not only her, of course—but the others didn't seem to feel the pain of that abandonment as deeply as she did. Or if they did, they didn't let anyone know.

"It is, isn't it?" Rose sat up and picked up her own Bible. "Maybe you should stop expecting to be left."

Ma had given them each a Bible and had written a verse for each on the flyleaf. Lilly turned there and read the verse even though she knew it by heart. Hebrews 13:5. "I will never leave thee, nor forsake thee." Then Ma had written her own words. *Lilly, I can't promise that Pa or I will always be with you, but I can assure you that God will never fail to keep His promise to be with you. My prayer is for you to surround yourself with others who will stand by you when we are gone.*

The words had stung Lilly when she'd first read them a few years ago. It had felt as if Ma was saying goodbye, as if she couldn't wait for that final farewell. Now she saw it only as Ma dealing with the inevitable, though the idea still pained Lilly.

She answered her sister. "I have you and Cora."

"Yes, you do, and we will always be here for each other so long as God grants us life. But don't you long for love like that which Cora has found with Wyatt?"

Lilly cocked her head toward the door—all that separated her from Caleb. Only there was so much more than a door between them. There was his warning that he wasn't offering more than the here and now. There was her fear of being left. No doubt Rose's statements contained much truth.

Lilly mused aloud. "I don't remember our birth parents, but I do remember standing beside Cora in the middle of the prairie and seeing nothing but grass and sky."

"I remember, too. Cora tried her best to comfort us."

"Do you remember when Ma found us?"

"Vaguely. I remember getting fed and feeling safe."

"For years I was so scared of being left that it must have driven Ma and Pa half mad."

Rose laughed softly. "Remember the little rag doll you clung to for so long? I wonder what happened to it."

Lilly snorted. "As if you don't know it's in my drawer. All tattered and torn."

"It was well loved."

"I guess I thought as long as I was holding it I was also holding on to Ma, because she'd made it. It doesn't make much sense now, but it did then."

"Do you think Caleb would stay if Teddy's leg worked?"

Lilly had been avoiding that question ever since she'd mentioned to Caleb that Teddy's leg was getting better and he'd ended the evening in response. He obviously did not welcome a reason to stay.

"I don't think so."

"Well, I'm sorry even though he is a Caldwell cowboy. I don't like to see you hurt."

"Who says I will be? Don't you think I've learned to be cautious?" She clapped her hand over her mouth as she realized her words had confirmed Rose's theory.

Rose chuckled. "Oh, indeed. But I think Caleb has managed to break through your defenses."

Lilly turned the pages of her Bible to signal the conversation was over. She was loath to admit it, but Rose was right. Despite Lilly's good intentions not to let herself be hurt again, something about Caleb had disarmed her and left her vulnerable.

It might be too late to prevent any damage, but she would take steps immediately to contain it to one memorable kiss, one day of wishing and dreaming.

If only she knew how to accomplish such a task.

The next morning she had her resolve firmly in place as she hurried out of her room. She called a quick "Good morning" to everyone in general. Using every ounce of self-control she could muster, she kept her gaze slightly to Caleb's right to avoid direct eye contact.

Normally she waited until after breakfast and after Caleb had ridden away to do the milking, but today, without a backward look, she hurried out to the barn, grateful for the chance to be alone.

Breakfast was ready when she returned with the milk. Caleb followed her to the storeroom to help strain the milk. It was a task she could have managed on her own, but she couldn't refuse his help without being rude.

"You left in a hurry this morning." He sounded both curious and cautious and his smile barely lifted his lips.

She turned to watch the milk run through the cloth. "I wanted to get an early start on the chores. There's a lot yet to do to get ready for winter."

"I see." He waited as if he was hoping she'd say more.

She didn't. How could she explain when caution warred with sweet thoughts of last evening's kiss?

"Have I offended you?" He kept his voice low so those in the other room wouldn't hear.

She jerked her eyes to his. "Offended me? How?"

His lips twisted into a crooked grin. "By kissing you.

By saying I couldn't promise you anything." He jammed his hands in the front pockets of his jeans. "Or maybe in other ways I haven't considered."

She chuckled. "None of the above." She grew serious. "But it seems to me neither of us is ready to think beyond today." At least in their relationship with each other.

He quirked an eyebrow in acknowledgment. "I don't blame you for wanting more."

In the way he left the sentence hanging, she understood he was wondering if she would say that was enough. But was it? Could she take temporary and not be hurt by it?

She was fully aware of the inescapable fact that she would pay a pretty penny in sorrow when he and Teddy left.

But why not enjoy what the present offered? Might just as well mourn a lot as a little.

"I don't know what I want." She headed for the door, ending the conversation.

If only she could as easily walk away from her thoughts.

Caleb reasoned with himself throughout the day as he did repairs on the oat bin at the Caldwell ranch.

He wasn't sorry he'd been honest with Lilly, telling her he could offer her nothing but the time he would be there. He could give no promises for the future. He clung to that fact as if it were a metal shield.

No expectations meant no failures.

He jerked back from nailing a board in place and stared out at the rolling hills. Did he avoid thinking of the future to make sure he couldn't fail?

Nah. He returned to his task. It was a practical decision.

He worked hard throughout the day, barely pausing to down water several times and grab a handful of sandwiches for dinner. He finished early and headed for the Bell farm.

Work hard, enjoy the evening with Teddy and the Bell family. A man could get used to that routine.

He snorted, realizing his thought was seriously at odds with his decision to avoid thinking about a future.

He shifted his attention to his surroundings. Ebner and the Caldwell cowboys had moved some of the cows down from the higher pastures. A dozen head grazed in a hollow to his right, another twenty or so on a grassy knoll to his left. The grass would prove adequate for several weeks unless it snowed a great deal.

The sky was clear and bright. He breathed in air heavy with the scent of fragrant grasses and ripe fall leaves. It was pretty and productive country. A man could look a long time to find a place that equaled it.

All his life he had imagined himself with a ranch of his own, a cozy home of his own and a family with which to fill it.

He sighed. He'd already tried that route. It was time to move on to something else.

But the feeling refused to be quenched.

The face that completed those dreams was not Amanda's, but rather it was Lilly's. Her lovely face smiled at him from inside his make-believe house.

"Hello."

A call behind him jerked him around in his saddle. What was Ebner doing out here? He'd said he would ride to the higher pastures and check on the cows.

Caleb reined in and waited for the foreman to reach him, though he could think of no one in the world he'd less like to see.

Ebner reached Caleb's side. "Howdy. Where you off to?"

"I'm done my work for the day." He wouldn't let Ebner know his destination.

"So if you're done, where you going now?"

"I thought you headed up into the hills. Did you run into trouble?" Was it possible to divert the man?

"Nah. But the boss and his wife should be returning this week. I figure if I can persuade the Bells to move on before he gets back he might be grateful enough to give me a nice fat reward."

The Bells! What did this man have in mind? "What kind of reward do you fancy?" He edged his horse around. He'd go back to the ranch before he'd let Ebner know his destination.

"I got my eye on a nice piece of land north of here. High in the mountains where a man can do what he wants and no one will say otherwise. Now, if I had me a few head of cows I might just say goodbye to this job and go claim that bit of land."

"Sounds like a fine plan."

Ebner cut off Caleb's retreat. "Why don't you ride along with me for a spell?"

Caleb considered his options. He could refuse and return to the ranch, but that would leave Ebner to go on his way to the Bells, and who knows what he might decide to do there. Besides, if he refused his boss, it might well get him fired.

Or he could ride along with Ebner and talk that man out of any mischief.

"Sure. Got nothing else to do at the moment." He hung back, letting Ebner lead the way.

They reached the crest of a hill that gave them a good view of the Bell farm. Fortunately, it was not so close as to draw the attention of those living there.

He made out the twins in the garden digging something. He couldn't see what from that distance, only that they were loading something into the wheelbarrow. Mrs. Bell was taking laundry off the line. Where was Mr. Bell? Caleb swung his gaze wider. There he was, fixing the fence on the chicken yard. He couldn't see Teddy and prayed he would stay out of sight until Ebner left.

"Those gals are sure pretty things. Too bad they're as pigheaded as the old man. You'd think they'd be willing to befriend the one person who decides what happens to them."

Caleb understood the man meant himself, not Mr. Caldwell. He stifled a shudder. To even think of Ebner with Lilly made him feel dirty all over.

Grub loped across the yard, tumbling over himself.

"That's the dumbest dog I ever seen." Ebner chuckled. "Not that I'm complainin'."

"Uh-huh." Caleb didn't mean to give the man a reason to think he agreed with him. Nor did he want to arouse suspicion because he said nothing.

"I keep asking myself what it would take to persuade this bunch to leave. It ain't like they've been made welcome."

Blossom limped after Grub.

Caleb groaned in the depths of his heart. Would Ebner recognize the pup? Worse, would Teddy be chasing after the two dogs?

Ebner leaned forward over his saddle. "Say, ain't that

the half-dead mutt you rescued? So you brought the thing here for the Bells to fix up, did ya?"

Before Caleb could answer, Teddy swung past the house and into plain view. If not for the crutches, Ebner might have thought it was any little boy visiting the Bells.

Ebner sat back. "Well, I'll be." He shifted to face Caleb, his face gouged with harsh lines. "Didn't I tell you to stay away from this bunch?"

Caleb kept his thoughts to himself. What he did on his own time was nobody's business but his.

Ebner's lips curled into a mocking grin. "Guess I can't blame you. I'd like to spend an evening or two with one of those pretty young things, too." The evil in the man's eyes made Caleb's fists into knots. But he faced the man without revealing what he was feeling.

Ebner turned toward the farm again, chuckling softly…a sound that grated across Caleb's nerves.

"You've been leaving your son here during the day and coming here every evening. Now ain't that nice. I could fire you for consorting with the enemy."

Caleb said nothing.

Ebner studied the farm long enough for tension to squeeze the back of Caleb's neck. He hadn't known Ebner long, but long enough to be aware that when the foreman spent more than a few minutes in thought someone wasn't going to like the words that came out of his mouth. Caleb knew he wouldn't like what the man had to say.

"I could fire you," Ebner repeated. "Or I could use this to my advantage."

Caleb clenched his teeth. He did not like the sound of that.

"Yup. Having you here every day might be a good

thing." He faced Caleb with narrowed eyes. "You can tell me what they're up to. Let me know when they're where I can do them the most damage." He stared down at the farm again. "I tried drowning those smelly little woolies, but those people came home in time to rescue them. But if they happen to go visiting and we know ahead of time…" He didn't finish his sentence. Instead he turned his horse and pressed right up to Caleb's side. "Do we understand each other?"

Caleb met him look for look, not blinking, not giving in to Ebner for even a heartbeat.

Ebner snorted. "I think you get my meaning. Just remember your job is at stake here." He spurred his horse and galloped away.

Caleb slowly brought his gaze back to the farm.

Rose was standing there, pointing in his direction. Lilly was turned toward him, her hand tented over her eyes.

How much had they seen? There was only one way to find out.

He rode to the farm, and Teddy hurried toward him. Caleb lifted him up to sit behind him on the horse. He hooked the crutches on the saddle horn and continued toward the garden, where he lowered Teddy to the ground.

"Son, go wait in the house." He dropped to his feet.

Teddy looked at him and then at the twins. Their calm expressions stilled any protest and Teddy hobbled away.

"Howdy," Caleb said. From the scowl on Rose's face and the uncertainty on Lilly's, he knew they'd seen him with Ebner, but he'd let one of them reveal how much they had seen and what they now thought.

"Never had any use for a Caldwell cowboy," Rose said.

"'Spect you've got good reason," he replied. Ebner

had made it clear he'd done everything he could to drive them out.

Lilly looked past him to where he and Ebner had been. "What does Ebner want?"

Rose snorted. "As if we don't know. He wants us out of here and will stop at nothing to accomplish that." She drilled Caleb with her look. "But you! After we've offered you hospitality and Lilly has helped your son."

Lilly's eyes met his, confused, silently asking for an explanation. Her uncertainty tore at his soul. If only he could promise to always protect her from men like Ebner... He'd give the only promise he could. "I work for the Caldwells, but that doesn't mean they have the right to tell me what I do in my own time. Ebner is the foreman. He doesn't own me." He drew himself tall. "I am not part of this feud, nor do I want to be."

"Words. Let's see if actions follow." Rose stomped away.

Lilly ducked her head.

"Lilly," he said, "I would never do anything to hurt you or your family."

He wanted to see her face, gauge what she was thinking. He caught her chin and lifted it. "Lilly, you believe me, don't you?"

For a moment more she kept her eyes lowered. The breeze caught her hair and blew strands across her face from her loose braid. She caught the wayward lengths and tucked them behind her ear. His fingers curled. What would it be like to see her hair unbraided and tumbling down her back?

He scrubbed his lips together and sighed. When he realized she was watching him, he brought his thoughts and attention back to her.

"I don't trust Ebner."

He waited, his hands at his side, as she searched for what she meant to say.

"I'm sure he wants you to be part of the Caldwell campaign against us. But I don't believe you will do anything to harm us while Teddy is here."

He rubbed his hands against his legs. "You think it's only for Teddy's sake?" He studied her a moment, relieved to see her shift her gaze away from him, revealing she wasn't being entirely honest with him or herself. "Do you really think I'd want harm to come to you or your family?"

Her eyes jerked back to his, full of what he could only think was longing. It hit him square in the chest and knocked his breath out.

What did she want from him?

He wanted to promise her the sun, the moon and her very own star. He forced his lungs to work and his thoughts to remain in the realm of reality. He couldn't promise her anything except for what he already had— the present.

She seemed aware of what he was thinking and gave a tight smile. "You couldn't stop Ebner even if you wanted to. Even if you were here to do it." She stepped aside and turned to the full wheelbarrow.

Turnips. They'd been digging turnips.

"But seeing as you'll soon be gone…" Her voice contained a shrug.

He opened his mouth to protest but closed it without saying a word. He wished he could promise he'd stay and help her, take care of her, protect her from men like Ebner. He wished not only that he could promise it, but that he could have faith he would follow through on it.

But his past had shown nothing but failure on his part. He didn't believe he could live up to his expectations, let alone the expectations of others.

Something Lilly had said sprang to his mind. Was it that he didn't have enough faith or that he was looking for faith in the wrong places? In his own strength and abilities?

But what else did he have?

If he couldn't protect and provide for those in his care, he would continue to suffer both loss and failure.

Still, he wanted to offer Lilly some kind of assurance.

"While I'm here, I won't let Ebner do anything harmful to your family."

She stopped picking up turnips and faced him. "Is that a promise?"

He nodded. "It's a promise." She didn't say whether or not she believed him, instead simply turning back to her task.

The sight of Amanda bleeding and dying filled his mind. He recalled Teddy, white with shock and fear.

He tried to ignore the heavy lump in the pit of his stomach.

He'd promised to protect them, too. And look how that had turned out.

Chapter Sixteen

Lilly followed Caleb as he pushed the barrow full of turnips to the root cellar. She waited outside while he dumped them into the bin.

His promise to see no harm came to them while he was there had made her smile. For a few days they could forget about the Caldwells.

She sighed. And then what? Things would be back to the way they had been. Nothing would have changed.

Wasn't she always saying she didn't want things to change? Except when it came to the Caldwells. If only they would just leave her family alone.

Rose came over. "You made him take the turnips inside, didn't you?"

Lilly chuckled. "I see no reason to do it if someone else will."

Rose stared at the doorway. "I don't trust the Caldwells."

"I don't either. But Caleb assured me he would see nothing happened while he's there."

"And you believe him?" Rose stared at her like she'd suddenly sprung an extra head.

"I do. He doesn't seem the kind of man to break a promise."

Rose stomped away.

Caleb stood in the doorway to the root cellar, a look of surprise and delight on his face. Then his expression gave way to guardedness. "I wouldn't intentionally break a promise." His words were low and husky. "But I failed to protect my wife and son."

A great need to comfort him welled up inside her and she followed her instincts. "Caleb, you can't blame yourself for what evil men do." As she spoke she rubbed his arm, relieved when she felt the stiffness in his muscles ease.

"But I do. I failed them."

"You must have loved her very much." Each word clawed its way out of her throat.

He swallowed hard. "We loved Teddy."

Her heart lurched at the wording of his reply. Did he mean he hadn't loved his wife? But how awful that would have been for both of them. It was certainly nothing for her to be pleased about.

She sought a way to comfort him and assure him he wasn't a failure. "Does not God promise to keep our feet from slipping and to put us on a solid rock?"

"Does it say that in the Bible?"

She nodded, trying to recall the exact verse. "I think it's in Psalm 40, but it's a theme repeated throughout the scriptures. He is able to keep us from falling, and that's in Jude."

"I'll have to find it and read it for myself." He rubbed at his neck. "But it doesn't explain what happened to Amanda."

"How do you explain evil in the world? And yet it exists." She could have told him some of the cruel things the Caldwells had done, but what would have been the point? He had firsthand experience with how cruel people could be.

They tidied up the garden tools and he went with her to bring in the cows.

Grub followed, getting in the way as he chased a butterfly and tripped in front of Maude, who mooed at him as she sidestepped to avoid him.

Teddy and Blossom followed as she led the cows to the barn and into their stalls.

Caleb took one of the buckets she had brought out. "I'll help. Which cow should I milk?"

Her mind went blank for the space of two full seconds.

"Do you object to my help?" He sounded hurt.

"Just surprised. Thanks for offering. You can milk Maude."

He took his place at the cow's side, and in moments the white streams plunked against the bottom of the empty pail.

At the sound, the cats ran into the barn. They saw Caleb doing the milking and skidded to a halt.

Her hungry cats were expecting fresh milk, so she hurried to Bossy's side and began to milk as well, squirting streams to each waiting cat.

Teddy giggled when one cat missed and got a faceful of milk.

Caleb attempted to squirt milk to the cats closest to him. He missed by a mile, sending Teddy into a fit of laughter that had him rolling on the floor. "Papa, you don't know how to milk a cow."

"Anyone can do it." Caleb tried a couple of more times

and missed, while Teddy continued to giggle. Then Caleb shifted the direction and shot a stream of milk at Teddy, managing to hit his open mouth.

Teddy's laughter ended on a gulp. He sat up, swallowed the milk and stared at his father.

Caleb laughed, a full-throated, deep-chested laugh that rang through the barn and echoed in the loft.

Teddy's eyes widened and he giggled so hard he got the hiccups.

Lilly grinned, leaning her forehead into Bossy's flank. It felt so good to see the pair relax and enjoy themselves. They both deserved a home and a family.

But Caleb had been clear as springwater that he would be moving on.

Unless something happened to change his mind. She guessed it would have to be something more than Teddy using his leg. He thought he'd failed his wife. And now Teddy. Would Caleb ever be willing to try again?

Oh, if only it would be so. For Caleb's sake. And Teddy's, too, of course.

And for her sake as well. She wanted to deny it, but she couldn't. Something in her heart cried out to know him more deeply and thoroughly. To hear him laugh more often. To talk about their faith.

They finished milking and turned the cows out.

She took the buckets of milk to the house, a smile clinging to her lips.

Rose noticed before Lilly had the presence of mind to change her expression. "Lilly, you are going to get your heart broken and you know it."

Lilly sobered. "I won't let that happen."

Only it was already too late, and there was absolutely

nothing she could do about it. She could not deny herself one moment of time with Caleb and Teddy.

She did her best to keep her distance the rest of the evening and to avoid looking at Caleb throughout the meal.

Then it was bedtime. She couldn't avoid being close to Caleb as they helped Teddy prepare for bed. She'd promised to continue writing the story they had begun. Almost every evening they'd added more to Tiny's adventures, things that the dog was scared of and what made him feel safe. Sometimes Teddy asked Lilly to correct a picture, so she knew he was truly involved in the spirit of the story.

Every evening she silently prayed that the story would help Teddy find the healing he needed as well, for she understood his little heart must be full of hurt and confusion after witnessing his mother's murder.

Tonight Teddy wanted to talk about what would happen if Tiny got hurt.

The request stunned her so much she didn't answer immediately. She glanced at Caleb and saw her surprise reflected in his face.

She brought her attention back to Teddy's request. "What sort of hurt?"

"A broken leg."

It appeared Tiny was going to mirror Teddy's injury. Where would this lead? She could only follow his direction and pray for wisdom as she did so. "Poor puppy." She drew the dog with a splint on one front leg. "What happened?"

"Take it off." He indicated the splint and she obediently erased it.

"Maybe it isn't broken." Teddy sounded confused.

Caleb met Lilly's gaze over Teddy's head as the boy rubbed his fingers along the picture of the dog. She felt Caleb's hope and fear, a reflection of her own. Silently she prayed. *God, help this little boy find healing.*

Teddy sat up. "I don't think it's broke. Just hurt."

"Can he walk on it?"

Teddy shook his head.

"Is he in pain?"

Again Teddy shook his head. "But he'd like to run and play with his boy."

The boy had never been given a name. Just "boy."

Teddy studied Lilly. "What can we do to help him?"

The question caught her off guard. She'd hoped Teddy would be the one to say how he or the puppy could be helped. She glanced to Caleb for guidance. When he shrugged, she understood what he couldn't say with Teddy listening...he'd already tried everything to no avail.

She glanced at the others in the room. Pa had nodded off in his chair. Rose had her nose buried in a book. Only Ma was paying attention, and she smiled her encouragement. *Follow your heart,* she'd say. Or would it be to follow her instincts? Either way Lilly needed to answer Teddy's question to the best of her meager abilities.

"Do you think Tiny would like to play a game? Or would that hurt his leg?"

Teddy considered the question. "He's afraid it will hurt."

"I see. Then we'll have to do our best to see what will work. Has Tiny tried taking little steps?"

Teddy shook his head. "That might not work, and if it didn't he'd fall down."

"Maybe the boy could help him."

"Maybe." Teddy sounded doubtful. "I think he has to keep resting until it's all better."

Teddy was clearly afraid. She feared pushing him too hard. "Then we'll let him rest. It's time for Tiny to go to bed. Maybe the boy should pray for Tiny's legs to get better." She drew a picture of the boy kneeling at his bedside with the dog curled up beside him.

"What will the boy say?"

"What would you say to your papa?"

Teddy turned to Caleb. "Papa, can you make Tiny better? Can you make him forget his leg doesn't remember how to work?" He had used the same words he used to describe his own leg.

Lilly's heart twisted at the agony in Caleb's face. She hadn't expected Teddy to be so direct.

Caleb swallowed hard. "Son, I'm afraid I can't make Tiny better."

"Well, who can?"

"Only God," Lilly said.

Teddy shifted his questioning eyes to Lilly. "Then I'm going to ask Him." He hesitated, stroking Blossom's head. He gave Lilly a shy look. "Will you help me pray?"

"I'd love to." The words caught in her throat. She often helped him say his good-night prayers, but this time felt different. She reached for his hands.

He squeezed his eyes shut.

"Dear Jesus," she said, and he repeated her words. Silently she added a few more of her own. *Help me guide this child.* "I know You love me always and forever," she prayed aloud.

"Always and forever? Even when I'm bad?" Teddy asked.

"Yes, even then, though He's sad when we do bad things because He knows bad things aren't good for us."

"Okay." Teddy bowed his head again and continued his prayer. "I know You love me. Even when I'm bad and I'll try not to be bad too often." Teddy's sweet trust tightened Lilly's throat, but she continued.

"Our friend, Tiny—" She'd almost said Teddy but had caught herself. "He has a hurt leg. Can You please help him?"

Teddy repeated the words.

"Thank You for always hearing me."

Teddy again repeated the words. Then he added, "Good night, God." He tilted his face up for a good-night kiss from Lilly.

She kissed his soft cheek and gave him a hug. Her heart swelled against her ribs with love for this child. She wanted to hold him tight and never let him go. But he wasn't hers. She forced herself to release him and leave his side, and then she went to the table and sat down.

Caleb tucked him in and kissed him good-night.

He joined her at the table.

She ached to squeeze his hand or pat his back to show she understood how difficult the past few minutes had been, but she was acutely conscious of the others, so she kept her hands clutched together in her lap.

"Teddy is telling you about himself through Tiny," Ma said. "It's a very clever way to help him."

Lilly pulled her emotions under control. "I just follow his lead." She meant both Teddy's and God's.

Ma folded up the mending she'd been doing and put it in the basket. "It's been a long day. I expect you're all ready for bed."

Lilly and Rose immediately headed for their room as

Ma wakened Pa. Just before she closed the door behind them, she glanced over her shoulder. Caleb was watching her, his eyes dark with—

She ducked inside and leaned against the door.

Rose looked at her. "What's wrong with you?"

"Apart from having a few sore muscles after digging in the garden all day?"

"You know that's not what I mean."

Lilly pushed away from the door and slipped out of her dress. "Right now it's enough." She didn't want to think of the rush and tangle of emotions that knotted her insides.

Rose grunted. But thankfully she did not press the matter.

A few minutes later Lilly lay in the darkness. What had she thought she'd seen in Caleb's eyes? Longing? But what could he long for that he couldn't have?

Her heart answered that question.

He had a boy who didn't walk and a heap of guilt over his perceived failures. No doubt he wished he could erase parts of his past.

If he could, would he wish for more than just that? A family, a home, love?

She turned on her side, facing the wall, and pressed her fist to her mouth. Those were her heart's wishes, not his. Wishes she must keep silent. Unless, as Rose continually reminded her, she wanted to be hurt.

This time she knew her pain would reach new depths, and she hugged her arms around her, wanting to prevent it.

Knowing she couldn't.

Throughout the next day, Caleb's thoughts bounced back and forth as he tackled the list of chores Ebner had given him. The list grew longer every day, as if Ebner hoped to force Caleb to quit in order to spend his evenings at the Bells.

By midmorning he was chopping wood and stacking it. His mind wandered to the time he'd spent with Lilly.

He'd heard Lilly say she trusted him. He liked that.

But guilt darkened his pleasure. Would he prove himself worthy of her trust?

She'd assured him God would keep him from failing. He scrubbed at the back of his neck. God surely didn't take responsibility from a man, leaving him free to live a lackadaisical life.

Chunks of wood flew before his ax as his thoughts continued to wander.

He'd made a promise to make sure the Caldwell cowboys didn't bother the Bells. The first promise he'd made since he vowed to himself that he would not give up looking for help for Teddy until his son could walk.

Would he fail to keep either of those promises?

Sweat trickled down his back and dripped from his forehead. He was chopping wood as fast as he could.

Teddy and Lilly had made up a story about a pretend dog, Tiny. Caleb had seen the similarities to Teddy's own situation and, as they'd bent over the paper, he'd held his breath and prayed for something wonderful to happen.

But Teddy had grown weary of the story without giving any suggestion that he knew how to fix Tiny.

Caleb jerked upright, the ax hanging from his hand. Something wonderful *had* happened. Last night, for the first time since Amanda's death, Teddy had not cried out in the night with a nightmare.

Caleb grinned. He hadn't even noticed. He could hardly wait to tell Lilly. She'd be as pleased as he was.

"Grinning like a fool don't get the work done." Ebner crossed toward the wood stack.

"Just taking a breather." Caleb swung the ax and split a log neatly.

Ebner moved close enough to force Caleb to stop working.

"You need something, boss?"

"Yeah. What can you tell me about the Bells? They got anything planned I should know about?"

Caleb planted one boot on the chopping block and considered the foreman. He wasn't about to tell the man what he thought. That he had no intention of spying for him. Instead, he took his time wiping his brow and answered, "Well, now. Seems to me they did mention they meant to finish digging the turnips. You should see the crop they grew. Some of those turnips were as big as a bucket. I imagine they'll taste real good about the middle of winter." He managed to answer the man's question without giving him any useful information.

Ebner made a rude noise. "Who cares about turnips?"

Caleb pretended surprise. "Why, I expect the Bells do, and likely people in town who buy vegetables from them do, too. Hear tell they give them away. Say, you ever buy stuff from them?"

"Anything I want from them, I'll take."

Caleb put another log in place and edged back, waiting for Ebner to move aside so he could swing the ax.

Instead, Ebner planted a boot where the ax would have landed. "I'm counting on you to keep an eye on them Bells and let us know when an opportune time arises for us to persuade them it's in their best interest to leave."

Caleb touched the brim of his hat in a little salute. Let the man think what he would of it. He could take it as agreement if he so chose. For Caleb it meant that though Ebner might be the boss, Caleb wouldn't be following an order like that.

Ebner gave Caleb a steely look and then walked away.

Caleb returned to chopping wood. It would be a frosty day in July before he'd do anything to help Ebner chase the Bells from their land.

His arms ached by the time he called it a day. There was more wood to chop, but even Ebner couldn't expect a man to keep at it any longer. He glanced about. No sign of the foreman. Good. He might be able to slip away without running into him.

He dashed to the well and pumped water. He downed several dippers full, then washed up as much as he could. By rights he should grab some clothes from the wagon when he got back to the Bells and take a trip down to the river for a good scrubbing.

He realized he was standing there grinning at the thought of seeing Lilly and her family, and he quickly sobered, lest anyone see him and draw their own conclusion.

A few minutes later he swung into his saddle and trotted from the yard. His nerves twitched until he was out of sight of the buildings, but even in the open he glanced over his shoulder repeatedly and checked the horizon for any sign of Ebner.

Not until he reached the Bell farm did he take a full, satisfying breath. He had not seen Ebner. Had not been reminded of what the man wanted.

"Papa, Papa." Teddy hurried toward him, swinging his crutches so fast Caleb feared he would fall.

"Slow down, son. There's no fire."

Teddy reached him. "But there will be."

"Will be what?"

"A fire. There's gonna be a fire tonight."

Lilly crossed the yard to join them. She smiled.

He forced himself to continue unsaddling his horse, though his hands felt a mile from his brain at the sight of the welcome light in her eyes. "What's this about a fire?" Caleb asked.

"And a party." Teddy practically danced a jig on his one foot. "A real party. Miss Lilly says they do it every year. Isn't that right, Lilly?"

He didn't correct Teddy about using Lilly's name as she ruffled Teddy's hair. "We've done it for a long time." She turned to Caleb. "We burn the cornstalks. It's such fun we started asking our friends to come. They seem to enjoy it."

"I see." He tried to imagine where he would fit in this picture. He was an old man compared to Lilly and her friends. Even compared to Wyatt. An old man with a child and heavy responsibilities.

Teddy pressed close to Caleb. "Lilly said everyone can come. Us, too. Right, Lilly?"

"Everyone is welcome." She met Caleb's eyes and no doubt read the eagerness in them. "You are most sincerely welcome." She lowered her eyes as pink stole up her throat and stained her cheeks in such a beguiling way he grinned and dipped his head to see full into her face.

"That sounds like an invitation I can't refuse."

She looked at him through the curtain of her lashes. "I'm glad."

"Me, too."

"I can stay up for the party, can't I?" Teddy asked. "Lilly said I could if you agreed."

"You may stay up for a reasonable amount of time." He finished caring for his mount.

Teddy hung his head. "I 'pose you decide what's reasonable."

Lilly laughed. "That's your papa's job. To take care of you."

Caleb held her assuring gaze. His heart beat hard against his ribs. His job. He needed to remember that his responsibilities must come before anything else.

Lilly patted Teddy's head and then rubbed Caleb's arm. "You remember that you have a very good papa who cares deeply for you."

Caleb stood motionless. Had she purposely praised him in response to what he'd said yesterday about his failures? Or had she spoken spontaneously?

She squeezed his arm. "Now, don't get all serious and cautious. This is an evening meant for fun and celebration."

"What're we celebrating?" Teddy asked.

"The harvest." Lilly swung her arms in an all-encompassing gesture. "The crops are in. The garden has filled our root cellar to bursting and there is still more to bring in. The sheep and pigs are ready to sell. And—" She caught Teddy's chin and tipped his face to grin at him. "We have friends and family to share our joy with."

Caleb held his breath, hoping she would touch his face as she had Teddy's, but she only smiled at him.

"Would you like to help us prepare for the party?"

He nodded. "What do you need done?"

The three of them left the barn. Blossom and Grub waited at the door and joined them. Blossom still limped when she walked, but she was improving every day.

"We need to get a place ready for the fire." Lilly led

them to a spot in the middle of the garden. "Right here, where we don't need to worry about the fire getting away."

"Do you want me to pull out the cornstalks?"

"Oh, no. That's part of the fun. But we need something to sit on." She pointed to the planks and lengths of logs and together they made a wide circle of benches.

Caleb's stomach rumbled. It had been hours since he'd grabbed a quick dinner, and it had already worn off.

Lilly heard and pressed her hand to her mouth to cover a giggle.

He rolled his eyes.

"We are going to eat," she assured him. "Everyone brings their own sandwiches and Ma makes us hot cocoa."

A wagon rumbled toward them.

"Here are the first ones." Lilly hurried toward the wagon. When she saw that Caleb was hesitating, she waved him forward.

Mr. and Mrs. Bell and Rose came from the house and joined them as they went to greet the visitors.

Lilly introduced the preacher's daughter, and several other young ladies. Caleb forgot most of their names almost as soon as they were given.

Behind them came a second wagon. With relief Caleb recognized Wyatt, Cora and Lonnie. At least he wouldn't be completely surrounded by strangers.

Lonnie and a Miss Ellen smiled shyly at each other and headed to the circle of benches.

Some young men arrived on horseback. Was one of these Lilly's beau? Or a man who wanted to be? She greeted them all exactly the same way and drew him forward to introduce him.

The crowd seemed made up of school chums and church friends. Caleb again felt old in comparison.

But Lilly didn't allow him time to worry about it. "Come on. We're going to start the fire."

Everyone gathered round with Mr. Bell in the center next to a small stack of kindling. He lifted a hand to signal for quiet and then spoke.

"Welcome to everyone. It's always a joy to celebrate our bounty with friends and neighbors."

Caleb noted that one bunch of neighbors was conspicuously absent—the Caldwells. Too bad they wouldn't forget their feud and join in on the fun.

Mr. Bell continued. "Let us pray." He removed his hat and the men in the crowd did the same.

"God of all the earth, You have blessed us abundantly in this land. You bring the rains. You give us the sunshine and You cause the seeds to break forth into new plants. Everywhere we see evidence of Your great love for us and we thank You. Amen."

Several echoed his amen.

"Let the fun begin." He lit the fire. "Now remember not to put too many stalks on at once. You want to enjoy a nice fire, not a scorching blaze that could get out of control."

"Come on." Lilly drew Caleb and Teddy with her toward the corn patch and they wrestled the stalks from the ground. "Knock off the dirt." They did so and then took their stalks to the fire.

One by one the young people did the same while Mr. and Mrs. Bell sat and watched. Dusk descended and the fire blazed brighter. Sparks flew upward.

Teddy sat by Mrs. Bell, her arm around him, and watched with amazement.

Caleb paused a moment, too, watching the light of the fire reflect in Lilly's face. She smiled at him. Flames burned through his veins.

But he dared not hope that she meant to encourage his interest. He could not allow himself to think this tender feeling, this sweet regard, this full-bodied enjoyment would someday grow into more.

He had followed his dreams once before and his dreams had proven to be made of dust.

Someone tossed another stalk into the fire and the flames shot into the sky. Lilly shrank back from the heat.

Caleb turned away.

He needed to quench this yearning of his soul before he failed, before she shrank from him as she had from the fire.

Chapter Seventeen

Lilly hurried after Caleb. She had sensed from the start of the evening that he was fighting a war with himself. But she was uncertain as to the cause. Did he fear enjoying himself? Perhaps he saw that as a way of inviting disaster. She reached him and caught his arm to bring his attention to her.

"Caleb, don't take things so seriously. This night is meant for fun."

Others dashed past them bearing stalks to toss on the fire, but she paid them no mind.

Caleb studied her for a long moment. "I can't lose sight of my responsibilities."

She pressed her hand more firmly to his arm. "I wouldn't for one moment think you should. I know there are things you must do for Teddy." If his leg didn't start to work then Caleb needed to take him east and seek help. "A father should always put his children first."

His expression softened and he covered her hand with his own. "On that we agree." His fingers curled about hers, offering much more than his words did, as if he understood her concern about a father's devotion.

She allowed herself a moment of sweet comfort before she returned to her original intent. "You wouldn't be neglecting Teddy by enjoying this evening."

He drew in a long breath while she held hers, waiting for him to come to his own conclusion. Then she filled her lungs, knowing even before he spoke that he would agree.

"Enjoy the evening, you say?"

"Your responsibilities will be waiting for you come morning, but there's nothing you can do at the moment."

He nodded and headed for the corn patch, her hand firmly clasped in his. "Then, by all means, let's enjoy the evening." He laughed, filling her heart with shimmering warmth.

They gathered cornstalks, throwing them on the fire and laughing at the way the flames rushed into the air. Teddy sat with Ma and Pa, watching and laughing.

Lilly found herself glancing at Caleb more frequently than not, each time catching his dark gaze and something more. She couldn't name it—hope, anticipation? But whatever it was made her aware of her own needs and wants and dreams in a way that made the flames pale in significance.

The night deepened. Cool air crept closer, drawing people toward the fire.

Pa moved to the center again. "Who's hungry?"

A general call indicated that everyone was.

"I'll ask the blessing and then we'll eat."

She bowed her head and added her own silent words of thanks to the prayer. Thanks for the way Caleb was enjoying himself. Thanks for her own enjoyment of the evening. A warning sounded in her brain, but tonight she would follow her own advice and enjoy herself without thinking of the consequences.

Rose and Ma had made sandwiches for the Bell family as well as Caleb and Teddy, and Rose brought them out as the guests retrieved their food from wagons and saddlebags.

Lilly sat between Caleb and Rose. Teddy sat on Caleb's other side.

She wondered how the boy managed to eat three sandwiches despite his constant chatter. For her part, she was content to be in this place at this time without considering what tomorrow might bring.

Harry Simmons sauntered over. "Mind if I join you?" he asked as he looked at Rose.

Lilly stared. Harry! She couldn't believe he had an interest in Rose. Unless Rose hid it well, she certainly didn't have any interest in him. But stranger things had happened.

She shifted so Rose could make room for Harry at her other side. The movement pressed Lilly close to Caleb. He angled his body so he could look directly at her.

"*The* Harry Simmons?" he whispered for her ears only.

"Pardon?" She didn't know what he meant.

He leaned closer. "Who sings like a bullfrog?"

Then she recalled what she had said about the poor man. But pleased he had remembered, she chuckled. "One and the same."

Rose had been listening to something Harry was saying, but she turned at the sound of Lilly's chuckle. "What's so funny?"

"I'll tell you later."

"Uh-huh."

She turned her attention back to the food, but her arm brushed Caleb's each time she lifted her hand to her mouth. She grew so aware of every movement she could hardly swallow. Her nerve endings tingled.

"Girls, let's get the hot cocoa," Ma said.

Lilly bounced to her feet and rushed after her. The distance gave her a chance to gain a tenuous control over her emotions.

They carried a big pot of the hot drink back with them and filled each one's cup. If Lilly's hand seemed a little shaky, no one seemed to notice.

Then she stood before Caleb and her tremors increased. She held her breath so as not to spill the hot liquid on him, and managed to fill his cup.

Only then did she meet his gaze. The firelight reflected in his eyes, burning away secrets and barriers. She felt as if she could see straight into his heart. Her breath stalled at the depth of longing and love she saw there.

Did he want her to be part of what she saw? Did he think she could satisfy at least part of his longing?

Rose nudged her and they moved on, filling Harry's cup and continuing on to the others.

But something had shifted inside Lilly. It no longer mattered if caring about Caleb brought her pain in the end. This moment, this evening, these past few days would be the source of so much joy that they would outweigh anything else.

Caleb ate the sandwiches offered him and drank the hot cocoa that Lilly had poured. *Enjoy the moment,* she'd told him. It was good advice. His responsibilities wouldn't suffer because of an evening of ignoring them.

He watched Lilly circle the crowd with Rose and her ma, ladling out hot cocoa for each.

He grinned as she made someone laugh and bent close to others as if sharing some heartfelt confession. He grew thoughtful. She'd done the same for him—made him laugh, made him share things from his heart. Made him care. It was her sweet way.

He should be worried about how she'd pulled so many feelings and confessions from him. Perhaps he should have been pulling them back.

But that night was made for enjoyment.

She finished with the cocoa, and Rose took the pot to the house. Lilly returned to his side and his heart filled with warmth.

Teddy leaned against Caleb.

"It's time for you to go to bed," he said to his son.

"Aww." But the protest was halfhearted.

Mrs. Bell pushed to her feet. "We're going in. The night is for young people like yourself. Let me take care of him tonight."

He turned to Teddy, but he didn't need to ask his son if he approved of the idea. Teddy had already taken Mrs. Bell's hand.

"I'll go with Grandma and Grandpa," he said. "You stay and have fun with Lilly." He patted Caleb's hand.

Lilly chuckled.

Caleb shrugged. He didn't mind that Teddy approved of his friendship with Lilly. In fact, it eased his mind greatly.

Someone pulled out a guitar and started strumming it. A young man took a mouth organ from his pocket and sat beside the guitar player, and they played a lively tune.

A young lady across the fire called out a song and

the musicians played it. Voices rang out in chorus. Caleb had already heard Lilly and her sisters sing, knew them to have fine voices, but sitting beside Lilly, he felt like the two of them sang a duet.

The fire threw off welcome heat and filled the area with dancing shadows. Stars rivaled the sparks for attention. It was a night made for love.

Whoa. Caleb was not letting his thoughts head down that trail. Love carried responsibility and risks.

And, his hopeful side suggested, joy and satisfaction.

Caleb argued back. It was a package deal. You couldn't have one without the other.

Then Harry Simmons joined the singing and Caleb's attention came back to his surroundings. He choked back a chuckle. The man indeed croaked like a frog. He nudged Lilly in the ribs and they grinned at each other.

No sooner had one song ended than someone called out a request and another began. Caleb knew many of the songs and sang along. He enjoyed listening to Lilly sing those he was unfamiliar with.

Someone requested "The Girl I Left Behind Me." He had forgotten the words. But as the crowd sang, each word wailed through his head. A girl with golden hair and eyes like diamonds. And a wish to get safely back to her. He closed his eyes as the ache inside him swelled with every note.

He would miss Lilly when he left. As the song said, like a bee that could no longer taste the honey, or a dove that had become a wanderer.

The song ended and for a moment people were quiet, allowing Caleb to consider what he was to do.

Not that he really had any choice. One promise he would never forget and for which he would never accept failure was getting help for Teddy. He would not stop until his son could again walk on two legs.

He needed to ignore the sweet call of Lilly's beauty and spirit in favor of his son's needs.

A reveler requested another song and the evening continued for some time.

However, the songs seemed to grow fuller and fuller of love and angst and sorrow, until Caleb thought his heart could not contain it.

Lilly edged closer. "Are you okay?"

He nodded, his heart too swollen to answer.

"Does this music make you miss Amanda?"

He jerked about to face her. The fire filled her eyes. "Amanda!" It shocked him that she'd thought that. "Amanda and I didn't—" He could hardly say they didn't love each other. Not only did it make him sound mean-spirited, but it besmirched her somehow. He shook his head. "We weren't like that."

From a few feet away Rose was watching them, but he was certain she couldn't hear their words over the music, so he continued. "All my life I've wanted what you have here—a home, a family, love. Now it is out of my reach."

She ducked her head before his intensity then slowly brought her gaze back to his, her face full of fierceness. "It sounds like you're giving up."

"I have given up on my dreams. All that matters now is getting help for Teddy." He scrubbed his lips together. It was no longer true. His dreams had never died. They'd only lain dormant. "You have made me wish things could be different."

She smiled so gently his throat tightened. "Caleb, maybe they can be different. Maybe you just have to be willing to look for ways to make it so."

He drank in her look of hope and encouragement. "Teddy didn't have a nightmare last night."

"Well, there you go. Things are changing for the better."

"If only he could walk."

Her eyes bored into his until he saw nothing else but her, heard no sound but the twinning of their breath. "If Teddy walked, what would you do?"

He stared as hope flourished like a drought-stricken plant soaked in life-giving water. Then he pushed reality into his thoughts.

"I've never considered it." He turned and faced the fire. He didn't dare let his thoughts drift in that direction. He might be tempted to take a wait-and-see attitude toward Teddy's healing.

She correctly read his withdrawal and turned her attention back to the sing-along. He couldn't help but notice that she shifted to her right, putting a few inches between them so their arms no longer were no longer brushing.

He should be glad. He didn't want to encourage her to think he was offering more than he was. All he could offer was friendship and gratitude.

But there was no gladness in his heart. Only a gut-wrenching regret.

The guitar player stood. "Best be going."

His announcement echoed around the circle and the company slowly drifted away except for Cora, Wyatt and Lonnie, who had planned to stay overnight.

Wyatt grabbed a shovel and tossed dirt on the fire. Caleb helped him. Each shovelful quenched the flames until nothing remained but the smell of smoke.

Caleb took the tools and carried them to the shed, his footsteps slow and heavy.

The flames in his own heart also needed to be put out. He had to set aside the dreams he had allowed to flare to life and again focus on the tasks before him, working to get enough money to take Teddy down east.

But the sweet fragrance of memory would remain.

Cora and Rose lay in their beds on either side of Lilly. Wyatt and Lonnie slept in the other room with Caleb, Teddy and Blossom. Lilly smiled with contentment. "It's almost like it used to be."

"It's nice," Cora said. "I miss you two."

Rose made a jeering sound. "From what Lonnie says, all you talk about is Wyatt. Wyatt this and Wyatt that."

Lilly chuckled. "He says Wyatt is just as bad. It's always Cora this and Cora that."

Cora laughed. "That doesn't mean I don't miss home at times. Lots of times."

Lilly sat up on one elbow. "Is it as you hoped?" What she meant was: Did the change make life better? Or did it make life scary? Did she ever wonder if Wyatt would leave her?

"I love Wyatt and can't imagine life without him. Every day is full of sweet surprises as we get to know each other better. More and more I am impressed with what a good, noble man he is. And my, what good times we have. He—"

Rose groaned. "We get the picture."

Cora laughed. "Sorry. Lonnie's right. I do talk about Wyatt a lot." Her voice grew serious. "There's one thing I want to say to you both. Don't ever be afraid to love."

Neither of the twins said anything. If Cora had pressed her, Lilly would have had to confess she was afraid of falling in love. What if it led to more disappointment?

Cora continued. "Don't let our past control your future."

"Funny, but I said the very same words to Caleb." The words were barely out of her mouth before she wished she'd held them back. Her sisters would demand details.

But maybe she'd said it because she wanted to talk about Caleb.

"I expect he has good reasons for his past to influence his future," Cora said, her voice thoughtful. "He's had to deal with a lot. How are your treatments working on Teddy's leg?"

"I see improvement in his muscle strength, but he won't use the leg. It seems to me he's afraid to, and I don't know how to help him deal with that." She told her sister about the story she and Teddy were making up and how she hoped talking about Tiny would give her clues that would help Teddy. "All he says is his leg has forgotten to work."

"So what are you going to do?" Cora asked.

Lilly smiled. Her big sister was back, even if only for the night. She'd always felt she could go to Cora for anything from a little scratch to a big fear. "I think I'll play some games with him. Something that will give him an opportunity to express whatever is holding him back." She had talked to him plenty over the past few days, saying much the same things as she had said to Caleb, only in simpler, more direct ways. Like bad things in the past don't mean bad things in the future, and how evil things make a person fearful, afraid to change or try new things.

With a start that almost brought a cry from her mouth—a cry that would surely have made her sisters demand an explanation—she realized she had been speaking from her heart and to her heart as she talked to Teddy.

She was afraid of things changing. She didn't want to try new things. Rose was right. Being abandoned on the prairie had left an indelible mark on her. Not that it surprised her that it had. It only surprised her that the event had the power to flavor every thought she had.

Was it something she could change, or was her past so much a part of her that it would always make her fearful of change and of trusting others?

Chapter Eighteen

"I hear there was a fire at the Bell place last night."
Ebner gave Caleb a look that made Caleb's skin tighten.
He wished the man would go away and leave him alone
to relive the joys of the previous evening. He didn't even
have to close his eyes to recall every detail—the way
the firelight had pooled in Lilly's eyes, the way she had
smiled when she'd talked to him, the way her eyes had
lowered with shyness and then blinked wide open with
assurance. The way his heart had willingly gone down
pleasant trails with her.

"Don't suppose you set it."

Caleb's muscles tensed with horror. "Nope." He managed to keep his tone neutral.

"Too bad. It's fine idea."

"Have you forgotten my son is staying there?" His
taut and commanding voice should have alerted Ebner
that he wouldn't tolerate putting Teddy at risk.

"He won't be there forever."

Caleb didn't like that answer. He would divert Ebner
as best he could while he was there, but then what? Ebner

meant to get the Bells to move by fair means or foul. And he guessed Ebner preferred the latter.

"What have you got against the Bells? It isn't like they own enough land to affect the Caldwell ranch. Just a few measly acres."

"It irks me that anyone could be so stubborn. The boss has tried to reason with them. He offered them ten times what the land is worth, but that old man refuses to budge. You know what he says?" Ebner snorted.

Caleb held his counsel, though he guessed the man didn't expect an answer.

"He says God meant the land to be put to good use and that's what he's done." Ebner snorted again. "Like he and God have a special arrangement." Ebner looked ready to gnaw the arm off someone.

Caleb backed away. "I best get to work. It won't get done on its own."

"Yeah. You do that." The man stomped away, muttering to himself.

Caleb shook his head. He didn't want Ebner to become a problem for either himself or for the Bells, though the Bells had already experienced trouble from him.

He tended the list of chores Ebner had assigned then headed for the woodpile.

Ebner rode into the yard and jumped from his horse. He jogged toward Caleb. "I got something for you to do."

Caleb groaned inwardly, but outwardly he kept the appearance of patience. Ebner had gone out of his way all week to keep Caleb from getting finished in time to have supper at the Bells'. Likely he meant to try again. "What do you need, boss?" he asked as Ebner drew closer.

"Need you to go to town. Get some oats from the feed store. Those horses coming in from working the range all summer deserve a good feed." Ebner headed away and then turned back. "Best see if the cook needs anything for the kitchen, too."

"Yes, boss." As Caleb trotted to the barn to hitch up the wagon, he did a little figuring. If all went well, he should be able to get to town, pick up whatever was needed, get home and unload the wagon and still get to the Bells' in decent time. Though he might not make it for supper.

Would Lilly be disappointed? Would she set aside a plate of food for him?

A few minutes later he was on his way. At the fork in the road, he took the right-hand one that led to town, but he glanced longingly to the left and wished he could follow it to the Bells' farm.

In Bar Crossing, he jumped down from his wagon and clambered up the steps, his boots ringing on the boards. He hurried for the door of the store, stepping aside to allow several young ladies out.

They studied him with interest. "Hello, Caleb," they chirruped.

He touched the brim of his hat. "Afternoon, ladies." They had been at the bonfire the night before.

One pretty little thing with eyes as dark as the night sky glanced past him. "You're alone?"

"I am." Why should she care?

The girl sidled up to him, her friends surrounding him. "Maybe you'd like some company while you're in town."

He scrambled for a way to inform them he had neither the time nor the interest without being rude. "Ma'am, I wish I had the time to enjoy your company." He let his glance skim over the four of them without meeting a single pair of eyes. "But the boss is mighty particular about me getting back in good time."

The girls stepped back, the dark-eyed one pouting openly.

As he reached the door, one of the others spoke loudly enough for him to hear. "I think there's something not quite right about a Caldwell cowboy courting Lilly Bell."

Courting? The word blared through his mind.

He gave the storekeeper the list the cook had given him.

"I hope you don't mind waiting," the man said. "I have three other orders to fill and I don't have anyone to help me today."

"I have to get some feed and a few others things, so I'll be busy for a while." Caleb left the store and jumped into the wagon. Surely the order would be filled by the time he had picked up the other things.

He smiled as he thought of returning to the Bells in a few hours. His mind scurried back to the conversation with the young ladies in front of the store.

Did he mean to court Lilly? Maybe he had been doing so without realizing it. He shook his head. As soon as he got his paycheck he would be going east with Teddy. There would be no time for courting.

He pulled up to the feed store and loaded the sacks of oats and then drove to the hardware to get nails and two new ax handles.

When he returned to the mercantile, the order was ready. He carried the boxes to the wagon, ready to be on his way.

He hadn't left town when someone flagged him down. "Mister, you got a loose wheel."

Sighing back his frustration, Caleb thanked the man and got off to inspect it. Indeed, the wheel was crooked.

He scrubbed at the back of his neck. This would mean a delay, but at least it hadn't happened out on the trail. He turned the wagon toward the blacksmith shop.

An hour later the wheel was repaired and he was again on his way. He glanced at the sun already half-way down to the horizon. Would he make it to the Bells' before dark?

"Let's play catch," Lilly said to Teddy as she tossed a ball back and forth from hand to hand.

"Okay." He grabbed his crutches and followed her out to the yard. He leaned on the crutches in order to free his hands.

Lilly tossed the ball gently to him. She had no wish to see him tumble to the ground, but she hoped to again see him use his right leg when he wasn't conscious of it.

If Teddy's leg would work again, Caleb wouldn't need to leave.

Would he then stay in the area? He'd hinted he might. She allowed herself to dream of the possibility.

He giggled as she missed his wide toss and had to chase after the ball. After that, it turned into a game of how far he could make Lilly run, until, panting for breath, she finally called a halt.

"Let's see if Blossom would like to play." She found a stick and handed it to Teddy. "Call her over and show her the stick, then toss it just a few feet away from you. Let's see if she will bring it back."

Teddy looked troubled. "Won't it hurt her to fetch it?"

"Don't throw it very far." This could be a chance to

talk to Teddy about injuries. "She needs to use her muscles to keep them strong."

"Won't she be afraid?"

"You mean of the pain?"

"I guess."

She squatted before him and held his shoulders. "Did your leg hurt a lot when it happened?"

He nodded.

"Are you afraid it will hurt if you walk on it now?"

He looked into her eyes as if seeking something.

She wanted to hug him, but she needed for him to think about her question. She'd seen enough evidence to be convinced he could use his leg if he tried. He had to get over his fear.

Teddy looked at the stick he was holding. "My mama's dead." The agony in Teddy's voice brought the sting of tears to Lilly's eyes and she hugged the child.

"I'm so sorry." She felt powerless in the face of his pain. The child had endured so much physically and emotionally. No wonder he feared to trigger any more pain by using his leg.

Rose wandered by. "Pa's out digging turnips." There were several rows still in the ground.

Lilly understood Rose's unspoken message. Pa shouldn't have been doing it on his own. In fact, since his fall from the ladder a few months ago, they'd done their best to persuade him to leave most of the physical work to them. Not that he had listened.

Lilly straightened. "Teddy, you stay here and play with Blossom while I help Rose and Pa." She grabbed a digging fork and hurried after Rose.

They knew better than to ask him to leave, so they

set to work alongside him. The more they dug, the less Pa would have to do.

An hour later, when they were down to their last ten feet, Lilly felt the ground rumble.

"Did you feel that?"

Rose nodded and they looked about for the source. Over the hill raced a herd of stampeding cows.

"The Caldwells." Rose spat out the words.

They raced for the house.

Lilly stopped. Where was Teddy? She spotted him up the hill, right in the path of the thundering cows. "Teddy!" she shrieked.

The boy stared at the approaching herd.

"Run, Teddy, run."

He took one step. Two. Then froze.

Lilly's heart stalled. He'd be trampled unless she could reach him. She picked up her skirts and tore across the yard, with Rose behind her hollering, "Hurry!" Then Lilly heard nothing but the pounding hooves, the snorting and bellowing of the cows.

She measured her progress against that of the cows and forced another burst of speed to her feet. She reached Teddy, snatched him into her arms and continued her headlong flight to the barn.

The ground shook. The air rang with a noise that she knew would fill her nightmares for days to come.

They reached the barn, falling through the slit in the door. She sat on the floor, rocking Teddy as the cows rushed past. The door shuddered as an animal banged into it. Something creaked from the pressure of the surging animals.

The pigs squealed. Chickens squawked. She wondered if any of them would survive.

Finally the noise lessened. A set of hooves cracked against the wall and then the thunder passed. Dust and the smell of cattle droppings filled the air.

She held Teddy, her arms locked in position. Weakness filled her until she thought she might throw up.

"Lilly, come quick." Rose's urgent voice gave strength to her limbs and she stood up and pushed the barn door open enough to exit easily.

Teddy's crutches lay nearby, one broken in two, the other soiled so badly it would require a good hard scrubbing.

Debris and disaster lay everywhere. The fence around the chicken pen was torn down. She saw at least three dead chickens. The garden was flattened, the turnips they'd dug but not picked up trampled to pieces. Ma's herb garden was a mess, the flower gardens by the house torn. One step of the porch was broken.

"Lilly." Rose waved from the garden, where she was bending over something.

The bottom fell out of Lilly's stomach. Pa lay on the ground before Rose.

Her feet leaden, her heart full of dread, she carried Teddy to the house. Ma's hand was clamped to her mouth, her eyes wide with shock.

Lilly put Teddy on a chair and led Ma to another. "Ma, you and Teddy stay here."

Ma's eyes focused on Teddy and she nodded. "Go see to things."

Lilly hurried from the house and did her best to avoid the cow droppings as she crossed to the garden. She knelt by Rose and looked at her pa. "How is he?"

Rose shook her head. "I don't know."

Pa groaned and tried to sit.

Lilly and Rose gently pushed him down.

"Pa, lie still until we see if you're injured." Lilly turned to Rose. "What happened?"

"He was right behind me, but when I got to the house he wasn't there." Her voice quavered and she reached for Lilly's hand. They held on tight, comforting each other.

"I tripped," Pa said. "Silly old man that I am."

"Did the cows—" Lilly couldn't finish the question. She couldn't bear the thought of Pa being trampled by the herd.

"Where are you hurt?" Rose asked.

"It hurts to breathe."

Rose and Lilly exchanged fearful looks. That could mean a number of things, from bruised ribs to severe internal injuries.

"Take me to your ma."

"You wait here while we get something to carry you on."

The fact that he didn't protest indicated how poorly he felt.

The girls hurried to the barn to get a piece of canvas and wrap it around two poles, and then they raced back. Neither of them spoke. Lilly knew Rose was as reluctant as she to express the truth—that Pa might be seriously injured. *Please God. Please God.* She uttered the silent prayer over and over, knowing God heard the cry of her heart.

They gently eased Pa to the makeshift stretcher and carried him to the house, where they laid him on the cot. Ma covered her mouth to muffle a cry as she rushed to his side.

"Bertie, Bertie, oh my dear." She bent over him, her hands hovering above him as if afraid to touch his skin.

Pa opened his eyes, full of stark pain. "Now, don't you worry. I'm okay." But the heavy tone of his words said otherwise.

Ma nodded and pulled herself together. "Girls, take Teddy and go outside while I see where your pa is injured."

Lilly took Teddy in her arms and the three of them left the house.

The devastation before them brought a groan to Lilly's lips. She would have sunk to the ground, but there was no place fit to sit. "It's awful," she whispered.

"Why'd those cows do that?" Teddy asked, his voice small and full of fear.

Rose grunted. "The Caldwell cowboys had a hand in this. That herd was purposely led here."

Lilly shushed her, tipping her head toward Teddy to indicate they should be cautious how they spoke around him.

Rose hushed, but her scowl informed Lilly what she was thinking.

"Where's Blossom?" Teddy's words rose with panic.

"I expect both she and Grub were smart enough to get out of the way." *Oh please, God. Let the pup be okay.*

"Blossom," Teddy called. "Come here, girl."

Lilly held her breath and waited. But there was no sign of either dog.

"Grub," Rose called. "How about some food?"

"Look." Lilly pointed toward Pa's workshed, which was relatively unharmed except for patches of green manure dotting it. Blossom stepped out, Grub at her tail. As soon as they saw it was safe to venture forward, they trotted across the yard.

She put Teddy on the ground and he wrapped his arms around his dog, laughing as she licked his face.

Ma opened the door and joined them on the step. "Your pa is badly bruised. I can't tell if he's injured inside. We'll just have to wait and see. I pray God will spare him."

Lilly took her hand on one side and Rose on the other. "Amen to that."

Ma looked about the yard. "Oh, my!"

There wasn't much else to say. Lilly added, "Rose, let's get started cleaning up. I'm going to get Teddy's crutch cleaned first. Teddy, you'll have to make do with one until your other can be repaired."

"Okay." He happily played with Blossom.

Halfway across the yard it hit her. Teddy had walked at least a step or two. His leg did work. For a second she rejoiced. Then she stepped in a fresh cow pie. "Ugh. It's going to take hours to clean this place."

"The sooner we get started, the sooner we finish," Rose said, her expression grim.

A tremor of fear skittered up Lilly's spine. "Rose, what are you thinking?"

"You have to ask?" She faced Lilly squarely. "What part did Caleb have in this?"

"Rose, how could you think that? Why, he'd never do anything to hurt...his son." She almost said he'd never hurt her. But could she be so certain? Hadn't he promised they'd be safe from a Caldwell attack while he was working there? Why hadn't he stopped this, or at least warned them it was coming? Perhaps tried to turn the cows away from the farm?

But he'd been conspicuously absent.

"I expect he was counting on one of us to make sure Teddy was okay." Rose looked about.

"I'm sure there's another explanation."

"I'm not planning to accept just any old reason." She kicked at a board torn from the chicken house. "Not after this."

Lilly scrubbed Teddy's crutch and took it to him. Then with shovel and wheelbarrow she tackled the cow manure. Green droppings smeared the outside of the barn that had been built just that summer. It would take a good rain to wash them away.

Meanwhile they would remain as a reminder of this dreadful day.

She and Rose repaired the chicken house and buried the dead chickens. They were about to start work on the fence when Ma called out.

"Pa says to salvage what you can of the turnips."

The girls crossed to the garden and picked through the damaged vegetables. Some could be used immediately. A few were whole, but most of them were trampled to a juicy waste.

All the while she secretly waited for Caleb to appear, and hoped he could provide an explanation of why this had happened.

She couldn't believe he'd had a part in it. But she'd been wrong before in trusting people.

Was she to be proven wrong again?

Chapter Nineteen

Caleb glanced at the sky, again assessing the amount of daylight he had left. He drove up to the Caldwell barn and unloaded the sacks of oats. He'd take care of the horse and wagon and then he would be on his way. He had a good chance of making it to the Bells before dusk descended.

A few minutes later he rode from the yard. He saw no sign of Ebner or any of the other cowboys who normally hung about the place.

As he neared the Bells' farm he saw evidence of many cows having trampled the grass. Odd they had bunched up together like that. Just that morning they had been scattered in small groups across a large area.

The closer he got, the more intense the signs grew. His jaws clenched. If he wasn't mistaken the herd had headed directly for the Bells'. What would have spooked them in such a fashion?

Or who? A shudder snaked across his shoulders. Why hadn't he seen Ebner back at the ranch?

At the top of the hill overlooking the farm, he could

see the cows had run right through the yard, trampling it into a dirty mess. Had Ebner done this?

Stampeding cows were dangerous. They could as easily trample a child as a flower. He scanned the yard in a quick second. No sign of Teddy. He spurred the horse forward, leaning over the saddle horn. *Teddy, Teddy,* he silently cried.

The boy was all he had left. If something happened to him—

He couldn't even finish the thought. He should have never left him there. Should have kept him at his side, no matter what.

When had the distance down the hill grown so far?

The horse's hooves pounded, the sound reverberating in his chest.

Then Teddy appeared, limping along, Blossom at his side, and Caleb sat back to catch his breath.

Anger pounded against the back of his eyes. His son could have been hurt. If this had been a deliberate action—

He rode more slowly toward the farm.

Rose and Lilly were kneeling in the garden. He couldn't be sure what they were doing, but they appeared to be picking up turnips. Strange. Why would they do that when there was so much cleaning up to do?

He dismounted when he reached his son, swung Teddy into his arms, and went to join Lilly and Rose.

Rose jolted to her feet, gave him a look of pure displeasure and stalked away.

He saw they weren't picking up turnips so much as looking for undamaged ones to salvage from the mashed mess. The cows had done this.

Lilly stared at him, her sorrowful expression tinted with both hope and despair.

"How did this happen?"

"You need to ask? Where were you that you didn't stop it? You promised."

Rose had not gone far, and was listening to every word. "Yes, let's hear your explanation."

He didn't want Teddy to hear this conversation. He put him down. "Go to the house." He waited until Teddy went inside, walking with one crutch, and shut the door.

"Ebner sent me to town." His suspicions grew. The blacksmith had wondered why the wheel had been loose, suggesting someone had deliberately tampered with it.

Ebner had planned it all along.

"I see now he meant to keep me out of the way because he knew I'd oppose him."

Rose snorted. "Well, I hope he's happy. The place is a mess. Pa is injured."

"He's injured? How badly?"

Lilly's eyes misted. "We don't know. He might have internal injuries."

"Lilly, you must believe I had nothing to do with this." She averted her eyes.

He knew she was having trouble believing him.

He wheeled around and headed for the house.

Rose trotted after him. "Where do you think you're going?"

"To check on your pa."

"Ma can do that."

Lilly followed hard on Caleb's heels. "Rose, for pity's sake. You can't blame Caleb for every evil the Caldwells have inflicted on us."

"Right now I can't see why not."

Caleb ducked into the house. Mr. Bell lay on the cot, pale as the sheets.

Mrs. Bell glanced up. Caleb had never seen her look so drawn and old.

"How is he?"

She responded the same way Lilly had. "We'll have to wait and see. I've given him something to ease the pain."

"I pray he'll recover."

"Thank you."

Caleb saw no accusation in Mrs. Bell's eyes and was grateful. He didn't dare look at Lilly again for fear of what he'd see.

"Can I leave Teddy here for a bit? I have something I need to take care of." He didn't wait for their answer, knowing Teddy would be well cared for in his absence. If they'd let him, he'd return and help clean the place up. But they might never want to see him around again. At least that was the impression Rose had given.

Did Lilly see things differently?

He'd soon find out.

He swung back into the saddle and retraced his route through the cow droppings, over the hill and onward to the Caldwells' ranch.

He rode directly to the cookhouse, where he guessed the men would be gathered. He swung down and stomped in.

Ebner looked up and glowered. "Thought you'd gone to join your friends."

"What you did was lower than a snake's belly. You chased a herd of cows over the land of an old man, an old woman and two innocent girls." He took a step forward, his fists clenched at his sides. "Even knowing my son is there, a crippled little boy who can't run from the stampede. That's about the most cowardly thing I've ever heard of." He would not mention Mr. Bell's condition, lest Ebner feel he should take advantage of the Bells while they were down and hurting. "I'll not work for an outfit like this."

A dozen men observed them. It helped ease Caleb's tension to see half of them hang their heads in shame. The other half, however, sneered. A cowardly, dangerous bunch.

"I'll take my wages now if you care to give me them."

Ebner rolled his shoulders. "'Fraid that's up to the boss."

"Right. When do you expect him back?"

"Say, didn't he and the missus ride in this afternoon?" The man who spoke had a face as cruel as a tornado, but he was one of those who hadn't looked pleased about Ebner's actions.

"Shut up, Stu," Ebner growled.

Caleb didn't nod his thanks to Stu. No point in making things worse for the man. "I'll be collecting my wages, then." He strode from the cookhouse, mounted the steps to the main house and banged on the door, ignoring Ebner as he hollered at him to stay away from there.

A man opened the door. "Mr. Caldwell?" The man had a fine head of silver hair and wore a suit that had obviously been tailored to fit him to perfection. He lacked the menacing air Caleb expected.

"Yes, what can I do for you?"

"Name's Caleb Craig. I've been working here a month, but I quit and I've come to collect my wages."

"You quit?"

"Yes, sir. I can't work for an outfit that deliberately

attacks innocent, helpless people. It goes against my grain."

"I see. Well, come in and we'll settle up."

Caleb followed the man across the hall to an office with a big mahogany desk, mahogany wainscoting and shelves lined with leather-bound books.

"Have a seat." Mr. Caldwell pointed toward a black leather armchair.

"I'll stand." He held his hat in hand.

"Suit yourself." He wrote on a piece of paper. "Perhaps you'd care to tell me what you're in such a high dungeon over."

Caleb considered whether or not to tell him, then decided it might help him judge the character of this man to see his reaction. "Your crew stampeded a herd of cows over the Bell farm, even knowing my son who has a crippled leg was there."

"Was your son injured further?"

"No, but it was no thanks to your cowboys." Again he decided against telling Mr. Caldwell about Mr. Bell's injuries. "I'll not be part of a crew that acts in such a cowardly way."

"You have proof my men did this?"

"Who else would?"

Mr. Caldwell gave him a piercing look. "Cows have been known to stampede for lots of reasons, many of them not man-made. It seems you're jumping to conclusions."

Caleb nodded. So that's the way it was to be. "I'll take my pay."

Mr. Caldwell handed him the paper. "Present that at the bank in town and they'll give you what's owed you."

"Thanks." He strode from the room without another

word and crossed the yard to his horse. He didn't say anything to Ebner, who followed him demanding to know what he had said to the boss.

He swung into the saddle and rode back toward the Bells'.

Could be they'd ask him to move on.

Welcome or not, he'd help them clean up before he left.

Was it just that morning he'd been smiling at what he'd interpreted as Lilly's acceptance of him?

Would she welcome him now or side with Rose in wishing him gone?

He'd soon enough know.

For the first time he looked at the script Mr. Caldwell had given him and sat back. Twice what he'd expected for a month's work.

His first instinct was to turn around and ride back, demand to know why he had given Caleb that generous amount. Was Mr. Caldwell trying to silence his criticism with a bribe? He stared at the paper for a minute. It was enough for him to go east with Teddy and see that special doctor.

Was this how it was meant to be?

He'd promised Lilly he'd make sure she and her family were safe while he was there. He'd failed. Again. He folded the script, tucked it deep into his pocket and rode on.

Dusk had fattened the shadows by the time he reached the Bells'. He put his horse in the barn, grabbed a shovel and set to work. He scooped and smoothed the dirt, then when he finished that, he lit a lantern and untangled the wire for the chicken yard.

Lilly came from the house. "Caleb, it's dark. Come inside for supper."

He stopped hammering. "You sure I'm welcome?"

She nodded. "Where did you go?"

"I went to the Caldwells' to quit."

Her eyes were wide, the lantern light revealing surprise and—dare he hope—gladness.

"What about taking Teddy east?"

"Mr. Caldwell paid me generously. I can afford to take him to that special doctor."

"The Caldwells are back?"

"Arrived today." He pulled at the wire, trying to untangle it so he could nail it to the post.

She grabbed the end and pulled it tight.

He drove in the nails and moved on to the next post. In a few minutes they had the chickens securely shut in.

There was something he needed to know. "You don't believe I had any part of this, do you?"

"No. After all, Teddy is here."

He leaned closer. "I wouldn't hurt you, either. Didn't I promise you that?"

She ducked her head. "I hope Pa will be okay."

He understood what she meant. She would be hurt if her pa was hurt.

"Come in for supper," she said again.

"I'll be there as soon as I put the tools away."

She didn't move. "A person can't always keep their promises." With that, she hurried to the house.

What good were promises if a man couldn't keep them? What sort of man failed repeatedly to protect those he cared for? If he'd been paying attention, he would have known Ebner meant to do something, but he'd walked around with his head in the clouds, thinking he could forget his past.

It was impossible to forget his failures.

A little later he went to the house and joined the family for supper, but the meal was somber with Mr. Bell lying on the nearby cot.

Lilly had a troubled sleep, awaking in a sweat with the sound of angry cows in her ears. Twice she woke when Rose called out, and she knew her sister's dreams were also troubled.

Finally she gave up on sleep and stared into the dark.

Her insides twisted and turned in turmoil.

Caleb had enough money to leave. He'd given no indication he wished it could be otherwise.

A blackness to rival that of the moonless night crept into her heart. He'd never given her any reason to think he would stay. Not even if Teddy used his leg again.

She gasped and sat up in bed then lay down again, waiting to see if she'd disturbed Rose. Thankfully Rose continued to breathe quietly, because she didn't want to discuss her latest thought with her sister.

Teddy had taken at least two steps on his leg. Would Caleb stay if he knew?

Or did he want a reason to leave?

Would he stay if she asked? Why would she? She hugged her arms about herself as the answer grew clear.

Because she cared for him and Teddy far more than she should have allowed herself to.

Cared? This feeling she had went far beyond that weak word. She loved them. The admission sang through her heart.

But love was so disruptive. It had taken Cora away.

Love often proved fickle. Karl had taught her that, though she'd never felt for him anything remotely like this feeling she had for Caleb.

But could love be trusted? Her birth father had given her that doubt.

The next morning, she rushed from the room to see how Pa was doing. He was sitting at the table.

"I'm fine," he said. "Just sore. Thank God for His mercies."

She raced around to hug him, then paused, afraid to hurt him, and settled for squeezing his shoulder. "I'm so grateful."

"Me, too," Rose echoed, patting Pa's arm.

"Grandpa is going to be okay, right?" Teddy said.

Ma ruffled his hair. "I believe he is."

Where was Caleb? Certainly not in the house. Lilly glanced out the window. With a broom and water, Caleb was scrubbing the soil off the side of the barn.

He came for breakfast when she called him, but he had little to say over the meal and returned to scrubbing the barn as soon as the meal ended.

He finished at noon. After he'd eaten, he made an announcement. "I'll be leaving this afternoon. I'll get whatever supplies we need, sell the horse and wagon at the livery stable then get the train headed east."

Teddy's face sagged. "We're leaving?"

Caleb planted his hand on his son's head to silence him.

"I'm most grateful for everything you've done." He pushed from the table, signaled Teddy to follow and left the house.

Lilly stared after him, every thought in her head frozen.

Rose sighed. "Well, that's the end of that."

"I'm sorry to see him go," Pa said. "He's a good man."

"I guess now that he's not a Caldwell cowboy he's okay," Rose allowed.

Lilly bolted to her feet and fled through the door. He couldn't leave without saying goodbye. That was the very worst way to end things.

As she approached the wagon she could hear Teddy asking, "But why do we have to go?"

"I'm taking you to see the doctor your grandparents found. He'll help your leg work again."

"No, Papa. We don't need to go."

Lilly reached them. She wanted to rush to Caleb's side and beg him to stay. But would her asking change his decision?

Teddy saw her. "Tell him, Lilly. Tell him I can walk."

Caleb turned to her then, allowing her to meet his eyes. In them she saw despair and determination. "He used his leg when the cows were coming. Seemed to work just fine."

"I'll show you." Teddy climbed from the wagon and took five faltering steps right into Lilly's arms. "See? It doesn't hurt anymore. I was scared it would, but it doesn't."

She hugged him tight, laughing and crying at the same time.

Teddy wiped her tears away. "Don't be sad."

"These are happy tears."

Teddy looked toward Caleb for an explanation.

Caleb leaned back, a wide grin on his face. "Son, it's something women do."

Teddy looked confused for a moment. "See, Papa?

We don't need a doctor. We can stay here. Can't we? Please say we can."

Teddy left Lilly's arms and walked to Caleb, who swept him into a bear hug. Tears glistened in Caleb's eyes.

"Papa, are those happy tears?"

"The happiest in the world."

"Can I go show Grandma and Grandpa?"

"Yes. But take your crutch just in case."

Teddy hopped away with a combination of leg and crutch movements.

Caleb wet his lips. "It isn't just about his leg."

Lilly waited for him to explain.

"I can't promise I can prevent disasters."

"Isn't that why we trust God to take care of us?"

"But a husband's job, a man's responsibility, is to protect and guard his loved ones. I have failed so many times."

"You can't hold yourself responsible for what happened to Amanda."

"Or what happened to you and your family?"

"I don't blame you."

He scrubbed at the back of his neck. "Life is full of so many risks."

"That's why we must leave the future to God."

He moved closer. "Do you really believe that?"

She nodded, somewhat confused by the question and by his nearness. They stood so close she could touch him with a mere flick of her hand and yet they were separated by so many doubts.

"Do you believe strongly enough to trust love?"

"I—" Had she not asked herself almost the same question? And now she saw the answer as plainly as if God had written it in visible letters across the sky. She gave a joyful little laugh. "Of course. Our future includes our responsibility and our relationships. How foolish I've been to think I had to guard my heart so tightly, when all along it was safe in God's keeping. Like it says in the Psalms, 'What time I am afraid, I will trust in Thee.'"

"Are you afraid of me?"

She shook her head.

"Even if I can't prevent the Caldwells from further mischief?"

She smiled up at him, her heart so ready to love that she could hardly contain the urge to hug him. "It wouldn't be fair to blame you for what others do." She touched his cheek. "It's not fair for you to blame yourself for what others do, either."

"I'm beginning to understand that." The air between them shimmered with unspoken promise and possibility.

"Lilly, I know you've been hurt before, but do you think you can learn to trust love?"

"I believe I already do."

"You do?" He swallowed audibly. "Dare I hope?"

Her smile came from a heart and soul overflowing with joy. "I believe you dare."

It took him about two seconds to understand her meaning, and then he laughed, a sound of joy she knew she would cherish forever.

He wrapped his arms about her. "Lilly Bell, sweetest thing I've ever found, I love you. I love you to the heights and depths of this world. I love you with every breath. I will love you as long as my life shall last and I pray God will give us both a long time to enjoy love." His smile faltered. "Am I getting ahead of myself?"

She chuckled softly. "No. I'd say you're right on target, because—" She cupped her hands to the back of his head. "Caleb Craig, I love you with everything I have and am. I trust your love." It was wholly true. Once she stopped holding on to her doubts, they had dissipated like early morning dew. "Nothing I have ever known compares to the love I feel for you."

"Are you going to marry him?" Teddy called from the corner of the wagon.

"Would that be okay with you?" she asked, amused that he had come back to spy on them.

"It would be just right."

"Son, go back to the house and let me ask her on my own."

Teddy studied his father for a moment and then nodded. "I guess you can do it without any help."

Lilly and Caleb held their laughter until Teddy reached the house.

Then Caleb sobered. "Lilly, will you marry me?"

"I thought you'd never ask."

"So did Teddy," he murmured before he claimed her lips.

Lilly sighed beneath his kiss. This was the love she had ached for since she was three years old. A love of her own. A love given by a man who would cherish her and care for her so long as their lives should last.

Epilogue

A month later, Lilly stood in the anteroom of the church.

Cora wiped a tear from her eye. "You look lovely in our dress." When Cora had married, the girls had agreed they would all wear the same wedding gown.

Rose adjusted the veil Lilly was wearing. "You are a beautiful bride."

Lilly hugged each of her sisters in turn. "You both look lovely, too." She sighed. "My only regret is how things are changing."

"It's time to grow up and move on," Cora said. "That's how life was meant to be." She turned to Rose. "I wonder who you'll find to marry."

Rose snorted. "Who says I plan to?"

Cora and Lilly both laughed.

Rose shrugged. "Look at me. Red hair like my head is on fire." She shrugged again.

Lilly could not stand to think of her twin sister being sad on her wedding day. "Rose, someday a man will come along who thinks your hair is the most beautiful thing he's ever seen. And he'll fall so madly in love with you he won't be able to think straight."

Rose laughed at Lilly's impassioned description of love.

Pa stepped into the room. He'd recovered his strength and showed no ill effects from the cattle stampede. "Are you girls ready?"

Together they said, "Yes, Pa."

He pulled them close and touched his forehead to each of theirs. "I've always known this day would come when one by one my girls would leave me. I've prayed you'd find good men and I've prayed I'd be strong and brave when I walked you down the aisle." He paused as his voice grew shaky. "I'm doing my best to live up to my plan."

They hugged their pa and then the organ music changed.

"It's time," he said.

Cora left the room to walk down the aisle and then Rose followed.

Pa held his arm out for Lilly to take. "You've found a good man."

"He found me," Lilly said.

"You found each other with God's help."

They stepped into the sanctuary. Lilly smiled at Teddy and Wyatt at Caleb's side and then she met Caleb's gaze and nothing else mattered.

She walked down the aisle and joined hands with him. Their hearts were already joined in joyful love. And now their lives would be joined as they began married life together.

They had decided to take a house in Bar Crossing for the winter so Teddy could start school without having to walk far. In the spring they'd find a bit of land and start a ranch, God willing.

One thing she'd learned was life was easier and happier if she entrusted her future to God.

She repeated her vows, as did Caleb.

"You may kiss the bride," the pastor said.

Caleb kissed her gently. She understood what he didn't need to say. He, too, had learned to forget the past, leave the future in God's hands and enjoy what the present had to offer.

"God has brought us to this day," he whispered.

"Blessed be His name." She would be forever grateful.

* * * * *

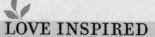
*When Susannah Peachy returns to her grandfather's
potato farm to help out after her grandmother is injured,
she's not ready to face Peter Lambright—the Amish
bachelor who broke her heart. But she doesn't know his
true reason for ending things…and it could make all the
difference for their future.*

Read on for a sneak peek at
An Unexpected Amish Harvest *by Carrie Lighte.*

"Time to get back to work," Marshall ordered, and the other men pushed their
chairs back and started filing out the door.

"But, *Groossdaadi*, Peter's not done with his pie yet," Susannah pointed
out. "And that's practically the main course of this meal."

Marshall glowered, but as he put his hat on, he told Peter, "We'll be in the
north field."

"I'll be right out," Peter said, shoveling another bite into his mouth and
triggering a coughing spasm.

"Take your time," Lydia told him once Marshall exited the house. "Sweet
things are meant to be savored."

Susannah was still seated beside him and Peter thought he noticed her
shake her head at her stepgrandmother, but maybe he'd imagined it. "This does
taste *gut*," he agreed.

"*Jah*. But it's not as gut as the pies your *mamm* used to make," Susannah
commented. "I mean, I really appreciate that Almeda made pies for us. But
your *mamm*'s were extraordinarily *appenditlich*. Especially her *blohbier* pies."

"*Jah*. I remember that time you traded me your entire lunch for a second
piece of her pie." Peter hadn't considered what he was disclosing until Susannah
knocked her knee against his beneath the table. It was too late. Lydia's ears had
already perked up.

"When was that?" she asked.

"It was on a *Sunndaag* last summer when some of us went on a picnic after
kurrich," Susannah immediately said. Which was true, although "some of us"
really meant "the two of us." Peter and Susannah had never picnicked with
anyone else when they were courting; Sundays had been the only chance they

had to be alone. Dorcas, the only person they'd told about their courtship, had frequently dropped off Susannah at the gorge, where Peter would be waiting for her.

"Ah, that's right. You and Dorcas loved going out to the gorge on *Sunndaag*," Lydia recalled. "I didn't realize you'd gone with a group."

Susannah started coughing into her napkin. Or was she trying not to laugh? Peter couldn't tell. *How could I have been so* dumm *as to blurt out something like that?* he lamented.

After Lydia excused herself, Peter mumbled quietly to Susannah, "Sorry about that. It just slipped out."

"It's okay. Sometimes things spring to my mind, too, and I say them without really thinking them through."

It felt strange to be sitting side by side with her, with no one else on the other side of the table. No one else in the room. It reminded Peter of when they'd sit on a rock by the creek in the gorge, dangling their feet into the water and chatting as they ate their sandwiches. And instead of pushing the romantic memory from his mind, Peter deliberately indulged it, lingering over his pie even though he knew Marshall would have something to say about his delay when he returned to the fields.

Susannah didn't seem in any hurry to get up, either. She was silent while he whittled his pie down to the last two bites. Then she asked, "How is your *mamm*? At the frolic, someone mentioned she's been…under the weather."

I'm sure they did, Peter thought, and instantly the nostalgic connection he felt with Susannah was replaced by insecurity about whatever rumors she'd heard about his mother. Peter could bear it if Marshall thought ill of him, but he didn't want Susannah to think his mother was lazy. "She's okay," he said and abruptly stood up, even as he was scooping the last bite of pie into his mouth. "I'd better get going or your *groossdaddi* won't let me take any more lunch breaks after this."

He'd only been half joking about Marshall, but Susannah replied, "Don't worry. Lydia would never let that happen." Standing, she caught his eye and added, "And neither would I."

Peering into her earnest golden-brown eyes, Peter was overcome with affection. *"Denki,"* he said and then forced himself to leave the house while his legs could still carry him out to the fields.

Don't miss
An Unexpected Amish Harvest *by Carrie Lighte,*
available September 2021 wherever
Love Inspired books and ebooks are sold.

LoveInspired.com

LIEXP0821

LOVE INSPIRED

INSPIRATIONAL ROMANCE

UPLIFTING STORIES OF FAITH, FORGIVENESS AND HOPE.

———————————

Join our social communities to connect with other readers who share your love!

Sign up for the Love Inspired newsletter at **LoveInspired.com** to be the first to find out about upcoming titles, special promotions and exclusive content.

———————————

HARLEQUIN

Heartfelt or thrilling, passionate or uplifting—Harlequin is more than just happily-ever-after.

With twelve different series to choose from and new books available every month, you are sure to find stories that will move you, uplift you, inspire and delight you.

Get 4 FREE REWARDS!

We'll send you 2 FREE Books plus 2 FREE Mystery Gifts.

Love Inspired books feature uplifting stories where faith helps guide you through life's challenges and discover the promise of a new beginning.

FREE
Value Over
$20

YES! Please send me 2 FREE Love Inspired Romance novels and my 2 FREE mystery gifts (gifts are worth about $10 retail). After receiving them, if I don't wish to receive any more books, I can return the shipping statement marked "cancel." If I don't cancel, I will receive 6 brand-new novels every month and be billed just $5.24 each for the regular-print edition or $5.99 each for the larger-print edition in the U.S., or $5.74 each for the regular-print edition or $6.24 each for the larger-print edition in Canada. That's a savings of at least 13% off the cover price. It's quite a bargain! Shipping and handling is just 50¢ per book in the U.S. and $1.25 per book in Canada.* I understand that accepting the 2 free books and gifts places me under no obligation to buy anything. I can always return a shipment and cancel at any time. The free books and gifts are mine to keep no matter what I decide.

Choose one: ☐ **Love Inspired Romance Regular-Print**
(105/305 IDN GNWC)

☐ **Love Inspired Romance Larger-Print**
(122/322 IDN GNWC)

Name (please print)

Address _____ Apt. #

City _____ State/Province _____ Zip/Postal Code

Email: Please check this box ☐ if you would like to receive newsletters and promotional emails from Harlequin Enterprises ULC and its affiliates. You can unsubscribe anytime.

Mail to the **Harlequin Reader Service:**
IN U.S.A.: P.O. Box 1341, Buffalo, NY 14240-8531
IN CANADA: P.O. Box 603, Fort Erie, Ontario L2A 5X3

Want to try 2 free books from another series? Call 1-800-873-8635 or visit www.ReaderService.com.